THE BIOGRAPHICAL EDITION
OF THE WORKS OF
ROBERT LOUIS STEVENSON

THE WRECKER

BIOGRAPHICAL EDITION

THE WRECKER

BY

ROBERT LOUIS STEVENSON

AND

LLOYD OSBOURNE

WITH A PREFACE BY MRS. STEVENSON

WILDSIDE PRESS

www.wildsidebooks.com

PREFACE

TO

THE BIOGRAPHICAL EDITION

O N Christmas day, 1888, we left Tahiti in
the yacht Casco, and after a wild voyage
of thirty days' duration arrived at Honolulu, with the intention of returning to England
by way of America after a brief period of rest.
"We will start next week," we said; "we will
start next month," — delaying our departure on
any pretext, for we knew that once back in England
our South Sea rovings would be over forever. Our
hearts followed every trading ship that left Honolulu. When the missionary vessel, the Morning
Star, began to get ready for sea we could bear it
no longer, and applied for passage to the Kingsmills. Knowing the life would be rougher than
anything we had yet experienced, and it being evident that my mother-in-law, wearying for home,
was disappointed by the change in our plans, it was
decided she should go back to Scotland to wait
there for our final return.

While my husband was trying to arrange matters with the Morning Star, — many difficulties were made, — he heard of a trading schooner, the Equator, bound for the Kingsmills. The more we learned of the Equator, the more eager we were to sail in her. We found the owner, Mr. Wightman of San Francisco, most obliging and liberal, and soon concluded a bargain with him by which we chartered the Equator, securing unusual privileges.

My husband's intention was to visit the Kingsmills, then Ponape, thence to Manila and to China, where we would take passage for England. The regular trading round of the Equator would carry us to Butaritari in the Kingsmills, and possibly to Ponape. We thought we might be dropped at either of these ports to take our chance of picking up a vessel en route for China or Manila. By the "charter party" of the Equator we agreed to pay a fixed sum down for the trip from Honolulu to Butaritari and through the Kingsmill group, with the proviso that whenever the ship's anchor went down, if for no more than five minutes, my husband should have the right to hold the ship there for three days without extra charge. At the same time we always tried to consider the owner's interests, not allowing ours to clash with his.

While we were submerged in preparations for

the voyage, Honolulu was thrilled by the landing of a number of castaways picked up on Midway Island by a passing vessel. This, in itself, was not so extraordinary, but the circumstances were unusual and mysterious. The story, which was far from convincing, as told by the captain of the wrecked ship, a barque called the Wandering Minstrel, was that he had fitted out his vessel in Hong Kong for the purpose of catching sharks. He meant, he said, to make spurious cod-liver oil from the livers of the sharks, and sell the dried fins to the Chinese. There were many discrepancies and evasions in his tale that I have forgotten; but it was plain that fishing for sharks was not the sole object of the Wandering Minstrel. The wages of the sailors, for one thing, were to be far beyond the usual rate of payment.

Almost nothing was saved from the stores of the Wandering Minstrel; the castaways were soon in desperate circumstances, and in no condition to make terms with a ship that answered their signals of distress. The captain of the rescuing vessel first ascertained exactly what amount of money had been saved from the wreck; it was just this sum, several thousand dollars — comprising all the sailors' wages as well as the entire means of the captain — that the stranger demanded as his price for carrying the miserable creatures to the nearest civilized port, where they were dumped, penniless, on the wharf. My husband tried in vain to solve the mystery of the Wandering Minstrel; and it was more or less in his mind when we started on our new cruise.

The Equator was a tiny boat to brave the seas upon, being a schooner of only sixty-four tons register; but it was soundly built, and the captain, Denny Reid, was a skilful mariner. I have just been reading a surprising article, published in the *Westminster Budget* of Feb. 22, 1895, by Lieut. Frank L. G. Harden, " supercargo of the Equator," entitled " The Dynasty of the Shark: a Personal Reminiscence of Robert Louis Stevenson." I never before heard of Lieut. Frank L. G. Harden, and he was certainly not supercargo of the Equator when we sailed in her. The captain was expected to attend to all business himself, and sold his goods in person from behind his counter in the trade room.

We took with us from Honolulu a Chinaman, named Ah Fu, whom we had picked up in the Marquesas. It seemed a good chance for Ah Fu to get back to his native land, as he wished to do, our intention then being to end our cruise in China. We also thought he might be useful to us, as indeed he was, — actually saving the ship one night in a storm, and, incidentally, every life on board. The Equator's cook was a runaway college lad, named McDonald, who knew Greek, but was an indifferent hand with the pots and pans. After one week of McDonald he was deposed in favor of Ah Fu. But a week of Ah Fu, whose really good French cooking did not please the captain, brought the reinstatement of McDonald. For the rest of the voyage, which lasted about three months, Ah Fu and McDonald were consigned to the galley alternate weeks. An artistic rivalry springing up between the two, we were treated to some wild inventions in the way of new dishes.

On our outward run we had true Pacific weather — perfect days and glorious nights — that swept us straight on our course. The little schooner, lying so low in the water, brought us close to the sea with a sort of intimacy that those on large ships, especially steamers, can never know. We began to feel that the sea belonged to us and we to the sea; and in our happiness remembered, with some qualms, the two importunate Belgians and the anæmic young Englishman who had begged permission to accompany us in any capacity. Years later I found the Englishman in London, managing a prosperous candy store on Regent Street. We learned afterwards that the Belgians were no better than pirates. They would take passage on a schooner from one island to another, poison all

on board just before making port, where they
would sell the schooner and repeat the process.
Unfortunately for their schemes, they allowed the
cook of a French vessel to survive long enough to
lodge information against them. After having
been tried and sentenced to death in Manila, they
somehow escaped execution, but are now safe behind the walls of a French prison.

After ten heavenly days my husband determined
to make his home forever in the islands, and to
that end projected the purchase of a schooner,
to be commanded by Captain Reid, which was to
be half yacht, half trader, and wholly self supporting. It was not our intention to live on board the
vessel indefinitely, but to pick it up at intervals,
making it a sort of floating home to which we could
constantly return. Elaborate plans were drawn,
with the enthusiastic co-operation of Captain Reid,
for a top-sail schooner of ninety tons to be called
the Northern Light. All details were arranged,
even to the rifle racks, the patent davits, the steam
launch, the library, and the price — fifteen thousand dollars.

My husband and my son had been continually
recurring, in their talk, to the mystery of the Wandering Minstrel; it now struck them that they
might collaborate on a novel, founded on the
episode of the wreck, which should bring in the

necessary sum. One fine moonlight night, the
fresh trade wind blowing in their faces, the two
men sat late on deck, inventing the plot of *The
Wrecker*. My husband, his mind filled with this
new and exciting enterprise, changed his plans,
determining to give up all the proposed Equator
cruise, except through the Kingsmills, and charter
the schooner thence to Samoa. Samoa was chosen
because it possessed a good service of mail steamers,
making serial publication of *The Wrecker* possible.
We were to stop in Samoa until the fifteen thousand dollars were earned and the schooner bought.

Our first port in the Kingsmills was Butaritari.
We stayed there some six weeks, while the Equator
roamed about the group, buying coprah. Captain
Reid had instructions from Mr. Wightman to make
the voyage as pleasant for us as possible; but his
own kind, generous, and delightful nature needed
no official promptings from his employer. He was
a small, fiery Scotch-Irishman, full of amusing
eccentricities, and always a most gay and charming
companion. Every evening Muggeree Bowyer,
our little native cabin boy, was called aft, made to
sing " Shoo, fly, don't bother me," given a dose of
a patent medicine called Kennedy's White Discovery, and after a spanking delivered in solemn
pretence over the captain's knee, sent to bed. It
often happened that all hands would be lined up

for their doses of Kennedy's Discovery or Mother Siegel's Syrup, and each man made to answer a question from the captain to prove that he had really disposed of the drug in a natural manner, and was not holding it in his mouth with the purpose of ejecting it when he got on deck.

Once the captain, fired, doubtless, by the pervading literary atmosphere, announced the fact that he was about to write a novel himself. Evening after evening he had his chapter ready to read aloud. If it pleased us he was delighted. If we laughed at it, as sometimes happened in spite of ourselves, he laughed with us. I never knew any one, except, perhaps, " Tommy Hadden," who was so disarming. While entirely devoted to us, we noted that his employer's interests always came first in any conflict of plans. As my husband meant he should be captain of the Northern Light, we watched him rather closely; and from the employer's point of view he stood the test triumphantly. As to his seamanship, there was no question of that; he had, as we knew, carried the little Equator safely through the great hurricane of March 16, 1889, arriving in Apia with his flag flying, without the loss of spar or sail — the only ship afloat except H. M. S. Calliope, within a radius of two hundred miles.

It is hard for me to believe that I could last have

heard of Denny Reid as lying in prison in Levuka, convicted of the fraudulent sale of a vessel. Out of the ship's company that sailed with us from Honolulu, the captain, as I have said, is a convict in Fiji. The mate, Anderson, a silent man with a cleft palate, known as the Sou'wegian, in contradistinction to Norwegian — he being a Swede — and several of the crew, including little Muggeree Bowyer, died of influenza on the return voyage to San Francisco; and about the same time La, a handsome young native sailor, was swept overboard and lost in a squall. I only know of one of the crew who escaped disaster, Sir Charles Self, a colonial lad who was studying navigation under Captain Reid. Sir Charles was not the proud bearer of an hereditary title, but was actually christened by that absurd name.

Just after our arrival in Butaritari, the king, a besotted, dull, obese man, lifted the taboo from strong drink, and the entire population went on a prolonged debauch. Those of the natives who had money thronged the bars of the two saloons, the " Sans Souci " and " The Land We Live in "; while the rest contented themselves with the fiery spirit made from the sap of the cocoanut blossom. This beverage, called sour toddy by the traders, causes the person intoxicated on it to " see ' red.' " Scenes of atrocious barbarity were common, and

our own safety seemed doubtful. We had rented
a little wooden house from an Hawaiian missionary, Maka, and kept Ah Fu on shore with us to
cook, thinking Butaritari a nice, quiet place for
literary work. As Maka's cottage was next dôor
to the " Sans Souci," our hopes in this direction
were hardly realized. Mr. Rick, Mr. Crawford's
agent in Butaritari, finally closed the doors of the
" Sans Souci "; but that only made matters worse,
so far as noise was concerned, as a crowd gathered
round the place, fighting and clamouring for drink.

Little work was done during our six weeks' stay
in Butaritari; but my husband took the occasion
to thoroughly study the methods of the South Sea
traders, of whom there were several on the island.
It slowly became evident to him that if he wished
to make a success of the Northern Light, and earn
any kind of interest on his investment, he must
necessarily do many things contrary to the dictates
of his conscience. South Sea trading could not
bear close examination. Without being actually
dishonest, it came a little too close to the line to
please us. Our fine scheme began to fade away,
and by the time we had made the tour of the group
it was practically abandoned; though my husband,
now interested in *The Wrecker,* still meant to
write the novel. We had talked and thought so
much of Samoa, however, that it came to seem the

natural termination of our cruise. My husband concluded to stop at one more island, and then charter the Equator for Samoa. So little had been accomplished in the way of work in Butaritari, that he proposed that we should be left in Apemama while the Equator made her final trip through the group.

Captain Reid expected to be gone about three weeks; but squalls and adverse winds drove him out of his course, so that more than six weeks had passed before his return, bringing us well into the hurricane season. Meanwhile, Tembinoka, absolute monarch of the three islands, Apemama, Kurai, and Araukai, had four houses moved from another part of the island to be set up for our use near some brackish water that filtered through the coral of the beach into a turbid pool rising and falling with the tides. Every evening an old man we called Uncle Barker, because his speech was like the barking of a dog, brought us green cocoanuts fresh from the trees for our drinking, so we need use the pool only for washing and bathing. Besides Uncle Barker, several slaves were given us, including three buxom young damsels who spent the most of their time frolicking in the pool. Our premises were enclosed within a taboo line which it was death for any native commoner, not connected with our family, to cross.

Here we lived in peace of mind for more than three weeks. At last a real beginning of *The Wrecker* was made, and several poems and many letters were written besides. Our houses were charming little basket-work affairs, something like bird cages, standing on stilts about four feet above the ground, with hanging lids for doors and windows; they were clean, airy, and quite large enough for our needs. Ah Fu, whom we had with us, as usual, baked bread and cakes and pies, and roasted the wild chickens he shot with the king's gun, all in one Dutch oven. A Dutch oven is nothing more than a shallow iron pot with a flat cover on which live coals may be piled. The king proved one of the most interesting men we had ever met, and exerted himself as he had probably never done in his life before to entertain his unexpected guests.

Week after week slipped by with no sign of the return of the Equator. To add to our anxiety our provisions began to run short, and a continued diet of wild chickens grew to be more distasteful than one would imagine. At the end of the fifth week the king's fishers caught several large turtles of the hawk-bill species, the kind whose shells are used commercially. Never was anything more welcome than the fresh turtle steaks that were sent up to us from the palace. Luckily, just as we had finished the turtles, the H. L. Tiernan, Captain Sachs, came in, and we were able to buy a couple of kegs of mess beef and some other small stores.

By this time we had about given up the Equator as lost, and my husband very nearly took passage on the Tiernan for Samoa. But the price asked seemed exorbitant; besides, the Equator might still be afloat, and we could not consider with equanimity Captain Reid's disappointment should he return and find us gone. Shortly after her departure from Apemama the Tiernan, lying becalmed with all hands asleep, was struck by a sudden squall and "turned turtle," losing sixteen lives. The mate, Edwin Lauterbach, swam to an overturned boat, righted it, and together with seventeen survivors, made shift, with a mat held up by hand for a sail and thwarts for oars, to reach land after several days of extreme hardship.

Our anxiety concerning the fate of the Equator was now becoming intense. We spent days scanning the seas through our glasses, while the king, with his "dogstars" (doctors) made a form of divination that we were not allowed to see. When six weeks had gone by, and we had lost hope, a sail appeared on the horizon; the ship drew nearer and cast anchor — the Equator at last! That night we sent off fireworks in honour of the captain's safe arrival, rather to Tembinoka's alarm, as he had many kegs of powder stored in some little wooden houses within the palace compound where we made our festivities.

We said farewell to the king with tears. " I think," said he, with pathetic dignity, " you never saw a king cry before." Tembinoka, in his realm of cocoanut and coral, had gradually pieced together for himself some conception of the universe. He called white men his " books "; was anxious in inquiring into the mainsprings of human action; was a philosopher, a cynic, and a poet. From his little corner he had learned to know the world, both its good side and its bad, and his strong, shrewd mind was insatiable for facts and prone to the right deductions. " I once kept a missionary here a year," he said, in his strange, hesitating, uncouth English that I make no attempt to render. " I had him teach me all he knew, and then sent him off with a handsome present. Every white man has something to teach me; but when I have learned it — here 's your present, my friend, and good by ! " I am glad to say we were not included in this category of speeded guests. The king's regard for us was genuine, and his affection and kindness unbounded.

A succession of storms followed us to Samoa, where we arrived in the early part of December, having lost our fore-topmast and stay-sail in a

squall that nearly sent us to the bottom. Had the
Equator not carried a cargo of some fifty tons
of coprah, which served to steady her, nothing
could have saved us. Further chapters of *The
Wrecker* were written in Apia in the house of
Mr. Harry Moors, the trader, mostly on his ve-
randah within a few steps of the sea. It was then
carried to Sydney, where my husband made the
acquaintance of "Tommy Hadden" (Jack Buckland). Poor Jack, several years ago, was robbed
by an executor of the estate of the little fortune
left him by his grandfather, and in his despair committed suicide. I often think of Jack's last visit
to Vailima, where he arrived accompanied by
innumerable "kautops" (retainers; I give Jack's
pronunciation of the native word) and laden
with the strangest presents for the family. For
my husband he brought a very expensive white
felt hat, "the latest novelty, just out from London"; to my daughter he gave the skull of an
immense shark, with a photograph of himself
which he proposed to have framed in blue velvet
and set between the jaws. There was an anvil for
my son, and for me four little silver saucepans, an
enormous, seamless steel frying-pan, and a brick of
mushroom spawn.

Jack, whose vanity was charmingly innocent,
was in the habit of continually presenting his photo-

graphs to every one he knew. When Lauterbach, mate of the H. L. Tiernan, took stock of the articles he had succeeded in saving after the ship sank, he had one case of wine, the ship's pet pig, an old mat, and Jack Buckland's photograph.

From Sydney the much-travelled manuscript returned to Samoa, where my husband had bought the lands of Vailima, and built his " big, beautiful, windy house." Here *The Wrecker,* after its many adventures, was finally completed in the autumn of the year 1891.

F. V. DE G. S.

CONTENTS

CONTENTS

THE WRECKER

PROLOGUE

IN THE MARQUESAS

IT was about three o'clock of a winter's afternoon in Tai-o-hae, the French capital and
port of entry of the Marquesas Islands. The
trades blew strong and squally; the surf roared
loud on the shingle beach; and the fifty-ton
schooner of war, that carries the flag and influence of France about the islands of the cannibal group, rolled at her moorings under Prison
Hill. The clouds hung low and black on the surrounding amphitheatre of mountains; rain had
fallen earlier in the day, real tropic rain, a water-
spout for violence; and the green and gloomy
brow of the mountain was still seamed with many
silver threads of torrent.

In these hot and healthy islands winter is but
a name. The rain had not refreshed, nor could
the wind invigorate, the dwellers of Tai-o-hae:
away at one end, indeed, the commandant was
directing some changes in the residency garden
beyond Prison Hill; and the gardeners, being
all convicts, had no choice but to continue to
obey. All other folks slumbered and took their
rest: Vaekehu, the native queen, in her trim

house under. the rustling palms; the Tahitian commissary, in his beflagged official residence; the merchants, in their deserted stores; and even the club-servant in the club, his head fallen forward on the bottle-counter, under the map of the world and the cards of navy officers. In the whole length of the single shore-side street, with its scattered board houses looking to the sea, its grateful shade of palms and green jungle of puraos, no moving figure could be seen. Only, at the end of the rickety pier, that once (in the prosperous days of the American rebellion) was used to groan under the cotton of John Hart, there might have been spied upon a pile of lumber the famous tatooed white man, the living curiosity of Tai-o-hae.

His eyes were open, staring down the bay. He saw the mountains droop, as they approached the entrance, and break down in cliffs; the surf boil white round the two sentinel islets; and between, on the narrow bight of blue horizon, Ua-pu upraise the ghost of her pinnacled mountain-tops. But his mind would take no account of these familiar features; as he dodged in and out along the frontier line of sleep and waking, memory would serve him with broken fragments of the past: brown faces and white, of skipper and shipmate, king and chief, would arise before his mind and vanish; he would recall old voyages, old landfalls in the hour of dawn; he would hear again the drums beat for a man-eating festival; perhaps he would summon up the form of that island princess for the love of whom he had submitted his body to the cruel hands of the tattooer, and now sat on the lumber, at the pier-end of Tai-o-hae, so strange a figure of a European. Or perhaps from yet further back, sounds and scents of England and his childhood might assail him: the merry clamour of cathedral bells, the broom upon the foreland, the song of the river on the weir.

It is bold water at the mouth of the bay; you can steer a ship about either sentinel, close enough to toss a biscuit on the rocks. Thus it chanced that, as the tattooed man sat dozing and dreaming, he was startled into wakefulness and animation by the appearance of a flying jib beyond the western islet. Two more head-sails followed; and before the tattooed man had scrambled to his feet, a topsail schooner, of some hundred tons, had luffed about the sentinel and was standing up the bay, close-hauled.

The sleeping city awakened by enchantment. Natives appeared upon all sides, hailing each other with the magic cry " Ehippy " — ship; the Queen stepped forth on her veranda, shading her eyes under a hand that was a miracle of the fine art of tattooing; the commandant broke from his domestic convicts and ran into the residency for his glass; the harbour master, who was also the gaoler, came speeding down the Prison Hill; the seventeen brown Kanakas and the French boatswain's mate, that make up the complement of the war-schooner, crowded on the forward deck; and the various English, Americans, Germans, Poles, Corsicans, and Scots — the merchants and the clerks of Tai-o-hae — deserted their places of business, and gathered, according to invariable custom, on the road before the club.

So quickly did these dozen whites collect, so short are the distances in Tai-o-hae, that they were already exchanging guesses as to the nationality and business of the strange vessel, before she had gone about upon her second board towards the anchorage. A moment after, English colours were broken out at the main truck.

"I told you she was a Johnny Bull — knew it by her head-sails," said an evergreen old salt, still qualified (if he could anywhere have found an owner unacquainted with his story) to adorn another quarter-deck and lose another ship.

"She has American lines, anyway," said the astute Scotch engineer of the gin-mill; "it's my belief she's a yacht."

"That's it," said the old salt, "a yacht! look at her davits, and the boat over the stern."

"A yacht in your eye!" said a Glasgow voice. "Look at her red ensign! A yacht! not much she is n't!"

"You can close the store, anyway, Tom," observed a gentlemanly German. "*Bon jour, mon Prince!*" he added, as a dark, intelligent native cantered by on a neat chestnut. "*Vous allez boire une verre de bière?*"

But Prince Stanilas Moanatini, the only reasonably busy human creature on the island, was riding hot-spur to view this morning's landslip on the mountain road: the sun already visibly declined; night was imminent; and if he would avoid the perils of darkness and precipice, and the fear of the dead, the haunters of the jungle, he must for once decline a hospitable invitation. Even had he been minded to alight, it presently appeared there would be difficulty as to the refreshment offered.

"Beer!" cried the Glasgow voice. "No such a thing; I tell you there 's only eight bottles in the club! Here 's the first time I 've seen British colours in this port! and the man that sails under them has got to drink that beer."

The proposal struck the public mind as fair, though far from cheering; for some time back, indeed, the very name of beer had been a sound of sorrow in the club, and the evenings had passed in dolorous computation.

"Here is Havens," said one, as if welcoming a fresh topic. "What do you think of her, Havens?"

"I don't think," replied Havens, a tall, bland, cool-looking, leisurely Englishman, attired in spotless duck, and deliberately dealing with a cigarette. "I may say I know. She 's consigned to me from Auckland by Donald & Edenborough. I am on my way aboard."

"What ship is she?" asked the ancient mariner.

"Have n't an idea," returned Havens. "Some tramp they have chartered."

With that, he placidly resumed his walk, and was soon seated in the stern-sheets of a whale-boat manned by uproarious Kanakas, himself daintily perched out of the way of the least maculation, giving his commands in an unobtrusive, dinner-table tone of voice, and sweeping neatly enough alongside the schooner.

A weather-beaten captain received him at the gangway.

"You are consigned to us, I think," said he. "I am Mr. Havens."

"That is right, sir," replied the captain, shaking hands. "You will find the owner, Mr. Dodd, below. Mind the fresh paint on the house."

Havens stepped along the alley-way, and descended the ladder into the main cabin.

"Mr. Dodd, I believe," said he, addressing a smallish, bearded gentleman, who sat writing at the table. "Why," he cried, "it is n't Loudon Dodd?"

"Myself, my dear fellow," replied Mr. Dodd, springing to his feet with companionable alacrity. "I had a half-hope it might be you, when I found your name on the papers. Well, there's no change in you; still the same placid, fresh-looking Britisher."

"I can't return the compliment; for you seem to have become a Britisher yourself," said Havens.

"I promise you, I am quite unchanged," returned Dodd. "The red tablecloth at the top of the stick is not my flag; it's my partner's. He is not dead, but sleepeth. There he is," he added, pointing to a bust which formed one of the numerous unexpected ornaments of that unusual cabin.

Havens politely studied it. "A fine bust," said he; "and a very nice-looking fellow."

"Yes; he's a good fellow," said Dodd. "He runs me now. It's all his money."

"He does n't seem to be particularly short of it," added the other, peering with growing wonder round the cabin.

"His money, my taste," said Dodd. "The black-walnut bookshelves are Old English; the books all mine, — mostly Renaissance French. You should see how the beach-combers wilt away when they go round them looking for a change of Seaside Library novels. The mirrors are genuine Venice; that's a good piece in the corner. The daubs are mine — and his; the mudding mine."

"Mudding? What is that?" asked Havens.

"These bronzes," replied Dodd. "I began life as a sculptor."

"Yes; I remember something about that," said the other. "I think, too, you said you were interested in Californian real estate."

"Surely, I never went so far as that," said Dodd. "Interested? I guess not. Involved, perhaps. I was born an artist; I never took an interest in anything but art. If I were to pile up this old schooner to-morrow," he added, "I declare I believe I would try the thing again!"

"Insured?" inquired Havens.

"Yes," responded Dodd. "There's some fool in 'Frisco who insures us, and comes down like a wolf on the fold on the profits; but we'll get even with him some day."

"Well, I suppose it's all right about the cargo," said Havens.

"O, I suppose so!" replied Dodd. "Shall we go into the papers?"

"We'll have all to-morrow, you know," said Havens; "and they'll be rather expecting you at the club. *C'est l'heure de l'absinthe.* Of course, Loudon, you'll dine with me later on."

Mr. Dodd signified his acquiescence; drew on his white coat, not without a trifling difficulty, for he was a man of middle age, and well-to-do; arranged his beard and moustaches at one of the Venetian mirrors; and, taking a broad felt hat, led the way through the trade-room into the ship's waist.

The stern boat was waiting alongside, — a boat of an elegant model, with cushions and polished hard-wood fittings.

"You steer," observed Loudon. "You know the best place to land."

"I never like to steer another man's boat," replied Havens.

"Call it my partner's, and cry quits," returned Loudon, getting nonchalantly down the side.

Havens followed and took the yoke lines without further protest. "I am sure I don't know how you make this pay," he said. "To begin with, she is too big for the trade, to my taste; and then you carry so much style."

"I don't know that she does pay," returned Loudon. "I never pretend to be a business man. My partner appears happy; and the money is all his, as I told you — I only bring the want of business habits."

"You rather like the berth, I suppose?" suggested Havens.

"Yes," said Loudon; "it seems odd, but I rather do."

While they were yet on board, the sun had dipped; the sunset gun (a rifle) cracked from the war-schooner, and the colours had been handed down. Dusk was deepening as they came ashore; and the *Cercle Internationale* (as the club is officially and significantly named) began to shine, from under its low verandas, with the light of many lamps. The good hours of the twenty-four drew on; the hateful, poisonous day-fly of Nukahiva was beginning to desist from its activity; the land-breeze came in refreshing draughts; and the club men gathered together for the hour of absinthe. To the commandant himself, to the man whom he was then contending with at billiards — a trader from the next island, honorary member of the club, and once carpenter's mate on board a Yankee war-ship — to the doctor of the port, to the Brigadier of Gendarmerie, to the opium farmer, and to all the white men whom the tide of commerce, or the chances of shipwreck and desertion, had stranded on the beach of Tai-o-hae, Mr. Loudon Dodd was formally presented; by all (since he was a man of pleasing exterior, smooth ways, and an unexceptionable flow of talk, whether in French or English) he was excellently well received; and presently, with one of the last eight bottles of beer on a table at his elbow, found himself the rather silent centre-piece of a voluble group on the veranda.

Talk in the South Seas is all upon one pattern; it is a wide ocean, indeed, but a narrow world: you shall never talk long and not hear the name of Bully Hayes, a naval hero whose exploits and deserved extinction left Europe cold; commerce will be touched on, copra, shell, perhaps cotton or fungus; but in a far-away dilettante fashion, as by men not deeply interested; through all, the names of schooners and their captains will keep coming and going, thick as may-flies; and news of the last shipwreck will be placidly exchanged and debated. To a stranger, this conversation will at first seem scarcely brilliant; but he will soon catch the tone; and by the time he shall have moved a year or so in the island world, and come across a good number of the schooners, so that every captain's name calls up a figure in pajamas or white duck, and becomes used to a certain laxity of moral tone which prevails (as in memory of Mr. Hayes) on smuggling, ship-scuttling, barratry, piracy, the labour trade, and other kindred fields of human activity, he will find Polynesia no less amusing and no less instructive than Pall Mall or Paris.

Mr. Loudon Dodd, though he was new to the group of the Marquesas, was already an old, salted trader; he knew the ships and the captains; he had assisted, in other islands, at the first steps of some career of which he now heard the culmination, or (*vice versa*) he had brought with him from further south the end of some story which had begun in Tai-o-hae. Among other matter of interest, like other arrivals in the South Seas, he had a wreck to announce. The *John T. Richards*, it appeared, had met the fate of other island schooners.

" Dickinson piled her up on Palmerston Island," Dodd announced.

" Who were the owners? " inquired one of the club men.

" O, the usual parties! " returned Loudon, — " Capsicum & Co."

A smile and a glance of intelligence went round the group; and perhaps Loudon gave voice to the general sentiment by remarking, " Talk of good business! I know nothing better than a schooner, a competent captain, and a sound, reliable reef."

" Good business! There's no such a thing! " said the Glasgow man. " Nobody makes anything but the missionaries — dash it! "

" I don't know," said another. " There's a good deal in opium."

" It's a good job to strike a tabooed pearl-island, say, about the fourth year," remarked a third; " skim the whole lagoon on the sly, and up stick and away before the French get wind of you."

" A pig nokket of cold is good," observed a German.

" There's something in wrecks, too," said Havens. " Look at that man in Honolulu, and the ship that went ashore on Waikiki Reef; it was blowing a kona, hard; and she began to break up as soon as she touched. Lloyd's agent had her sold inside an hour; and before dark, when she went to pieces in earnest, the man that bought her had feathered his nest. Three more hours of daylight, and he might have retired from business. As it was, he built a house on Beretania Street, and called it for the ship."

"Yes, there's something in wrecks sometimes," said the Glasgow voice; "but not often."

"As a general rule, there's deuced little in anything," said Havens.

"Well, I believe that's a Christian fact," cried the other. "What I want is a secret; get hold of a rich man by the right place, and make him squeal."

"I suppose you know it's not thought to be the ticket," returned Havens.

"I don't care for that; it's good enough for me," cried the man from Glasgow, stoutly. "The only devil of it is, a fellow can never find a secret in a place like the South Seas: only in London and Paris."

"McGibbon's been reading some dime novel, I suppose," said one club man.

"He's been reading *Aurora Floyd*," remarked another.

"And what if I have?" cried McGibbon. "It's all true. Look at the newspapers! It's just your confounded ignorance that sets you snickering. I tell you, it's as much a trade as underwriting, and a dashed sight more honest."

The sudden acrimony of these remarks called Loudon (who was a man of peace) from his reserve. "It's rather singular," said he, "but I seem to have practised about all these means of livelihood."

"Tit you effer vind a nokket?" inquired the inarticulate German, eagerly.

"No. I have been most kinds of fool in my time," returned Loudon, "but not the gold-digging variety. Every man has a sane spot somewhere."

"Well, then," suggested some one, "did you ever smuggle opium?"

"Yes, I did," said Loudon.

"Was there money in that?"

"All the way," responded Loudon.

"And perhaps you bought a wreck?" asked another.

"Yes, sir," said Loudon.

"How did that pan out?" pursued the questioner.

"Well, mine was a peculiar kind of wreck," replied Loudon. "I don't know, on the whole, that I can recommend that branch of industry."

"Did she break up?" asked some one.

"I guess it was rather I that broke down," says Loudon. "Head not big enough."

"Ever try the blackmail?" inquired Havens.

"Simple as you see me sitting here!" responded Dodd.

"Good business?"

"Well, I'm not a lucky man, you see," returned the stranger. "It ought to have been good."

"You had a secret?" asked the Glasgow man.

"As big as the State of Texas."

"And the other man was rich?"

" He was n't exactly Jay Gould, but I guess he could buy these islands if he wanted."

" Why, what was wrong, then? Could n't you get hands on him?"

" It took time, but I had him cornered at last; and then —— "

" What then?"

" The speculation turned bottom up. I became the man's bosom friend."

" The deuce you did!"

" He could n't have been particular, you mean?" asked Dodd, pleasantly. " Well, no; he's a man of rather large sympathies."

" If you're done talking nonsense, Loudon," said Havens, " let's be getting to my place for dinner."

Outside, the night was full of the roaring of the surf. Scattered lights glowed in the green thicket. Native women came by twos and threes out of the darkness, smiled and ogled the two whites, perhaps wooed them with a strain of laughter, and went by again, bequeathing to the air a heady perfume of palm-oil and frangipani blossom. From the club to Mr. Havens's residence was but a step or two, and to any dweller in Europe they must have seemed steps in fairyland. If such an one could but have followed our two friends into the wide-verandaed house, sat down with them in the cool trellised room, where the wine shone on the lamp-lighted tablecloth; tasted of their exotic food — the raw fish, the breadfruit, the cooked bananas, the roast pig served with the inimitable miti, and that king of delicacies, palm-tree salad; seen and heard by fits and starts, now peering round the corner of the door, now railing within against invisible assistants, a certain comely young native lady in a sacque, who seemed too modest to be a member of the family, and too imperious to be less; and then if such an one were whisked again, through space to Upper Tooting, or wherever else he honoured the domestic gods, "I have had a dream," I think he would say, as he sat up, rubbing his eyes, in the familiar chimney-corner chair, "I have had a dream of a place, and I declare I believe it must be heaven." 'But to Dodd and his entertainer, all this amenity of the tropic night and all these dainties of the island table, were grown things of custom; and they fell to meat like men who were hungry, and drifted into idle talk like men who were a trifle bored.

The scene in the club was referred to.

"I never heard you talk so much nonsense, Loudon," said the host.

"Well, it seemed to me there was sulphur in the air, so I talked for talking," returned the other. "But it was none of it nonsense."

"Do you mean to say it was true?" cried Havens, — "that about the opium and the wreck, and the blackmailing and the man who became your friend?"

"Every last word of it," said Loudon.

"You seem to have been seeing life," returned the other.

"Yes, it's a queer yarn," said his friend; "if you think you would like, I'll tell it you."

Here follows the yarn of Loudon Dodd, not as he told it to his friend, but as he subsequently wrote it.

THE YARN

CHAPTER I

A SOUND COMMERCIAL EDUCATION

THE beginning of this yarn is my poor father's character. There never was a better man, nor a handsomer, nor (in my view) a more unhappy — unhappy in his business, in his pleasures, in his place of residence, and (I am sorry to say it) in his son. He had begun life as a land-surveyor, soon became interested in real estate, branched off into many other speculations, and had the name of one of the smartest men in the State of Muskegon. "Dodd has a big head," people used to say; but I was never so sure of his capacity. His luck, at least, was beyond doubt for long; his assiduity, always. He fought in that daily battle of money-grubbing, with a kind of sad-eyed loyalty like a martyr's; rose early, ate fast, came home dispirited and over-weary, even from success; grudged himself all pleasure, if his nature was capable of taking any, which I sometimes wondered; and laid out, upon some deal in wheat or corner in aluminium, the essence of which was little better than highway robbery, treasures of conscientiousness and self-denial.

2

Unluckily, I never cared a cent for anything but art, and never shall. My idea of man's chief end was to enrich the world with things of beauty, and have a fairly good time myself while doing so. I do not think I mentioned that second part, which is the only one I have managed to carry out; but my father must have suspected the suppression, for he branded the whole affair as self-indulgence.

"Well," I remember crying once, "and what is your life? You are only trying to get money, and to get it from other people at that."

He sighed bitterly (which was very much his habit), and shook his poor head at me. "Ah, Loudon, Loudon!" said he, "you boys think yourselves very smart. But, struggle as you please, a man has to work in this world. He must be an honest man or a thief, Loudon."

You can see for yourself how vain it was to argue with my father. The despair that seized upon me after such an interview was, besides, embittered by remorse; for I was at times petulant, but he invariably gentle; and I was fighting, after all, for my own liberty and pleasure, he singly for what he thought to be my good. And all the time he never despaired. "There is good stuff in you, Loudon," he would say; "there is the right stuff in you. Blood will tell, and you will come right in time. I am not afraid my boy will ever disgrace me; I am only vexed he should sometimes talk nonsense." And then he would pat my shoulder or my hand with a kind of motherly way he had, very affecting in a man so strong and beautiful.

As soon as I had graduated from the high school, he packed me off to the Muskegon Commercial Academy. You are a foreigner, and you will have a difficulty in accepting the reality of this seat of education. I assure you before I begin that I am wholly serious. The place really existed, possibly exists to-day: we were proud of it in the State, as something exceptionally nineteenth century and civilised; and my father, when he saw me to the cars, no doubt considered he was putting me in a straight line for the Presidency and the New Jerusalem.

"Loudon," said he, "I am now giving you a chance that Julius Cæsar could not have given to his son — a chance to see life as it is, before your own turn comes to start in earnest. Avoid rash speculation, try to behave like a gentleman; and if you will take my advice, confine yourself to a safe, conservative business in railroads. Breadstuffs are tempting, but very dangerous; I would not try breadstuffs at your time of life; but you may feel your way a little in other commodities. Take a pride to keep your books posted, and never throw good money after bad. There, my dear boy. kiss me good-bye; and never forget that you are an only chick, and that your dad watches your career with fond suspense."

The commercial college was a fine, roomy establishment, pleasantly situate among woods. The air was healthy, the food excellent, the premium high. Electric wires connected it (to use the words of the prospectus) with "the various world centres." The reading-room was well supplied with "commercial organs." The talk was that of Wall Street; and the pupils (from fifty to a hundred lads) were principally engaged in rooking or trying to rook one another for nominal sums in what was called "college paper." We had class hours, indeed, in the morning, when we studied German, French, book-keeping, and the like goodly matters; but the bulk of our day and the gist of the education centred in the exchange, where we were taught to gamble in produce and securities. Since not one of the participants possessed a bushel of wheat or a dollar's worth of stock, legitimate business was of course impossible from the beginning. It was cold-drawn gambling, without colour or disguise. Just that which is the impediment and destruction of all genuine commercial enterprise, just that we were taught with every luxury of stage effect. Our simulacrum of a market was ruled by the real markets outside, so that we might experience the course and vicissitude of prices. We must keep books, and our ledgers were overhauled at the month's end by the principal or his assistants. To add a spice of verisimilitude, "college paper" (like poker chips) had an actual marketable value. It was bought for each pupil by anxious parents and guardians at the rate of one cent for the dollar. The same pupil, when his education was complete, resold, at the same figure, so much as was left him to the college; and even in the midst of his curriculum, a successful operator would sometimes realise a proportion of his holding, and stand a

supper on the sly in the neighbouring hamlet.
In short, if there was ever a worse education, it
must have been in that academy where Oliver met
Charlie Bates.

When I was first guided into the exchange to
have my desk pointed out by one of the assistant
teachers, I was overwhelmed by the clamour and
confusion. Certain blackboards at the other end
of the building were covered with figures continually replaced. As each new set appeared, the
pupils swayed to and fro, and roared out aloud
with a formidable and to me quite meaningless
vociferation; leaping at the same time upon the
desks and benches, signalling with arms and heads,
and scribbling briskly in note-books. I thought I
had never beheld a scene more disagreeable; and
when I considered that the whole traffic was illu-
sory, and all the money then upon the market would
scarce have sufficed to buy a pair of skates, I was
at first astonished, although not for long. Indeed,
I had no sooner called to mind how grown-up men
and women of considerable estate will lose their
temper about half-penny points, than (making an
immediate allowance for my fellow-students) I
transferred the whole of my astonishment to the
assistant teacher, who — poor gentleman — had
quite forgot to show me to my desk, and stood in
the midst of this hurly-burly, absorbed and seemingly transported.

"Look, look," he shouted in my ear; "a falling
market! The bears have had it all their own way
since yesterday."

" It can't matter," I replied, making him hear with difficulty, for I was unused to speak in such a babel, " since it is all fun."

" True," said he; " and you must always bear in mind that the real profit is in the book-keeping. I trust, Dodd, to be able to congratulate you upon your books. You are to start in with ten thousand dollars of college paper, a very liberal figure, which should see you through the whole curriculum, if you keep to a safe, conservative business. . . . Why, what 's that? " he broke off, once more attracted by the changing figures on the board. " Seven, four, three! Dodd, you are in luck: this is the most spirited rally we have had this term. And to think that the same scene is now transpiring in New York, Chicago, St. Louis, and rival business centres! For two cents, I would try a flutter with the boys myself," he cried, rubbing his hands; " only it 's against the regulations."

" What would you do, sir? " I asked.

" Do? " he cried with glittering eyes. " Buy for all I was worth! "

" Would that be a safe, conservative business? " I inquired, as innocent as a lamb.

He looked daggers at me. " See that sandy-haired man in glasses? " he asked, as if to change the subject. " That 's Billson, our most prominent undergraduate. We build confidently on Billson's future. You could not do better, Dodd, than follow Billson."

Presently after, in the midst of a still growing tumult, the figures coming and going more busily than ever on the board, and the hall resounding like Pandemonium with the howls of operators, the assistant teacher left me to my own resources at my desk. The next boy was posting up his ledger, figuring his morning's loss, as I discovered later on; and from this ungenial task he was readily diverted by the sight of a new face.

" Say, Freshman," he said, "what's your name? What? Son of Big Head Dodd? What's your figure? Ten thousand? O, you're away up! What a soft-headed clam you must be to touch your books!"

I asked him what else I could do, since the books were to be examined once a month.

" Why, you galoot, you get a clerk!" cries he. " One of our dead beats — that's all they're here for. If you're a successful operator, you need never do a stroke of work in this old college."

The noise had now become deafening; and my new friend, telling me that some one had certainly "gone down," that he must know the news, and that he would bring me a clerk when he returned, buttoned his coat and plunged into the tossing throng. It proved that he was right: some one had gone down; a prince had fallen in Israel; the corner in lard had proved fatal to the mighty; and the clerk who was brought back to keep my books, spare me all work, and get all my share of the education, at a thousand dollars a month, college paper (ten dollars, United States currency), was no other than the prominent Billson whom I could do no better than follow. The poor lad

was very unhappy. It's the only good thing I
have to say for Muskegon Commercial College,
that we were all, even the small fry, deeply mor-
tified to be posted as defaulters; and the collapse
of a merchant prince like Billson, who had ridden
pretty high in his days of prosperity, was, of
course, particularly hard to bear. But the spirit
of make-believe conquered even the bitterness of
recent shame; and my clerk took his orders, and
fell to his new duties, with decorum and civility.

Such were my first impressions in this absurd
place of education; and to be frank, they were
far from disagreeable. As long as I was rich,
my evenings and afternoons would be my own;
the clerk must keep my books, the clerk could do
the jostling and bawling in the exchange; and I
could turn my mind to landscape-painting and
Balzac's novels, which were then my two pre-
occupations. To remain rich, then, became my
problem; or, in other words, to do a safe, conservative line of business. I am looking for that
line still; and I believe the nearest thing to it in
this imperfect world is the sort of speculation
sometimes insidiously proposed to childhood, in
the formula, "Heads, I win; tails, you lose."
Mindful of my father's parting words, I turned
my attention timidly to railroads; and for a
month or so maintained a position of inglorious
security, dealing for small amounts in the most
inert stocks, and bearing (as best I could) the
scorn of my hired clerk. One day I had ventured
a little further by way of experiment; and, in

the sure expectation they would continue to go
down, sold several thousand dollars of Pan-Handle
Preference (I think it was). I had no sooner
made this venture, than some fools in New York
began to bull the market; Pan-Handles rose like
a balloon; and in the inside of half an hour I
saw my position compromised. Blood will tell,
as my father said; and I stuck to it gallantly:
all afternoon I continued selling that infernal
stock, all afternoon it continued skying. I suppose I had come (a frail cockle-shell) athwart
the hawse of Jay Gould; and, indeed, I think I
remember that this vagary in the market proved
subsequently to be the first move in a considerable deal. That evening, at least, the name of
H. Loudon Dodd held the first rank in our col-
legiate gazette, and I and Billson (once more
thrown upon the world) were competing for the
same clerkship. The present object takes the
present eye. My disaster, for the moment, was
the more conspicuous; and it was I that got the
situation. So you see, even in Muskegon Commercial College, there were lessons to be learned.

For my own part, I cared very little whether
I lost or won at a game so random, so complex,
and so dull; but it was sorry news to write to
my poor father, and I employed all the resources
of my eloquence. I told him (what was the truth)
that the successful boys had none of the education; so that if he wished me to learn, he should
rejoice at my misfortune. I went on (not very
consistently) to beg him to set me up again, when

I would solemnly promise to do a safe business in reliable railroads. Lastly (becoming somewhat carried away), I assured him I was totally unfit for business, and implored him to take me away from this abominable place, and let me go to Paris to study art. He answered briefly, gently, and sadly, telling me the vacation was near at hand, when we would talk things over.

When the time came, he met me at the depot, and I was shocked to see him looking older. He seemed to have no thought but to console me and restore (what he supposed I had lost) my courage. I must not be down-hearted; many of the best men had made a failure in the beginning. I told him I had no head for business, and his kind face darkened. "You must not say that, Loudon," he replied; "I will never believe my son to be a coward."

"But I don't like it," I pleaded. "It hasn't got any interest for me, and art has. I know I could do more in art," and I reminded him that a successful painter gains large sums; that a picture of Meissonier's would sell for many thousand dollars.

"And do you think, Loudon," he replied, "that a man who can paint a thousand dollar picture has not grit enough to keep his end up in the stock market? No, sir; this Mason (of whom you speak) or our own American Bierstadt — if you were to put them down in a wheat pit to-morrow, they would show their mettle. Come, Loudon, my dear; Heaven knows I have no thought but your own good, and I will offer you a bargain. I start you again next term with ten thousand dollars; show yourself a man, and double it, and then (if you still wish to go to Paris, which I know you won't) I'll let you go. But to let you run away as if you were whipped, is what I am too proud to do."

My heart leaped at this proposal, and then sank again. It seemed easier to paint a Meissonier on the spot than to win ten thousand dollars on that mimic stock exchange. Nor could I help reflecting on the singularity of such a test for a man's capacity to be a painter. I ventured even to comment on this.

He sighed deeply. "You forget, my dear," said he, "I am a judge of the one, and not of the other. You might have the genius of Bierstadt himself, and I would be none the wiser."

"And then," I continued, "it's scarcely fair. The other boys are helped by their people, who telegraph and give them pointers. There's Jim Costello, who never budges without a word from his father in New York. And then, don't you see, if anybody is to win, somebody must lose?"

"I'll keep you posted," cried my father, with unusual animation; "I did not know it was allowed. I'll wire you in the office cipher, and we'll make it a kind of partnership business, Loudon: — Dodd & Son, eh?" and he patted my shoulder and repeated, "Dodd & Son, Dodd & Son," with the kindliest amusement.

If my father was to give me pointers, and the

commercial college was to be a stepping-stone to Paris, I could look my future in the face. The old boy, too, was so pleased at the idea of our association in this foolery that he immediately plucked up spirit. Thus it befell that those who had met at the depot like a pair of mutes, sat down to table with holiday faces.

And now I have to introduce a new character that never said a word nor wagged a finger, and yet shaped my whole subsequent career. You have crossed the States, so that in all likelihood you have seen the head of it, parcel-gilt and curiously fluted, rising among trees from a wide plain; for this new character was no other than the State capitol of Muskegon, then first projected. My father had embraced the idea with a mixture of patriotism and commercial greed both perfectly genuine. He was of all the committees, he had subscribed a great deal of money, and he was making arrangements to have a finger in most of the contracts. Competitive plans had been sent in; at the time of my return from college my father was deep in their consideration; and as the idea entirely occupied his mind, the first evening did not pass away before he had called me into council. Here was a subject at last into which I could throw myself with pleasurable zeal. Architecture was new to me, indeed; but it was at least an art; and for all the arts I had a taste naturally classical and that capacity to take delighted pains which some famous idiot has supposed to be synonymous with genius. I threw myself headlong into my father's work, acquainted myself with all the plans, their merits and defects, read besides in special books, made myself a master of the theory of strains, studied the current prices of materials, and (in one word) "devilled" the whole business so thoroughly, that when the plans came up for consideration, Big Head Dodd was supposed to have earned fresh laurels. His arguments carried the day, his choice was approved by the committee, and I had the anonymous satisfaction to know that arguments and choice were wholly mine. In the recasting of the plan which followed, my part was even larger; for I designed and cast with my own hand a hot-air grating for the offices, which had the luck or merit to be accepted. The energy and aptitude which I displayed throughout delighted and surprised my father, and I believe, although I say it whose tongue should be tied, that they alone prevented Muskegon capitol from being the eyesore of my native State.

Altogether, I was in a cheery frame of mind when I returned to the commercial college; and my earlier operations were crowned with a full measure of success. My father wrote and wired to me continually. "You are to exercise your own judgment, Loudon," he would say. "All that I do is to give you the figures; but whatever operation you take up must be upon your own responsibility, and whatever you earn will be entirely due to your own dash and forethought." For all that, it was always clear what he intended me to do, and I was always careful to do it. Inside of a month I was at the head of seventeen or eighteen thousand dollars, college paper. And here I fell a victim to one of the vices of the system. The paper (I have already explained) had a real value of one per cent; and cost, and could be sold, for currency. Unsuccessful speculators were thus always selling clothes, books, banjos, and sleeve-links, in order to pay their differences; the successful, on the other hand, were often tempted to realise, and enjoy some return upon their profits. Now I wanted thirty dollars' worth of artist-truck, for I was always sketching in the woods; my allowance was for the time exhausted; I had begun to regard the exchange (with my father's help) as a place where money was to be got for stooping; and in an evil hour I realised three thousand dollars of the college paper and bought my easel.

It was a Wednesday morning when the things arrived, and set me in the seventh heaven of satisfaction. My father (for I can scarcely say myself) was trying at this time a " straddle " in wheat between Chicago and New York; the operation so called is, as you know, one of the most tempting and least safe upon the chess-board of finance. On the Thursday, luck began to turn against my father's calculations; and by the Friday evening, I was posted on the boards as a defaulter for the second time. Here was a rude blow: my father would have taken it ill enough in any case; for however much a man may resent the incapacity of an only son, he will feel his own more sensibly. But it chanced that, in our bitter cup of failure, there was one ingredient that might truly be called poisonous. He had been keeping the run of my position; he missed the three thousand dollars, paper; and in his view, I had stolen thirty dollars, currency. It was an extreme view perhaps; but in some senses, it was just; and my father, although (to my judgment) quite reckless of honesty in the essence of his operations, was the soul of honour as to their details. I had one grieved letter from him, dignified and tender; and during the rest of that wretched term, working as a clerk, selling my clothes and sketches to make futile speculations, my dream of Paris quite vanished, I was cheered by no word of kindness and helped by no hint of counsel from my father.

All the time he was no doubt thinking of little else but his son, and what to do with him. I believe he had been really appalled by what he regarded as my laxity of principle, and began to think it might be well to preserve me from temptation; the architect of the capitol had, besides, spoken obligingly of my design; and while he was thus hanging between two minds, Fortune suddenly stepped in, and Muskegon State capitol reversed my destiny.

"Loudon," said my father, as he met me at the depot, with a smiling countenance, "if you were to go to Paris, how long would it take you to become an experienced sculptor?"

"How do you mean, father?" I cried. "Experienced?"

"A man that could be entrusted with the highest styles," he answered: "the nude, for instance; and the patriotic and emblematical styles."

"It might take three years," I replied.

"You think Paris necessary?" he asked. "There are great advantages in our own country; and that man Prodgers appears to be a very clever sculptor, though I suppose he stands too high to go around giving lessons."

"Paris is the only place," I assured him.

"Well, I think myself it will sound better," he admitted. "A Young Man, a Native of this State, Son of a Leading Citizen, Studies Prosecuted under the Most Experienced Masters in Paris," he added, relishingly.

"But, my dear dad, what is it all about?" I interrupted. "I never even dreamed of being a sculptor."

"Well, here it is," said he. "I took up the statuary contract on our new capitol; I took it up at first as a deal; and then it occurred to me it would be better to keep it in the family. It meets your idea; there's considerable money in the thing; and it's patriotic. So, if you say the word, you shall go to Paris, and come back in three years to decorate the capitol of your native State. It's a big chance for you, Loudon; and I'll tell you what — every dollar you earn, I'll put another alongside of it. But the sooner you go, and the harder you work, the better; for if the first half-dozen statues are n't on a line with public taste in Muskegon, there will be trouble."

CHAPTER II

ROUSSILLON WINE

MY mother's family was Scotch, and it was judged fitting I should pay a visit on my way Paris-ward to my uncle Adam Loudon, a wealthy retired grocer of Edinburgh. He was very stiff and very ironical; he fed me well, lodged me sumptuously, and seemed to take it out of me all the time, cent per cent, in secret entertainment which caused his spectacles to glitter and his mouth to twitch. The ground of this ill-suppressed mirth (as well as I could make out) was simply the fact that I was an American. "Well," he would say, drawing out the word to infinity, "and I suppose now in your country, things will be so and so." And the whole group of my cousins would titter joyously. Repeated receptions of this sort must be at the root, I suppose, of what they call the Great American Jest; and I know I was myself goaded into saying that my friends went naked in the summer months, and that the Second Methodist Episcopal Church in Muskegon was decorated with scalps. I cannot say that these flights had any great success; they seemed to awaken little more surprise than the fact that my father was a Republican or that I had been taught in school to spell *colour* without the *u*. If I had told them (what was after all the truth) that my father had paid a considerable annual sum to have me brought up in a gambling hell, the tittering and grinning of this dreadful family might perhaps have been excused.

I cannot deny but I was sometimes tempted to knock my uncle Adam down; and indeed I believe it must have come to a rupture at last, if they had not given a dinner-party at which I was the lion. On this occasion, I learned (to my surprise and relief) that the incivility to which I had been subjected was a matter for the family circle and might be regarded almost in the light of an endearment. To strangers, I was presented with consideration; and the account given of "my American brother-in-law, poor Janie's man, James K. Dodd, the well-known millionaire of Muskegon," was calculated to enlarge the heart of a proud son.

An aged assistant of my grandfather's, a pleasant, humble creature with a taste for whisky, was at first deputed to be my guide about the city. With this harmless but hardly aristocratic companion, I went to Arthur's Seat and the Calton Hill, heard the band play in the Princes Street Gardens, inspected the regalia and the blood of Rizzio, and fell in love with the great castle on its .cliff, the innumerable spires of churches, the stately buildings, the broad prospects, and those narrow and crowded lanes of the old town where my ancestors had lived and died in the days before Columbus.

But there was another curiosity that interested me more deeply — my grandfather, Alexander Loudon. In his time, the old gentleman had been a working mason, and had risen from the ranks more, I think, by shrewdness than by merit. In his appearance, speech, and manners, he bore broad marks of his origin, which were gall and wormwood to my uncle Adam. His nails, in spite of anxious supervision, were often in conspicuous mourning; his clothes hung about him in bags and wrinkles like a ploughman's Sunday coat; his accent was rude, broad, and dragging: take him at his best, and even when he could be induced to hold his tongue, his mere presence in a corner of the drawing-room, with his open-air wrinkles, his scanty hair, his battered hands, and the cheerful craftiness of his expression, advertised the whole gang of us for a self-made family. My aunt might mince and my cousins bridle; but there was no getting over the solid, physical fact of the stonemason in the chimney-corner.

That is one advantage of being an American: it never occurred to me to be ashamed of my grandfather, and the old gentleman was quick to mark the difference. He held my mother in tender memory, perhaps because he was in the habit of daily contrasting her with Uncle Adam, whom he detested to the point of frenzy; and he set down to inheritance from his favourite my own becoming treatment of himself. On our walks abroad,

which soon became daily, he would sometimes
(after duly warning me to keep the matter dark
from " Aadam ") skulk into some old familiar
pot-house; and there (if he had the luck to en-
counter any of his veteran cronies) he would present me to the company with manifest pride, casting
at the same time a covert slur on the rest of his
descendants. " This is my Jeannie's yin," he would
say. " He 's a fine fallow, him." The purpose of
our excursions was not to seek antiquities or to
enjoy famous prospects, but to visit one after another a series of doleful suburbs, for which it was
the old gentleman's chief claim to renown that he
had been the sole contractor, and too often the
architect besides. I have rarely seen a more shocking exhibition: the bricks seemed to be blushing
in the walls, and the slates on the roof to have
turned pale with shame; but I was careful not to
communicate these impressions to the aged artificer at my side; and when he would direct my
attention to some fresh monstrosity — perhaps with
the comment, " There 's an idee of mine's: it 's
cheap and tasty, and had a graand run; the idee
was soon stole, and there 's whole deestricts near
Glesgie with the goathic adeetion and that plunth,"
— I would civilly make haste to admire and (what
I found particularly delighted him) to inquire into
the cost of each adornment. It will be conceived
that Muskegon capitol was a frequent and a welcome ground of talk; I drew him all the plans
from memory; and he, with the aid of a narrow
volume full of figures and tables, which answered

(I believe) to the name of Molesworth, and was his constant pocket companion, would draw up rough estimates and make imaginary offers on the various contracts. Our Muskegon builders he pronounced a pack of cormorants; and the congenial subject, together with my knowledge of architectural terms, the theory of strains, and the prices of materials in the States, formed a strong bond of union between what might have been otherwise an ill-assorted pair, and led my grandfather to pronounce me, with emphasis, "a real intalligent kind of a cheild." Thus a second time, as you will presently see, the capitol of my native State had influentially affected the current of my life.

I left Edinburgh, however, with not the least idea that I had done a stroke of excellent business for myself, and singly delighted to escape out of a somewhat dreary house and plunge instead into the rainbow city of Paris. Every man has his own romance; mine clustered exclusively about the practice of the arts, the life of Latin Quarter students, and the world of Paris as depicted by that grimy wizard, the author of the *Comédie Humaine*. I was not disappointed — I could not have been; for I did not see the facts, I brought them with me ready-made. Z. Marcas lived next door to me in my ungainly, ill-smelling hotel of the Rue Racine; I dined at my villainous restaurant with Lousteau and with Rastignac: if a curricle nearly ran me down at a street-crossing, Maxime de Trailles would be the driver. I dined,

I say, at a poor restaurant and lived in a poor hotel; and this was not from need, but sentiment. My father gave me a profuse allowance, and I might have lived (had I chosen) in the Quartier de l'Etoile and driven to my studies daily. Had I done so, the glamour must have fled: I should still have been but Loudon Dodd; whereas now I was a Latin Quarter student, Murger's successor, living in flesh and blood the life of one of those romances I had loved to read, to re-read, and to dream over, among the woods of Muskegon.

At this time we were all a little Murger-mad in the Latin Quarter. The play of the *Vie de Bohème* (a dreary, snivelling piece) had been produced at the Odéon, had run an unconscionable time — for Paris, and revived the freshness of the legend. The same business, you may say, or there and thereabout, was being privately enacted in consequence in every garret of the neighbourhood, and a good third of the students were consciously impersonating Rodolphe or Schaunard to their own incommunicable satisfaction. Some of us went far, and some farther. I always looked with awful envy (for instance) on a certain countryman of my own, who had a studio in the Rue Monsieur le Prince, wore boots, and long hair in a net, and could be seen tramping off, in this guise, to the worst eating-house of the quarter, followed by a Corsican model, his mistress, in the conspicuous costume of her race and calling. It takes some greatness of soul to carry even folly to such heights as these; and for my own part, I had to content myself by pretending very arduously to be poor, by wearing a smoking-cap on the streets, and by pursuing, through a series of misadventures, that extinct mammal, the grisette. The most grievous part was the eating and the drinking. I was born with a dainty tooth and a palate for wine; and only a genuine devotion to romance could have supported me under the cat-civets that I had to swallow, and the red ink of Bercy I must wash them down withal. Every now and again, after a hard day at the studio, where I was steadily and far from unsuccessfully industrious, a wave of distaste would overbear me; I would slink away from my haunts and companions, indemnify myself for weeks of self-denial with fine wines and dainty dishes; seated perhaps on a terrace, perhaps in an arbour in a garden, with a volume of one of my favourite authors propped open in front of me, and now consulted awhile, and now forgotten: — so remain, relishing my situation, till night fell and the lights of the city kindled; and thence stroll homeward by the river-side, under the moon or stars, in a heaven of poetry and digestion.

One such indulgence led me in the course of my second year into an adventure which I must relate: indeed, it is the very point I have been aiming for, since that was what brought me in acquaintance with Jim Pinkerton. I sat down alone to dinner one October day when the rusty leaves were falling and scuttling on the boulevard, and the minds of impressionable men inclined in about an equal degree towards sadness and conviviality. The restaurant was no great place, but boasted a considerable cellar and a long printed list of vintages. This I was perusing with the double zest of a man who is fond of wine and a lover of beautiful names, when my eye fell (near the end of the card) on that not very famous or familiar brand, Roussillon. I remember it was a wine I had never tasted, ordered a bottle, found it excellent, and when I had discussed the contents, called (according to my habit) for a final pint. It appears they did not keep Roussillon in half-bottles. "All right," said I. "Another bottle." The tables at this eating-house are close together; and the next thing I can remember, I was in somewhat loud conversation with my nearest neighbours. From these I must have gradually extended my attentions; for I have a clear recollection of gazing about a room in which every chair was half turned round and every face turned smilingly to mine. I can even remember what I was saying at the moment; but after twenty years, the embers of shame are still alive; and I prefer to give your imagination the cue, by simply mentioning that my muse was the patriotic. It had been my design to adjourn for coffee in the company of some of these new friends; but I was no sooner on the sidewalk than I found myself unaccountably alone. The circumstance scarce surprised me at the time, much less now; but I was somewhat chagrined a little after to find I had walked into a kiosque. I began to wonder if I were any the worse for my last bottle, and decided to steady myself with coffee and brandy. In the Café de la Source, where I went for this restorative, the fountain was playing, and (what greatly surprised me) the mill and the various mechanical figures on the rockery appeared to have been freshly repaired and performed the most enchanting antics. The café was extraordinarily hot and bright, with every detail of a conspicuous clearness, from the faces of the guests to the type of the newspapers on the tables, and the whole apartment swang to and fro like a hammock, with an exhilarating motion. For some while I was so extremely pleased with these particulars that I thought I could never be weary of beholding them : then dropped of a sudden into a causeless sadness ; and then, with the same swiftness and spontaneity, arrived at the conclusion that I was drunk and had better get to bed.

It was but a step or two to my hotel, where I got my lighted candle from the porter and mounted the four flights to my own room. Although I could not deny that I was drunk, I was at the same time lucidly rational and practical. I had but one preoccupation — to be up in time on the morrow for my work ; and when I observed the clock on my chimney-piece to have stopped, I decided to go down-stairs again and give directions to the porter. Leaving the candle burning and my door open, to be a guide to me on my return, I set forth accordingly. The house was quite dark ; but as there were only the three doors on each landing, it was impossible to wander, and I had nothing to do but descend the stairs until I saw the glimmer

of the porter's night light. I counted four flights:
no porter. It was possible, of course, that I had
reckoned incorrectly; so I went down another and
another, and another, still counting as I went,
until I had reached the preposterous figure of
nine flights. It was now quite clear that I had
somehow passed the porter's lodge without remarking it; indeed, I was, at the lowest figure,
five pairs of stairs below the street, and plunged
in the very bowels of the earth. That my hotel
should thus be founded upon catacombs was a
discovery of considerable interest; and if I had
not been in a frame of mind entirely businesslike,
I might have continued to explore all night this
subterranean empire. But I was bound I must
be up betimes on the next morning, and for that
end it was imperative that I should find the porter. I faced about accordingly, and counting with
painful care, remounted towards the level of the
street. Five, six, and seven flights I climbed, and
still there was no porter. I began to be weary of
the job, and reflecting that I was now close to my
own room, decided I should go to bed. Eight, nine,
ten, eleven, twelve, thirteen flights I mounted; and
my open door seemed to be as wholly lost to me
as the porter and his floating dip. I remembered
that the house stood but six stories at its highest
point, from which it appeared (on the most moderate computation) I was now three stories higher
than the roof. My original sense of amusement
was succeeded by a not unnatural irritation. " My
room has just *got* to be here," said I, and I stepped

towards the door with outspread arms. There was no door and no wall; in place of either there yawned before me a dark corridor, in which I continued to advance for some time without encountering the smallest opposition. And this in a house whose extreme area scantily contained three small rooms, a narrow landing, and the stair! The thing was manifestly nonsense; and you will scarcely be surprised to learn that I now began to lose my temper. At this juncture I perceived a filtering of light along the floor, stretched forth my hand which encountered the knob of a door-handle, and without further ceremony entered a room. A young lady was within; she was going to bed, and her toilet was far advanced, or the other way about, if you prefer.

"I hope you will pardon this intrusion," said I; "but my room is No. 12, and something has gone wrong with this blamed house."

She looked at me a moment: and then, "If you will step outside for a moment, I will take you there," says she.

Thus, with perfect composure on both sides, the matter was arranged. I waited awhile outside her door. Presently she rejoined me, in a dressing-gown, took my hand, led me up another flight, which made the fourth above the level of the roof, and shut me into my own room, where (being quite weary after these contraordinary explorations) I turned in, and slumbered like a child.

I tell you the thing calmly, as it appeared to

me to pass; but the next day, when I awoke and put memory in the witness-box, I could not conceal from myself that the tale presented a good many improbable features. I had no mind for the studio, after all, and went instead to the Luxembourg gardens, there, among the sparrows and the statues and the falling leaves, to cool and clear my head. It is a garden I have always loved. You sit there in a public place of history and fiction. Barras and Fouché have looked from these windows. Lousteau and De Banville (one as real as the other) have rhymed upon these benches. The city tramples by without the railings to a lively measure; and within and about you, trees rustle, children and sparrows utter their small cries, and the statues look˜ on for ever. Here, then, in a seat opposite the gallery entrance, I set to work on the events of the last night, to disengage (if it were possible) truth from fiction.

The house, by daylight, had proved to be six stories high, the same as ever. I could find, with all my architectural experience, no room in its altitude for those interminable stairways, no width between its walls for that long corridor, where I had tramped at night. And there was yet a greater difficulty. I had read somewhere an aphorism that everything may be false to itself save human nature. A house might elongate or enlarge itself — or seem to do so to a gentleman who had been dining. The ocean might dry up, the rocks melt in the sun, the stars fall from heaven like autumn apples; and there was nothing in these incidents to boggle the philosopher. But the case of the young lady stood upon a different foundation. Girls were not good enough, or not good that way, or else they were too good. I was ready to accept any of these views: all pointed to the same conclusion, which I was thus already on the point of reaching, when a fresh argument occurred, and instantly confirmed it. I could remember the exact words we had each said; and I had spoken, and she had replied, in English. Plainly, then, the whole affair was an illusion: catacombs, and stairs, and charitable lady, all were equally the stuff of dreams.

I had just come to this determination, when there blew a flaw of wind through the autumnal gardens; the dead leaves showered down, and a flight of sparrows, thick as a snowfall, wheeled above my head with sudden pipings. This agreeable bustle was the affair of a moment, but it startled me from the abstraction into which I had fallen, like a summons. I sat briskly up, and as I did so, my eyes rested on the figure of a lady in a brown jacket and carrying a paint-box. By her side walked a fellow some years older than myself, with an easel under his arm; and alike by their course and cargo I might judge they were bound for the gallery, where the lady was, doubtless, engaged upon some copying. You can imagine my surprise when I recognised in her the heroine of my adventure. To put the matter beyond question, our eyes met, and she, seeing herself remembered and recalling the trim in which

I had last beheld her, looked swiftly on the ground with just a shadow of confusion.

I could not tell you to-day if she were plain or pretty; but she had behaved with so much good sense, and I had cut so poor a figure in her presence, that I became instantly fired with the desire to display myself in a more favourable light. The young man besides was possibly her brother; brothers are apt to be hasty, theirs being a part in which it is possible, at a comparatively early age, to assume the dignity of manhood; and it occurred to me it might be wise to forestall all possible complications by an apology.

On this reasoning I drew near to the gallery door, and had hardly got in position before the young man came out. Thus it was that I came face to face with my third destiny; for my career has been entirely shaped by these three elements, — my father, the capitol of Muskegon, and my friend, Jim Pinkerton. As for the young lady with whom my mind was at the moment chiefly occupied, I was never to hear more of her from that day forward: an excellent example of the Blind Man's Buff that we call life.

CHAPTER III

TO INTRODUCE MR. PINKERTON

THE stranger, I have said, was some years older than myself: a man of a good stature, a very lively face, cordial, agitated manners, and a grey eye as active as a fowl's.

"May I have a word with you?" said I.

"My dear sir," he replied, "I don't know what it can be about, but you may have a hundred if you like."

"You have just left the side of a young lady," I continued, "towards whom I was led (very unintentionally) into the appearance of an offence. To speak to herself would be only to renew her embarrassment, and I seize the occasion of making my apology, and declaring my respect, to one of my own sex who is her friend, and perhaps," I added, with a bow, "her natural protector."

"You are a countryman of mine; I know it!" he cried: "I am sure of it by your delicacy to a lady. You do her no more than justice. I was introduced to her the other night at tea, in the apartment of some people, friends of mine; and meeting her again this morning, I could not do

less than carry her easel for her. My dear sir,
what is your name?"

I was disappointed to find he had so little bond
with my young lady; and but that it was I who
had sought the acquaintance, might have been
tempted to retreat. At the same time, something
in the stranger's eye engaged me.

"My name," said I, "is Loudon Dodd; I am
a student of sculpture here from Muskegon."

"Of sculpture?" he cried, as though that would
have been his last conjecture. "Mine is James
Pinkerton; I am delighted to have the pleasure
of your acquaintance."

"Pinkerton!" it was now my turn to exclaim.
"Are you Broken-Stool Pinkerton?"

He admitted his identity with a laugh of boyish
delight; and indeed any young man in the quarter might have been proud to own a sobriquet thus
gallantly acquired.

In order to explain the name, I must here
digress into a chapter of the history of manners
in the nineteenth century, very well worth commemoration for its own sake. In some of the
studios at that date, the hazing of new pupils was
both barbarous and obscene. Two incidents following one on the heels of the other tended to
produce an advance in civilisation by the means
(as so commonly happens) of a passing appeal
to savage standards. The first was the arrival of
a little gentleman from Armenia. He had a fez
upon his head and (what nobody counted on) a
dagger in his pocket. The hazing was set about

in the customary style, and, perhaps in virtue of the victim's head-gear, even more boisterously than usual. He bore it at first with an inviting patience; but upon one of the students proceeding to an unpardonable freedom, plucked out his knife and suddenly plunged it in the belly of the jester. This gentleman, I am pleased to say, passed months upon a bed of sickness, before he was in a position to resume his studies. The second incident was that which had earned Pinkerton his reputation. In a crowded studio, while some very filthy brutalities were being practised on a trembling debutant, a tall, pale fellow sprang from his stool and (without the smallest preface or explanation) sang out, "All English and Americans to clear the shop!" Our race is brutal, but not filthy; and the summons was nobly responded to. Every Anglo-Saxon student seized his stool; in a moment the studio was full of bloody coxcombs, the French fleeing in disorder for the door, the victim liberated and amazed. In this feat of arms, both English-speaking nations covered themselves with glory; but I am proud to claim the author of the whole for an American, and a patriotic American at that, being the same gentleman who had subsequently to be held down in the bottom of a box during a performance of *L'Oncle Sam*, sobbing at intervals, "My country, O my country!" While yet another (my new acquaintance, Pinkerton) was supposed to have made the most conspicuous figure in the actual battle. At one blow, he had broken his own stool and sent the

4

largest of his opponents back-foremost through what we used to call "a conscientious nude." It appears that, in the continuation of his flight, this fallen warrior issued on the boulevard still framed in the burst canvas.

It will be understood how much talk the incident aroused in the students' quarter, and that I was highly gratified to make the acquaintance of my famous countryman. It chanced I was to see more of the quixotic side of his character before the morning was done; for as we continued to stroll together, I found myself near the studio of a young Frenchman whose work I had promised to examine, and in the fashion of the quarter carried up Pinkerton along with me. Some of my comrades of this date were pretty obnoxious fellows. I could almost always admire and respect the grown-up practitioners of art in Paris; but many of those who were still in a state of pupilage were sorry specimens, so much so that I used often to wonder where the painters came from, and where the brutes of students went to. A similar mystery hangs over the intermediate stages of the medical profession, and must have perplexed the least observant. The ruffian, at least, whom I now carried Pinkerton to visit, was one of the most crapulous in the quarter. He turned out for our delectation a huge "crust" (as we used to call it) of St. Stephen, wallowing in red upon his belly in an exhausted receiver, and a crowd of Hebrews in blue, green, and yellow, pelting him — apparently with buns; and while we gazed upon this contrivance, regaled us with a piece of his own recent biography, of which his mind was still very full, and which he seemed to fancy represented him in a heroic posture. I was one of those cosmopolitan Americans, who accept the world (whether at home or abroad) as they find it, and whose favourite part is that of the spectator; yet even I was listening with ill-suppressed disgust, when I was aware of a violent plucking at my sleeve.

" Is he saying he kicked her down-stairs? " asked Pinkerton, white as St. Stephen.

" Yes," said I : " his discarded mistress ; and then he pelted her with stones. I suppose that 's what gave him the idea for his picture. He has just been alleging the pathetic excuse that she was old enough to be his mother."

Something like a sob broke from Pinkerton. " Tell him," he gasped — " I can't speak this language, though I understand a little ; I never had any proper education — tell him I 'm going to punch his head."

" For God's sake, do nothing of the sort! " I cried. " They don't understand that sort of thing here." And I tried to bundle him out.

" Tell him first what we think of him," he objected. " Let me tell him what he looks in the eyes of a pure-minded American."

" Leave that to me," said I, thrusting Pinkerton clear through the door.

" *Qu'est-ce qu'il a ?* " [1] inquired the student.

[1] " *What 's the matter with him ?* "

"*Monsieur se sent mal au cœur d'avoir trop regardé votre croûte*,"[1] said I, and made my escape, scarce with dignity, at Pinkerton's heels.

"What did you say to him?" he asked.

"The only thing that he could feel," was my reply.

After this scene, the freedom with which I had ejected my new acquaintance, and the precipitation with which I had followed him, the least I could do was to propose luncheon. I have forgot the name of the place to which I led him, nothing loath; it was on the far side of the Luxembourg at least, with a garden behind, where we were speedily set face to face at table, and began to dig into each other's history and character, like terriers after rabbits, according to the approved fashion of youth.

Pinkerton's parents were from the old country; there too, I incidentally gathered, he had himself been born, though it was a circumstance he seemed prone to forget. Whether he had run away, or his father had turned him out, I never fathomed; but about the age of twelve, he was thrown upon his own resources. A travelling tin-type photographer picked him up, like a haw out of a hedgerow, on a wayside in New Jersey; took a fancy to the urchin; carried him on with him in his wandering life; taught him all he knew himself — to take tin-types (as well as I can make out) and doubt the Scriptures; and died at last in Ohio at the

---

[1] "*The gentleman is sick at his stomach from having looked too long at your daub.*"

corner of a road. "He was a grand specimen,"
cried Pinkerton; "I wish you could have seen
him, Mr. Dodd. He had an appearance of magnanimity that used to remind me of the patriarchs."
On the death of this random protector, the boy
inherited the plant and continued the business.
"It was a life I could have chosen, Mr. Dodd!"
he cried. "I have been in all the finest scenes of
that magnificent continent that we were born to
be the heirs of. I wish you could see my collection
of tin-types; I wish I had them here. They were
taken for my own pleasure and to be a memento;
and they show Nature in her grandest as well as
her gentlest moments." As he tramped the Western States and Territories, taking tin-types, the
boy was continually getting hold of books, good,
bad, and indifferent, popular and abstruse, from
the novels of Sylvanus Cobb to Euclid's Elements,
both of which I found (to my almost equal wonder) he had managed to peruse: he was taking
stock by the way, of the people, the products, and
the country, with an eye unusually observant and
a memory unusually retentive; and he was collecting for himself a body of magnanimous and semi-
intellectual nonsense, which he supposed to be the
natural thoughts and to contain the whole duty
of the born American. To be pure-minded, to be
patriotic, to get culture and money with both hands
and with the same irrational fervour — these appeared to be the chief articles of his creed. In
later days (not of course upon this first occasion)
I would sometimes ask him why; and he had his

answer pat. "To build up the type!" he would
cry. "We're all committed to that; we're all
under bond to fulfil the American Type! Loudon, the hope of the world is there. If we fail, like
these old feudal monarchies, what is left?"

The trade of a tin-typer proved too narrow for
the lad's ambition; it was insusceptible of expan-
sion, he explained; it was not truly modern; and
by a sudden conversion of front, he became a rail-
road scalper. The principles of this trade I never
clearly understood; but its essence appears to be
to cheat the railroads out of their due fare. "I
threw my whole soul into it; I grudged myself
food and sleep while I was at it; the most practised hands admitted I had caught on to the idea
in a month and revolutionised the practice inside
of a year," he said. "And there's interest in it,
too. It's amusing to pick out some one going by,
make up your mind about his character and tastes,
dash out of the office and hit him flying with an
offer of the very place he wants to go to. I don't
think there was a scalper on the continent made
fewer blunders. But I took it only as a stage. I
was saving every dollar; I was looking ahead. I
knew what I wanted — wealth, education, a refined home, and a conscientious, cultured lady for
a wife; for, Mr. Dodd " — this with a formidable
outcry — " every man is bound to marry above
him: if the woman's not the man's superior, I
brand it as mere sensuality. There was my idea,
at least. That was what I was saving for; and
enough, too! But it isn't every man, I know that

— it 's far from every man — could do what I did: close up the livest agency in St. Jo, where he was coining dollars by the pot, set out alone, without a friend or a word of French, and settle down here to spend his capital learning art."

" Was it an old taste? " I asked him, " or a sudden fancy? "

" Neither, Mr. Dodd," he admitted. " Of course, I had learned in my tin-typing excursions to glory and exult in the works of God. But it was n't that. I just said to myself, What is most wanted in my age and country? More culture and more art, I said; and I chose the best place, saved my money, and came here to get them."

The whole attitude of this young man warmed and shamed me. He had more fire in his little toe than I in my whole carcase; he was stuffed to bursting with the manly virtues; thrift and courage glowed in him; and even if his artistic vocation seemed (to one of my exclusive tenets) not quite clear, who could predict what might be accomplished by a creature so full-blooded and so inspired with animal and intellectual energy? So, when he proposed that I should come and see his work (one of the regular stages of a Latin Quarter friendship) I followed him with interest and hope.

He lodged parsimoniously at the top of a tall house near the Observatory, in a bare room, principally furnished with his own trunks and papered with his own despicable studies. No man has less taste for disagreeable duties than myself; perhaps there is only one subject on which I cannot flatter a man without a blush; but upon that, upon all that touches art, my sincerity is Roman. Once and twice I made the circuit of his walls in silence, spying in every corner for some spark of merit; he, meanwhile, following close at my heels, reading the verdict in my face with furtive glances, presenting some fresh study for my inspection with undisguised anxiety, and (after it had been silently weighed in the balances and found wanting) whisking it away with an open gesture of despair. By the time the second round was completed, we were both extremely depressed.

"O!" he groaned, breaking the long silence, "it's quite unnecessary you should speak!"

"Do you want me to be frank with you? I think you are wasting time," said I.

"You don't see any promise?" he inquired, beguiled by some return of hope, and turning upon me the embarrassing brightness of his eye. "Not in this still-life here, of the melon? One fellow thought it good."

It was the least I could do to give the melon a more particular examination; which, when I had done, I could but shake my head. "I am truly sorry, Pinkerton," said I, "but I can't advise you to persevere."

He seemed to recover his fortitude at the moment, rebounding from disappointment like a man of india-rubber. "Well," said he, stoutly, "I don't know that I'm surprised. But I'll go on with the course; and throw my whole soul into it, too. You mustn't think the time is lost. It's all cul-

ture; it will help me to extend my relations when
I get back home; it may fit me for a position on
one of the illustrateds; and then I can always
turn dealer," he said, uttering the monstrous proposition, which was enough to shake the Latin
Quarter to the dust, with entire simplicity. " It's
all experience, besides"; he continued, "and it
seems to me there's a tendency to underrate experience, both as net profit and investment. Never
mind. That's done with. But it took courage for
you to say what you did, and I'll never forget it.
Here's my hand, Mr. Dodd. I'm not your equal
in culture or talent —— "

"You know nothing about that," I interrupted.
"I have seen your work, but you have n't seen
mine."

"No more I have," he cried; "and let's go
see it at once! But I know you are away up. I
can feel it here."

To say truth, I was almost ashamed to introduce him to my studio — my work, whether ab-
solutely good or bad, being so vastly superior to
his. But his spirits were now quite restored; and
he amazed me, on the way, with his light-hearted
talk and new projects. So that I began at last to
understand how matters lay: that this was not an
artist who had been deprived of the practice of his
single art; but only a business man of very extended interests, informed (perhaps something of
the most suddenly) that one investment out of
twenty had gone wrong.

As a matter of fact besides (although I never

suspected it) he was already seeking consolation with another of the muses, and pleasing himself with the notion that he would repay me for my sincerity, cement our friendship, and (at one and the same blow) restore my estimation of his talents. Several times already, when I had been speaking of myself, he had pulled out a writing-pad and scribbled a brief note; and now, when we entered the studio, I saw it in his hand again, and the pencil go to his mouth, as he cast a comprehensive glance round the uncomfortable building.

"Are you going to make a sketch of it?" I could not help asking, as I unveiled the Genius of Muskegon.

"Ah, that's my secret," said he. "Never you mind. A mouse can help a lion."

He walked round my statue and had the design explained to him. I had represented Muskegon as a young, almost a stripling, mother, with something of an Indian type; the babe upon her knees was winged, to indicate our soaring future; and her seat was a medley of sculptured fragments, Greek, Roman, and Gothic, to remind us of the older worlds from which we trace our generation.

"Now, does this satisfy you, Mr. Dodd?" he inquired, as soon as I had explained to him the main features of the design.

"Well," I said, "the fellows seem to think it's not a bad *bonne femme* for a beginner. I don't think it's entirely bad, myself. Here is the best point; it builds up best from here. No, it seems to me it has a kind of merit," I admitted; "but I mean to do better."

"Ah, that's the word!" cried Pinkerton. "There's the word I love!" and he scribbled in his pad.

"What in creation ails you?" I inquired. "It's the most commonplace expression in the English language."

"Better and better!" chuckled Pinkerton. "The unconsciousness of genius. Lord, but this is coming in beautiful!" and he scribbled again.

"If you're going to be fulsome," said I, "I'll close the place of entertainment." And I threatened to replace the veil upon the Genius.

"No, no," said he. "Don't be in a hurry. Give me a point or two. Show me what's particularly good."

"I would rather you found that out for yourself," said I.

"The trouble is," said he, "that I've never turned my attention to sculpture, beyond, of course, admiring it, as everybody must who has a soul. So do just be a good fellow, and explain to me what you like in it, and what you tried for, and where the merit comes in. It'll be all education for me."

"Well, in sculpture, you see, the first thing you have to consider is the masses. It's, after all, a kind of architecture," I began, and delivered a lecture on that branch of art, with illustrations from my own masterpiece there present, all of which, if you don't mind, or whether you mind or not, I mean to conscientiously omit. Pinkerton listened with a fiery interest, questioned me with a certain uncultivated shrewdness, and continued to scratch down notes, and tear fresh sheets from his pad. I found it inspiring to have my words thus taken down like a professor's lecture; and having had no previous experience of the press, I was unaware that they were all being taken down wrong. For the same reason (incredible as it must appear in an American) I never entertained the least suspicion that they were destined to be dished up with a sauce of penny-a-lining gossip; and myself, my person, and my works of art butchered to make a holiday for the readers of a Sunday paper. Night had fallen over the Genius of Muskegon before the issue of my theoretic eloquence was stayed, nor did I separate from my new friend without an appointment fc. the morrow.

I was indeed greatly taken with this first view of my countryman, and continued, on further acquaintance, to be interested, amused, and attracted by him in about equal proportions. I must not say he had a fault, not only because my mouth is sealed by gratitude, but because those he had sprang merely from his education, and you could see he had cultivated and improved them like virtues. For all that, I can never deny he was a troublous friend to me, and the trouble began early.

It may have been a fortnight later that I divined the secret of the writing-pad. My wretch (it leaked out) wrote letters for a paper in the West, and had filled a part of one of them with descriptions of myself. I pointed out to him that he had no right to do so without asking my permission.

" Why, this is just what I hoped!" he exclaimed. " I thought you did n't seem to catch on; only it seemed too good to be true."

" But, my good fellow, you were bound to warn me," I objected.

" I know it 's generally considered etiquette," he admitted; " but between friends, and when it was only with a view of serving you, I thought it would n't matter. I wanted it (if possible) to come on you as a surprise; I wanted you just to waken, like Lord Byron, and find the papers full of you. You must admit it was a natural thought. And no man likes to boast of a favour beforehand."

" But heavens and earth! how do you know I think it a favour?" I cried.

He became immediately plunged in despair. " You think it a liberty," said he; " I see that. I would rather have cut off my hand. I would stop it now, only it 's too late; it 's published by now. And I wrote it with so much pride and pleasure!"

I could think of nothing but how to console him. " O, I dare say it 's all right," said I. " I know you meant it kindly, and you would be sure to do it in good taste."

" That you may swear to," he cried. " It 's a pure, bright, A number 1 paper; the St. Jo *Sunday Herald*. The idea of the series was quite my own; I interviewed the editor, put it to him

straight; the freshness of the idea took him, and
I walked out of that office with the contract in my
pocket, and did my first Paris letter that evening
in St. Jo. The editor did no more than glance
his eye down the head-lines. 'You 're the man for
us,' said he."

I was certainly far from reassured by this sketch
of the class of literature in which I was to make
my first appearance; but I said no more, and possessed my soul in patience, until the day came when
I received a copy of a newspaper marked in the
corner, "Compliments of J. P." I opened it with
sensible shrinkings; and there, wedged between
an account of a prize-fight and a skittish article
upon chiropody — think of chiropody treated with
a leer! — I came upon a column and a half in which
myself and my poor statue were embalmed. Like
the editor with the first of the series, I did but
glance my eye down the head-lines and was more
than satisfied.

ANOTHER OF PINKERTON'S SPICY CHATS.

ART PRACTITIONERS IN PARIS.

MUSKEGON'S COLUMNED CAPITOL.

SON OF MILLIONAIRE DODD,

PATRIOT AND ARTIST.

"HE MEANS TO DO BETTER."

In the body of the text besides, my eye caught,
as it passed, some deadly expressions: "Figure
somewhat fleshy," "bright, intellectual smile,"

" the unconsciousness of genius," " ' Now, Mr.
Dodd,' resumed the reporter, ' what would be your
idea of a distinctively American quality in sculpture?' " It was true the question had been asked;
it was true, alas! that I had answered; and now
here was my reply, or some strange hash of it,
gibbeted in the cold publicity of type. I thanked
God that my French fellow-students were ignorant of English; but when I thought of the British
— of Myner (for instance) or the Stennises — I
think I could have fallen on Pinkerton and beat
him.

To divert my thoughts (if it were possible) from
this calamity, I turned to a letter from my father
which had arrived by the same post. The envelope
contained a strip of newspaper-cutting; and my
eye caught again, " Son of Millionaire Dodd —
Figure somewhat fleshy," and the rest of the degrading nonsense. What would my father think
of it? I wondered, and opened his manuscript.
" My dearest boy," it began, " I send you a cutting,
which has pleased me very much, from a St. Joseph
paper of high standing. At last you seem to be
coming fairly to the front; and I cannot but reflect
with delight and gratitude how very few youths
of your age occupy nearly two columns of press-
matter all to themselves. I only wish your dear
mother had been here to read it over my shoulder;
but we will hope she shares my grateful emotion
in a better place. Of course I have sent a copy to
your grandfather and uncle in Edinburgh; so you
can keep the one I enclose. This Jim Pinkerton

seems a valuable acquaintance; he has certainly great talent; and it is a good general rule to keep in with pressmen."

I hope it will be set down to the right side of my account, but I had no sooner read these words, so touchingly silly, than my anger against Pinkerton was swallowed up in gratitude. Of all the circumstances of my career, my birth, perhaps, excepted, not one had given my poor father so profound a pleasure as this article in the *Sunday Herald*. What a fool, then, was I, to be lamenting! when I had at last, and for once, and at the cost of only a few blushes, paid back a fraction of my debt of gratitude. So that, when I next met Pinkerton, I took things very lightly; my father was pleased, and thought the letter very clever, I told him; for my own part, I had no taste for publicity: thought the public had no concern with the artist, only with his art; and though I owned he had handled it with great consideration, I should take it as a favour if he never did it again.

"There it is," he said, despondingly. • "I 've hurt you. You can't deceive me, Loudon. It 's the want of tact, and it 's incurable." He sat down, and leaned his head upon his hand. "I had no advantages when I was young, you see," he added.

"Not in the least, my dear fellow," said I. "Only the next time you wish to do me a service, just speak about my work; leave my wretched person out, and my still more wretched conversation; and above all," I added, with an irrepressible shudder, " don't tell them how I said it! There's that phrase, now: 'With a proud, glad smile.' Who cares whether I smiled or not?"

" O, there now, Loudon, you're entirely wrong," he broke in. " That's what the public likes; that's the merit of the thing, the literary value. It's to call up the scene before them; it's to enable the humblest citizen to enjoy that afternoon the same as I did. Think what it would have been to me when I was tramping around with my tin-types to find a column and a half of real, cultured conversation — an artist, in his studio abroad, talking of his art — and to know how he looked as he did it, and what the room was like, and what he had for breakfast; and to tell myself, eating tinned beans beside a creek, that if all went well, the same sort of thing would, sooner or later, happen to myself: why, Loudon, it would have been like a peephole into heaven!"

" Well, if it gives so much pleasure," I admitted, " the sufferers should n't complain. Only give the other fellows a turn."

The end of the matter was to bring myself and the journalist in a more close relation. If I know anything at all of human nature — and the *if* is no mere figure of speech, but stands for honest doubt — no series of benefits conferred, or even dangers shared, would have so rapidly confirmed our friendship as this quarrel avoided, this fundamental difference of taste and training accepted and condoned.

5

CHAPTER IV

IN WHICH I EXPERIENCE EXTREMES OF FORTUNE

WHETHER it came from my training and repeated bankruptcy at the commercial college, or by direct inheritance from old Loudon, the Edinburgh mason, there can be no doubt about the fact that I was thrifty. Looking myself impartially over, I believe that is my only manly virtue. During my first two years in Paris I not only made it a point to keep well inside of my allowance, but accumulated considerable savings in the bank. You will say, with my masquerade of living as a penniless student, it must have been easy to do so: I should have had no difficulty, however, in doing the reverse. Indeed, it is wonderful I did not; and early in the third year, or soon after I had known Pinkerton, a singular incident proved it to have been equally wise. Quarter-day came, and brought no allowance. A letter of remonstrance was despatched, and for the first time in my experience, remained unanswered. A cablegram was more effectual; for it brought me at least a promise of attention. " Will write at once," my father telegraphed; but I waited long for his letter. I was puzzled, angry, and alarmed; but thanks to my previous thrift, I cannot say that I was ever practically embarrassed. The embarrassment, the distress, the agony, were all for my unhappy father at home in Muskegon, struggling for life and fortune against untoward chances, returning at night from a day of ill-starred shifts and ventures, to read and perhaps to weep over that last harsh letter from his only child, to which he lacked the courage to reply.

Nearly three months after time, and when my economies were beginning to run low, I received at last a letter with the customary bills of exchange.

"My dearest boy," it ran, "I believe, in the press of anxious business, your letters and even your allowance have been somewhile neglected. You must try to forgive your poor old dad, for he has had a trying time; and now when it is over, the doctor wants me to take my shotgun and go to the Adirondacks for a change. You must not fancy I am sick, only over-driven and under the weather. Many of our foremost operators have gone down: John T. M'Brady skipped to Canada with a trunkful of boodle; Billy Sandwith, Charlie Downs, Joe Kaiser, and many others of our leading men in this city bit the dust. But Big-Head Dodd has again weathered the blizzard, and I think I have fixed things so that we may be richer than ever before autumn.

"Now I will tell you, my dear, what I propose. You say you are well advanced with your first statue; start in manfully and finish it, and if your teacher — I can never remember how to spell his name — will send me a certificate that it is up to market standard, you shall have ten thousand dollars to do what you like with, either at home or in Paris. I suggest, since you say the facilities for work are so much greater in that city, you would do well to buy or build a little home; and the first thing you know, your dad will be dropping in for a luncheon. Indeed, I would come now, for I am beginning to grow old, and I long to see my dear boy; but there are still some operations that want watching and nursing. Tell your friend, Mr. Pinkerton, that I read his letters every week; and though I have looked in vain lately for my Loudon's name, still I learn something of the life he is leading in that strange, old world, depicted by an able pen."

Here was a letter that no young man could possibly digest in solitude. It marked one of those junctures when the confidant is necessary; and the confidant selected was none other than Jim Pinkerton. My father's message may have had an influence in this decision; but I scarce suppose so, for the intimacy was already far advanced. I had a genuine and lively taste for my compatriot; I laughed at, I scolded, and I loved him. He, upon his side, paid me a kind of dog-like service of admiration, gazing at me from afar off as at one who had liberally enjoyed those "advantages" which he envied for himself. He followed at heel; his laugh was ready chorus; our friends gave him the nickname of " The Henchman." It was in this insidious form that servitude approached me.

Pinkerton and I read and re-read the famous news: he, I can swear, with an enjoyment as unalloyed and far more vocal than my own. The statue was nearly done: a few days' work sufficed to prepare it for exhibition; the master was approached; he gave his consent; and one cloudless morning of May beheld us gathered in my studio for the hour of trial. The master wore his many-hued rosette; he came attended by two of my French fellow-pupils — friends of mine and both considerable sculptors in Paris at this hour. " Corporal John " (as we used to call him), breaking for once those habits of study and reserve which have since carried him so high in the opinion of the world, had left his easel of a morning to countenance a fellow-countryman in some suspense. My dear old Romney was there by particular request; for who that knew him would think a pleasure quite complete unless he shared it, or not support a mortification more easily if he were present to console? The party was completed by John Myner, the Englishman; by the brothers Stennis, — Stennis-*ainé* and Stennis-*frère,* as they used to figure on their accounts at Barbizon — a pair of hare-brained Scots; and by the inevitable Jim, as white as a sheet and bedewed with the sweat of anxiety.

I suppose I was little better myself when I unveiled the Genius of Muskegon. The master walked about it seriously; then he smiled.

"It is already not so bad," said he, in that funny
English of which he was so proud. "No, already
not so bad."

We all drew a deep breath of relief; and Corporal John (as the most considerable junior present) explained to him it was intended for a public
building, a kind of prefecture ——

"*Hé! Quoi?*" cried he, relapsing into French.
"*Qu'est-ce que vous me chantez-là?* O, in Amé-
rica," he added, on further information being hastily furnished. "That is anozer sing. O véry
good, véry good."

The idea of the required certificate had to be
introduced to his mind in the light of a pleasantry
— the fancy of a nabob little more advanced than
the red Indians of "Fénnimore Cooperr"; and
it took all our talents combined to conceive a form
of words that would be acceptable on both sides.
One was found, however: Corporal John en-
grossed it in his undecipherable hand, the master
lent it the sanction of his name and flourish, I
slipped it into an envelope along with one of the
two letters I had ready prepared in my pocket,
and as the rest of us moved off along the boulevard to breakfast, Pinkerton was detached in a
cab and duly committed it to the post.

The breakfast was ordered at Lavenue's, where
no one need be ashamed to entertain even the master; the table was laid in the garden; I had chosen
the bill of fare myself; on the wine question, we
held a council of war with the most fortunate
results; and the talk, as soon as the master laid

aside his painful English, became fast and furious.
There were a few interruptions, indeed, in the
way of toasts. The master's health had to be
drunk, and he responded in a little well-turned
speech, full of neat allusions to my future and to
the United States; my health followed; and then
my father's must not only be proposed and drunk,
but a full report must be despatched to him at
once by cablegram — an extravagance which was
almost the means of the master's dissolution.
Choosing Corporal John to be his confidant (on
the ground, I presume, that he was already too
good an artist to be any longer an American except
in name) he summed up his amazement in one
oft-repeated formula — " *C'est barbare!* " Apart
from these genial formalities, we talked, talked of
art, and talked of it as only artists can. Here in
the South Seas we talk schooners most of the time;
in the quarter we talked art with the like unflag-
ging interest, and perhaps as much result.

Before very long, the master went away; Corporal John (who was already a sort of young master) followed on his heels; and the rank and file
were naturally relieved by their departure. We
were now among equals; the bottle passed, the
conversation sped. I think I can still hear the
Stennis brothers pour forth their copious tirades;
Dijon, my portly French fellow-student, drop wit-
ticisms well conditioned like himself; and another
(who was weak in foreign languages) dash hotly
into the current of talk with some " *Je trove que
pore oon sontimong de delicacy, Corot* . . . ," or

some *"Pour moi Corot est le plou . . . "*; and
then, his little raft of French foundering at once,
scramble silently to shore again. He at least
could understand; but to Pinkerton, I think· the
noise, the wine, the sun, the shadows of the leaves,
and the esoteric glory of being seated at a foreign
festival, made up the whole available means of
entertainment.

We sat down about half-past eleven; I suppose
it was two when, some point arising and some particular picture being instanced, an adjournment
to the Louvre was proposed. I paid the score, and
in a moment we were trooping down the Rue de
Renne. It was smoking hot; Paris glittered with
that superficial brilliancy which is so agreeable to
the man in high spirits, and in moods of dejection
so depressing; the wine sang in my ears, it danced
and brightened in my eyes. The pictures that we
saw that afternoon, as we sped briskly and loqua-
ciously through the immortal galleries, appear to
me, upon a retrospect, the loveliest of all; the comments we exchanged to have touched the highest
mark of criticism, grave or gay.

It was only when we issued again. from the
museum that a difference of race broke up the
party. Dijon proposed an adjournment to a café,
there to finish the afternoon on beer; the elder
Stennis, revolted at the thought, moved for the
country, a forest if possible, and a long walk. At
once the English speakers rallied to the name of
any exercise; even to me, who have been often
twitted with my sedentary habits, the thought of

country air and stillness proved invincibly attractive. It appeared, upon investigation, we had just time to hail a cab and catch one of the fast trains for Fontainebleau. Beyond the clothes we stood in, all were destitute of what is called (with dainty vagueness) personal effects; and it was earnestly mooted, on the other side, whether we had not time to call upon the way and pack a satchel? But the Stennis boys exclaimed upon our effeminacy. They had come from London, it appeared, a week before with nothing but great-coats and tooth-brushes. No baggage — there was the secret of existence. It was expensive, to be sure; for every time you had to comb your hair, a barber must be paid, and every time you changed your linen, one shirt must be bought and another thrown away; but anything was better (argued these young gentlemen) than to be the slaves of haversacks. " A fellow has to get rid gradually of all material attachments; that was manhood " (said they); " and as long as you were bound down to anything, — house, umbrella, or portmanteau, — you were still tethered by the umbilical cord." Something engaging in this theory carried the most of us away. The two Frenchmen, indeed, retired, scoffing, to their bock; and Romney, being too poor to join the excursion on his own resources and too proud to borrow, melted unobtrusively away. Meanwhile the remainder of the company crowded the benches of a cab; the horse was urged (as horses have to be) by an appeal to the pocket of the driver; the train caught by the inside of a

minute; and in less than an hour and a half we were
breathing deep of the sweet air of the forest and
stretching our legs up the hill from Fontainebleau
octroi, bound for Barbizon. That the leading
members of our party covered the distance in fifty-
one minutes and a half is (I believe) one of the
historic landmarks of the colony; but you will
scarce be surprised to learn that I was somewhat
in the rear. Myner, a comparatively philosophic
Briton, kept me company in my deliberate advance; the glory of the sun's going down, the fall
of the long shadows, the inimitable scent and the
inspiration of the woods, attuned me more and
more to walk in a silence which progressively in-
fected my companion; and I remember that, when
at last he spoke, I was startled from a deep
abstraction.

" Your father seems to be a pretty good kind of
a father," said he. " Why don't he come to see
you?" I was ready with some dozen of reasons,
and had more in stock; but Myner, with that
shrewdness which made him feared and admired,
suddenly fixed me with his eyeglass, and asked,
" Ever press him?"

The blood came in my face. No; I had never
pressed him; I had never even encouraged him to
come. I was proud of him; proud of his handsome looks, of his kind, gentle ways, of that bright
face he could show when others were happy;
proud, too (meanly proud, if you like) of his great
wealth and startling liberalities. And yet he would
have been in the way of my Paris life, of much of

which he would have disapproved. I had feared to expose to criticism his innocent remarks on art; I had told myself, I had even partly believed, he did not want to come; I had been (and still am) convinced that he was sure to be unhappy out of Muskegon; in short, I had a thousand reasons, good and bad, not all of which could alter one iota of the fact that I knew he only waited for my invitation.

" Thank you, Myner," said I; " you 're a much better fellow than ever I supposed. I 'll write to-night."

" O, you 're a pretty decent sort yourself," returned Myner, with more than his usual flippancy of manner, but (as I was gratefully aware) not a trace of his occasional irony of meaning.

Well, these were brave days, on which I could dwell for ever. Brave, too, were those that followed, when Pinkerton and I walked Paris and the suburbs, viewing and pricing houses for my new establishment, or covered ourselves with dust and returned laden with Chinese gods and brass warming-pans from the dealers in antiquities. I found Pinkerton well up in the situation of these establishments as well as in the current prices, and with quite a smattering of critical judgment; it turned out he was investing capital in pictures and curiosities for the States, and the superficial thoroughness of the creature appeared in the fact that, although he would never be a connoisseur, he was already something of an expert. The things themselves left him as near as may be cold; but he had a joy of his own in understanding how to buy and sell them.

In such engagements the time passed until I might very well expect an answer from my father. Two mails followed each other, and brought nothing. By the third I received a long and almost incoherent letter of remorse, encouragement, consolation, and despair. From this pitiful document, which (with a movement of piety) I burned as soon as I had read it, I gathered that the bubble of my father's wealth was burst, that he was now both penniless and sick; and that I, so far from expecting ten thousand dollars to throw away in juvenile extravagance, must look no longer for the quarterly remittances on which I lived. My case was hard enough; but I had sense enough to perceive, and decency enough to do my duty. I sold my curiosities, or rather I sent Pinkerton to sell them; and he had previously bought and now disposed of them so wisely that the loss was trifling. This, with what remained of my last allowance, left me at the head of no less than five thousand francs. Five hundred I reserved for my own immediate necessities; the rest I mailed inside of the week to my father at Muskegon, where they came in time to pay his funeral expenses.

The news of his death was scarcely a surprise and scarce a grief to me. I could not conceive my father a poor man. He had led too long a life of thoughtless and generous profusion to endure the change; and though I grieved for myself, I was able to rejoice that my father had been taken from the battle. I grieved, I say, for myself; and it is probable there were at the same date many thousands of persons grieving with less cause. I had lost my father; I had lost the allowance; my whole fortune (including what had been returned from Muskegon) scarce amounted to a thousand francs; and to crown my sorrows, the statuary contract had changed hands. The new contractor had a son of his own, or else a nephew; and it was signified to me, with business-like plainness, that I must find another market for my pigs. In the meanwhile I had given up my room, and slept on a truckle-bed in a corner of the studio, where as I read myself to sleep at night, and when I awoke in the morning, that now useless bulk, the Genius of Muskegon, was ever present to my eyes. Poor stone lady! born to be enthroned under the gilded, echoing dome of the new capitol, whither was she now to drift? for what base purposes be ultimately broken up, like an unseaworthy ship? and what should befall her ill-starred artificer, standing, with his thousand francs, on the threshold of a life so hard as that of the unbefriended sculptor?

It was a subject often and earnestly debated by myself and Pinkerton. In his opinion, I should instantly discard my profession. " Just drop it, here and now," he would say. " Come back home with me, and let's throw our whole soul into business. I have the capital; you bring the culture. *Dodd & Pinkerton* — I never saw a better name for an advertisement; and you can't think, Loudon, how much depends upon a name." On my side, I would admit that a sculptor should possess one of three things — capital, influence, or an energy only to be qualified as hellish. The two first I had now lost; to the third I never had the smallest claim; and yet I wanted the cowardice (or perhaps it was the courage) to turn my back on my career without a fight. I told him, besides, that however poor my chances were in sculpture, I was convinced they were yet worse in business, for which I equally lacked taste and aptitude. But upon this head, he was my father over again; assured me that I spoke in ignorance; that any intelligent and cultured person was bound to succeed; that I must, besides, have inherited some of my father's fitness; and, at any rate, that I had been regularly trained for that career in the commercial college.

"Pinkerton," I said, "can't you understand that, as long as I was there, I never took the smallest interest in any stricken thing? The whole affair was poison to me."

"It's not possible," he would cry; "it can't be; you couldn't live in the midst of it and not feel the charm; with all your poetry of soul, you couldn't help! Loudon," he would go on, "you drive me crazy. You expect a man to be all broken up about the sunset, and not to care a dime for a place where fortunes are fought for and made and lost all day; or for a career that consists in studying up life till you have it at your finger-ends, spying out every cranny where you can get your hand in and a dollar out, and standing there in the midst — one foot on bankruptcy, the other on a borrowed dollar, and the whole thing spinning round you like a mill — raking in the stamps, in spite of fate and fortune."

To this romance of dickering I would reply with the romance (which is also the virtue) of art; reminding him of those examples of constancy through many tribulations, with which the rôle of Apollo is illustrated; from the case of Millet, to those of many of our friends and comrades, who had chosen this agreeable mountain-path through life, and were now bravely clambering among rocks and brambles, penniless and hopeful.

"You will never understand it, Pinkerton," I would say. "You look to the result, you want to see some profit of your endeavours: that is why you could never learn to paint, if you lived to be Methusalem. The result is always a fizzle: the eyes of the artist are turned in; he lives for a frame of mind. Look at Romney, now. There is the nature of the artist. He has n't a cent; and if you offered him to-morrow the command of an army, or the presidentship of the United States, he would n't take it, and you know he would n't."

"I suppose not," Pinkerton would cry, scouring his hair with both his hands; "and I can't see why; I can't see what in fits he would be after, not to; I don't seem to rise to these views. Of course, it's the fault of not having had advantages in early life; but, Loudon, I'm so miserably low, that it seems to me silly. The fact is," he might add with a smile, "I don't seem to have

the least use for a frame of mind without square
meals; and you can't get it out of my head that
it's a man's duty to die rich, if he can."

" What for?" I asked him once.

" O, I don't know," he replied. " Why in snakes
should anybody want to be a sculptor, if you come
to that? I would love to sculp myself. But what
I can't see is why you should want to do nothing
else. It seems to argue a poverty of nature."

Whether or not he ever came to understand me
— and I have been so tossed about since then that
I am not very sure I understand myself — he soon
perceived that I was perfectly in earnest; and after
about ten days of argument, suddenly dropped the
subject, and announced that he was wasting capital, and must go home at once. No doubt he
should have gone long before, and had already lingered over his intended time for the sake of our
companionship and my misfortune; but man is so
unjustly minded that the very fact, which ought
to have disarmed, only embittered my vexation.
I resented his departure in the light of a desertion; I would not say, but doubtless I betrayed
it; and something hang-dog in the man's face and
bearing led me to believe he was himself remorse-
ful. It is certain at least that, during the time of
his preparations, we drew sensibly apart — a circumstance that I recall with shame. On the last
day, he had me to dinner at a restaurant which
he knew I had formerly frequented, and had only
forsworn of late from considerations of economy. He seemed ill at ease; I was myself both

sorry and sulky; and the meal passed with little conversation.

"Now, Loudon," said he, with a visible effort, after the coffee was come and our pipes lighted, "you can never understand the gratitude and loyalty I bear you. You don't know what a boon it is to be taken up by a man that stands on the pinnacle of civilisation; you can't think how it's refined and purified me, how it's appealed to my spiritual nature; and I want to tell you that I would die at your door like a dog."

I don't know what answer I tried to make, but he cut me short.

"Let me say it out!" he cried. "I revere you for your whole-souled devotion to art; I can't rise to it, but there's a strain of poetry in my nature, Loudon, that responds to it. I want you to carry it out, and I mean to help you."

"Pinkerton, what nonsense is this?" I interrupted.

"Now don't get mad, Loudon; this is a plain piece of business," said he; "it's done every day; it's even typical. How are all those fellows over here in Paris, Henderson, Sumner, Long? — it's all the same story: a young man just plum full of artistic genius on the one side, a man of business on the other who doesn't know what to do with his dollars —— "

"But, you fool, you're as poor as a rat," I cried.

"You wait till I get my irons in the fire!" returned Pinkerton. "I'm bound to be rich; and

6

I tell you I mean to have some of the fun as I
go along. Here's your first allowance; take it
at the hand of a friend; I'm one that holds
friendship sacred as you do yourself. It's only
a hundred francs; you'll get the same every
month, and as soon as my business begins to
expand we'll increase it to something fitting.
And so far from it being a favour, just let me
handle your statuary for the American market,
and I'll call it one of the smartest strokes of
business in my life."

It took me a long time, and it had cost us both
much grateful and painful emotion, before I had
finally managed to refuse his offer and compounded
for a bottle of particular wine. He dropped the
subject at last suddenly with a " Never mind;
that's all done with," nor did he again refer to
the subject, though we passed together the rest
of the afternoon, and I accompanied him, on his
departure, to the doors of the waiting-room at
St. Lazare. I felt myself strangely alone; a voice
told me that I had rejected both the counsels of
wisdom and the helping hand of friendship; and
as I passed through the great bright city on my
homeward way, I measured it for the first time
with the eye of an adversary.

CHAPTER V

IN WHICH I AM DOWN ON MY LUCK
IN PARIS

IN no part of the world is starvation an agreeable business; but I believe it is admitted there is no worse place to starve in than this city of Paris. The appearances of life are there so especially gay, it is so much a magnified beergarden, the houses are so ornate, the theatres so numerous, the very pace of the vehicles is so brisk, that a man in any deep concern of mind or pain of body is constantly driven in upon himself. In his own eyes, he seems the one serious creature moving in a world of horrible unreality; voluble people issuing from a café, the queue at theatre doors, Sunday cabfuls of second-rate pleasure-seekers, the bedizened ladies of the pavement, the show in the jewellers' windows — all the familiar sights contributing to flout his own unhappiness, want, and isolation. At the same time, if he be at all after my pattern, he is perhaps supported by a childish satisfaction: this is life at last, he may tell himself; this is the real thing; the bladders on which I was set swimming are now empty, my own weight depends upon the ocean; by my own exertions I must perish or succeed; and I am now enduring in the vivid fact, what I so much delighted to read of in the case of Lousteau or Lucien, Rodolphe or Schaunard.

Of the steps of my misery, I cannot tell at length. In ordinary times what were politically called "loans" (although they were never meant to be repaid) were matters of constant course among the students, and many a man has partly lived on them for years. But my misfortune befell me at an awkward juncture. Many of my friends were gone; others were themselves in a precarious situation. Romney (for instance) was reduced to tramping Paris in a pair of country sabots, his only suit of clothes so imperfect (in spite of cunningly adjusted pins) that the authorities at the Luxembourg suggested his withdrawal from the gallery. Dijon, too, was on a lee shore, designing clocks and gas-brackets for a dealer; and the most he could do was to offer me a corner of his studio where I might work. My own studio (it will be gathered) I had by that time lost; and in the course of my expulsion the Genius of Muskegon was finally separated from her author. To continue to possess a full-sized statue, a man must have a studio, a gallery, or at least the freedom of a back garden. He cannot carry it about with him, like a satchel, in the bottom of a cab, nor can he cohabit in a garret, ten by fifteen, with so momentous a companion. It was my first idea to leave her behind at my departure. There, in her birthplace, she might lend an inspiration, methought, to my successor. But the proprietor, with whom I had unhappily quarrelled, seized the occasion to be disagreeable, and called upon me to remove my property. For a man in such straits as I now found myself, the hire of a lorry was a consideration; and yet even that I could have faced, if I had had anywhere to drive to after it was hired. Hysterical laughter seized upon me, as I beheld (in imagination) myself, the waggoner, and the Genius of Muskegon, standing in the public view of Paris, without the shadow of a destination; perhaps driving at last to the nearest rubbish-heap, and dumping there, among the ordures of a city, the beloved child of my invention. From these extremities I was relieved by a seasonable offer; and I parted from the Genius of Muskegon for thirty francs. Where she now stands, under what name she is admired or criticised, history does not inform us; but I like to think she may adorn the shrubbery of some suburban tea-garden, where holiday shop-girls hang their hats upon the mother, and their swains (by way of an approach of gallantry) identify the winged infant with the god of love.

In a certain cabman's eating-house on the outer boulevard I got credit for my midday meal. Supper I was supposed not to require, sitting down nightly to the delicate table of some rich acquaintances. This arrangement was extremely ill-considered. My fable, credible enough at first, and so long as my clothes were in good order, must have seemed worse than doubtful after my coat became frayed about the edges, and my boots began to squelch and pipe along the restaurant floors. The allowance of one meal a day besides, though suitable enough to the state of my finances, agreed poorly with my stomach. The restaurant was a place I had often visited experimentally, to taste the life of students then more unfortunate than myself; and I had never in those days entered it without disgust, or left it without nausea. It was strange to find myself sitting down with avidity, rising up with satisfaction, and counting the hours that divided me from my return to such a table. But hunger is a great magician; and so soon as I had spent my ready cash, and could no longer fill up on bowls of chocolate or hunks of bread, I must depend entirely on that cabman's eating-house, and upon certain rare, long-expected, long-remembered windfalls. Dijon (for instance) might get paid for some of his pot-boiling work, or else an old friend would pass through Paris; and then I would be entertained to a meal after my own soul, and contract a Latin Quarter loan, which would keep me in tobacco and my morning coffee for a fortnight. It might be thought the latter would appear the more important. It might be supposed that a life, led so near the confines of actual famine, should have dulled the nicety of my palate. On the contrary, the poorer a man's diet, the more sharply is he set on dainties. The last of my ready cash, about thirty francs, was deliberately squandered on a single dinner; and a great part of my time when I was alone was passed upon the details of imaginary feasts.

One gleam of hope visited me — an order for a bust from a rich Southerner. He was free-handed, jolly of speech, merry of countenance; kept me in good-humour through the sittings, and when they were over, carried me off with him to dinner and the sights of Paris. I ate well; I laid on flesh; by all accounts, I made a favourable likeness of the being, and I confess I thought my future was assured. But when the bust was done, and I had despatched it across the Atlantic, I could never so much as learn of its arrival. The blow felled me; I should have lain down and tried no stroke to right myself, had not the honour of my country been involved. For Dijon improved the opportunity in the European style; informing me (for the first time) of the manners of America: how it was a den of banditti without the smallest rudiment of law or order, and debts could be there only collected with a shotgun. " The whole world knows it," he would say; " you are alone, *mon petit Loudon*, you are alone to be in ignorance of these facts. The judges of the Supreme Court fought but the other day with stilettos on the bench at Cincinnati. You should read the little book of one of my friends: *Le Touriste dans le Far-West;* you will see it all there in good French." At last, incensed by days of such discussion, I undertook to prove to him the contrary, and put the affair in the hands of my late father's lawyer. From him I had the gratification of hearing, after a due

interval, that my debtor was dead of the yellow
fever in Key West, and had left his affairs in
some confusion. I suppress his name; for though
he treated me with cruel nonchalance, it is probable he meant to deal fairly in the end.

Soon after this a shade of change in my re-
ception at the cabman's eating-house marked the
beginning of a new phase in my distress. The
first day, I told myself it was but fancy; the next,
I made quite sure it was a fact; the third, in
mere panic I stayed away, and went for forty-
eight hours fasting. This was an act of great
unreason; for the debtor who stays away is but
the more remarked, and the boarder who misses
a meal is sure to be accused of infidelity. On the
fourth day, therefore, I returned, inwardly quaking. The proprietor looked askance upon my entrance; the waitresses (who were his daughters)
neglected my wants and sniffed at the affected
joviality of my salutations; last and most plain,
when I called for a *suisse* (such as was being
served to all the other diners) I was bluntly told
there were no more. It was obvious I was near
the end of my tether; one plank divided me from
want, and now I felt it tremble. I passed a sleepless night, and the first thing in the morning took
my way to Myner's studio. It was a step I had
long meditated and long refrained from; for I
was scarce intimate with the Englishman; and
though I knew him to possess plenty of money,
neither his manner nor his reputation were the
least encouraging to beggars.

I found him at work on a picture, which I was able conscientiously to praise, dressed in his usual tweeds, plain, but pretty fresh, and standing out in disagreeable contrast to my own withered and degraded outfit. As we talked, he continued to shift his eyes watchfully between his handiwork and the fat model, who sat at the far end of the studio in a state of nature, with one arm gallantly arched above her head. My errand would have been difficult enough under the best of circumstances: placed between Myner, immersed in his art, and the white, fat, naked female in a ridiculous attitude, I found it quite impossible. Again and again I attempted to approach the point, again and again fell back on commendations of the picture; and it was not until the model had enjoyed an interval of repose, during which she took the conversation in her own hands and regaled us (in a soft, weak voice) with details as to her husband's prosperity, her sister's lamented decline from the paths of virtue, and the consequent wrath of her father, a peasant of stern principles, in the vicinity of Chalons on the Marne; — it was not, I say, until after this was over, and I had once more cleared my throat for the attack, and once more dropped aside into some commonplace about the picture, that Myner himself brought me suddenly and vigorously to the point.

"You did n't come here to talk this rot," said he.

"No," I replied sullenly; "I came to borrow money."

He painted awhile in silence.

"I don't think we were ever very intimate?" he asked.

"Thank you," said I. "I can take my answer," and I made as if to go, rage boiling in my heart.

"Of course you can go if you like," said Myner; "but I advise you to stay and have it out."

"What more is there to say?" I cried. "You don't want to keep me here for a needless humiliation?"

"Look here, Dodd, you must try and command your temper," said he. "This interview is of your own seeking, and not mine; if you suppose it's not disagreeable to me, you're wrong; and if you think I will give you money without knowing thoroughly about your prospects, you take me for a fool. Besides," he added, "if you come to look at it, you've got over the worst of it by now: you have done the asking, and you have every reason to know I mean to refuse. I hold out no false hopes, but it may be worth your while to let me judge."

Thus — I was going to say — encouraged, I stumbled through my story; told him I had credit at the cabman's eating-house, but began to think it was drawing to a close; how Dijon lent me a corner of his studio, where I tried to model ornaments, figures for clocks, Time with the scythe, Leda and the swan, musketeers for candlesticks, and other kickshaws, which had never (up to that day) been honoured with the least approval.

"And your room?" asked Myner.

"O, my room is all right, I think," said I.

" She is a very good old lady, and has never even mentioned her bill."

" Because she is a very good old lady, I don't see why she should be fined," observed Myner.

" What do you mean by that? " I cried.

" I mean this," said he. " The French give a great deal of credit amongst themselves; they find it pays on the whole, or the system would hardly be continued; but I can't see where *we* come in; I can't see that it 's honest of us Anglo-Saxons to profit by their easy ways, and then skip over the channel or (as you Yankees do) across the Atlantic."

" But I 'm not proposing to skip," I objected.

" Exactly," he replied. " And should n't you? There 's the problem. You seem to me to have a lack of sympathy for the proprietors of cabmen's eating-houses. By your own account you 're not getting on: the longer you stay, it 'll only be the more out of the pocket of the dear old lady at your lodgings. Now I 'll tell you what I 'll do: if you consent to go, I 'll pay your passage to New York, and your railway fare and expenses to Muskegon (if I have the name right) where your father lived, where he must have left friends, and where, no doubt, you 'll find an opening. I don't seek any gratitude, for of course you 'll think me a beast; but I do ask you to pay it back when you are able. At any rate, that 's all I can do. It might be different if I thought you a genius, Dodd; but I don't, and I advise you not to."

" I think that was uncalled for, at least," said I.

" I dare say it was," he returned, with the same steadiness. " It seemed to me pertinent; and besides, when you ask me for money upon no security, you treat me with the liberty of a friend, and it 's to be presumed that I can do the like. But the point is, do you accept? "

" No, thank you," said I; " I have another string to my bow."

" All right," says Myner. " Be sure it 's honest."

" Honest? honest? " I cried. " What do you mean by calling my honesty in question? "

" I won't, if you don't like it," he replied. " You seem to think honesty as easy as Blind Man's Buff: I don't. It 's some difference of definition."

I went straight from this irritating interview, during which Myner had never discontinued painting, to the studio of my old master. Only one card remained for me to play, and I was now resolved to play it: I must drop the gentleman and the frock-coat, and approach art in the workman's tunic.

" *Tiens*, this little Dodd! " cried the master; and then, as his eye fell on my dilapidated clothing, I thought I could perceive his countenance to darken.

I made my plea in English; for I knew, if he were vain of anything, it was of his achievement of the island tongue. " Master," said I, " will you take me in your studio again? but this time as a workman."

" I sought your fazér was immensely reech," said he.

I explained to him that I was now an orphan and penniless.

He shook his head. " I have betterr workmen waiting at my door," said he; " far betterr workmen."

" You used to think something of my work, sir," I pleaded.

" Somesing, somesing—yés!" he cried; "énough for a son of a reech man — not énough for an orphan. Besides, I sought you might learn to be an artist; I did not sink you might learn to be a workman."

On a certain bench on the outer boulevard, not far from the tomb of Napoleon, a bench shaded at that date by a shabby tree, and commanding a view of muddy roadway and blank wall, I sat down to wrestle with my misery. The weather was cheerless and dark; in three days I had eaten but once; I had no tobacco; my shoes were soaked, my trousers horrid with mire; my humour and all the circumstances of the time and place lugubriously attuned. Here were two men who had both spoken fairly of my work while I was rich and wanted nothing; now that I was poor and lacked all: " no genius," said the one; " not enough for an orphan," the other; and the first offered me my passage like a pauper immigrant, and the second refused me a day's wage as a hewer of stone — plain dealing for an empty belly. They had not been insincere in the past; they were not insincere to-day: change of circumstance had introduced a new criterion: that was all.

But if I acquitted my two Job's comforters of insincerity, I was yet far from admitting them infallible. Artists had been contemned before, and had lived to turn the laugh on their contemners. How old was Corot before he struck the vein of his own precious metal? When had a young man been more derided (or more justly so) than the god of my admiration, Balzac? Or if I required a bolder inspiration, what had I to do but turn my head to where the gold dome of the Invalides glittered against inky squalls, and recall the tale of him sleeping there: from the day when a young artillery-sub could be giggled at and nicknamed Puss-in-Boots by frisky misses; on to the days of so many crowns and so many victories, and so many hundred mouths of cannon, and so many thousand war-hoofs trampling the roadways of astonished Europe eighty miles in front of the grand army? To go back, to give up, to proclaim myself a failure, an ambitious failure, first a rocket, then a stick! I, Loudon Dodd, who had refused all other livelihoods with scorn, and been advertised in the St. Joseph *Sunday Herald* as a patriot and an artist, to be returned upon my native Muskegon like damaged goods, and go the circuit of my father's acquaintance, cap in hand, and begging to sweep offices! No, by Napoleon! I would die at my chosen trade; and the two who had that day flouted me should live to envy my success, or to weep tears of unavailing penitence behind my pauper coffin.

Meantime, if my courage was still undimin-

ished, I was none the nearer to a meal. At no
great distance my cabman's eating-house stood,
at the tail of a muddy cab-rank, on the shores of
a wide thoroughfare of mud, offering (to fancy)
a face of ambiguous invitation. I might be received, I might once more fill my belly there; on
the other hand, it was perhaps this day the bolt
was destined to fall, and I might be expelled instead, with vulgar hubbub. It was policy to make
the attempt, and I knew it was policy; but I had
already, in the course of that one morning, endured
too many affronts, and I felt I could rather starve
than face another. I had courage and to spare for
the future, none left for that day; courage for the
main campaign, but not a spark of it for that pre-
liminary skirmish of the cabman's restaurant. I
continued accordingly to sit upon my bench, not
far from the ashes of Napoleon, now drowsy, now
light-headed, now in complete mental obstruction,
or only conscious of an animal pleasure in quies-
cence; and now thinking, planning, and remembering with unexampled clearness, telling myself
tales of sudden wealth, and gustfully ordering and
greedily consuming imaginary meals : in the course
of which I must have dropped asleep.

It was towards dark that I was suddenly recalled
to famine by a cold souse of rain, and sprang shivering to my feet. For a moment I stood bewildered : the whole train of my reasoning and
dreaming passed afresh through my mind; I was
again tempted, drawn as if with cords, by the
image of the cabman's eating-house, and again

recoiled from the possibility of insult. "*Qui dort dine*," thought I to myself; and took my homeward way with wavering footsteps, through rainy streets in which the lamps and the shop-windows now began to gleam; still marshalling imaginary dinners as I went.

"Ah, Monsieur Dodd," said the porter, "there has been a registered letter for you. The facteur will bring it again to-morrow."

A registered letter for me, who had been so long without one? Of what it could possibly contain, I had no vestige of a guess; nor did I delay myself guessing; far less form any conscious plan of dishonesty: the lies flowed from me like a natural secretion.

"O," said I, "my remittance at last! What a bother I should have missed it! Can you lend me a hundred francs until to-morrow?"

I had never attempted to borrow from the porter till that moment: the registered letter was, besides, my warranty; and he gave me what he had — three napoleons and some francs in silver. I pocketed the money carelessly, lingered awhile chaffing, strolled leisurely to the door; and then (fast as my trembling legs could carry me) round the corner to the Café de Cluny. French waiters are deft and speedy: they were not deft enough for me; and I had scarce decency to let the man set the wine upon the table or put the butter alongside the bread, before my glass and my mouth were filled. Exquisite bread of the Café Cluny, exquisite first glass of old Pomard tingling to my wet feet, in-

describable first olive culled from the *hors d'œuvre*
— I suppose, when I come to lie dying, and the
lamp begins to grow dim, I shall still recall your
savour. Over the rest of that meal, and the rest
of the evening, clouds lie thick: clouds perhaps of
Burgundy; perhaps, more properly, of famine and
repletion.

I remember clearly, at least, the shame, the
despair, of the next morning, when I reviewed
what I had done, and how I had swindled the poor,
honest porter; and, as if that were not enough,
fairly burnt my ships, and brought bankruptcy
home to that last refuge, my garret. The porter
would expect his money; I could not pay him;
here was scandal in the house; and I knew right
well, the cause of scandal would have to pack.
" What do you mean by calling my honesty in
question? " I had cried the day before, turning
upon Myner. Ah, that day before! the day before Waterloo, the day before the Flood; the day
before I had sold the roof over my head, my
future, and my self-respect, for a dinner at the
Café Cluny!

In the midst of these lamentations the famous
registered letter came to my door, with healing
under its seals. It bore the postmark of San Francisco, where Pinkerton was already struggling to
the neck in multifarious affairs: it renewed the
offer of an allowance, which his improved estate
permitted him to announce at the figure of two
hundred francs a month; and in case I was in some
immediate pinch, it enclosed an introductory draft

for forty dollars. There are a thousand excellent reasons why a man, in this self-helpful epoch, should decline to be dependent on another; but the most numerous and cogent considerations all bow to a necessity as stern as mine; and the banks were scarce open ere the draft was cashed.

It was early in December that I thus sold myself into slavery; and for six months I dragged a slowly lengthening chain of gratitude and uneasiness. At the cost of some debt I managed to excel myself and eclipse the Genius of Muskegon, in a small but highly patriotic *Standard Bearer* for the Salon; whither it was duly admitted, where it stood the proper length of days entirely unremarked, and whence it came back to me as patriotic as before. I threw my whole soul (as Pinkerton would have phrased it) into clocks and candlesticks; the devil a candlestick-maker would have anything to say to my designs. Even when Dijon, with his infinite good-humour and infinite scorn for all such journey-work, consented to peddle them in indiscriminately with his own, the dealers still detected and rejected mine. Home they returned to me, true as the Standard Bearer; who now, at the head of quite a regiment of lesser idols, began to grow an eyesore in the scanty studio of my friend. Dijon and I have sat by the hour, and gazed upon that company of images. The severe, the frisky, the classical, the Louis Quinze, were there — from Joan of Arc in her soldierly cuirass to Leda with the swan; nay, and God forgive me for a man that knew better! the

humourous was represented also. We sat and
gazed, I say; we criticised, we turned them hither
and thither; even upon the closest inspection they
looked quite like statuettes; and yet nobody would
have a gift of them!

Vanity dies hard; in some obstinate cases it out-
lives the man: but about the sixth month, when
I already owed near two hundred dollars to
Pinkerton, and half as much again in debts scattered about Paris, I awoke one morning with a
horrid sentiment of oppression, and found I was
alone: my vanity had breathed her last during the
night. I dared not plunge deeper in the bog; I
saw no hope in my poor statuary; I owned myself
beaten at last; and sitting down in my nightshirt
beside the window, whence I had a glimpse of the
tree-tops at the corner of the boulevard, and where
the music of its early traffic fell agreeably upon
my ear, I penned my farewell to Paris, to art, to
my whole past life, and my whole former self. " I
give in," I wrote. " When the next allowance
arrives, I shall go straight out West, where you
can do what you like with me."

It is to be understood that Pinkerton had
been, in a sense, pressing me to come from the
beginning; depicting his isolation among new acquaintances, " who have none of them your culture," he wrote; expressing his friendship in
terms so warm that it sometimes embarrassed me
to think how poorly I could echo them; dwelling
upon his need for assistance; and the next moment
turning about to commend my resolution and press

me to remain in Paris. " Only remember, Loudon," he would write, "if you ever *do* tire of it,
there's plenty work here for you — honest, hard,
well-paid work, developing the resources of this
practically virgin State. And of course I need n't
say what a pleasure it would be to me if we were
going at it *shoulder to shoulder.*" I marvel (looking back) that I could so long have resisted these
appeals, and continued to sink my friend's money
in a manner that I knew him to dislike. At least,
when I did awake to any sense of my position, I
awoke to it entirely; and determined not only to
follow his counsel for the future, but even as
regards the past, to rectify his losses. For in this
juncture of affairs I called to mind that I was not
without a possible resource, and resolved, at whatever cost of mortification, to beard the Loudon
family in their historic city.

In the excellent Scots' phrase, I made a moonlight flitting, a thing never dignified, but in my
case unusually easy. As I had scarce a pair of
boots worth portage, I deserted the whole of my
effects without a pang. Dijon fell heir to Joan
of Arc, the Standard Bearer, and the Musketeers.
He was present when I bought and frugally stocked
my new portmanteau; and it was at the door of
the trunk shop that I took my leave of him, for
my last few hours in Paris must be spent alone.
It was alone (and at a far higher figure than my
finances warranted) that I discussed my dinner;
alone that I took my ticket at St. Lazare; all
alone, though in a carriage full of people, that I

watched the moon shine on the Seine flood with its tufted islets, on Rouen with her spires, and on the shipping in the harbour of Dieppe. When the first light of the morning called me from troubled slumbers on the deck, I beheld the dawn at first with pleasure; I watched with pleasure the green shores of England rising out of rosy haze; I took the salt air with delight into my nostrils; and then all came back to me; that I was no longer an artist, no longer myself; that I was leaving all I cared for, and returning to all that I detested, the slave of debt and gratitude, a public and a branded failure.

From this picture of my own disgrace and wretchedness, it is not wonderful if my mind turned with relief to the thought of Pinkerton, waiting for me, as I knew, with unwearied affection, and regarding me with a respect that I had never deserved, and might therefore fairly hope that I should never forfeit. The inequality of our relation struck me rudely. I must have been stupid, indeed, if I could have considered the history of that friendship without shame — I, who had given so little, who had accepted and profited by so much. I had the whole day before me in London, and I determined (at least in words) to set the balance somewhat straighter. Seated in a corner of a public place, and calling for sheet after sheet of paper, I poured forth the expression of my gratitude, my penitence for the past, my resolutions for the future. Till now, I told him, my course had been mere selfishness. I had been selfish to my father and to my friend, taking their help, and denying them (what was all they asked) the poor gratification of my company and countenance.

Wonderful are the consolations of literature! As soon ãs that letter was written and posted, the consciousness of virtue glowed in my veins like some rare vintage.

CHAPTER VI

IN WHICH I GO WEST

I REACHED my uncle's door next morning in time to sit down with the family to breakfast. More than three years had intervened almost without mutation in that stationary household, since I had sat there first, a young American freshman, bewildered among unfamiliar dainties, finnan haddock, kippered salmon, baps and mutton ham, and had wearied my mind in vain to guess what should be under the tea-cozy. If there were any change at all, it seemed that I had risen in the family esteem. My father's death once fittingly referred to, with a ceremonial lengthening of Scotch upper lips and wagging of the female head, the party launched at once (God help me) into the more cheerful topic of my own successes. They had been so pleased to hear such good accounts of me; I was quite a great man now; where was that beautiful statue of the Genius of Something or other? " You have n't it here? not here? Really?" asks the sprightliest of my cousins, shaking curls at me; as though it were likely I had brought it in the cab, or kept it concealed about my person like a birthday surprise. In the bosom of this family, unaccustomed to the

tropical nonsense of the West, it became plain the
Sunday Herald and poor, blethering Pinkerton
had been accepted for their face. It is not possible to invent a circumstance that could have
more depressed me; and I am conscious that I
behaved all through that breakfast like a whipt
schoolboy.

At length, the meal and family prayers being
both happily over, I requested the favour of an
interview with Uncle Adam on "the state of my
affairs." At sound of this ominous expression,
the good man's face conspicuously lengthened; and
when my grandfather, having had the proposition
repeated to him (for he was hard of hearing) announced his intention of being present at the interview, I could not but think that Uncle Adam's
sorrow kindled into momentary irritation. Nothing, however, but the usual grim cordiality appeared upon the surface; and we all three passed
ceremoniously to the adjoining library, a gloomy
theatre for a depressing piece of business. My
grandfather charged a clay pipe, and sat tremu-
lously smoking in a corner of the fireless chimney;
behind him, although the morning was both chill
and dark, the window was partly open and the
blind partly down: I cannot depict what an air
he had of being out of place, like a man ship-
wrecked there. Uncle Adam had his station at
the business table in the midst. Valuable rows
of books looked down upon the place of torture;
and I could hear sparrows chirping in the garden,
and my sprightly cousin already banging the piano

and pouring forth an acid stream of song from the drawing-room overhead.

It was in these circumstances that, with all brevity of speech and a certain boyish sullenness of manner, looking the while upon the floor, I informed my relatives of my financial situation: the amount I owed Pinkerton; the hopelessness of any maintenance from sculpture; the career offered me in the States; and how, before becoming more beholden to a stranger, I had judged it right to lay the case before my family.

"I am only sorry you did not come to me at first," said Uncle Adam. "I take the liberty to say it would have been more decent."

"I think so too, Uncle Adam," I replied; "but you must bear in mind I was ignorant in what light you might regard my application."

"I hope I would never turn my back on my own flesh and blood," he returned with emphasis; but to my anxious ear, with more of temper than affection. "I could never forget you were my sister's son. I regard this as a manifest duty. I have no choice but to accept the entire responsibility of the position you have made."

I did not know what else to do but murmur "Thank you."

"Yes," he pursued, "and there is something providential in the circumstance that you come at the right time. In my old firm there is a vacancy; they call themselves Italian Warehousemen now," he continued, regarding me with a twinkle of humour; "so you may think yourself in luck: we were only grocers in my day. I shall place you there to-morrow."

"Stop a moment, Uncle Adam," I broke in. "This is not at all what I am asking. I ask you to pay Pinkerton, who is a poor man. I ask you to clear my feet of debt, not to arrange my life or any part of it."

"If I wished to be harsh, I might remind you that beggars cannot be choosers," said my uncle; "and as to managing your life, you have tried your own way already, and you see what you have made of it. You must now accept the guidance of those older and (whatever you may think of it) wiser than yourself. All these schemes of your friend (of whom I know nothing, by the bye) and talk of openings in the West, I simply disregard. I have no idea whatever of your going troking across a continent on a wild-goose chase. In this situation, which I am fortunately able to place at your disposal, and which many a well-conducted young man would be glad to jump at, you will receive, to begin with, eighteen shillings a week."

"Eighteen shillings a week!" I cried. "Why, my poor friend gave me more than that for nothing!"

"And I think it is this very friend you are now trying to repay?" observed my uncle, with an air of one advancing a strong argument.

"Aadam!" said my grandfather.

"I'm vexed you should be present at this business," quoth Uncle Adam, swinging rather obsequiously towards the stonemason; "but I must remind you it is of your own seeking."

"Aadam!" repeated the old man.

"Well, sir, I am listening," says my uncle.

My grandfather took a puff or two in silence; and then, "Ye 're makin' an awful poor appearance, Aadam," said he.

My uncle visibly reared at the affront. "I 'm sorry you should think so," said he, "and still more sorry you should say so before present company."

"A believe that; A ken that, Aadam," returned old Loudon, drily; "and the curiis thing is, I 'm no very carin'. See here, ma man," he continued, addressing himself to me. "A 'm your grandfaither, am n't I not? Never you mind what Aadam says. A 'll see justice din ye. A 'm rich."

"Father," said Uncle Adam, "I would like one word with you in private."

I rose to go.

"Set down upon your hinderlands," cried my grandfather, almost savagely. "If Aadam has anything to say, let him say it. It 's me that has the money here; and by Gravy! I 'm goin' to be obeyed."

Upon this scurvy encouragement, it appeared that my uncle had no remark to offer: twice challenged to "speak out and be done with it," he twice sullenly declined; and I may mention that about this period of the engagement, I began to be sorry for him.

"See here, then, Jeannie's yin!" resumed my grandfather. "A'm going to give ye a set-off. Your mither was always my fav'rite, for A never could agree with Aadam. A like ye fine yoursel'; there's nae noansense aboot ye; ye've a fine nayteral idee of builder's work; ye've been to France, where they tell me they're grand at the stuccy. A splendid thing for ceilin's, the stuccy! and it's a vailyable disguise, too; A don't believe there's a builder in Scotland has used more stuccy than me. But as A was sayin', if ye'll follie that trade, with the capital that A'm goin' to give ye, ye may live yet to be as rich as mysel'. Ye see, ye would have always had a share of it when A was gone; it appears ye're needin' it now; well, ye'll get the less, as is only just and proper."

Uncle Adam cleared his throat. "This is very handsome, father," said he; "and I am sure Loudon feels it so. Very handsome, and as you say, very just; but will you allow me to say that it had better, perhaps, be put in black and white?"

The enmity always smouldering between the two men at this ill-judged interruption almost burst in flame. The stonemason turned upon his offspring, his long upper lip pulled down, for all the world, like a monkey's. He stared awhile in virulent silence; and then, "Get Gregg!" said he.

The effect of these words was very visible. "He will be gone to his office," stammered my uncle.

"Get Gregg!" repeated my grandfather.

"I tell you, he will be gone to his office," reiterated Adam.

"And I tell ye, he's takin' his smoke," retorted the old man.

"Very well, then," cried my uncle, getting to his feet with some alacrity, as upon a sudden change of thought, "I will get him myself."

"Ye will not!" cried my grandfather. "Ye will sit there upon your hinderland."

"Then how the devil am I to get him?" my uncle broke forth, with not unnatural petulance.

My grandfather (having no possible answer) grinned at his son with the malice of a schoolboy; then he rang the bell.

"Take the garden key," said Uncle Adam to the servant; "go over to the garden, and if Mr. Gregg the lawyer is there (he generally sits under the red hawthorn), give him old Mr. Loudon's compliments, and will he step in here for a moment?"

"Mr. Gregg the lawyer!" At once I understood (what had been puzzling me) the significance of my grandfather and the alarm of my poor uncle: the stonemason's will, it was supposed, hung trembling in the balance.

"Look here, grandfather," I said, "I did n't want any of this. All I wanted was a loan of (say) two hundred pounds. I can take care of myself; I have prospects and opportunities, good friends in the States —— "

The old man waved me down. "It's me that speaks here," he said curtly; and we waited the coming of the lawyer in a triple silence. He appeared at last, the maid ushering him in — a spectacled, dry but not ungenial looking man.

"Here, Gregg," cried my grandfather. "Just a question. What has Aadam got to do with my will?"

"I'm afraid I don't quite understand," said the lawyer, staring.

"What has he got to do with it?" repeated the old man, smiting with his fist upon the arm of his chair. "Is my money mine's, or is it Aadam's? Can Aadam interfere?"

"O, I see," said Mr. Gregg. "Certainly not. On the marriage of both of your children a certain sum was paid down and accepted in full of legitim. You have surely not forgotten the circumstance, Mr. Loudon?"

"So that, if I like," concluded my grandfather, hammering out his words, "I can leave every doit I die possessed of to the Great Magunn?" — meaning probably the Great Mogul.

"No doubt of it," replied Gregg, with a shadow of a smile.

"Ye hear that, Aadam?" asked my grandfather.

"I may be allowed to say I had no need to hear it," said my uncle.

"Very well," says my grandfather. "You and Jeannie's yin can go for a bit walk. Me and Gregg has business."

When once I was in the hall alone with Uncle Adam, I turned to him, sick at heart. "Uncle Adam," I said, "you can understand, better than I can say, how very painful all this is to me."

"Yes, I am sorry you have seen your grandfather in so unamiable a light," replied this ex-

traordinary man. " You should n't allow it to
affect your mind though. He has sterling qualities, quite an extraordinary character; and I have
no fear but he means to behave handsomely to
you."

His composure was beyond my imitation: the
house could not contain me, nor could I even
promise to return to it: in concession to which
weakness, it was agreed that I should call in about
an hour at the office of the lawyer, whom (as he
left the library) Uncle Adam should waylay and
inform of the arrangement. I suppose there was
never a more topsy-turvy situation: you would
have thought it was I who had suffered some
rebuff, and that iron-sided Adam was a generous
conqueror who scorned to take advantage.

It was plain enough that I was to be endowed:
to what extent and upon what conditions I was
now left for an hour to meditate in the wide and
solitary thoroughfares of the new town, taking
counsel with street-corner statues of George IV.
and William Pitt, improving my mind with the
pictures in the window of a music-shop, and renewing my acquaintance with Edinburgh east
wind. By the end of the hour I made my way
to Mr. Gregg's office, where I was placed, with
a few appropriate words, in possession of a cheque
for two thousand pounds and a small parcel of
architectural works.

" Mr. Loudon bids me add," continued the lawyer, consulting a little sheet of notes, " that although these volumes are very valuable to the

practical builder, you must be careful not to lose
originality. He tells you also not to be 'hadden
doun ' — his own expression — by the theory of
strains, and that Portland cement, properly sanded,
will go a long way."

I smiled, and remarked that I supposed it would.

" I once lived in one of my excellent client's
houses," observed the lawyer; " and I was tempted,
in that case, to think it had gone far enough."

" Under these circumstances, sir," said I, " you
will be rather relieved to hear that I have no intention of becoming a builder."

At this, he fairly laughed; and, the ice being
broken, I was able to consult him as to my conduct. He insisted I must return to the house, at
least, for luncheon, and one of my walks with
Mr. Loudon. " For the evening, I will furnish you
with an excuse, if you please," said he, " by asking you to a bachelor dinner with myself. But
the luncheon and the walk are unavoidable. He
is an old man, and, I believe, really fond of you;
he would naturally feel aggrieved if there were
any appearance of avoiding him; and as for Mr.
Adam, do you know, I think your delicacy out
of place. . . . And now, Mr. Dodd, what are you
to do with this money? "

Ay, there was the question. With two thousand pounds — fifty thousand francs — I might
return to Paris and the arts, and be a prince
and millionaire in that thrifty Latin Quarter. I
think I had the grace, with one corner of my
mind, to be glad that I had sent the London

letter: I know very well that with the rest and worst of me, I repented bitterly of that precipitate act. On one point, however, my whole multiplex estate of man was unanimous: the letter being gone, there was no help but I must follow. The money was accordingly divided into two unequal shares: for the first, Mr. Gregg got me a bill in the name of Dijon to meet my liabilities in Paris; for the second, as I had already cash in hand for the expenses of my journey, he supplied me with drafts on San Francisco.

The rest of my business in Edinburgh, not to dwell on a very agreeable dinner with the lawyer or the horrors of the family luncheon, took the form of an excursion with the stonemason, who led me this time to no suburb or work of his old hands, but with an impulse both natural and pretty, to that more enduring home which he had chosen for his clay. It was in a cemetery, by some strange chance, immured within the bulwarks of a prison; standing, besides, on the margin of a cliff, crowded with elderly stone memorials, and green with turf and ivy. The east wind (which I thought too harsh for the old man) continually shook the boughs, and the thin sun of a Scottish summer drew their dancing shadows.

"I wanted ye to see the place," said he. "Yon's the stane. *Euphemia Ross:* that was my goodwife, your grandmither — hoots! I'm wrong; that was my first yin; I had no bairns by her; — yours is the second, *Mary Murray, Born 1819, Died 1850:* that's her — a fine, plain, decent sort

8

of a creature, tak' her athegether. *Alexander Loudon, Born Seventeen Ninety-Twa, Died —* and then a hole in the ballant: that's me. Alexander's my name. They ca'd me Ecky when I was a boy. Eh, Ecky! ye're an awful auld man!"

I had a second and sadder experience of graveyards at my next alighting-place, the city of Muskegon, now rendered conspicuous by the dome of the new capitol encaged in scaffolding. It was late in the afternoon when I arrived, and raining; and as I walked in great streets, of the very name of which I was quite ignorant — double, treble, and quadruple lines of horse-cars jingling by — hundred-fold wires of telegraph and telephone matting heaven above my head — huge, staring houses, garish and gloomy, flanking me from either hand — the thought of the Rue Racine, ay, and of the cabman's eating-house, brought tears to my eyes. The whole monotonous Babel had grown, or I should rather say swelled, with such a leap since my departure, that I must continually inquire my way, and the very cemetery was brand new. Death, however, had been active; the graves were already numerous, and I must pick my way in the rain, among the tawdry sepulchres of millionaires, and past the plain, black crosses of Hungarian labourers, till chance or instinct led me to the place that was my father's. The stone had been erected (I knew already) "by admiring friends"; I could now judge their taste in monuments; their taste in literature, methought, I could imagine, and I refrained from drawing near enough to read the terms of the inscription. But the name was in larger letters and stared at me — *James K. Dodd.* What a singular thing is a name, I thought; how it clings to a man, and continually misrepresents, and then survives him; and it flashed across my mind, with a mixture of regret and bitter mirth, that I had never known, and now probably never should know, what the *K* had represented. King, Kilter, Kay, Kaiser, I went, running over names at random, and then stumbled with ludicrous misspelling on Kornelius, and had nearly laughed aloud. I have never been more childish; I suppose (although the deeper voices of my nature seemed all dumb) because I have never been more moved. And at this last incongruous antic of my nerves, I was seized with a panic of remorse and fled the cemetery.

Scarce less funereal was the rest of my experience in Muskegon, where, nevertheless, I lingered, visiting my father's circle, for some days. It was in piety to him I lingered; and I might have spared myself the pain. His memory was already quite gone out. For his sake, indeed, I was made welcome; and for mine the conversation rolled awhile with laborious effort on the virtues of the deceased. His former comrades dwelt, in my company, upon his business talents or his generosity for public purposes; when my back was turned, they remembered him no more. My father had loved me; I had left him alone to live and die among the indifferent; now I returned to find him

dead and buried and forgotten. Unavailing penitence translated itself in my thoughts to fresh resolve. There was another poor soul who loved
me: Pinkerton. I must not be guilty twice of the
same error.

A week perhaps had been thus wasted, nor
had I prepared my friend for the delay. Accordingly, when I had changed trains at Council Bluffs,
I was aware of a man appearing at the end of the
car with a telegram in his hand and inquiring
whether there were any one aboard " of the name
of *London* Dodd? " I thought the name near
enough, claimed the despatch, and found it was
from Pinkerton: " What day do you arrive?
Awfully important." I sent him an answer giving
day and hour, and at Ogden found a fresh despatch
awaiting me: " That will do. Unspeakable relief. Meet you at Sacramento." In Paris days
I had a private name for Pinkerton: " The Irrepressible " was what I had called him in hours of
bitterness; and the name rose once more on my
lips. What mischief was he up to now? What
new bowl was my benignant monster brewing
for his Frankenstein? In what new imbroglio
should I alight on the Pacific coast? My trust in
the man was entire, and my distrust perfect. I
knew he would never mean amiss; but I was convinced he would almost never (in my sense) do
aright.

I suppose these vague anticipations added a
shade of gloom to that already gloomy place
of travel: Nebraska, Wyoming, Utah, Nevada,

scowled in my face at least, and seemed to point me back again to that other native land of mine, the Latin Quarter. But when the Sierras had been climbed, and the train, after so long beating and panting, stretched itself upon the downward track — when I beheld that vast extent of prosperous country rolling seaward from the woods and the blue mountains, that illimitable spread of rippling corn, the trees growing and blowing in the merry weather, the country boys thronging aboard the train with figs and peaches, and the conductors, and the very darky stewards, visibly exulting in the change — up went my soul like a balloon; Care fell from his perch upon my shoulders; and when I spied my Pinkerton among the crowd at Sacramento, I thought of nothing but to shout and wave for him, and grasp him by the hand, like what he was — my dearest friend.

" O Loudon! " he cried. " Man, how I 've pined for you! And you have n't come an hour too soon. You 're known here and waited for; I 've been booming you already; you 're billed for a lecture to-morrow night; *Student Life in Paris, Grave and Gay:* twelve hundred places booked at the last stock! Tut, man, you 're looking thin! Here, try a drop of this." And he produced a case bottle, staringly labelled PINKERTON'S THIRTEEN STAR GOLDEN STATE BRANDY, WARRANTED ENTIRE.

" God bless me! " said I, gasping and winking after my first plunge into this fiery fluid. " And what does ' Warranted Entire ' mean? "

"Why, Loudon! you ought to know that!"
cried Pinkerton.   "It's real, copper-bottomed
English; you see it on all the old-time wayside
hostelries over there."

"But if I'm not mistaken, it means something
Warranted Entirely different," said I, "and ap-
plies to the public house, and not the beverages
sold."

"It's very possible," said Jim, quite unabashed.
"It's effective, anyway; and I can tell you, sir,
it has boomed that spirit: it goes now by the gross
of cases. By the way, I hope you won't mind;
I've got your portrait all over San Francisco for
the lecture, enlarged from that carte de visit:
*H. Loudon Dodd, the Americo-Parisienne Sculp-
tor.*   Here's a proof of the small handbills; the
posters are the same, only in red and blue, and the
letters fourteen by one."

I looked at the handbill, and my head turned.
What was the use of words? why seek to explain
to Pinkerton the knotted horrors of "Americo-
Parisienne"? He took an early occasion to point
it out as "rather a good phrase; gives the two
sides at a glance: I wanted the lecture written up to that."   Even after we had reached
San Francisco, and at the actual physical shock
of my own effigy placarded on the streets I
had broken forth in petulant words, he never
comprehended in the least the ground of my
aversion.

"If I had only known you disliked red lettering!" was as high as he could rise.   "You are

perfectly right: a clear-cut black is preferable, and shows a great deal further. The only thing that pains me is the portrait: I own I thought that a success. I 'm dreadfully and truly sorry, my dear fellow: I see now it 's not what you had a right to expect; but I did it, Loudon, for the best; and the press is all delighted."

At the moment, sweeping through green tule swamps, I fell direct on the essential. "But, Pinkerton," I cried, "this lecture is the maddest of your madnesses. How can I prepare a lecture in thirty hours?"

"All done, Loudon!" he exclaimed in triumph. "All ready. Trust me to pull a · piece of business through. You 'll find it all type-written in my desk at home. I put the best talent of San Francisco on the job: Harry Miller, the brightest pressman in the city."

And so he rattled on, beyond reach of my modest protestations, blurting out his complicated interests, crying up his new acquaintances, and ever and again hungering to introduce me to some "whole-souled, grand fellow, as sharp as a needle," from whom, and the very thought of whom, my spirit shrank instinctively.

Well, I was in for it: in for Pinkerton, in for the portrait, in for the type-written lecture. One promise I extorted — that I was never again to be committed in ignorance; even for that, when I saw how its extortion puzzled and depressed the Irrepressible, my soul repented me; and in all else I suffered myself to be led uncomplaining at his

chariot wheels. The Irrepressible, did I say? The
Irresistible were nigher truth.

But the time to have seen me was when I sat
down to Harry Miller's lecture. He was a face-
tious dog, this Harry Miller; he had a gallant way
of skirting the indecent which (in my case) produced physical nausea; and he could be sentimental
and even melodramatic about grisettes and starv-
ing genius. I found he had enjoyed the benefit
of my correspondence with Pinkerton: adventures
of my own were here and there horridly misrep-
resented, sentiments of my own echoed and exaggerated till I blushed to recognise them. I will do
Harry Miller justice: he must have had a kind of
talent, almost of genius; all attempts to lower his
tone proving fruitless, and the Harry-Millerism
ineradicable. Nay, the monster had a certain key
of style, or want of style, so that certain milder
passages, which I sought to introduce, discorded
horribly, and impoverished (if that were possible)
the general effect.

By an early hour of the numbered evening I
might have been observed at the sign of the *Poodle
Dog*, dining with my agent: so Pinkerton delighted to describe himself. Thence, like an ox to
the slaughter, he led me to the hall, where I stood
presently alone, confronting assembled San Francisco, with no better allies than a table, a glass of
water, and a mass of manuscript and type-work,
representing Harry Miller and myself. I read the
lecture; for I had lacked both time and will to get
the trash by heart — read it hurriedly, humbly,

and with visible shame. Now and then I would
catch in the auditorium an eye of some intelligence,
now and then, in the manuscript, would stumble
on a richer vein of Harry Miller, and my heart
would fail me, and I gabbled. The audience
yawned, it stirred uneasily, it muttered, grumbled,
and broke forth at last in articulate cries of " Speak
up!" and " Nobody can hear!" I took to skip-
ping, and being extremely ill-acquainted with the
country, almost invariably cut in again in the un-
intelligible midst of some new topic. What struck
me as extremely ominous, these misfortunes were
allowed to pass without a laugh. Indeed, I was
beginning to fear the worst, and even personal
indignity, when all at once the humour of the
thing broke upon me strongly. I could have
laughed aloud; and being again summoned to
speak up, I faced my patrons for the first time with
a smile. " Very well," I said, " I will try; though
I don't suppose anybody wants to hear, and I
can't see why anybody should." Audience and
lecturer laughed together till the tears ran down;
vociferous and repeated applause hailed my impromptu sally. Another hit which I made but a
little after, as I turned three pages of the copy:
" You see I am leaving out as much as I possibly
can," increased the esteem with which my patrons
had begun to regard me; and when I left the stage
at last, my departing form was cheered with laughter, stamping, shouting, and the waving of hats.

Pinkerton was in the waiting-room, feverishly
jotting in his pocket-book. As he saw me enter,

he sprang up, and I declare, the tears were trickling on his cheeks.

"My dear boy," he cried, "I can never forgive myself, and you can never forgive me. Never mind: I did it for the best. And how nobly you clung on! I dreaded we should have had to return the money at the doors."

"It would have been more honest if we had," said I.

The pressmen followed me, Harry Miller in the front ranks; and I was amazed to find them, on the whole, a pleasant set of lads, probably more sinned against than sinning, and even Harry Miller apparently a gentleman. I had in oysters and champagne — for the receipts were excellent — and being in a high state of nervous tension, kept the table in a roar. Indeed, I was never in my life so well inspired as when I described my vigil over Harry Miller's literature or the series of my emotions as I faced the audience. The lads vowed I was the soul of good company and the prince of lecturers; and — so wonderful an institution is the popular press — if you had seen the notices next day in all the papers, you must have supposed my evening's entertainment an unqualified success.

I was in excellent spirits when I returned home that night, but the miserable Pinkerton sorrowed for us both.

"O, Loudon," he said, "I shall never forgive myself. When I saw you did n't catch on to the idea of the lecture, I should have given it myself!"

CHAPTER VII

IRONS IN THE FIRE

Opes Strepitumque

THE food of the body differs not so greatly for the fool or the sage, the elephant or the cock-sparrow; and similar chemical elements, variously disguised, support all mortals. A brief study of Pinkerton in his new setting convinced me of a kindred truth about that other and mental digestion, by which we extract what is called " fun for our money " out of life. In the same spirit as a schoolboy, deep in Mayne Reid, handles a dummy gun and crawls among imaginary forests, Pinkerton sped through Kearney Street upon his daily business, representing to himself a highly coloured part in life's performance, and happy for hours if he should have chanced to brush against a millionaire. Reality was his romance; he gloried to be thus engaged; he wallowed in his business. Suppose a man to dig up a galleon on the Coromandel coast, his rakish schooner keeping the while an offing under easy sail, and he, by the blaze of a great fire of wreckwood, to measure ingots by the bucketful on the uproarious beach: such an one might realise a greater material spoil; he should have no more profit of romance than Pinkerton when he cast up his weekly balance-sheet in a bald office. Every dollar gained was like something brought ashore from a mysterious deep; every venture made was like a diver's plunge; and as he thrust his bold hand into the plexus of the money-market, he was delightedly aware of how he shook the pillars of existence, turned out men (as at a battle-cry) to labour in far countries, and set the gold twitching in the drawers of millionaires.

I could never fathom the full extent of his speculations; but there were five separate businesses which he avowed and carried like a banner. The *Thirteen Star Golden State Brandy, Warranted Entire* (a very flagrant distillation) filled a great part of his thoughts and was kept before the public in an eloquent but misleading treatise: *Why Drink French Brandy? A Word to the Wise.* He kept an office for advertisers, counselling, designing, acting as middleman with printers and bill-stickers, for the inexperienced or the uninspired: the dull haberdasher came to him for ideas, the smart theatrical agent for his local knowledge; and one and all departed with a copy of his pamphlet: *How, When, and Where; or, the Advertiser's Vade-Mecum.* He had a tug chartered every Saturday afternoon and night, carried people outside the Heads, and provided them with lines and bait for six hours' fishing, at the rate of five dollars a person. I am told that some of them (doubtless adroit anglers) made a profit on the transaction.

Occasionally he bought wrecks and condemned vessels; these latter (I cannot tell you how) found their way to sea again under aliases, and continued to stem the waves triumphantly enough under the colours of Bolivia or Nicaragua. Lastly, there was a certain agricultural engine, glorying in a great deal of vermilion and blue paint, and filling (it appeared) a "long-felt want," in which his interest was something like a tenth.

This for the face or front of his concerns. "On the outside," as he phrased it, he was variously and mysteriously engaged. No dollar slept in his possession; rather he kept all simultaneously flying like a conjurer with oranges. My own earnings, when I began to have a share, he would but show me for a moment, and disperse again, like those illusive money gifts which are flashed in the eyes of childhood only to be entombed in the missionary box. And he would come down radiant from a weekly balance-sheet, clap me on the shoulder, declare himself a winner by Gargantuan figures, and prove destitute of a quarter for a drink.

"What on earth have you done with it?" I would ask.

"Into the mill again; all re-invested!" he would cry, with infinite delight. Investment was ever his word. He could not bear what he called gambling. "Never touch stocks, Loudon," he would say; "nothing but legitimate business." And yet, Heaven knows, many an indurated gambler might have drawn back appalled at the first hint of some of Pinkerton's investments! One, which I succeeded in tracking home, and instance for a specimen, was a seventh share in the charter of a certain ill-starred schooner bound for Mexico, to smuggle weapons on the one trip, and cigars upon the other. The latter end of this enterprise, involving (as it did) shipwreck, confiscation, and a lawsuit with the underwriters, was too painful to be dwelt upon at length. " It 's proved a disappointment," was as far as my friend would go with me in words; but I knew, from observation, that the fabric of his fortunes tottered. For the rest, it was only by accident I got wind of the transaction; for Pinkerton, after a time, was shy of introducing me to his arcana: the reason you are to hear presently.

The office which was (or should have been) the point of rest for so many evolving dollars stood in the heart of the city: a high and spacious room, with many plate-glass windows. A glazed cabinet of polished redwood offered to the eye a regiment of some two hundred bottles, conspicuously labelled. These were all charged with Pinkerton's Thirteen Star, although from across the room it would have required an expert to distinguish them from the same number of bottles of Courvoisier. I used to twit my friend with this resemblance, and propose a new edition of the pamphlet, with the title thus improved: *Why Drink French Brandy, when we give you the same labels?* The doors of the cabinet revolved all day upon their hinges; and if there entered any one

who was a stranger to the merits of the brand,
he departed laden with a bottle. When I used to
protest at this extravagance, "My dear Loudon,"
Pinkerton would cry, "you don't seem to catch
on to business principles! The prime cost of the
spirit is literally nothing. I could n't find a cheaper
advertisement if I tried." Against the side post
of the cabinet there leaned a gaudy umbrella, preserved there as a relic. It appears that when
Pinkerton was about to place Thirteen Star upon
the market, the rainy season was at hand. He lay
dark, almost in penury, awaiting the first shower,
at which, as upon a signal, the main thoroughfares became dotted with his agents, vendors of
advertisements; and the whole world of San
Francisco, from the business man fleeing for the
ferry-boat, to the lady waiting at the corner for
her car, sheltered itself under umbrellas with this
strange device: *Are you wet? Try Thirteen Star.*
"It was a mammoth boom," said Pinkerton, with
a sigh of delighted recollection. "There was n't
another umbrella to be seen. I stood at this window, Loudon, feasting my eyes; and I declare, I
felt like Vanderbilt." And it was to this neat
application of the local climate that he owed, not
only much of the sale of Thirteen Star, but the
whole business of his advertising agency.

The large desk (to resume our survey of the
office) stood about the middle, knee-deep in stacks
of handbills and posters, of *Why Drink French
Brandy?* and *The Advertiser's Vade-Mecum.* It
was flanked upon the one hand by two female

type-writers, who rested not between the hours
of nine and four, and upon the other by a model
of the agricultural machine. The walls, where
they were not broken by telephone boxes and a
couple of photographs — one representing the
wreck of the *James L. Moody* on a bold and broken
coast, the other the Saturday tug alive with amateur fishers — almost disappeared under oil-paint-
ings gaudily framed. Many of these were relics
of the Latin Quarter, and I must do Pinkerton
the justice to say that none of them were bad,
and some had remarkable merit. They went off
slowly but for handsome figures; and their places
were progressively supplied with the work of local
artists. These last it was one of my first duties
to review and criticise. Some of them were villainous, yet all were saleable. I said so; and the
next moment saw myself, the figure of a miserable
renegade, bearing arms in the wrong camp. I was
to look at pictures thenceforward, not with the eye
of the artist, but the dealer; and I saw the stream
widen that divided me from all I loved.

" Now, Loudon," Pinkerton had said, the morning after the lecture, " now, Loudon, we can go at
it shoulder to shoulder. This is what I have longed
for: I wanted two heads and four arms; and now
I have 'em. You 'll find it 's just the same as art
— all observation and imagination; only more
movement. Just wait till you begin to feel the
charm!"

I might have waited long. Perhaps I lack a
sense; for our whole existence seemed to me one

dreary bustle, and the place we bustled in fitly to be
called the Place of Yawning. I slept in a little
den behind the office; Pinkerton, in the office itself,
stretched on a patent sofa which sometimes collapsed, his slumbers still further menaced by an
imminent clock with an alarm. Roused by this
diabolical contrivance, we rose early, went forth
early to breakfast, and returned by nine to what
Pinkerton called work, and I distraction. Masses
of letters must be opened, read, and answered;
some by me at a subsidiary desk which had been
introduced on the morning of my arrival; others
by my bright-eyed friend, pacing the room like a
caged lion as he dictated to the tinkling type-
writers. Masses of wet proof had to be overhauled
and scrawled upon with a blue pencil — " rustic "
— " six-inch caps " — " bold spacing here " — or
sometimes terms more fervid, as for instance this,
which I remember Pinkerton to have spirted on
the margin of an advertisement of Soothing Syrup:
" Throw this all down. Have you never printed an
advertisement? I 'll be round in half an hour."
The ledger and sale-book, besides, we had always
with us. Such was the backbone of our occupation,
and tolerable enough; but the far greater proportion of our time was consumed by visitors, whole-
souled, grand fellows no doubt, and as sharp as
a needle, but to me unfortunately not diverting.
Some were apparently half-witted, and must be
talked over by the hour before they could reach
the humblest decision, which they only left the
office to return again (ten minutes later) and re-

scind. Others came with a vast show of hurry and despatch, but I observed it to be principally show. The agricultural model for instance, which was practicable, proved a kind of fly-paper for these busybodies. I have seen them blankly turn the crank of it for five minutes at a time, simulating (to nobody's deception) business interest: " Good thing this, Pinkerton? Sell much of it? Ha! Could n't use it, I suppose, as a medium of advertisement for my article? " — which was perhaps toilet soap. Others (a still worse variety) carried us to neighbouring saloons to dice for cocktails and (after the cocktails were paid) for dollars on a corner of the counter. The attraction of dice for all these people was indeed extraordinary: at a certain club, where I once dined in the character of " my partner, Mr. Dodd," the dice-box came on the table with the wine, an artless substitute for after-dinner wit.

Of all our visitors, I believe I preferred Emperor Norton; the very mention of whose name reminds me I am doing scanty justice to the folks of San Francisco. In what other city would a harmless madman who supposed himself emperor of the two Americas have been so fostered and encouraged? Where else would even the people of the streets have respected the poor soul's illusion? Where else would bankers and merchants have received his visits, cashed his cheques, and submitted to his small assessments? Where else would he have been suffered to attend and address the exhibition days of schools and colleges? where

else, in God's green earth, have taken his pick of
restaurants, ransacked the bill of fare, and departed scathless? They tell me he was even an
exacting patron, threatening to withdraw his custom when dissatisfied; and I can believe it, for
his face wore an expression distinctly gastronom-
ical. Pinkerton had received from this monarch
a cabinet appointment; I have seen the brevet,
wondering mainly at the good-nature of the printer
who had executed the forms, and I think my friend
was at the head either of foreign affairs or education: it mattered, indeed, nothing, the prestation
being in all offices identical. It was at a comparatively early date that I saw Jim in the exercise of
his public functions. His Majesty entered the
office — a portly, rather flabby man, with the face
of a gentleman, rendered unspeakably pathetic and
absurd by the great sabre at his side and the pea-
cock's feather in his hat.

"I have called to remind you, Mr. Pinkerton,
that you are somewhat in arrear of taxes," he
said, with old-fashioned, stately courtesy.

"Well, Your Majesty, what is the amount?"
asked Jim; and when the figure was named (it
was generally two or three dollars), paid upon the
nail and offered a bonus in the shape of Thirteen
Star.

"I am always delighted to patronise native in-
dustries," said Norton the First. "San Francisco
is public-spirited in what concerns its Emperor;
and indeed, sir, of all my domains, it is my favourite city."

"Come," said I, when he was gone, "I prefer that customer to the lot."

"It's really rather a distinction," Jim admitted. "I think it must have been the umbrella racket that attracted him."

We were distinguished under the rose by the notice of other and greater men. There were days when Jim wore an air of unusual capacity and resolve, spoke with more brevity like one pressed for time, and took often on his tongue such phrases as "Longhurst told me so this morning," or "I had it straight from Longhurst himself." It was no wonder, I used to think, that Pinkerton was called to council with such Titans; for the creature's quickness and resource were beyond praise. In the early days when he consulted me without reserve, pacing the room, projecting, ciphering, extending hypothetical interests, trebling imaginary capital, his "engine" (to renew an excellent old word) labouring full steam ahead, I could never decide whether my sense of respect or entertainment were the stronger. But these good hours were destined to curtailment.

"Yes, it's smart enough," I once observed. "But, Pinkerton, do you think it's honest?"

"You don't think it's honest!" he wailed. "O dear me, that ever I should have heard such an expression on your lips!"

At sight of his distress, I plagiarised unblushingly from Myner. "You seem to think honesty as simple as Blind Man's Buff," said I. "It's a

more delicate affair than that: delicate as any
art."

"O well! at that rate!" he exclaimed, with
complete relief. "That 's casuistry."

"I am perfectly certain of one thing: that what
you propose is dishonest," I returned.

"Well, say no more about it. That 's settled,"
he replied.

Thus, almost at a word, my point was carried.
But the trouble was that such differences continued to recur, until we began to regard each
other with alarm. If there were one thing Pinkerton valued himself upon, it was his honesty;
if there were one thing he clung to, it was my
good opinion; and when both were involved, as
was the case in these commercial cruces, the man
was on the rack. My own position, if you consider how much I owed him, how hateful is the
trade of fault-finder, and that yet I lived and
fattened on these questionable operations, was
perhaps equally distressing. If I had been more
sterling or more combative things might have
gone extremely far. But, in truth, I was just
base enough to profit by what was not forced
on my attention, rather than seek scenes: Pinkerton quite cunning enough to avail himself of
my weakness; and it was a relief to both when
he began to involve his proceedings in a decent
mystery.

Our last dispute, which had a most unlooked-
for consequence, turned on the refitting of condemned ships. He had bought a miserable hulk,

and came, rubbing his hands, to inform me she was already on the slip, under a new name, to be repaired. When first I had heard of this industry I suppose I scarcely comprehended; but much discussion had sharpened my faculties, and now my brow became heavy.

"I can be no party to that, Pinkerton," said I.

He leaped like a man shot. "What next?" he cried. "What ails you, anyway? You seem to me to dislike everything that's profitable."

"This ship has been condemned by Lloyd's agent," said I.

"But I tell you it's a deal. The ship's in splendid condition; there's next to nothing wrong with her but the garboard streak and the sternpost. I tell you Lloyd's is a ring like everybody else; only it's an English ring, and that's what deceives you. If it was American, you would be crying it down all day. It's Anglomania, common Anglomania," he cried, with growing irritation.

"I will not make money by risking men's lives," was my ultimatum.

"Great Cæsar! isn't all speculation a risk? Isn't the fairest kind of shipowning to risk men's lives? And mining — how's that for risk? And look at the elevator business — there's danger, if you like! Didn't I take my risk when I bought her? She might have been too far gone; and where would I have been? Loudon," he cried, "I tell you the truth: you're too full of refinement for this world!"

"I condemn you out of your own lips," I replied. "'The fairest kind of shipowning,' says you. If you please, let us only do the fairest kind of business."

The shot told, the Irrepressible was silenced; and I profited by the chance, to pour in a broadside of another sort. He was all sunk in money-getting, I pointed out; he never dreamed of anything but dollars. Where were all his generous, progressive sentiments? Where was his culture? I asked. And where was the American Type?

"It's true, Loudon," he cried, striding up and down the room, and wildly scouring at his hair. "You're perfectly right. I'm becoming materialised. O, what a thing to have to say, what a confession to make! Materialised! Me! Loudon, this must go on no longer. You've been a loyal friend to me once more; give me your hand! — you've saved me again. I must do something to rouse the spiritual side: something desperate; study something, something dry and tough. What shall it be? Theology? Algebra? What's Algebra?"

"It's dry and tough enough," said I; "$a^2 + 2ab + b^2$."

"It's stimulating, though?" he inquired.

I told him I believed so, and that it was considered fortifying to Types.

"Then, that's the thing for me. I'll study Algebra," he concluded.

The next day, by application to one of his typewriting women, he got word of a young lady, one

Miss Mamie McBride, who was willing and able to conduct him in these bloomless meadows; and, her circumstances being lean, and terms consequently moderate, he and Mamie were soon in agreement for two lessons in the week. He took fire with unexampled rapidity; he seemed unable to tear himself away from the symbolic art; an hour's lesson occupied the whole evening; and the original two was soon increased to four, and then to five. I bade him beware of female blandishments. "The first thing you know, you'll be falling in love with the algebraist," said I.

"Don't say it even in jest," he cried. "She's a lady I revere. I could no more lay a hand upon her than I could upon a spirit. Loudon, I don't believe God ever made a purer-minded woman."

Which appeared to me too fervent to be reassuring.

Meanwhile I had been long expostulating with my friend upon a different matter. "I'm the fifth wheel," I kept telling him. "For any use I am, I might as well be in Senegambia. The letters you give me to attend to might be answered by a sucking child. And I tell you what it is, Pinkerton: either you've got to find me some employment, or I'll have to start in and find it for myself."

This I said with a corner of my eye in the usual quarter, toward the arts, little dreaming what destiny was to provide.

"I've got it, Loudon," Pinkerton at last replied. "Got the idea on the Potrero cars. Found

I had n't a pencil, borrowed one from the conductor, and figured on it roughly all the way in
town. I saw it was the thing at last; gives you
a real show. All your talents and accomplish-
ments come in. Here 's a sketch advertisement.
Just run your eye over it. '*Sun, Ozone, and
Music!* PINKERTON'S HEBDOMADARY
PICNICS!' (That 's a good, catching phrase,
'hebdomadary,' though it 's hard to say. I made
a note of it when I was looking in the diction-
ary how to spell *hectagonal.* 'Well, you 're a
boss word,' I said. 'Before you 're very much
older, I 'll have you in type as long as yourself.'
And here it is, you see.) '*Five dollars a head,
and ladies free.* MONSTER OLIO OF ATTRAC-
TIONS.' (How does that strike you?) '*Free
luncheon under the greenwood tree. Dance on
the elastic sward. Home again in the Bright
Evening Hours. Manager and Honorary Steward, H. Loudon Dodd, Esq., the well-known
connoisseur.*'"

Singular how a man runs from Scylla to
Charybdis! I was so intent on securing the dis-
appearance of a single epithet that I accepted the
rest of the advertisement and all that it involved
without discussion. So it befell that the words
"well-known connoisseur" were deleted; but that
H. Loudon Dodd became manager and honorary
steward of Pinkerton's Hebdomadary Picnics, soon
shortened, by popular consent, to the Dromedary.

By eight o'clock, any Sunday morning, I was to
be observed by an admiring public on the wharf.

The garb and attributes of sacrifice consisted of
a black frock-coat, rosetted, its pockets bulging
with sweetmeats and inferior cigars, trousers of
light blue, a sik hat like a reflector, and a var-
nished wand. A goodly steamer guarded my one
flank, panting and throbbing, flags fluttering fore
and aft of her, illustrative of the Dromedary and
patriotism. My other flank was ·covered by the
ticket-office, strongly held by a trusty character
of the Scots persuasion, rosetted like his superior
and smoking a cigar to mark the occasion festive.
At half-past, having assured myself that all was
well with the free luncheons, I lit a cigar myself,
and awaited the strains of the " Pioneer Band."
I had never to wait long — they were German and
punctual — and by a few minutes after the half-
hour, I would hear them booming down street with
a long military roll of drums, some score of gratuitous asses prancing at the head in bearskin hats
and buckskin aprons, and conspicuous with resplendent axes.   The band, of course, we paid
for; but so strong is the San Franciscan passion
for public masquerade, that the asses (as I say)
were all gratuitous, pranced for the love of it,
and cost us nothing but their luncheon.

The musicians formed up in the bows of my
steamer, and struck into a skittish polka; the
asses mounted guard upon the gangway and the
ticket-office; and presently after, in family parties
of father, mother, and children, in the form of
duplicate lovers or in that of solitary youth, the
public began to descend upon us by the carful

at a time; four to six hundred perhaps, with a strong German flavour, and all merry as children. When these had been shepherded on board, and the inevitable belated two or three had gained the deck amidst the cheering of the public, the hawser was cast off, and we plunged into the bay.

And now behold the honorary steward in the hour of duty and glory: see me circulate amid the crowd, radiating affability and laughter, liberal with my sweetmeats and cigars. I say unblushing things to hobbledehoy girls, tell shy young persons this is the married peoples' boat, roguishly ask the abstracted if they are thinking of their sweethearts, offer Paterfamilias a cigar, am struck with the beauty and grow curious about the age of mamma's youngest who (I assure her gaily) will be a man before his mother; or perhaps it may occur to me, from the sensible expression of her face, that she is a person of good counsel, and I ask her earnestly if she knows any particularly pleasant place on the Saucelito or San Rafael coast, for the scene of our picnic is always supposed to be uncertain. The next moment I am back at my giddy badinage with the young ladies, wakening laughter as I go, and leaving in my wake applausive comments of "Isn't Mr. Dodd a funny gentleman?" and "O, I think he's just too nice!"

An hour having passed in this airy manner, I start upon my rounds afresh, with a bag full of coloured tickets, all with pins attached, and all with legible inscriptions: "Old Germany," "California," "True Love," "Old Fogies," "La Belle France," "Green Erin," "The Land of Cakes," "Washington," "Blue Jay," "Robin Red-Breast," — twenty of each denomination; for when it comes to the luncheon, we sit down by twenties. These are distributed with anxious tact — for indeed this is the most delicate part of my functions — but outwardly with reckless unconcern, amidst the gayest flutter and confusion; and are immediately after sported upon hats and bonnets, to the extreme diffusion of cordiality, total strangers hailing each other by "the number of their mess" — so we humorously name it — and the deck ringing with cries of, "Here, all Blue Jays to the rescue!" or, "I say, am I alone in this blame' ship? Ain't there no more Californians?"

By this time we are drawing near to the appointed spot. I mount upon the bridge, the observed of all observers.

"Captain," I say, in clear, emphatic tones, heard far and wide, "the majority of the company appear to be in favour of the little cove beyond One Tree Point."

"All right, Mr. Dodd," responds the captain, heartily; "all one to me. I am not exactly sure of the place you mean; but just you stay here and pilot me."

I do, pointing with my wand. I do pilot him, to the inexpressible entertainment of the picnic; for I am (why should I deny it?) the popular man. We slow down off the mouth of a grassy valley, watered by a brook, and set in pines and redwoods. The anchor is let go; the boats are lowered, two of them already packed with the materials of an impromptu bar; and the Pioneer Band, accompanied by the resplendent asses, fill the other, and move shoreward to the inviting strains of *Buffalo Gals, won't you come out to-night?* It is a part of our programme that one of the asses shall, from sheer clumsiness, in the course of this embarkation, drop a dummy axe into the water: whereupon the mirth of the picnic can hardly be assuaged. Upon one occasion, the dummy axe floated, and the laugh turned rather the wrong way.

In from ten to twenty minutes the boats are alongside again, the messes are marshalled separately on the deck, and the picnic goes ashore, to find the band and the impromptu bar awaiting them. Then come the hampers, which are piled upon the beach, and surrounded by a stern guard of stalwart asses, axe on shoulder. It is here I take my place, note-book in hand, under a banner bearing the legend, "Come here for hampers." Each hamper contains a complete outfit for a separate twenty, cold provender, plates, glasses, knives, forks, and spoons: an agonised printed appeal from the fevered pen of Pinkerton, pasted on the inside of the lid, beseeches that care be taken of the glass and silver. Beer, wine, and lemonade are flowing already from the bar, and the various clans of twenty file away into the woods, with bottles under their arms, and the hampers strung upon a stick. Till one they feast there, in a very moderate seclusion, all being within earshot of the band. From one till four, dancing takes place upon the grass; the bar does a roaring business, and the honorary steward, who has already exhausted himself to bring life into the dullest of the messes, must now indefatigably dance with the plainest of the women. At four a bugle-call is sounded; and by half-past behold us on board again, pioneers, corrugated iron bar, empty bottles, and all; while the honorary steward, free at last, subsides into the captain's cabin over a brandy and soda and a book. Free at last, I say, yet there remains before him the frantic leave-takings at the pier, and a sober journey up to Pinkerton's office with two policemen and the day's takings in a bag.

What I have here sketched was the routine. But we appealed to the taste of San Francisco more distinctly in particular fêtes. "Ye Olde Time Pycke-Nycke," largely advertised in handbills beginning "Oyez, Oyez!" and largely frequented by knights, monks, and cavaliers, was drowned out by unseasonable rain, and returned to the city one of the saddest spectacles I ever remember to have witnessed. In pleasing contrast, and certainly our chief success, was "The Gathering of the Clans," or Scottish picnic. So many milk-white knees were never before simultaneously exhibited in public, and to judge by the prevalence of "Royal Stewart" and the number of eagle's feathers, we were a high-born company. I threw forward the Scottish flank of my own ancestry,

and passed muster as a clansman with applause.
There was, indeed, but one small cloud on this
red-letter day. I had laid in a large supply of
the national beverage, in the shape of *The "Rob
Roy MacGregor O" Blend, Warranted Old and
Vatted;* and this must certainly have been a
generous spirit, for I had some anxious work
between four and half-past, conveying on board
the inanimate forms of chieftains.

To one of our ordinary festivities, where he was
the life and soul of his own mess, Pinkerton himself came incognito, bringing the algebraist on his
arm. Miss Mamie proved to be a well-enough-
looking mouse, with a large, limpid eye, very good
manners, and a flow of the most correct expressions I have ever heard upon the human lip. As
Pinkerton's incognito was strict, I had little opportunity to cultivate the lady's acquaintance; but
I was informed afterwards that she considered me
" the wittiest gentleman she had ever met." " The
Lord mend your taste in wit!" thought I; but
I cannot conceal that such was the general impression. One of my pleasantries even went the
round of San Francisco, and I have heard it
(myself all unknown) bandied in saloons. To be
unknown began at last to be a rare experience:
a bustle woke upon my passage; above all, in
humble neighbourhoods. "Who's that?" one
would ask, and the other would cry, "That!
Why, Dromedary Dodd!" or with withering
scorn, "Not know Mr. Dodd of the Picnics?
Well!" and indeed I think it marked a rather

barren destiny; for our picnics, if a trifle vulgar, were as gay and innocent as the age of gold; I am sure no people divert themselves so easily and so well: and even with the cares of my steward-ship, I was often happy to be there.

Indeed, there were but two drawbacks in the least considerable. The first was my terror of the hobbledehoy girls, to whom (from the demands of my situation) I was obliged to lay myself so open. The other, if less momentous, was more mortifying. In early days, at my mother's knee, as a man may say, I had acquired the unenviable accomplishment (which I have never since been able to lose) of singing *Just before the Battle*. I have what the French call a fillet of voice, my best notes scarce audible about a dinner-table, and the upper register rather to be regarded as a higher power of silence: experts tell me besides that I sing flat; nor, if I were the best singer in the world, does *Just before the Battle* occur to my mature taste as the song that I would choose to sing. In spite of all which considerations, at one picnic, memorably dull, and after I had exhausted every other art of pleasing, I gave, in desperation, my one song. From that hour my doom was gone forth. Either we had a chronic passenger (though I could never detect him), or the very wood and iron of the steamer must have retained the tradition. At every successive picnic word went round that Mr. Dodd was a singer; that Mr. Dodd sang *Just before the Battle*, and finally that now was the time when Mr. Dodd sang *Just before the Battle;* so that the thing became a fixture like the dropping of the dummy axe, and you are to conceive me, Sunday after Sunday, piping up my lamentable ditty and covered, when it was done, with gratuitous applause. It is a beautiful trait in human nature that I was invariably offered an encore.

I was well paid, however, even to sing. Pinkerton and I, after an average Sunday, had five hundred dollars to divide. Nay, and the picnics were the means, although indirectly, of bringing me a singular windfall. This was at the end of the season, after the "Grand Farewell Fancy Dress Gala." Many of the hampers had suffered severely; and it was judged wiser to save storage, dispose of them, and lay in a fresh stock when the campaign re-opened. Among my purchasers was a workingman of the name of Speedy, to whose house, after several unavailing letters, I must proceed in person, wondering to find myself once again on the wrong side, and playing creditor to some one else's debtor. Speedy was in the belligerent stage of fear. He could not pay. It appeared he had already resold the hampers, and he defied me to do my worst. I did not like to lose my own money; I hated to lose Pinkerton's; and the bearing of my creditor incensed me.

"Do you know, Mr. Speedy, that I can send you to the penitentiary?" said I, willing to read him a lesson.

The dire expression was overheard in the next room. A large, fresh, motherly Irishwoman ran forth upon the instant, and fell to besiege me with caresses and appeals. " Sure now, and ye could n't have the heart to ut, Mr. Dodd, you, that 's so well known to be a pleasant gentleman; and it 's a pleasant face ye have, and the picture of me own brother that 's dead and gone. It 's a truth that he 's been drinking. Ye can smell it off of him, more blame to him. But, indade, and there 's nothing in the house beyont the furnicher, and Thim Stock. It 's the stock that ye 'll be taking, dear. A sore penny it has cost me, first and last, and by all tales, not worth an owld tobacco pipe." Thus adjured, and somewhat embarrassed by the stern attitude I had adopted, I suffered myself to be invested with a considerable quantity of what is called wild-cat stock, in which this excellent if illogical female had been squandering her hard-earned gold. It could scarce be said to better my position, but the step quieted the woman; and, on the other hand, I could not think I was taking much risk, for the shares in question (they were those of what I will call the Catamount Silver Mine) had fallen some time before to the bed-rock quotation, and now lay perfectly inert, or were only kicked (like other waste paper) about the kennel of the exchange by bankrupt speculators.

A month or two after, I perceived by the stock-list that Catamount had taken a bound; before afternoon, " thim stock " were worth a quite considerable pot of money; and I learned, upon inquiry, that a bonanza had been found in a condemned lead, and the mine was now expected to do wonders. Remarkable to philosophers how bonanzas are found in condemned leads, and how the stock is always at freezing-point immediately before! By some stroke of chance, the Speedys had held on to the right thing; they had escaped the syndicate; yet a little more, if I had not come to dun them, and Mrs. Speedy would have been buying a silk dress. I could not bear, of course, to profit by the accident, and returned to offer restitution. The house was in a bustle; the neighbours (all stock-gamblers themselves) had crowded to condole; and Mrs. Speedy sat with streaming tears, the centre of a sympathetic group. " For fifteen year, I 've been at ut," she was lamenting, as I entered, " and grudging the babes the very milk, more shame to me! to pay their dhirty assessments. And now, my dears, I should be a lady, and driving in my coach, if all had their rights; and a sorrow on that man, Dodd! As soon as I set eyes on him, I seen the divil was in the house."

It was upon these words that I made my entrance, which was therefore dramatic enough, though nothing to what followed. For when it appeared that I was come to restore the lost fortune, and when Mrs. Speedy (after copiously weeping on my bosom) had refused the restitution, and when Mr. Speedy (summoned to that end from a camp of the Grand Army of the Republic) had added his refusal, and when I had insisted, and they had insisted, and the neighbours had applauded and supported each of us in turn; and when at last it was agreed we were to hold the stock together, and share the proceeds in three parts — one for me, one for Mr. Speedy, and one for his spouse — I will leave you to conceive the enthusiasm that reigned in that small, bare apartment, with the sewing-machine in the one corner, and the babes asleep in the other, and pictures of Garfield and the Battle of Gettysburg on the yellow walls. Port wine was had in by a sympathiser, and we drank it mingled with tears.

" And I dhrink to your health, my dear," sobbed Mrs. Speedy, especially affected by my gallantry in the matter of the third share; " and I 'm sure we all dhrink to his health — Mr. Dodd of the picnics, no gentleman better known than him; and it 's my prayer, dear, the good God may be long spared to see ye in health and happiness! "

In the end I was the chief gainer; for I sold my third while it was worth five thousand dollars, but the Speedys more adventurously held on until the syndicate reversed the process, when they were happy to escape with perhaps a quarter of that sum. It was just as well; for the bulk of the money was (in Pinkerton's phrase) reinvested; and when next I saw Mrs. Speedy, she was still gorgeously dressed from the proceeds of the late success, but was already moist with tears over the new catastrophe. " We 're froze out, me darlin'! All the money we had, dear, and the sewing-machine, and Jim's uniform, was in the Golden West; and the vipers has put on a new assessment."

By the end of the year, therefore, this is how I stood. I had made

By Catamount Silver Mine	$5,000
By the picnics	3,000
By the lecture	600
By profit and loss on capital in Pinkerton's business	1,350
	$9,950

to which must be added

What remained of my grandfather's donation . .	8,500
	$18,450

It appears, on the other hand, that

I had spent	4,000
Which thus left me to the good	$14,450

A result on which I am not ashamed to say I looked with gratitude and pride. Some eight thousand (being late conquest) was liquid and actually tractile in the bank; the rest whirled beyond reach and even sight (save in the mirror of a balance-sheet) under the compelling spell of wizard Pinkerton. Dollars of mine were tacking off the shores of Mexico, in peril of the deep and the guardacostas; they rang on saloon-counters in the city of Tombstone, Arizona; they shone in faro-tents among the mountain diggings: the imagination flagged in following them, so wide were they diffused, so briskly they span to the turning of the wizard's crank. But here, there, or everywhere I could still tell myself it was all mine, and what was more convincing, draw substantial dividends. My fortune, I called it; and it represented, when expressed in dollars or even

British pounds, an honest pot of money; when extended into francs, a veritable fortune. Perhaps I have let the cat out of the bag; perhaps you see already where my hopes were pointing, and begin to blame my inconsistency. But I must first tell you my excuse, and the change that had befallen Pinkerton.

About a week after the picnic to which he escorted Mamie, Pinkerton avowed the state of his affections. From what I had observed on board the steamer, where methought Mamie waited on him with her limpid eyes, I encouraged the bashful lover to proceed; and the very next evening he was carrying me to call on his affianced.

" You must befriend her, Loudon, as you have always befriended me," he said, pathetically.

" By saying disagreeable things? I doubt if that be the way to a young lady's favour," I replied; " and since this picnicking I begin to be a man of some experience."

" Yes, you do nobly there; I can't describe how I admire you," he cried. " Not that she will ever need it; she has had every advantage. God knows what I have done to deserve her. O man, what a responsibility this is for a rough fellow and not always truthful! "

" Brace up, old man, brace up! " said I.

But when we reached Mamie's boarding-house, it was almost with tears that he presented me. " Here is Loudon, Mamie," were his words. " I want you to love him; he has a grand nature."

"You are certainly no stranger to me, Mr. Dodd," was her gracious expression. "James is never weary of descanting on your goodness."

"My dear lady," said I, "when you know our friend a little better, you will make a large allowance for his warm heart. My goodness has consisted in allowing him to feed and clothe and toil for me when he could ill afford it. If I am now alive, it is to him I owe it; no man had a kinder friend. You must take good care of him," I added, laying my hand on his shoulder, "and keep him in good order, for he needs it."

Pinkerton was much affected by this speech, and so, I fear, was Mamie. I admit it was a tactless performance. "When you know our friend a little better," was not happily said, and even "keep him in good order, for he needs it" might be construed into matter of offence; but I lay it before you in all confidence of your acquittal: was the general tone of it "patronising"? Even if such was the verdict of the lady, I cannot but suppose the blame was neither wholly hers nor wholly mine; I cannot but suppose that Pinkerton had already sickened the poor woman of my very name, so that if I had come with the songs of Apollo, she must still have been disgusted.

Here, however, were two finger-posts to Paris. Jim was going to be married, and so had the less need of my society. I had not pleased his bride, and so was, perhaps, better absent. Late one evening I broached the idea to my friend. It had been a great day for me; I had just banked my five

thousand catamountain dollars; and as Jim had
refused to lay a finger on the stock, risk and profit
were both wholly mine, and I was celebrating the
event with stout and crackers. I began by telling
him that if it caused him any pain or any anxiety
about his affairs, he had but to say the word, and
he should hear no more of my proposal. He was
the truest and best friend I ever had or was ever
like to have; and it would be a strange thing if
I refused him any favour he was sure he wanted.
At the same time I wished him to be sure; for my
life was wasting in my hands. I was like one from
home; all my true interests summoned me away.
I must remind him, besides, that he was now about
to marry and assume new interests, and that our
extreme familiarity might be even painful to his
wife. — " O no, Loudon, I feel you are wrong
there," he interjected warmly, " she *does* appreciate your nature." — So much the better, then,
I continued; and went on to point out that our
separation need not be for long; that, in the way
affairs were going, he might join me in two years
with a fortune, small, indeed, for the States, but in
France almost conspicuous; that we might unite
our resources, and have one house in Paris for the
winter and a second near Fontainebleau for summer, where we could be as happy as the day was
long, and bring up little Pinkertons as practical,
artistic workmen, far from the money-hunger of
the West. " Let me go then," I concluded; " not
as a deserter, but as the vanguard, to lead the march
of the Pinkerton men."

So I argued and pleaded, not without emotion;
my friend sitting opposite, resting his chin upon
his hand and (but for that single interjection)
silent. " I have been looking for this, Loudon,"
said he, when I had done. " It does pain me, and
that 's the fact — I 'm so miserably selfish. And
I believe it 's a death blow to the picnics; for it 's
idle to deny that you were the heart and soul of
them with your wand and your gallant bearing,
and wit and humour and chivalry, and throwing
that kind of society atmosphere about the thing.
But for all that, you 're right, and you ought to go.
You may count on forty dollars a week; and if
Depew City — one of nature's centres for this
State — pan out the least as I expect, it may be
double. But it 's forty dollars anyway; and to
think that two years ago you were almost reduced
to beggary!"

" I *was* reduced to it," said I.

" Well, the brutes gave you nothing, and I 'm
glad of it now!" cried Jim. " It 's the triumphant
return I glory in! Think of the master, and that
cold-blooded Myner too! Yes, just let the Depew
City boom get on its legs, and you shall go; and
two years later, day for day, I 'll shake hands with
you in Paris, with Mamie on my arm, God bless
her!"

We talked in this vein far into the night. I was
myself so exultant in my new-found liberty, and
Pinkerton so proud of my triumph, so happy in my
happiness, in so warm a glow about the gallant little
woman of his choice, and the very room so filled

with castles in the air and cottages at Fontainebleau, that it was little wonder if sleep fled our
eyelids, and three had followed two upon the office
clock before Pinkerton unfolded the mechanism
of his patent sofa.

CHAPTER VIII

FACES ON THE CITY FRONT

IT is very much the custom to view life as if it were exactly ruled in two, like sleep and waking; the provinces of play and business standing separate. The business side of my career in San Francisco has been now disposed of; I approach the chapter of diversion; and it will be found they had about an equal share in building up the story of the Wrecker — a gentleman whose appearance may be presently expected.

With all my occupations, some six afternoons and two or three odd evenings remained at my disposal every week: a circumstance the more agreeable as I was a stranger in a city singularly picturesque. From what I had once called myself, *The Amateur Parisian,* I grew (or declined) into a water-side prowler, a lingerer on wharves, a frequenter of shy neighbourhoods, a scraper of acquaintance with eccentric characters. I visited Chinese and Mexican gambling-hells, German secret societies, sailors' boarding-houses, and " dives " of every complexion of the disreputable and dangerous. I have seen greasy Mexican hands pinned to the table with a knife for cheating, seamen (when blood-money ran high) knocked down upon the public street and carried insensible on board short-handed ships, shots exchanged and the smoke (and the company) dispersing from the doors of the saloon. I have heard cold-minded Polacks debate upon the readiest method of burning San Francisco to the ground, hot-headed working men and women bawl and swear in the tribune at the Sand Lot, and Kearney himself open his subscription for a gallows, name the manufacturers who were to grace it with their dangling bodies, and read aloud to the delighted multitude a telegram of adhesion from a member of the State legislature: all which preparations of proletarian war were (in a moment) breathed upon and abolished by the mere name and fame of Mr. Coleman. That lion of the Vigilantes had but to rouse himself and shake his ears, and the whole brawling mob was silenced. I could not but reflect what a strange manner of man this was, to be living unremarked there as a private merchant, and to be so feared by a whole city; and if I was disappointed, in my character of looker-on, to have the matter end ingloriously without the firing of a shot or the hanging of a single millionaire, philosophy tried to tell me that this sight was truly the more picturesque. In a thousand towns and different epochs I might have had occasion to behold the cowardice and carnage of street fighting; where else, but only there and then, could I have enjoyed a view of Coleman (the intermittent despot) walking meditatively up-hill in a quiet part of town, with a very rolling gait, and slapping gently his great thigh?

Minora canamus. This historic figure stalks
silently through a corner of the San Francisco of
my memory: the rest is bric-a-brac, the reminis-
cences of a vagrant sketcher. My delight was
much in slums. *Little Italy* was a haunt of mine;
there I would look in at the windows of small
eating-shops, transported bodily from Genoa or
Naples, with their macaroni, and chianti flasks and
portraits of Garibaldi, and coloured political cari-
catures; or (entering in) hold high debate with
some ear-ringed fisher of the bay as to the designs
of " Mr. Owstria " and " Mr. Rooshia." I was
often to be observed (had there been any to observe me) in that dispeopled, hill-side solitude of
Little Mexico, with its crazy wooden houses, endless crazy wooden stairs, and perilous mountain
goat-paths in the sand. Chinatown by a thousand
eccentricities drew and held me; I could never
have enough of its ambiguous, interracial atmosphere, as of a vitalised museum; never wonder
enough at its outlandish, necromantic-looking vege-
tables set forth to sell in commonplace American
shop-windows, its temple doors open and the scent
of the joss-sticks streaming forth on the American
air, its kites of Oriental fashion hanging fouled
in Western telegraph-wires, its flights of paper
prayers which the trade-wind hunts and dissipates
along Western gutters. I was a frequent wan-
derer on North Beach, gazing at the straits, and
the huge Cape-Horners creeping out to sea, and
imminent Tamalpais. Thence, on my homeward
way, I might visit that strange and filthy shed,

earth-paved and walled with the cages of wild
animals and birds, where at a ramshackle counter,
amid the yells of monkeys, and a poignant atmosphere of menagerie, forty-rod whisky was admin-
istered by a proprietor as dirty as his beasts. Nor
did I even neglect Nob Hill, which is itself a kind
of slum, being the habitat of the mere millionaire.
There they dwell upon the hill-top, high raised
above man's clamour, and the trade-wind blows
between their palaces about deserted streets.

But San Francisco is not herself only. She is
not only the most interesting city in the Union,
and the hugest smelting-pot of races and the
precious metals. She keeps, besides, the doors of
the Pacific, and is the port of entry to another
world and an earlier epoch in man's history.
Nowhere else shall you observe (in the ancient
phrase) so many tall ships as here convene from
round the Horn, from China, from Sydney, and
the Indies; but scarce remarked amid that crowd
of deep-sea giants, another class of craft, the Island
schooner, circulates: low in the water, with lofty
spars and dainty lines, rigged and fashioned like
a yacht, manned with brown-skinned, soft-spoken,
sweet-eyed native sailors, and equipped with their
great double-ender boats that tell a tale of boister-
ous sea-beaches. These steal out and in again,
unnoted by the world or even the newspaper
press, save for the line in the clearing column,
" Schooner So-and-so for Yap and South Sea
Islands " — steal out with nondescript cargoes
of tinned salmon, gin, bolts of gaudy cotton

stuff, women's hats, and Waterbury watches, to return, after a year, piled as high as to the eaves of the house with copra, or wallowing deep with the shells of the tortoise or the pearl oyster. To me, in my character of the Amateur Parisian, this island traffic, and even the island world, were beyond the bounds of curiosity, and how much more of knowledge. I stood there on the extreme shore of the West and of to-day. Seventeen hundred years ago, and seven thousand miles to the east, a legionary stood, perhaps, upon the wall of Antoninus, and looked northward toward the mountains of the Picts. For all the interval of time and space, I, when I looked from the cliff-house on the broad Pacific, was that man's heir and analogue: each of us standing on the verge of the Roman Empire (or, as we now call it, Western civilisation), each of us gazing onward into zones unromanised. But I was dull. I looked rather backward, keeping a kind eye on Paris; and it required a series of converging incidents to change my attitude of nonchalance for one of interest, and even longing, which I little dreamed that I should live to gratify.

The first of these incidents brought me in acquaintance with a certain San Francisco character, who had something of a name beyond the limits of the city, and was known to many lovers of good English. I had discovered a new slum, a place of precarious, sandy cliffs, deep, sandy cuttings, solitary, ancient houses, and the butt-ends of streets. It was already environed. The ranks of the street-lamps threaded it unbroken. The city, upon all sides of it, was tightly packed, and growled with traffic. To-day, I do not doubt the very landmarks are all swept away; but it offered then, within narrow limits, a delightful peace, and (in the morning, when I chiefly went there) a seclusion almost rural. On a steep sand-hill, in this neighbourhood, toppled, on the most insecure foundation, a certain row of houses, each with a bit of garden, and all (I have to presume) inhabited. Thither I used to mount by a crumbling footpath, and in front of the last of the houses, would sit down to sketch. The very first day I saw I was observed, out of the ground-floor window, by a youngish, good-looking fellow, pre- maturely bald, and with an expression both lively and engaging. The second, as we were still the only figures in the landscape, it was no more than natural that we should nod. The third, he came fairly out from his entrenchments, praised my sketch, and with the impromptu cordiality of ar- tists carried me into his apartment; where I sat presently in the midst of a museum of strange objects, — paddles and battle-clubs and baskets, rough-hewn stone images, ornaments of threaded shell, cocoanut bowls, snowy cocoanut plumes — evidences and examples of another earth, another climate, another race, and another (if a ruder) culture. Nor did these objects lack a fitting com- mentary in the conversation of my new acquaint- ance. Doubtless you have read his book. You know already how he tramped and starved, and

had so fine a profit of living, in his days among
the islands; and, meeting him, as I did, one artist with another, after months of offices and picnics, you can imagine with what charm he would
speak, and with what pleasure I would hear. It
was in such talks, which we were both eager to
repeat, that I first heard the names — first fell
under the spell — of the islands; and it was from
one of the first of them that I returned (a happy
man) with *Omoo* under one arm, and my friend's
own adventures under the other.

The second incident was more dramatic, and had,
besides, a bearing on my future. I was standing,
one day, near a boat-landing under Telegraph Hill.
A large barque, perhaps of eighteen hundred tons,
was coming more than usually close about the point
to reach her moorings; and I was observing her
with languid inattention, when I observed two men
to stride across the bulwarks, drop into a shore
boat, and, violently dispossessing the boatman of
his oars, pull toward the landing where I stood.
In a surprisingly short time they came tearing up
the steps; and I could see that both were too well
dressed to be foremast hands — the first even with
research, and both, and specially the first, appeared
under the empire of some strong emotion.

" Nearest police officer! " cried the leader.

" This way," said I, immediately falling in with
their precipitate pace. " What 's wrong? What
ship is that? "

" That 's the *Gleaner*," he replied. " I am chief
officer, this gentleman 's third; and we 've to get

in our depositions before the crew. You see they
might corral us with the captain; and that's no
kind of berth for me. I've sailed with some hard
cases in my time, and seen pins flying like sand on
a squally day — but never a match to our old man.
It never let up from the Hook to the Farallones;
and the last man was dropped not sixteen hours
ago. Packet rats our men were, and as tough a
crowd as ever sand-bagged a man's head in; but
they looked sick enough when the captain started
in with his fancy shooting."

"O, he's done up," observed the other. "He
won't go to sea no more."

"You make me tired," retorted his superior.
"If he gets ashore in one piece and isn't lynched
in the next ten minutes, he'll do yet. The owners
have a longer memory than the public; they'll
stand by him; they don't find as smart a captain
every day in the year."

"O, he's a son of a gun of a fine captain,
there ain't no doubt of that," concurred the other,
heartily. "Why, I don't suppose there's been no
wages paid aboard that *Gleaner* for three trips."

"No wages?" I exclaimed, for I was still a
novice in maritime affairs.

"Not to sailor-men before the mast," agreed
the mate. "Men cleared out; wasn't the soft
job they maybe took it for. She isn't the first
ship that never paid wages."

I could not but observe that our pace was progressively relaxing; and indeed I have often wondered since whether the hurry of the start were

not intended for the gallery alone. Certain it is
at least, that when we had reached the police office,
and the mates had made their deposition, and told
their horrid tale of five men murdered, some with
savage passion, some with cold brutality, between
Sandy Hook and San Francisco, the police were
despatched in time to be too late. Before we arrived, the ruffian had slipped out upon the dock,
had mingled with the crowd, and found a refuge
in the house of an acquaintance; and the ship was
only tenanted by his late victims. Well for him
that he had been thus speedy. For when word
began to go abroad among the shore-side characters, when the last victim was carried by to the
hospital, when those who had escaped (as by
miracle) from that floating shambles, began to
circulate and show their wounds in the crowd, it
was strange to witness the agitation that seized
and shook that portion of the city. Men shed
tears in public; bosses of lodging-houses, long
inured to brutality, and above all, brutality to
sailors, shook their fists at heaven: if hands could
have been laid on the captain of the *Gleaner*, his
shrift would have been short. That night (so
gossip reports) he was headed up in a barrel and
smuggled across the bay: in two ships already
he had braved the penitentiary and the gallows;
and yet, by last accounts, he now commands another on the Western Ocean.

As I have said, I was never quite certain
whether Mr. Nares (the mate) did not intend
that his superior should escape. It would have

been like his preference of loyalty to law; it would have been like his prejudice, which was all in favour of the after-guard. But it must remain a matter of conjecture only. Well as I came to know him in the sequel, he was never communicative on that point, nor indeed on any that concerned the voyage of the *Gleaner*. Doubtless he had some reason for his reticence. Even during our walk to the police office, he debated several times with Johnson, the third officer, whether he ought not to give up himself, as well as to denounce the captain. He had decided in the negative, arguing that " it would probably come to nothing, and even if there was a stink, he had plenty good friends in San Francisco." And to nothing it came; though it must have very nearly come to something, for Mr. Nares disappeared immediately from view and was scarce less closely hidden than his captain.

Johnson, on the other hand, I often met. I could never learn this man's country; and though he himself claimed to be American, neither his English nor his education warranted the claim. In all likelihood he was of Scandinavian birth and blood, long pickled in the forecastles of English and American ships. It is possible that, like so many of his race in similar positions, he had already lost his native tongue. In mind, at least, he was quite denationalised; thought only in English — to call it so; and though by nature one of the mildest, kindest, and most feebly playful of mankind, he had been so long accustomed to the

cruelty of sea-discipline, that his stories (told perhaps with a giggle) would sometimes turn me chill.
In appearance, he was tall, light of weight, bold
and high-bred of feature, dusky-haired, and with
a face of a clean even brown: the ornament of
outdoor men. Seated in a chair, you might have
passed him off for a baronet or a military officer;
but let him rise, and it was Fo'c's'le Jack that came
rolling toward you, crab-like; let him but open
his lips, and it was Fo'c's'le Jack that piped and
drawled his ungrammatical gibberish. He had
sailed (among other places) much among the
islands; and after a Cape Horn passage with its
snow-squalls and its frozen sheets, he announced
his intention of "taking a turn among them Kanakas." I thought I should have lost him soon; but
according to the unwritten usage of mariners, he
had first to dissipate his wages. "Guess I'll have
to paint this town red," was his hyperbolical expression; for sure no man ever embarked upon
a milder course of dissipation, most of his days
being passed in the little parlour behind Black
Tom's public house, with a select corps of old
particular acquaintances, all from the South Seas,
and all patrons of a long yarn, a short pipe, and
glasses round.

Black Tom's, to the front, presented the appearance of a fourth-rate saloon, devoted to Kanaka
seamen, dirt, negrohead tobacco, bad cigars, worse
gin, and guitars and banjos in a state of decline.
The proprietor, a powerful coloured man, was at
once a publican, a ward politician, leader of some

brigade of "lambs" or "smashers," at the wind of whose clubs the party bosses and the mayor were supposed to tremble, and (what hurt nothing) an active and reliable crimp. His front quarters, then, were noisy, disreputable, and not even safe. I have seen worse frequented saloons where there were fewer scandals; for Tom was often drunk himself; and there is no doubt the Lambs must have been a useful body, or the place would have been closed. I remember one day, not long before an election, seeing a blind man, very well dressed, led up to the counter and remain a long while in consultation with the negro. The pair looked so ill-assorted, and the awe with which the drinkers fell back and left them in the midst of an impromptu privacy was so unusual in such a place, that I turned to my next neighbour with a question. He told me the blind man was a dis-. tinguished party boss, called by some the King of San Francisco, but perhaps better known by his picturesque Chinese nickname of the Blind White Devil. "The Lambs must be wanted pretty bad, I guess," my informant added. I have here a sketch of the Blind White Devil leaning on the counter; on the next page, and taken the same hour, a jotting of Black Tom threatening a whole crowd of customers with a long Smith and Wesson: to such heights and depths we rose and fell in the front parts of the saloon.

Meanwhile, away in the back quarters, sat the small informal South Sea club, talking of another world and surely of a different century. Old schooner captains they were, old South Sea traders, cooks, and mates: fine creatures, softened by residence among a softer race: full men besides, though not by reading, but by strange experience; and for days together I could hear their yarns with an unfading pleasure. All had indeed some touch of the poetic; for the beach-comber, when not a mere ruffian, is the poor relation of the artist. Even through Johnson's inarticulate speech, his " O yes, there ain't no harm in them Kanakas," or, " O yes, that 's a son of a gun of a fine island, mountainious right down; I did n't never ought to have left that island," there pierced a certain gusto of appreciation: and some of the rest were master-talkers. From their long tales, their traits of character and unpremeditated landscape, there began to piece itself together in my head some image of the islands and the island life: precipitous shores, spired mountain-tops, the deep shade of hanging forests, the unresting surf upon the reef, and the unending peace of the lagoon; sun, moon, and stars of an imperial brightness; man moving in these scenes scarce fallen, and woman lovelier than Eve; the primal curse abrogated, the bed made ready for the stranger, life set to perpetual music, and the guest welcomed, the boat urged, and the long night beguiled, with poetry and choral song. A man must have been an unsuccessful artist; he must have starved on the streets of Paris; he must have been yoked to a commercial force like Pinkerton, before he can conceive the longings that at times assailed me.

The draughty, rowdy city of San Francisco, the bustling office where my friend Jim paced like a caged lion daily between ten and four, even (at times) the retrospect of Paris, faded in comparison. Many a man less tempted would have thrown up all to realise his visions; but I was by nature unadventurous and uninitiative: to divert me from all former paths and send me cruising through the isles of paradise, some force external to myself must be exerted; Destiny herself must use the fitting wedge; and little as I deemed it, that tool was already in her hand of brass.

I sat, one afternoon, in the corner of a great, glassy, silvered saloon, a free lunch at my one elbow, at the other a "conscientious nude" from the brush of local talent; when, with the tramp of feet and a sudden buzz of voices, the swing-doors were flung broadly open and the place carried as by storm. The crowd which thus entered (mostly seafaring men, and all prodigiously excited) contained a sort of kernel or general centre of interest, which the rest merely surrounded and advertised, as children in the Old World surround and escort the Punch-and-Judy man; and word went round the bar like wildfire, that these were Captain Trent and the survivors of the British brig _Flying Scud,_ picked up by a British war-ship on Midway Island, arrived that morning in San Francisco Bay, and now fresh from making the necessary declarations. Presently I had a good sight of them: four brown, seamanlike fellows, standing by the counter, glass in hand, the centre of a score of questioners. One

was a Kanaka — the cook, I was informed; one
carried a cage with a canary, which occasionally
trilled into thin song; one had his left arm in
a sling and looked gentlemanlike, and somewhat
sickly, as though the injury had been severe and
he was scarce recovered; and the captain himself
— a red-faced, blue-eyed, thick-set man of five and
forty — wore a bandage on his right hand. The
incident struck me; I was struck particularly to
see captain, cook, and foremast hands walking the
street and visiting saloons in company; and, as
when anything impressed me, I got my sketch-book
out, and began to steal a sketch of the four castaways. The crowd, sympathising with my design,
made a clear lane across the room; and I was thus
enabled, all unobserved myself, to observe with a
still-growing closeness the face and the demeanour
of Captain Trent.

Warmed by whisky and encouraged by the
eagerness of the bystanders, that gentleman was
now rehearsing the history of his misfortune. It
was but scraps that reached me: how he " filled
her on the starboard tack," and how " it came up
sudden out of the nor'nor'west," and " there she
was, high and dry." Sometimes he would appeal to
one of the men — " That was how it was, Jack? "
— and the man would reply, " That was the way of
it, Captain Trent." Lastly, he started a fresh tide
of popular sympathy by enunciating the sentiment,
" Damn all these Admiralty Charts, and that 's
what I say! " From the nodding of heads and the
murmurs of assent that followed, I could see that

Captain Trent had established himself in the public
mind as a gentleman and a thorough navigator:
about which period, my sketch of the four men and
the canary-bird being finished, and all (especially
the canary-bird) excellent likenesses, I buckled up
my book, and slipped from the saloon.

Little did I suppose that I was leaving Act I,
Scene I, of the drama of my life; and yet the scene,
or rather the captain's face, lingered for some time
in my memory. I was no prophet, as I say; but
I was something else: I was an observer; and one
thing I knew, I knew when a man was terrified.
Captain Trent, of the British brig *Flying Scud,*
had been glib; he had been ready; he had been
loud; but in his blue eyes I could detect the chill,
and in the lines of his countenance spy the agitation of perpetual terror. Was he trembling for
his certificate? In my judgment, it was some
livelier kind of fear that thrilled in the man's
marrow as he turned to drink. Was it the result
of recent shock, and had he not yet recovered the
disaster to his brig? I remembered how a friend
of mine had been in a railway accident, and shook
and started for a month; and although Captain
Trent of the *Flying Scud* had none of the appearance of a nervous man, I told myself, with incom-
plete conviction, that his must be a similar case.

CHAPTER IX

THE WRECK OF THE "FLYING SCUD"

THE next morning I found Pinkerton, who had risen before me, seated at our usual table, and deep in the perusal of what I will call the *Daily Occidental*. This was a paper (I know not if it be so still) that stood out alone among its brethren in the West; the others, down to their smallest item, were defaced with capitals, head-lines, alliterations, swaggering misquotations, and the shoddy picturesque and unpathetic pathos of the Harry Millers: the *Occidental* alone appeared to be written by a dull, sane, Christian gentleman, singly desirous of communicating knowledge. It had not only this merit, which endeared it to me, but was admittedly the best informed on business matters, which attracted Pinkerton.

"Loudon," said he, looking up from the journal, "you sometimes think I have too many irons in the fire. My notion, on the other hand, is, when you see a dollar lying, pick it up! Well, here I've tumbled over a whole pile of 'em on a reef in the middle of the Pacific."

"Why, Jim, you miserable fellow!" I exclaimed; "have n't we Depew City, one of God's green centres for this State? have n't we —— "

"Just listen to this," interrupted Jim. "It's miserable copy; these *Occidental* reporter fellows have no fire; but the facts are right enough, I guess." And he began to read:

"WRECK OF THE BRITISH BRIG 'FLYING SCUD'

"H. B. M. S. *Tempest*, which arrived yesterday at this port, brings Captain Trent and four men of the British brig *Flying Scud*, cast away February 12th on Midway Island, and most providentially rescued the next day. The *Flying Scud* was of 200 tons burthen, owned in London, and has been out nearly two years tramping. Captain Trent left Hong Kong December 8th, bound for this port in rice and a small mixed cargo of silks, teas, and China notions, the whole valued at $10,000, fully covered by insurance. The log shows plenty of fine weather, with light airs, calms, and squalls. In lat. 28 N., long. 177 W., his water going rotten, and misled by Hoyt's *North Pacific Directory*, which informed him there was a coaling station on the island, Captain Trent put in to Midway Island. He found it a literal sandbank, surrounded by a coral reef mostly submerged. Birds were very plenty, there was good fish in the lagoon, but no firewood; and the water, which could be obtained by digging, brackish. He found good holding-ground off the north end of the larger bank in fifteen fathoms water; bottom sandy, with coral patches. Here he was detained seven days by a calm, the crew suffering severely from the water, which was gone quite bad; and it was only on the evening of the 12th, that a little wind sprang up, coming puffy out of N. N. E. Late as it was, Captain Trent immediately weighed anchor and attempted to get out. While the vessel was beating up to the passage, the wind took a sudden lull and then veered squally into N., and even N. N. W., driving the brig ashore on the sand at about twenty minutes before six o'clock. John Wallen, a native of Finland, and Charles Holdorsen, a native of Sweden, were drowned alongside, in attempting to lower a boat, neither being able to swim, the squall very dark, and the noise of the breakers drowning everything. At the same time John Brown, another of the crew, had his arm broken by the falls. Captain Trent further informed the OCCIDENTAL reporter, that the brig struck heavily at first bows on, he supposes upon coral ; that she then drove over the obstacle, and now lies in sand, much down by the head and with a list to starboard. In the first collision she must have sustained some damage, as she was making water forward. The rice will probably be all destroyed ; but the more valuable part of the cargo is fortunately in the afterhold. Captain Trent was preparing his long-boat for sea, when the providential arrival of the *Tempest*, pursuant to Admiralty orders to call at islands in her course for castaways, saved the gallant captain from all further danger. It is scarcely necessary to add that both the officers and men of the unfortunate vessel speak in high terms of the kindness they received on board the man-of-war. We print a list of the survivors : Jacob Trent, master, of Hull, England ; Elias Goddedaal, mate, native of Christian-sand, Sweden ; Ah Wing, cook, native of Sana, China ; John Brown, native of Glasgow, Scotland ; John Hardy, native of London, England. The *Flying Scud* is ten years old, and this morning will be sold as she stands, by order of Lloyd's agent, at public auction for the benefit of the underwriters. The auction will take place in the Merchants' Exchange at ten o'clock.

" *Farther Particulars.* — Later in the afternoon the OCCI-DENTAL reporter found Lieutenant Sebright, first officer of H. B. M. S. *Tempest*, at the Palace Hotel. The gallant officer was somewhat pressed for time, but confirmed the account given by Captain Trent in all particulars. He added that the *Flying Scud* is in an excellent berth, and except in the highly improbable event of a heavy N. W. gale, might last until next winter."

" You will never know anything of literature," said I, when Jim had finished. " That is a good, honest, plain piece of work, and tells the story clearly. I see only one mistake : the cook is not a Chinaman ; he is a Kanaka, and I think a Hawaiian."

"Why, how do you know that?" asked Jim.

"I saw the whole gang yesterday in a saloon," said I. "I even heard the tale, or might have heard it, from Captain Trent himself, who struck me as thirsty and nervous."

"Well, that's neither here nor there," cried Pinkerton. "The point is, how about these dollars lying on a reef?"

"Will it pay?" I asked.

"Pay like a sugar trust!" exclaimed Pinkerton. "Don't you see what this British officer says about the safety? Don't you see the cargo's valued at ten thousand? Schooners are begging just now; I can get my pick of them at two hundred and fifty a month; and how does that foot up? It looks like three hundred per cent to me."

"You forget," I objected, "the captain himself declares the rice is damaged."

"That's a point, I know," admitted Jim. "But the rice is the sluggish article, anyway; it's little more account than ballast; it's the tea and silks that I look to: all we have to find is the proportion, and one look at the manifest will settle that. I've rung up Lloyd's on purpose; the captain is to meet me there in an hour, and then I'll be as posted on that brig as if I built her. Besides, you've no idea what pickings there are about a wreck — copper, lead, rigging, anchors, chains, even the crockery, Loudon!"

"You seem to me to forget one trifle," said I. "Before you pick that wreck, you've got to buy her, and how much will she cost?"

"One hundred dollars," replied Jim, with the promptitude of an automaton.

"How on earth do you guess that?" I cried.

"I don't guess; I know it," answered the Commercial Force. "My dear boy, I may be a galoot about literature, but you'll always be an outsider in business. How do you suppose I bought the *James L. Moody* for two hundred and fifty, her boats alone worth four times the money? Because my name stood first in the list. Well, it stands there again; I have the naming of the figure, and I name a small one because of the distance: but it would n't matter what I named; that would be the price."

"It sounds mysterious enough," said I. "Is this public auction conducted in a subterranean vault? Could a plain citizen — myself, for instance — come and see?"

"O, everything's open and above board," he cried indignantly. "Anybody can come, only nobody bids against us, and if he did, he would get frozen out. It's been tried before now, and once was enough. We hold the plant; we've got the connection; we can afford to go higher than any outsider; there's two million dollars in the ring; and we stick at nothing. Or suppose anybody did buy over our head — I tell you, Loudon, he would think this town gone crazy; he could no more get business through on the city front than I can dance; schooners, divers, men — all he wanted — the prices would fly right up and strike him."

"But how did you get in?" I asked. "You were once an outsider like your neighbours, I suppose?"

"I took hold of that thing, Loudon, and just studied it up," he replied. "It took my fancy; it was so romantic, and then I saw there was boodle in the thing; and I figured on the business till no man alive could give me points. Nobody knew I had an eye on wrecks till one fine morning I dropped in upon Douglas B. Longhurst in his den, gave him all the facts and figures, and put it to him straight: 'Do you want me in this ring? or shall I start another?' He took half an hour, and when I came back, 'Pink,' says he, 'I've put your name on.' The first time I came to the top, it was that *Moody* racket; now it's the *Flying Scud*."

Whereupon Pinkerton, looking at his watch, uttered an exclamation, made a hasty appointment with myself for the doors of the Merchants' Exchange, and fled to examine manifests and interview the skipper. I finished my cigarette with the deliberation of a man at the end of many picnics; reflecting to myself that of all forms of the dollar hunt, this wrecking had by far the most address to my imagination. Even as I went down town, in the brisk bustle and chill of the familiar San Francisco thoroughfares, I was haunted by a vision of the wreck, baking so far away in the strong sun, under a cloud of sea-birds; and even then, and for no better reason, my heart inclined towards the adventure. If not myself, something that was mine, some one at least in my employment should voyage to that ocean-bounded pin-point and descend to that deserted cabin.

Pinkerton met me at the appointed moment, pinched of lip and more than usually erect of bearing, like one conscious of great resolves.

" Well? " I asked.

" Well," said he, " it might be better, and it might be worse. This Captain Trent is a remarkably honest fellow — one out of a thousand. As soon as he knew I was in the market, he owned up about the rice in so many words. By his calculation, if there 's thirty mats of it saved, it 's an outside figure. However, the manifest was cheerier. There 's about five thousand dollars of the whole value in silks and teas and nut-oils and that, all in the lazarette, and as safe as if it was in Kearney Street. The brig was new coppered a year ago. There 's upwards of a hundred and fifty fathom away-up chain. It 's not a bonanza, but there 's boodle in it; and we 'll try it on."

It was by that time hard on ten o'clock, and we turned at once into the place of sale. The *Flying Scud,* although so important to ourselves, appeared to attract a very humble share of popular attention. The auctioneer was surrounded by perhaps a score of lookers-on, big fellows, for the most part, of the true Western build, long in the leg, broad in the shoulder, and adorned (to a plain man's taste) with needless finery. A jaunty, ostentatious comradeship prevailed. Bets were flying, and nicknames. " The boys " (as they would

12

have called themselves) were very boyish; and it was plain they were here in mirth, and not on business. Behind, and certainly in strong contrast to these gentlemen, I could detect the figure of my friend Captain Trent, come (as I could very well imagine that a captain would) to hear the last of his old vessel. Since yesterday, he had rigged himself anew in ready-made black clothes, not very aptly fitted; the upper left-hand pocket showing a corner of silk handkerchief, the lower, on the other side, bulging with papers. Pinkerton had just given this man a high character. Certainly he seemed to have been very frank, and I looked at him again to trace (if possible) that virtue in his face. It was red and broad and flustered and (I thought) false. The whole man looked sick with some unknown anxiety; and as he stood there, unconscious of my observation, he tore at his nails, scowled on the floor, or glanced suddenly, sharply, and fearfully at passers-by. I was still gazing at the man in a kind of fascination, when the sale began.

Some preliminaries were rattled through, to the irreverent, uninterrupted gambolling of the boys; and then, amid a trifle more attention, the auctioneer sounded for some two or three minutes the pipe of the charmer. Fine brig — new copper — valuable fittings — three fine boats — remarkably choice cargo — what the auctioneer would call a perfectly safe investment; nay, gentlemen, he would go further, he would put a figure on it: he had no hesitation (had that bold auctioneer)

in putting it in figures; and in his view, what
with this and that, and one thing and another,
the purchaser might expect to clear a sum equal
to the entire estimated value of the cargo; or,
gentlemen, in other words, a sum of ten thousand
dollars. At this modest computation the roof immediately above the speaker's head (I suppose,
through the intervention of a spectator of ventri-
loquial taste) uttered a clear "Cock-a-doodle-
doo!" — whereat all laughed, the auctioneer
himself obligingly joining.

"Now, gentlemen, what shall we say," resumed
that gentleman, plainly ogling Pinkerton, — "what
shall we say for this remarkable opportunity?"

"One hundred dollars," said Pinkerton.

"One hundred dollars from Mr. Pinkerton,"
went the auctioneer, "one hundred dollars. No
other gentleman inclined to make any advance?
One hundred dollars, only one hundred dollars . . ."

The auctioneer was droning on to some such
tune as this, and I, on my part, was watching
with something between sympathy and amazement
the undisguised emotion of Captain Trent, when
we were all startled by the interjection of a bid.

"And fifty," said a sharp voice.

Pinkerton, the auctioneer, and the boys, who
were all equally in the open secret of the ring,
were now all equally and simultaneously taken
aback.

"I beg your pardon," said the auctioneer.
"Anybody bid?"

"And fifty," reiterated the voice, which I was now able to trace to its origin, on the lips of a small, unseemly rag of human-kind. The speaker's skin was grey and blotched; he spoke in a kind of broken song, with much variety of key; his gestures seemed (as in the disease called St. Vitus's dance) to be imperfectly under control; he was badly dressed; he carried himself with an air of shrinking assumption, as though he were proud to be where he was and to do what he was doing, and yet half expected to be called in question and kicked out. I think I never saw a man more of a piece; and the type was new to me; I had never before set eyes upon his parallel, and I thought instinctively of Balzac and the lower regions of the *Comédie Humaine*.

Pinkerton stared a moment on the intruder with no friendly eye, tore a leaf from his note-book, and scribbled a line in pencil, turned, beckoned a messenger boy, and whispered "To Longhurst." Next moment, the boy had sped upon his errand, and Pinkerton was again facing the auctioneer.

"Two hundred dollars," said Jim.

"And fifty," said the enemy.

"This looks lively," whispered I to Pinkerton.

"Yes; the little beast means cold drawn biz," returned my friend. "Well, he'll have to have a lesson. Wait till I see Longhurst. Three hundred," he added aloud.

"And fifty," came the echo.

It was about this moment when my eye fell again on Captain Trent. A deeper shade had

mounted to his crimson face: the new coat was
unbuttoned and all flying open; the new silk handkerchief in busy requisition; and the man's eye,
of a clear sailor blue, shone glassy with excitement. He was anxious still, but now (if I could
read a face) there was hope in his anxiety.

"Jim," I whispered, "look at Trent. Bet you
what you please, he was expecting this."

"Yes," was the reply, "there's some blame'
thing going on here." And he renewed his bid.

The figure had run up into the neighoburhood
of a thousand when I was aware of a sensation
in the faces opposite, and looking over my shoulder, saw a very large, bland, handsome man come
strolling forth and make a little signal to the
auctioneer.

"One word, Mr. Borden," said he; and then to
Jim, "Well, Pink, where are we up to now?"

Pinkerton gave him the figure. "I ran up to
that on my own responsibility, Mr. Longhurst,"
he added, with a flush. "I thought it the square
thing."

"And so it was," said Mr. Longhurst, patting
him kindly on the shoulder, like a gratified uncle.
"Well, you can drop out now; we take hold
ourselves. You can run it up to five thousand;
and if he likes to go beyond that, he's welcome
to the bargain."

"By the bye, who is he?" asked Pinkerton.
"He looks away down."

"I've sent Billy to find out." And at the very
moment Mr. Longhurst received from the hands of

one of the expensive young gentlemen a folded paper. It was passed round from one to another till it came to me, and I read: " Harry D. Bellairs, Attorney-at-Law; defended Clara Varden; twice nearly disbarred."

" Well, that gets me!" observed Mr. Longhurst. "Who can have put up a shyster [1] like that? Nobody with money, that's a sure thing. Suppose you tried a big bluff? I think I would, Pink. Well, ta-ta! Your partner, Mr. Dodd? Happy to have the pleasure of your acquaintance, sir." And the great man withdrew.

" Well, what do you think of Douglas B?" whispered Pinkerton, looking reverently after him as he departed. " Six foot of perfect gentleman and culture to his boots."

During this interview the auction had stood transparently arrested, the auctioneer, the spectators, and even Bellairs, all well aware that Mr. Longhurst was the principal, and Jim but a speaking-trumpet. But now that the Olympian Jupiter was gone, Mr. Borden thought proper to affect severity.

" Come, come, Mr. Pinkerton. Any advance?" he snapped.

And Pinkerton, resolved on the big bluff, replied, " Two thousand dollars."

Bellairs preserved his composure. " And fifty," said he. But there was a stir among the onlookers, and what was of more importance, Captain Trent had turned pale and visibly gulped.

[1] A low lawyer.

"Pitch it in again, Jim," said I. "Trent is veakening."

"Three thousand," said Jim.

"And fifty," said Bellairs.

And then the bidding returned to its original novement by hundreds and fifties; but I had been ible in the meanwhile to draw two conclusions. n the first place, Bellairs had made his last advance with a smile of gratified vanity; and I :ould see the creature was glorying in the *kudos*)f an unusual position and secure of ultimate suc- :ess. In the second, Trent had once more changed :olour at the thousand leap, and his relief, when le heard the answering fifty, was manifest and inaffected. Here then was a problem: both were)resumably in the same interest, yet the one was lot in the confidence of the other. Nor was this ill. A few bids later it chanced that my eye en- :ountered that of Captain Trent, and his, which glittered with excitement, was instantly, and I thought guiltily, withdrawn. He wished, then, to conceal his interest? As Jim had said, there was some blamed thing going on. And for certain, here were these two men, so strangely united, so strangely divided, both sharp-set to keep the wreck from us, and that at an exorbitant figure.

Was the wreck worth more than we supposed? A sudden heat was kindled in my brain; the bids were nearing Longhurst's limit of five thousand; another minute, and all would be too late. Tear- ing a leaf from my sketch-book, and inspired (I suppose) by vanity in my own powers of infer-

ence and observation, I took the one mad decision
of my life. "*If you care to go ahead,*" I wrote,
"*I'm in for all I'm worth.*"

Jim read, and looked round at me like one bewildered; then his eyes lightened, and turning
again to the auctioneer, he bid, "Five thousand
one hundred dollars."

"And fifty," said monotonous Bellairs.

Presently Pinkerton scribbled, "*What can it
be?*" and I answered, still on paper: "*I can't
imagine; but there's something. Watch Bellairs;
he'll go up to the ten thousand; see if he don't.*"

And he did, and we followed. Long before this,
word had gone abroad that there was battle royal:
we were surrounded by a crowd that looked on
wondering; and when Pinkerton had offered ten
thousand dollars (the outside value of the cargo,
even were it safe in San Francisco Bay), and
Bellairs, smirking from ear to ear to be the centre
of so much attention, had jerked out his answering, "And fifty," wonder deepened to excitement.

"Ten thousand one hundred," said Jim; and
even as he spoke, he made a sudden gesture with
his hand, his face changed, and I could see that
he had guessed, or thought that he had guessed,
the mystery. As he scrawled another memoran-
dum in his note-book, his hand shook like a
telegraph-operator's.

"*Chinese ship,*" ran the legend; and then, in
big, tremulous half-text, and with a flourish that
overran the margin, "*Opium!*"

To be sure! thought I: this must be the secret.

I knew that scarce a ship came in from any Chinese port, but she carried somewhere, behind a bulkhead, or in some cunning hollow of the beams, a nest of the valuable poison. Doubtless there was some such treasure on the *Flying Scud*. How much was it worth? We knew not, we were gambling in the dark; but Trent knew, and Bellairs; and we could only watch and judge.

By this time neither Pinkerton nor I were of sound mind. Pinkerton was beside himself, his eyes like lamps. I shook in every member. To any stranger entering (say) in the course of the fifteenth thousand, we should probably have cut a poorer figure than Bellairs himself. But we did not pause; and the crowd watched us, now in silence, now with a buzz of whispers.

Seventeen thousand had been reached, when Douglas B. Longhurst, forcing his way into the opposite row of faces, conspicuously and repeatedly shook his head at Jim. Jim's answer was a note of two words: "*My racket!*" which, when the great man had perused, he shook his finger warningly, and departed, I thought, with a sorrowful countenance.

Although Mr. Longhurst knew nothing of Bellairs, the shady lawyer knew all about the Wrecker Boss. He had seen him enter the ring with manifest expectation; he saw him depart, and the bids continue, with manifest surprise and disappointment. "Hullo!" he plainly thought, "this is not the ring I'm fighting, then?" And he determined to put on a spurt.

"Eighteen thousand," said he.

"And fifty," said Jim, taking a leaf out of his adversary's book.

"Twenty thousand," from Bellairs.

"And fifty," from Jim, with a little nervous titter.

And with one consent they returned to the old pace, only now it was Bellairs who took the hundreds, and Jim who did the fifty business. But by this time our idea had gone abroad. I could hear the word "opium" pass from mouth to mouth; and by the looks directed at us, I could see we were supposed to have some private information. And here an incident occurred highly typical of San Francisco. Close at my back there had stood for some time a stout, middle-aged gentleman, with pleasant eyes, hair pleasantly grizzled, and a ruddy, pleasing face. All of a sudden, he appeared as a third competitor, skied the *Flying Scud* with four fat bids of a thousand dollars each, and then as suddenly fled the field, remaining thenceforth (as before) a silent, interested spectator.

Ever since Mr. Longhurst's useless intervention, Bellairs had seemed uneasy; and at this new attack, he began (in his turn) to scribble a note between the bids. I imagined naturally enough that it would go to Captain Trent; but when it was done, and the writer turned and looked behind him in the crowd, to my unspeakable amazement, he did not seem to remark the captain's presence.

"Messenger boy, messenger boy!" I heard him say. "Somebody call me a messenger boy."

At last somebody did, but it was not the captain. *"He's sending for instructions,"* I wrote to Pinkerton. *"For money,"* he wrote back. *"Shall I strike out? I think this is the time."*

I nodded.

" Thirty thousand," said Pinkerton, making a leap of close upon three thousand dollars.

I could see doubt in Bellairs's eye; then, sudden resolution. " Thirty-five thousand," said he.

" Forty thousand," said Pinkerton.

There was a long pause, during which Bellairs's countenance was as a book; and then, not much too soon for the impending hammer, " Forty thousand and five dollars," said he.

Pinkerton and I exchanged eloquent glances. We were of one mind. Bellairs had tried a bluff; now he perceived his mistake, and was bidding against time; he was trying to spin out the sale until the messenger boy returned.

" Forty-five thousand dollars," said Pinkerton: his voice was like a ghost's and tottered with emotion.

" Forty-five thousand and five dollars," said Bellairs.

" Fifty thousand," said Pinkerton.

" I beg your pardon, Mr. Pinkerton. Did I hear you make an advance, sir? " asked the auctioneer.

" I — I have a difficulty in speaking," gasped Jim. " It 's fifty thousand, Mr. Borden."

Bellairs was on his feet in a moment. " Auc-

tioneer," he said, "I have to beg the favour of
three moments at the telephone. In this matter,
I am acting on behalf of a certain party to whom
I have just written —— "

" I have nothing to do with any of this," said
the auctioneer, brutally. " I am here to sell this
wreck. Do you make any advance on fifty
thousand ? "

" I have the honour to explain to you, sir," returned Bellairs, with a miserable assumption of
dignity. " Fifty thousand was the figure named
by my principal; but if you will give me the small
favour of two moments at the telephone —— "

" O, nonsense ! " said the auctioneer. " If you
make no advance, I 'll knock it down to Mr.
Pinkerton."

" I warn you," cried the attorney, with sudden
shrillness. " Have a care what you 're about. You
are here to sell for the underwriters, let me tell
you — not to act for Mr. Douglas Longhurst. This
sale has been already disgracefully interrupted to
allow that person to hold a consultation with his
minions. It has been much commented on."

" There was no complaint at the time," said
the auctioneer, manifestly discountenanced. " You
should have complained at the time."

" I am not here to conduct this sale," replied
Bellairs; " I am not paid for that."

" Well, I am, you see," retorted the auctioneer,
his impudence quite restored; and he resumed his
sing-song. " Any advance on fifty thousand dollars? No advance on fifty thousand? No advance,

gentlemen? Going at fifty thousand, the wreck of the brig *Flying Scud* — going — going — gone!"

"My God, Jim, can we pay the money?" I cried, as the stroke of the hammer seemed to recall me from a dream.

"It 's got to be raised," said he, white as a sheet. "It 'll be a hell of a strain, Loudon. The credit 's good for it, I think; but I shall have to get around. Write me a cheque for your stuff. Meet you at the Occidental in an hour."

I wrote my cheque at a desk, and I declare I could never have recognised my signature. Jim was gone in a moment; Trent had vanished even earlier; only Bellairs remained exchanging insults with the auctioneer; and behold! as I pushed my way out of the exchange, who should run full tilt into my arms, but the messenger boy?

It was by so near a margin that we became the owners of the *Flying Scud*.

CHAPTER X

IN WHICH THE CREW VANISH

AT the door of the exchange, I found myself alongside of the short, middle-aged gentleman who had made an appearance, so vigorous and so brief, in the great battle.

" Congratulate you, Mr. Dodd," he said. " You and your friend stuck to your guns nobly."

" No thanks to you, sir," I replied, " running us up a thousand at a time, and tempting all the speculators in San Francisco to come and have a try."

" O, that was temporary insanity," said he; " and I thank the higher powers I am still a free man. Walking this way, Mr. Dodd? I 'll walk along with you. It 's pleasant for an old fogy like myself to see the young bloods in the ring; I 've done some pretty wild gambles in my time in this very city, when it was a smaller place and I was a younger man. Yes, I know you, Mr. Dodd. By sight, I may say I know you extremely well, you and your followers, the fellows in the kilts, eh? Pardon me. But I have the misfortune to own a little box on the Saucelito shore. I 'll be glad to see you there any Sunday — without the fellows in kilts, you know; and I can give you a bottle of wine, and show you the best collection of Arctic

voyages in the States. Morgan is my name —
Judge Morgan — a Welshman and a forty-niner."

" O, if you 're a pioneer," cried I, " come to me,
and I 'll provide you with an axe."

" You 'll want your axes for yourself, I fancy,"
he returned, with one of his quick looks. " Unless
you have private knowledge, there will be a good
deal of rather violent wrecking to do before you
find that — opium, do you call it? "

" Well, it 's either opium, or we are stark, staring mad," I replied. " But I assure you we have
no private information. We went in (as I suppose
you did yourself) on observation."

" An observer, sir? " inquired the judge.

" I may say it is my trade — or, rather, was,"
said I.

" Well, now, and what did you think of Bellairs? " he asked.

" Very little indeed," said I.

" I may tell you," continued the judge, " that
to me, the employment of a fellow like that appears
inexplicable. I knew him; he knows me too; he
has often heard from me in court; and I assure
you the man is utterly blown upon; it is not safe
to trust him with a dollar; and here we find him
dealing up to fifty thousand. I can't think who
can have so trusted him, but I am very sure it
was a stranger in San Francisco."

" Some one for the owners, I suppose," said I.

" Surely not! " exclaimed the judge. " Owners
in London can have nothing to say to opium
smuggled between Hong Kong and San Francisco.

I should rather fancy they would be the last to hear of it — until the ship was seized. No; I was thinking of the captain. But where would he get the money? above all, after having laid out so much to buy the stuff in China. Unless, indeed, he were acting for some one in 'Frisco; and in that case — here we go round again in the vicious circle — Bellairs would not have been employed."

"I think I can assure you it was not the captain," said I; "for he and Bellairs are not acquainted."

"Was n't that the captain, with the red face and coloured handkerchief? He seemed to me to follow Bellairs's game with the most thrilling interest," objected Mr. Morgan.

"Perfectly true," said I; "Trent is deeply interested; he very likely knew Bellairs, and he certainly knew what he was there for; but I can put my hand in the fire that Bellairs did n't know Trent."

"Another singularity," observed the judge. "Well, we have had a capital forenoon. But you take an old lawyer's advice, and get to Midway Island as fast as you can. There 's a pot of money on the table, and Bellairs and Co. are not the men to stick at trifles."

With this parting counsel, Judge Morgan shook hands and made off along Montgomery Street, while I entered the Occidental Hotel, on the steps of which we had finished our conversation. I was well known to the clerks, and as soon as it was understood that I was there to wait for Pinkerton and lunch, I was invited to a seat inside the counter. Here, then, in a retired corner, I was beginning to come a little to myself after these so violent experiences, when who should come hurrying in, and (after a moment with a clerk) fly to one of the telephone boxes but Mr. Henry D. Bellairs in person? Call it what you will, but the impulse was irresistible, and I rose and took a place immediately at the man's back. It may be some excuse that I had often practised this very innocent form of eavesdropping upon strangers, and for fun. Indeed, I scarce know anything that gives a lower view of man's intelligence than to overhear (as you thus do) one side of a communication.

" Central," said the attorney, "2241 and 584 B" (or some such numbers) — " Who 's that? — All right — Mr. Bellairs — Occidental; the wires are fouled in the other place — Yes, about three minutes — Yes — Yes — Your figure, I am sorry to say — No — I had no authority — Neither more nor less — I have every reason to suppose so — O, Pinkerton, Montana Block — Yes — Yes — Very good, sir — As you will, sir — Disconnect 584 B."

Bellairs turned to leave; at sight of me behind him, up flew his hands, and he winced and cringed, as though in fear of bodily attack. " O, it 's you! " he cried; and then, somewhat recovered, " Mr. Pinkerton's partner, I believe? I am pleased to see you, sir — to congratulate you on your late success." And with that he was gone, obsequiously bowing as he passed.

And now a madcap humour came upon me. It

was plain Bellairs had been communicating with his principal; I knew the number, if not the name; should I ring up at once, it was more than likely he would return in person to the telephone; why should not I dash (vocally) into the presence of this mysterious person, and have some fun for my money? I pressed the bell.

"Central," said I, "connect again 2241 and 584 B."

A phantom central repeated the numbers; there was a pause, and then "Two two four one," came in a tiny voice into my ear — a voice with the English sing-song — the voice plainly of a gentleman. "Is that you again, Mr. Bellairs?" it trilled. "I tell you it's no use. Is that you, Mr. Bellairs? Who is that?"

"I only want to put a single question," said I, civilly. "Why do you want to buy the *Flying Scud?*"

No answer came. The telephone vibrated and hummed in miniature with all the numerous talk of a great city; but the voice of 2241 was silent. Once and twice I put my question; but the tiny, sing-song English voice, I heard no more. The man, then, had fled? fled from an impertinent question? It scarce seemed natural to me; unless on the principle that the wicked fleeth when no man pursueth. I took the telephone list and turned the number up: "2241, Mrs. Keane, res. 942 Mission Street." And that, short of driving to the house and renewing my impertinence in person, was all that I could do.

Yet, as I resumed my seat in the corner of the office, I was conscious of a new element of the uncertain, the underhand, perhaps even the dangerous, in our adventure; and there was now a new picture in my mental gallery, to hang beside that of the wreck under its canopy of sea-birds and of Captain Trent mopping his red brow — the picture of a man with a telephone dice-box to his ear, and at the small voice of a single question, struck suddenly as white as ashes.

From these considerations I was awakened by the striking of the clock. An hour and nearly twenty minutes had elapsed since Pinkerton departed for the money: he was twenty minutes behind time; and to me who knew so well his gluttonous despatch of business and had so frequently admired his iron punctuality, the fact spoke volumes. The twenty minutes slowly stretched into an hour; the hour had nearly extended to a second; and I still sat in my corner of the office, or paced the marble pavement of the hall, a prey to the most wretched anxiety and penitence. The hour for lunch was nearly over before I remembered that I had not eaten. Heaven knows I had no appetite; but there might still be much to do — it was needful I should keep myself in proper trim, if it were only to digest the now too probable bad news; and leaving word at the office for Pinkerton, I sat down to table and called for soup, oysters, and a pint of champagne.

I was not long set, before my friend returned.

He looked pale and rather old, refused to hear of food, and called for tea.

"I suppose all 's up?" said I, with an incredible sinking.

"No," he replied; "I 've pulled it through, Loudon; just pulled it through. I could n't have raised another cent in all 'Frisco. People don't like it; Longhurst even went back on me; said he was n't a three-card-monte man."

"Well, what 's the odds?" said I. "That 's all we wanted, is n't it?"

"Loudon, I tell you I 've had to pay blood for that money," cried my friend, with almost savage energy and gloom. "It 's all on ninety days, too; I could n't get another day — not another day. If we go ahead with this affair, Loudon, you 'll have to go yourself and make the fur fly. I 'll stay of course — I 've got to stay and face the trouble in this city; though, I tell you, I just long to go. I would show these fat brutes of sailors what work was; I would be all through that wreck and out at the other end, before they had boosted themselves upon the deck! But you 'll do your level best, Loudon; I depend on you for that. You must be all fire and grit and dash from the word ' go.' That schooner and the boodle on board of her are bound to be here before three months, or it 's B. U. S. T. — bust."

"I 'll swear I 'll do my best, Jim; I 'll work double tides," said I. "It is my fault that you are in this thing, and I 'll get you out again or

kill myself. But what is that you say? 'If we
go ahead?' Have we any choice, then?"

"I'm coming to that," said Jim. "It is n't that
I doubt the investment. Don't blame yourself for
that; you showed a fine, sound business instinct:
I always knew it was in you, but then it ripped
right out. I guess that little beast of an attorney
knew what he was doing; and he wanted nothing
better than to go beyond. No, there's profit in
the deal; it's not that; it's these ninety-day bills,
and the strain I've given the credit, for I've been
up and down, borrowing, and begging and bribing
to borrow. I don't believe there's another man
but me in 'Frisco," he cried, with a sudden fervour of self-admiration, "who could have raised
that last ten thousand! — Then there's another
thing. I had hoped you might have peddled that
opium through the islands, which is safer and
more profitable. But with this three-month limit,
you must make tracks for Honolulu straight, and
communicate by steamer. I'll try to put up something for you there; I'll have a man spoken to
who's posted on that line of biz. Keep a bright
lookout for him as soon's you make the islands;
for it's on the cards he might pick you up at sea
in a whale-boat or a steam-launch, and bring the
dollars right on board."

It shows how much I had suffered morally during my sojourn in San Francisco, that even now,
when our fortunes trembled in the balance, I should
have consented to become a smuggler and (of
all things) a smuggler of opium. Yet I did, and

that in silence; without a protest, not without a twinge.

"And suppose," said I, "suppose the opium is so securely hidden that I can't get hands on it."

"Then you will stay there till that brig is kindling-wood, and stay and split that kindling-wood with your penknife," cried Pinkerton. "The stuff is there; we know that; and it must be found. But all this is only the one string to our bow — though I tell you I've gone into it head-first, as if it was our bottom dollar. Why, the first thing I did before I'd raised a cent, and with this other notion in my head already — the first thing I did was to secure the schooner. The *Norah Creina*, she is, sixty-four tons, quite big enough for our purpose since the rice is spoiled, and the fastest thing of her tonnage out of San Francisco. For a bonus of two hundred, and a monthly charter of three, I have her for my own time; wages and provisions, say four hundred more: a drop in the bucket. They began firing the cargo out of her (she was part loaded) near two hours ago; and about the same time John Smith got the order for the stores. That's what I call business."

"No doubt of that," said I. "But the other notion."

"Well, here it is," said Jim. "You agree with me that Bellairs was ready to go higher?"

I saw where he was coming. "Yes, — and why should n't he?" said I. "Is that the line?"

"That's the line, Loudon Dodd," assented Jim.

"If Bellairs and his principal have any desire to go me better, I'm their man."

A sudden thought, a sudden fear, shot into my mind. What if I had been right? What if my childish pleasantry had frightened the principal away, and thus destroyed our chance? Shame closed my mouth; I began instinctively a long course of reticence; and it was without a word of my meeting with Bellairs, or my discovery of the address in Mission Street, that I continued the discussion.

"Doubtless fifty thousand was originally mentioned as a round sum," said I, "or at least, so Bellairs supposed. But at the same time it may be an outside sum; and to cover the expenses we have already incurred for the money and the schooner — I am far from blaming you; I see how needful it was to be ready for either event — but to cover them we shall want a rather large advance."

"Bellairs will go to sixty thousand; it's my belief, if he were properly handled, he would take the hundred," replied Pinkerton. "Look back on the way the sale ran at the end."

"That is my own impression as regards Bellairs," I admitted. "The point I am trying to make is that Bellairs himself may be mistaken; that what he supposed to be a round sum was really an outside figure."

"Well, Loudon, if that is so," said Jim, with extraordinary gravity of face and voice, "if that is so, let him take the *Flying Scud* at fifty

thousand, and joy go with her! I prefer the
loss."

"Is that so, Jim? Are we dipped as bad as
that?" I cried.

"We've put our hand further out than we can
pull it in again, Loudon," he replied. "Why,
man, that fifty thousand dollars, before we get
clear again, will cost us nearer seventy. Yes, it
figures up overhead to more than ten per cent a
month; and I could do no better, and there is n't
the man breathing could have done as well. It
was a miracle, Loudon. I could n't but admire
myself. O, if we had just the four months! And
you know, Loudon, it may still be done. With
your energy and charm, if the worst comes to the
worst, you can run that schooner as you ran one
of your picnics; and we may have luck. And, O,
man! if we do pull it through, what a dashing
operation it will be! What an advertisement!
what a thing to talk of, and remember all our
lives! However," he broke off suddenly, "we
must try the safe thing first. Here's for the
shyster!"

There was another struggle in my mind, whether
I should even now admit my knowledge of the
Mission Street address. But I had let the favourable moment slip. I had now, which made it the
more awkward, not merely the original discovery,
but my late suppression to confess. I could not
help reasoning, besides, that the more natural
course was to approach the principal by the road
of his agent's office; and there weighed upon my

spirits a conviction that we were already too late, and that the man was gone two hours ago. Once more, then, I held my peace; and after an exchange of words at the telephone to assure ourselves he was at home, we set out for the attorney's office.

The endless streets of any American city pass, from one end to another, through strange degrees and vicissitudes of splendour and distress, running under the same name between monumental warehouses, the dens and taverns of thieves, and the sward and shrubbery of villas. In San Francisco, the sharp inequalities of the ground, and the sea bordering on so many sides, greatly exaggerate these contrasts. The street for which we were now bound took its rise among blowing sands, somewhere in view of the Lone Mountain Cemetery; ran for a term across that rather windy Olympus of Nob Hill, or perhaps just skirted its frontier; passed almost immediately after through a stage of little houses, rather impudently painted, and offering to the eye of the observer this diagnostic peculiarity, that the huge brass plates upon the small and highly coloured doors bore only the first names of ladies — Norah or Lily or Florence; traversed Chinatown, where it was doubtless undermined with opium cellars, and its blocks pierced, after the similitude of rabbit-warrens, with a hundred doors and passages and galleries; enjoyed a glimpse of high publicity at the corner of Kearney; and proceeded, among dives and warehouses, towards the City Front and the region of the water-rats. In this last stage of its career, where it was both grimy and solitary, and alternately quiet and roaring to the wheels of drays, we found a certain house of some pretension to neatness, and furnished with a rustic outside stair. On the pillar of the stair a black plate bore in gilded lettering this device: " Harry D. Bellairs, Attorney-at-law. Consultations, 9 to 6." On ascending the stairs, a door was found to stand open on the balcony, with this further inscription, " Mr. Bellairs In."

" I wonder what we do next," said I.

" Guess we sail right in," returned Jim, and suited the action to the word.

The room in which we found ourselves was clean, but extremely bare. A rather old-fashioned secretaire stood by the wall, with a chair drawn to the desk; in one corner was a shelf with half-a-dozen law books; and I can remember literally not another stick of furniture. One inference imposed itself: Mr. Bellairs was in the habit of sitting down himself and suffering his clients to stand. At the far end, and veiled by a curtain of red baize, a second door communicated with the interior of the house. Hence, after some coughing and stamping, we elicited the shyster, who came timorously forth, for all the world like a man in fear of bodily assault, and then, recognising his guests, suffered from what I can only call a nervous paroxysm of courtesy.

" Mr. Pinkerton and partner!" said he. " I will go and fetch you seats."

"Not the least," said Jim. "No time. Much rather stand. This is business, Mr. Bellairs. This morning, as you know, I bought the wreck, *Flying Scud.*"

The lawyer nodded.

"And bought her," pursued my friend, "at a figure out of all proportion to the cargo and the circumstances, as they appeared?"

"And now you think better of it, and would like to be off with your bargain? I have been figuring upon this," returned the lawyer. "My client, I will not hide from you, was displeased with me for putting her so high. I think we were both too heated, Mr. Pinkerton: rivalry — the spirit of competition. But I will be quite frank — I know when I am dealing with gentlemen — and I am almost certain, if you leave the matter in my hands, my client would relieve you of the bargain, so as you would lose" — he consulted our faces with gimlet-eyed calculation — "nothing," he added shrilly.

And here Pinkerton amazed me.

"That's a little too thin," said he. "I have the wreck. I know there's boodle in her, and I mean to keep her. What I want is some points which may save me needless expense, and which I am prepared to pay for, money down. The thing for you to consider is just this: am I to deal with you, or direct with your principal? If you are prepared to give me the facts right off, why, name your figure. Only one thing!" added Jim, holding a finger up, "when I say 'money down,' I mean bills payable when the ship returns, and if the information proves reliable. I don't buy pigs in pokes."

I had seen the lawyer's face light up for a moment, and then, at the sound of Jim's proviso, miserably fade. " I guess you know more about this wreck than I do, Mr. Pinkerton," said he. " I only know that I was told to buy the thing, and tried, and could n't."

· " What I like about you, Mr. Bellairs, is that you waste no time," said Jim. " Now then; your client's name and address."

" On consideration," replied the lawyer, with indescribable furtivity, " I cannot see that I am entitled to communicate my client's name. I will sound him for you with pleasure, if you care to instruct me; but I cannot see that I can give you his address."

" Very well," said Jim, and put his hat on. " Rather a strong step, is n't it?" (Between every sentence was a clear pause.) " Not think better of it? Well, come — call it a dollar!"

" Mr. Pinkerton, sir!" exclaimed the offended attorney; and indeed, I myself was almost afraid that Jim had mistaken his man and gone too far.

" No present use for a dollar?" says Jim. " Well, look here, Mr. Bellairs: we 're both busy men, and I 'll go to my outside figure with you right away —— "

" Stop this, Pinkerton," I broke in. " I know the address: 924 Mission Street."

I do not know whether Pinkerton or Bellairs was the more taken aback.

" Why in snakes did n't you say so, Loudon? "
cried my friend.

" You did n't ask for it before," said I, colouring
to my temples under his troubled eyes.

It was Bellairs who broke silence, kindly supply-
ing me with all that I had yet to learn. " Since
you know Mr. Dickson's address," said he, plainly
burning to be rid of us, " I suppose I need detain
you no longer."

I do not know how Pinkerton felt, but I had
death in my soul as we came down the outside
stair, from the den of this blotched spider. My
whole being was strung, waiting for Jim's first
question, and prepared to blurt out, I believe,
almost with tears, a full avowal. But my friend
asked nothing.

" We must hack it," said he, tearing off in the
direction of the nearest stand. " No time to be
lost. You saw how I changed ground. No use in
paying the shyster's commission."

Again I expected a reference to my suppression;
again I was disappointed. It was plain Jim feared
the subject, and I felt I almost hated him for that
fear. At last, when we were already in the hack
and driving towards Mission Street, I could bear
my suspense no longer.

" You do not ask me about that address,"
said I.

" No," said he, quickly and timidly. " What
was it? I would like to know."

The note of timidity offended me like a buffet;
my temper rose as hot as mustard. " I must re-

quest you do not ask me," said I. " It is a matter
I cannot explain."

The moment the foolish words were said, that
moment I would have given worlds to recall
them: how much more, when Pinkerton, patting
my hand, replied: "All right, dear boy; not
another word; that's all done. I'm convinced
it's perfectly right." To return upon the subject was beyond my courage; but I vowed inwardly that I should do my utmost in the
future for this mad speculation, and that I would
cut myself in pieces before Jim should lose one
dollar.

We had no sooner arrived at the address than
I had other things to think of.

"Mr. Dickson? He's gone," said the landlady.

Where had he gone?

"I'm sure I can't tell you," she answered. "He
was quite a stranger to me."

"Did he express his baggage, ma'am?" asked
Pinkerton.

"Hadn't any," was the reply. "He came last
night and left again to-day with a satchel."

"When did he leave?" I inquired.

"It was about noon," replied the landlady.
"Some one rang up the telephone, and asked for
him; and I reckon he got some news, for he left
right away, although his rooms were taken by the
week. He seemed considerable put out: I reckon
it was a death."

My heart sank; perhaps my idiotic jest had indeed driven him away; and again I asked myself,

Why? and whirled for a moment in a vortex of untenable hypotheses.

"What was he like, ma'am?" Pinkerton was asking, when I returned to consciousness of my surroundings.

"A clean-shaved man," said the woman, and could be led or driven into no more significant description.

"Pull up at the nearest drug-store," said Pinkerton to the driver; and when there, the telephone was put in operation, and the message sped to the Pacific Mail Steamship Company's office — this was in the days before Spreckels had arisen — "When does the next China steamer touch at Honolulu?"

"The *City of Pekin;* she cast off the dock to-day, at half-past one," came the reply.

"It's a clear case of bolt," said Jim. "He's skipped, or my name's not Pinkerton. He's gone to head us off at Midway Island."

Somehow I was not so sure; there were elements in the case, not known to Pinkerton — the fears of the captain, for example — that inclined me otherwise; and the idea that I had terrified Mr. Dickson into flight, though resting on so slender a foundation, clung obstinately in my mind. "Shouldn't we see the list of passengers?" I asked.

"Dickson is such a blamed common name," returned Jim; "and then, as like as not, he would change it."

At this I had another intuition. A negative of

a street scene, taken unconsciously when I was absorbed in other thoughts, rose in my memory with not a feature blurred: a view, from Bellairs's door as we were coming down, of muddy roadway, passing drays, matted telegraph wires, a Chinaboy with a basket on his head, and (almost opposite) a corner grocery with the name of Dickson in great gilt letters.

" Yes," said I, " you are right; he would change it. And anyway, I don't believe it was his name at all; I believe he took it from a corner grocery beside Bellairs's."

" As like as not," said Jim, still standing on the sidewalk with contracted brows.

" Well, what shall we do next? " I asked.

" The natural thing would be to rush the schooner," he replied. " But I don't know. I telephoned the captain to go at it head down and heels in air; he answered like a little man; and I guess he 's getting around. I believe, Loudon, we 'll give Trent a chance. Trent was in. it; he was in it up to the neck; even if he could n't buy, he could give us the straight tip."

" I think so too," said I. " Where shall we find him? "

" British consulate of course," said Jim. " And that 's another reason for taking him first. We can hustle that schooner up all evening; but when the consulate 's shut, it 's shut."

At the consulate, we learned that Captain Trent had alighted (such is I believe the classic phrase) at the What Cheer House. To that large and unaristocratic hostelry we drove, and addressed ourselves to a large clerk, who was chewing a tooth-pick and looking straight before him.

"Captain Jacob Trent?"

"Gone," said the clerk.

"Where has he gone?" asked Pinkerton.

"Cain't say," said the clerk.

"When did he go?" I asked.

"Don't know," said the clerk, and with the simplicity of a monarch offered us the spectacle of his broad back.

What might have happened next I dread to pic-ture, for Pinkerton's excitement had been growing steadily, and now burned dangerously high; but we were spared extremities by the intervention of a second clerk.

"Why! Mr. Dodd!" he exclaimed, running forward to the counter. "Glad to see you, sir! Can I do anything in your way?"

How virtuous actions blossom! Here was a young man to whose pleased ears I had rehearsed *Just before the Battle, Mother,* at some weekly picnic; and now, in that tense moment of my life, he came (from the machine) to be my helper.

"Captain Trent of the wreck? O yes, Mr. Dodd; he left about twelve; he and another of the men. The Kanaka went earlier by the *City of Pekin;* I know that; I remember expressing his chest. Captain Trent's? I'll inquire, Mr. Dodd. Yes, they were all here. Here are the names on the register; perhaps you would care to look at them while I go and see about the baggage?"

I drew the book toward me, and stood looking at the four names all written in the same hand, rather a big and rather a bad one: Trent, Brown, Hardy, and (instead of Ah Sing) Jos. Amalu.

"Pinkerton," said I, suddenly, "have you that *Occidental* in your pocket?"

"Never left me," said Pinkerton, producing the paper.

I turned to the account of the wreck. "Here," said I; "here's the name. 'Elias Goddedaal, mate.' Why do we never come across Elias Goddedaal?"

"That's so," said Jim. "Was he with the rest in that saloon when you saw them?"

"I don't believe it," said I. "They were only four, and there was none that behaved like a mate."

At this moment the clerk returned with his report.

"The captain," it appeared, "came with some kind of an express waggon, and he and the man took off three chests and a big satchel. Our porter helped to put them on, but they drove the cart themselves. The porter thinks they went down town. It was about one."

"Still in time for the *City of Pekin*," observed Jim.

"How many of them were here?" I inquired.

"Three, sir, and the Kanaka," replied the clerk. "I can't somehow find out about the third, but he's gone too."

"Mr. Goddedaal, the mate, was n't here then?"
I asked.

"No, Mr. Dodd, none but what you see," says
the clerk.

"Nor you never heard where he was?"

"No. Any particular reason for finding these
men, Mr. Dodd?" inquired the clerk.

"This gentleman and I have bought the wreck,"
I explained; "we wished to get some information, and it is very annoying to find the men all
gone."

A certain group had gradually formed about us,
for the wreck was still a matter of interest; and
at this, one of the bystanders, a rough seafaring
man, spoke suddenly.

"I guess the mate won't be gone," said he.
"He's main sick; never left the sick-bay aboard
the *Tempest;* so they tell *me.*"

Jim took me by the sleeve. "Back to the consulate," said he.

But even at the consulate nothing was known
of Mr. Goddedaal. The doctor of the *Tempest*
had certified him very sick; he had sent his
papers in, but never appeared in person before
the authorities.

"Have you a telephone laid on to the *Tempest?*" asked Pinkerton.

"Laid on yesterday," said the clerk.

"Do you mind asking, or letting me ask?
We are very anxious to get hold of Mr. Goddedaal."

"All right," said the clerk, and turned to the

telephone. "I'm sorry," he said presently, "Mr. Goddedaal has left the ship, and no one knows where he is."

"Do you pay the men's passage home?" I inquired, a sudden thought striking me.

"If they want it," said the clerk; "sometimes they don't. But we paid the Kanaka's passage to Honolulu this morning; and by what Captain Trent was saying, I understand the rest are going home together."

"Then you have n't paid them?" said I.

"Not yet," said the clerk.

"And you would be a good deal surprised, if I were to tell you they were gone already?" I asked.

"O, I should think you were mistaken," said he.

"Such is the fact, however," said I.

"I am sure you must be mistaken," he repeated.

"May I use your telephone one moment?" asked Pinkerton; and as soon as permission had been granted, I heard him ring up the printing-office where our advertisements were usually handled. More I did not hear; for suddenly recalling the big, bad hand in the register of the What Cheer House, I asked the consulate clerk if he had a specimen of Captain Trent's writing. Whereupon I learned that the captain could not write, having cut his hand open a little before the loss of the brig; that the latter part of the log even had been written up by Mr. Goddedaal, and that Trent had always signed with his left hand. By the time I had gleaned this information, Pinkerton was ready.

"That's all that we can do. Now for the schooner," said he; "and by to-morrow evening I lay hands on Goddedaal, or my name's not Pinkerton."

"How have you managed?" I inquired.

"You'll see before you get to bed," said Pinkerton. "And now, after all this backwarding and forwarding, and that hotel clerk, and that bug Bellairs, it'll be a change and a kind of consolation to see the schooner. I guess things are humming there."

But on the wharf, when we reached it, there was no sign of bustle, and but for the galley smoke, no mark of life on the *Norah Creina*. Pinkerton's face grew pale, and his mouth straightened, as he leaped on board.

"Where's the captain of this ——?" and he left the phrase unfinished, finding no epithet sufficiently energetic for his thoughts.

It did not appear whom or what he was addressing; but a head, presumably the cook's, appeared in answer at the galley door.

"In the cabin, at dinner," said the cook deliberately, chewing as he spoke.

"Is that cargo out?"

"No, sir."

"None of it?"

"O, there's some of it out. We'll get at the rest of it livelier to-morrow, I guess."

"I guess there 'll be something broken first," said Pinkerton, and strode to the cabin.

Here we found a man, fat, dark, and quiet, seated gravely at what seemed a liberal meal. He looked up, upon our entrance; and seeing Pinkerton continue to stand facing him in silence, hat on head, arms folded, and lips compressed, an expression of mingled wonder and annoyance began to dawn upon his placid face.

"Well," said Jim. "And so this is what you call rushing around?"

"Who are you?" cries the captain.

"Me! I 'm Pinkerton!" retorted Jim, as though the name had been a talisman.

"You 're not very civil, whoever you are," was the reply. But still a certain effect had been produced, for he scrambled to his feet, and added hastily, "A man must have a bit of dinner, you know, Mr. Pinkerton."

"Where 's your mate?" snapped Jim.

"He 's up town," returned the other.

"Up town!" sneered Pinkerton. "Now I 'll tell you what you are: you 're a Fraud; and if I was n't afraid of dirtying my boot, I would kick you and your dinner into that dock."

"I 'll tell you something, too," retorted the captain, duskily flushing. "I would n't sail this ship for the man you are, if you went upon your knees. I 've dealt with gentlemen up to now."

"I can tell you the names of a number of gentlemen you 'll never deal with any more, and that 's the whole of Longhurst's gang," said

Jim. " I 'll put your pipe out in that quarter, my
friend. Here, rout out your traps as quick as
look at it, and take your vermin along with
you. I 'll have a captain in, this very night,
that 's a sailor, and some sailors to work for
him."

" I 'll go when I please, and that 's to-morrow
morning," cried the captain after us, as we departed for the shore.

" There 's something gone wrong with the world
to-day; it must have come bottom up!" wailed
Pinkerton. "Bellairs, and then the hotel clerk, and
now This Fraud! And what am I to do for a
captain, Loudon, with Longhurst gone home an
hour ago, and the boys all scattered?"

" I know," said I. "Jump in!" And then to
the driver: "Do you know Black Tom's?"

Thither then we rattled; passed through the
bar, and found (as I had hoped) Johnson in the
enjoyment of club life. The table had been thrust
upon one side; a South Sea merchant was discoursing music from a mouth-organ in one corner; and in the middle of the floor Johnson and
a fellow-seaman, their arms clasped about each
other's bodies, somewhat heavily danced. The
room was both cold and close; a jet of gas,
which continually menaced the heads of the performers, shed a coarse illumination; the mouth-
organ sounded shrill and dismal; and the faces
of all concerned were church-like in their gravity.
It were, of course, indelicate to interrupt these
solemn frolics; so we edged ourselves to chairs.

for all the world like belated comers in a concert-room, and patiently waited for the end. At length the organist, having exhausted his supply of breath, ceased abruptly in the middle of a bar. With the cessation of a strain, the dances likewise came to a full stop, swayed a moment, still embracing, and then separated and looked about the circle for applause.

"Very well danced!" said one; but it appears the compliment was not strong enough for the performers, who (forgetful of the proverb) took up the tale in person.

"Well!" said Johnson. "I may n't be no sailor, but I can dance!"

And his late partner, with an almost pathetic conviction, added, "My foot is as light as a feather."

Seeing how the wind set, you may be sure I added a few words of praise before I carried Johnson alone into the passage: to whom, thus mollified, I told so much as I judged needful of our situation, and begged him, if he would not take the job himself, to find me a smart man.

"Me!" he cried. "I could n't no more do it than I could try to go to hell!"

"I thought you were a mate," said I.

"So I am a mate," giggled Johnson, "and you don't catch me shipping noways else. But I'll tell you what, I believe I can get you Arty Nares: you seen Arty: first-rate navigator and a son of a gun for style." And he proceeded to explain

to me that Mr. Nares, who had the promise of
a fine barque in six months, after things had
quieted down, was in the meantime living very
private, and would be pleased to have a change
of air.

I called out Pinkerton and told him. " Nares!"
he cried, as soon as I had come to the name. " I
would jump at the chance of a man that had had
Nares's trousers on! Why, Loudon, he's the
smartest deep-water mate out of San Francisco,
and draws his dividends regular in service and
out." This hearty indorsation clinched the proposal; Johnson agreed to produce Nares before
six the following morning; and Black Tom, being called into the consultation, promised us four
smart hands for the same hour, and even (what
appeared to all of us excessive) promised them
sober.

The streets were fully lighted when we left
Black Tom's: street after street sparkling with
gas or electricity, line after line of distant luminaries climbing the steep sides of hills towards
the overvaulting darkness; and on the other hand,
where the waters of the bay invisibly trembled, a
hundred riding lanterns marked the position of a
hundred ships. The sea-fog flew high in heaven;
and at the level of man's life and business it was
clear and chill. By silent consent, we paid the
hack off, and proceeded arm in arm towards the
Poodle Dog for dinner.

At one of the first hoardings, I was aware of
a bill-sticker at work: it was a late hour for this

employment, and I checked Pinkerton until the sheet should be unfolded. This is what I read:

TWO HUNDRED DOLLARS REWARD.

OFFICERS AND MEN OF THE

WRECKED BRIG FLYING SCUD

APPLYING,

PERSONALLY OR BY LETTER,

AT THE OFFICE OF JAMES PINKERTON, MONTANA BLOCK,

BEFORE NOON TO-MORROW, TUESDAY, 12TH,

WILL RECEIVE

TWO HUNDRED DOLLARS REWARD.

" This is your idea, Pinkerton! " I cried.

" Yes. They 've lost no time; I 'll say that for them — not like the Fraud," said he. " But mind you, Loudon, that 's not half of it. The cream of the idea 's here : we know our man 's sick; well, a copy of that has been mailed to every hospital, every doctor, and every drug-store in San Francisco."

Of course, from the nature of our business, Pinkerton could do a thing of the kind at a figure extremely reduced; for all that, I was appalled at the extravagance, and said so.

" What matter a few dollars now? " he replied sadly. " It 's in three months that the pull comes, Loudon."

We walked on again in silence, not without a shiver. Even at the Poodle Dog, we took our food with small appetite and less speech; and it was not until he was warmed with a third glass of champagne that Pinkerton cleared his throat and looked upon me with a deprecating eye.

"Loudon," said he, "there was a subject you did n't wish to be referred to. I only want to do so indirectly. It was n't " — he faltered — " it was n't because you were dissatisfied with me? " he concluded, with a quaver.

" Pinkerton! " cried I.

" No, no, not a word just now," he hastened to proceed. " Let me speak first. I appreciate, though I can't imitate, the delicacy of your nature; and I can well understand you would rather die than speak of it, and yet might feel disappointed. I did think I could have done better myself. But when I found how tight money was in this city, and a man like Douglas B. Longhurst — a forty-niner, the man that stood at bay in a corn patch for five hours against the San Diablo squatters — weakening on the operation, I tell you, Loudon, I began to despair; and — I may have made mistakes, no doubt there are thousands who could have done better — but I give you a loyal hand on it, I did my best."

" My poor Jim," said I, " as if I ever doubted you! as if I did n't know you had done wonders! All day I 've been admiring your energy and resource. And as for that affair —— "

" No, Loudon, no more, not a word more! I don't want to hear," cried Jim.

" Well, to tell you the truth, I don't want to tell you," said I; " for it 's a thing I 'm ashamed of."

" Ashamed, Loudon? O, don't say that; don't

use such an expression even in jest!" protested Pinkerton.

"Do you never do anything you're ashamed of?" I inquired.

"No," says he, rolling his eyes. "Why? I'm sometimes sorry afterwards, when it pans out different from what I figured. But I can't see what I would want to be ashamed for."

I sat awhile considering with admiration the simplicity of my friend's character. Then I sighed. "Do you know, Jim, what I'm sorriest for?" said I. "At this rate, I can't be best man at your marriage."

"My marriage!" he repeated, echoing the sigh. "No marriage for me now. I'm going right down to-night to break it to her. I think that's what's shaken me all day. I feel as if I had had no right (after I was engaged) to operate so widely."

"Well, you know, Jim, it was my doing, and you must lay the blame on me," said I.

"Not a cent of it!" he cried. "I was as eager as yourself, only not so bright at the beginning. No; I've myself to thank for it; but it's a wrench."

While Jim departed on his dolorous mission, I returned alone to the office, lit the gas, and sat down to reflect on the events of that momentous day: on the strange features of the tale that had been so far unfolded, the disappearances, the terrors, the great sums of money; and on the dangerous and ungrateful task that awaited me in the immediate future.

It is difficult, in the retrospect of such affairs, to avoid attributing to ourselves in the past a measure of the knowledge we possess to-day. But I may say, and yet be well within the mark, that I was consumed that night with a fever of suspicion and curiosity; exhausted my fancy in solutions, which I still dismissed as incommensurable with the facts; and in the mystery by which I saw myself surrounded, found a precious stimulus for my courage and a convenient soothing draught for conscience. Even had all been plain sailing, I do not hint that I should have drawn back. Smuggling is one of the meanest of crimes, for by that we rob a whole country *pro rata*, and are therefore certain to impoverish the poor: to smuggle opium is an offence particularly dark, since it stands related not so much to murder, as to massacre. Upon all these points I was quite clear; my sympathy was all in arms against my interest; and had not Jim been involved, I could have dwelt almost with satisfaction on the idea of my failure. But Jim, his whole fortune, and his marriage, depended upon my success; and I preferred the interests of my friend before those of all the islanders in the South Seas. This is a poor, private morality, if you like; but it is mine, and the best I have; and I am not half so much ashamed of having embarked at all on this adventure, as I am proud that (while I was in it, and for the sake of my friend) I was up early and down late, set my own hand to everything, took dangers as they came, and for once in my life played the man

throughout. At the same time, I could have desired another field of energy; and I was the more
grateful for the redeeming element of mystery.
Without that, though I might have gone ahead
and done as well, it would scarce have been with
ardour; and what inspired me that night with an
impatient greed of the sea, the island, and the
wreck, was the hope that I might stumble there
upon the answer to a hundred questions, and learn
why Captain Trent fanned his red face in the
exchange, and why Mr. Dickson fled from the
telephone in the Mission Street lodging-house.

CHAPTER XI

IN WHICH JIM. AND I TAKE DIFFERENT WAYS

I WAS unhappy when I closed my eyes; and it was to unhappiness that I opened them again next morning, to a confused sense of some calamity still inarticulate, and to the consciousness of jaded limbs and of a swimming head. I must have lain for some time inert and stupidly miserable, before I became aware of a reiterated knocking at the door; with which discovery all my wits flowed back in their accustomed channels, and I remembered the sale, and the wreck, and Goddedaal, and Nares, and Johnson, and Black Tom, and the troubles of yesterday, and the manifold engagements of the day that was to come. The thought thrilled me like a trumpet in the hour of battle. In a moment, I had leaped from bed, crossed the office where Pinkerton lay in a deep trance of sleep on the convertible sofa, and stood in the doorway, in my night gear, to receive our visitors.

Johnson was first, by way of usher, smiling. From a little behind, with his Sunday hat tilted forward over his brow, and a cigar glowing between his lips, Captain Nares acknowledged our previous acquaintance with a succinct nod. Behind him again, in the top of the stairway, a knot of sailors, the new crew of the *Norah Creina*, stood polishing the wall with back and elbow. These I left without, to their reflections. But our two officers I carried at once into the office, where (taking Jim by the shoulder) I shook him slowly into consciousness. He sat up, all abroad for the moment, and stared on the new captain.

"Jim," said I, "this is Captain Nares. Captain, Mr. Pinkerton."

Nares repeated his curt nod, still without speech; and I thought he held us both under a watchful scrutiny.

"O!" says Jim, "this is Captain Nares, is it? Good-morning, Captain Nares. Happy to have the pleasure of your acquaintance, sir. I know you well by reputation."

Perhaps, under the circumstances of the moment, this was scarce a welcome speech. At least, Nares received it with a grunt.

"Well, Captain," Jim continued, "you know about the size of the business? You 're to take the *Norah Creina* to Midway Island, break up a wreck, call at Honolulu, and back to this port? I suppose that 's understood?"

"Well," returned Nares, with the same unamiable reserve, "for a reason, which I guess you know, the cruise may suit me; but there 's a point or two to settle. We shall have to talk, Mr. Pinkerton. But whether I go or not, somebody will; there 's no sense in losing time; and you might give Mr. Johnson a note, let him take the hands

right down, and set to to overhaul the rigging.
The beasts look sober," he added, with an air of
great disgust, "and need putting to work to keep
them so."

This being agreed upon, Nares watched his sub-
ordinate depart and drew a visible breath.

"And now we 're alone and can talk," said he.
"What 's this thing about? It 's been advertised
like Barnum's museum; that poster of yours has
set the Front talking; that 's an objection in itself,
for I 'm laying a little dark just now; and anyway,
before I take the ship, I require to know what I 'm
going after."

Thereupon Pinkerton gave him the whole tale,
beginning with a businesslike precision, and working himself up, as he went on, to the boiling-point
of narrative enthusiasm. Nares sat and smoked,
hat still on head, and acknowledged each fresh feature of the story with a frowning nod. But his
pale blue eyes betrayed him, and lighted visibly.

"Now you see for yourself," Pinkerton concluded: "there 's every last chance that Trent has
skipped to Honolulu, and it won't take much of
that fifty thousand dollars to charter a smart
schooner down to Midway. Here 's where I want
a man!" cried Jim, with contagious energy. "That
wreck 's mine; I 've paid for it, money down; and
if it 's got to be fought for, I want to see it fought
for lively. If you 're not back in ninety days, I
tell you plainly, I 'll make one of the biggest busts
ever seen upon this coast; it 's life or death for
Mr. Dodd and me. As like as not, it 'll come to

grapples on the island; and when I heard your name last night — and a blame' sight more this morning when I saw the eye you 've got in your head — I said, ' Nares is good enough for me!' "

" I guess," observed Nares, studying the ash of his cigar, " the sooner I get that schooner outside the Farallones, the better you 'll be pleased."

" You 're the man I dreamed of!" cried Jim, bouncing on the bed. " There 's not five per cent of fraud in all your carcase."

" Just hold on," said Nares. " There 's another point. I heard some talk about a supercargo."

" That 's Mr. Dodd, here, my partner," replied Jim.

" I don't see it," returned the captain, drily. " One captain 's enough for any ship that ever I was aboard."

" Now, don't you start disappointing me," said Pinkerton; " for you 're talking without thought. I 'm not going to give you the run of the books of this firm, am I? I guess not. Well, this is not only a cruise; it 's a business operation; and that 's in the hands of my partner. You sail that ship, you see to breaking up that wreck and keeping the men upon the jump, and you 'll find your hands about full. Only, no mistake about one thing: it has to be done to Mr. Dodd's satisfaction; for it 's Mr. Dodd that 's paying."

" I 'm accustomed to give satisfaction," said Mr. Nares, with a dark flush.

" And so you will here!" cried Pinkerton. " I

understand you. You're prickly to handle, but you're straight all through."

"The position's got to be understood, though," returned Nares, perhaps a trifle mollified. "My position, I mean. I'm not going to ship sailing-master; it's enough out of my way already, to set a foot on this mosquito schooner."

"Well, I'll tell you," retorted Jim, with an indescribable twinkle: "you just meet me on the ballast, and we'll make it a barquentine."

Nares laughed a little; tactless Pinkerton had once more gained a victory in tact. "Then there's another point," resumed the captain, tacitly relinquishing the last. "How about the owners?"

"O, you leave that to me; I'm one of Longhurst's crowd, you know," said Jim, with sudden bristling vanity. "Any man that's good enough for me, is good enough for them."

"Who are they?" asked Nares.

"M'Intyre and Spittal," said Jim.

"O, well, give me a card of yours," said the captain: "you need n't bother to write; I keep M'Intyre and Spittal in my vest-pocket."

Boast for boast; it was always thus with Nares and Pinkerton — the two vainest men of my acquaintance. And having thus reinstated himself in his own opinion, the captain rose, and, with a couple of his stiff nods, departed.

"Jim," I cried, as the door closed behind him, "I don't like that man."

"You've just got to, Loudon," returned Jim. "He's a typical American seaman — brave as a lion, full of resource, and stands high with his owners. He's a man with a record."

"For brutality at sea," said I.

"Say what you like," exclaimed Pinkerton, "it was a good hour we got him in: I'd trust Mamie's life to him to-morrow."

"Well, and talking of Mamie?" says I.

Jim paused with his trousers half on. "She's the gallantest little soul God ever made!" he cried. "Loudon, I meant to knock you up last night, and I hope you won't take it unfriendly that I didn't. I went in and looked at you asleep; and I saw you were all broken up, and let you be. The news would keep, anyway; and even you, Loudon, couldn't feel it the same way as I did."

"What news?" I asked.

"It's this way," says Jim. "I told her how we stood, and that I backed down from marrying. 'Are you tired of me?' says she: God bless her! Well, I explained the whole thing over again, the chance of smash, your absence unavoidable, the point I made of having you for the best man, and that. 'If you're not tired of me, I think I see one way to manage,' says she. 'Let's get married to-morrow, and Mr. Loudon can be best man before he goes to sea.' That's how she said it, crisp and bright, like one of Dickens's characters. It was no good for me to talk about the smash. 'You'll want me all the more,' she said. Loudon, I only pray I can make it up to her; I prayed for it last night beside your bed, while you lay sleeping — for you, and Mamie and myself; and — I

don't know if you quite believe in prayer, I'm a
bit Ingersollian myself — but a kind of sweetness
came over me, and I could n't help but think it was
an answer. Never was a man so lucky! You and
me and Mamie; it's a triple cord, Loudon. If
either of you were to die! And she likes you so
much, and thinks you so accomplished and dis-
tingué-looking, and was just as set as I was to
have you for best man. 'Mr. Loudon,' she calls
you; seems to me so friendly! And she sat up till
three in the morning fixing up a costume for the
marriage; it did me good to see her, Loudon, and
to see that needle going, going, and to say 'All
this hurry, Jim, is just to marry you!' I could n't
believe it; it was so like some blame' fairy story.
To think of those old tin-type times about turned
my head; I was so unrefined then, and so illiter-
ate, and so lonesome; and here I am in clover,
and I'm blamed if I can see what I've done to
deserve it."

So he poured forth with innocent volubility the
fulness of his heart; and I, from these irregular
communications, must pick out, here a little and
there a little, the particulars of his new plan. They
were to be married, sure enough, that day; the
wedding breakfast was to be at Frank's; the evening to be passed in a visit of God-speed aboard the
Norah Creina; and then we were to part, Jim and
I, he to his married life, I on my sea-enterprise.
If ever I cherished an ill-feeling for Miss Mamie,
I forgave her now; so brave and kind, so pretty
and venturesome, was her decision. The weather

frowned overhead with a leaden sky, and San
Francisco had never (in all my experience) looked
so bleak, and gaunt, and shoddy, and crazy, like a
city prematurely old; but through all my wander-
ings and errands to and fro, by the dock-side or in
the jostling street, among rude sounds and ugly
sights, there ran in my mind, like a tiny strain of
music, the thought of my friend's happiness.

For that was indeed a day of many and incongruous occupations. Breakfast was scarce swallowed,
before Jim must run to the City Hall and Frank's
about the cares of marriage, and I hurry to John
Smith's upon the account of stores, and thence, on
a visit of certification, to the *Norah Creina.* Methought she looked smaller than ever, sundry great
ships overspiring her from close without. She was
already a nightmare of disorder; and the wharf
alongside was piled with a world of casks, and
cases, and tins, and tools, and coils of rope, and
miniature barrels of giant powder, such as it
seemed no human ingenuity could stuff on board
of her. Johnson was in the waist, in a red shirt
and dungaree trousers, his eye kindled with activity. With him I exchanged a word or two;
thence stepped aft along the narrow alleyway
between the house and the rail, and down the
companion to the main cabin, where the captain
sat with the commissioner at wine.

I gazed with disaffection at the little box which
for many a day I was to call home. On the starboard was a stateroom for the captain; on the port,
a pair of frowsy berths, one over the other, and

abutting astern upon the side of an unsavoury cupboard. The walls were yellow and damp, the floor black and greasy; there was a prodigious litter of straw, old newspapers, and broken packing-cases; and by way of ornament, only a glass-rack, a thermometer presented " with compliments " of some advertising whisky-dealer, and a swinging lamp. It was hard to foresee that, before a week was up, I should regard that cabin as cheerful, lightsome, airy, and even spacious.

I was presented to the commissioner, and to a young friend of his whom he had brought with him for the purpose (apparently) of smoking cigars; and after we had pledged one another in a glass of California port, a trifle sweet and sticky for a morning beverage, the functionary spread his papers on the table, and the hands were summoned. Down they trooped, accordingly, into the cabin; and stood eyeing the ceiling or the floor, the picture of sheepish embarrassment, and with a common air of wanting to expectorate and not quite daring. In admirable contrast, stood the Chinese cook, easy, dignified, set apart by spotless raiment, the hidalgo of the seas.

I dare say you never had occasion to assist at the farce which followed. Our shipping laws in the United States (thanks to the inimitable Dana) are conceived in a spirit of paternal stringency, and proceed throughout on the hypothesis that poor Jack is an imbecile, and the other parties to the contract, rogues and ruffians. A long and wordy paper of precautions, a fo'c's'le bill of rights, must

be read separately to each man. I had now the
benefit of hearing it five times in brisk succession;
and you would suppose I was acquainted with its
contents. But the commissioner (worthy man)
spends his days in doing little else; and when we
bear in mind the parallel case of the irreverent
curate, we need not be surprised that he took the
passage *tempo prestissimo,* in one roulade of gabble
— that I, with the trained attention of an educated
man, could gather but a fraction of its import —
and the sailors nothing. No profanity in giving
orders, nó sheath-knives, Midway Island and any
other port the master may direct, not to exceed
six calendar months, and to this port to be paid
off: so it seemed to run, with surprising verbiage;
so ended. And with the end, the commissioner, in
each case, fetched a deep breath, resumed his natural voice, and proceeded to business. " Now, my
man," he would say, " you ship A. B. at so many
dollars, American gold coin. Sign your name
here, if you have one, and can write." Whereupon,
and the name (with infinite hard breathing) being
signed, the commissioner would proceed to fill in
the man's appearance, height, etc., on the official
form. In this task of literary portraiture he seemed
to rely wholly upon temperament; for I could not
perceive him to cast one glance on any of his
models. He was assisted, however, by a running
commentary from the captain: " Hair blue and
eyes red, nose five foot seven, and stature broken "
— jests as old, presumably, as the American marine; and, like the similar pleasantries of the

billiard board, perennially relished. The highest
note of humour was reached in the case of the
Chinese cook, who was shipped under the name
of " One Lung," to the sound of his own protests
and the self-approving chuckles of the functionary.

" Now, Captain," said the latter, when the men
were gone, and he had bundled up his papers,
" the law requires you to carry a slop-chest and a
chest of medicines."

" I guess I know that," said Nares.

" I guess you do," returned the commissioner,
and helped himself to port.

But when he was gone, I appealed to Nares on
the same subject, for I was well aware we carried
none of these provisions.

" Well," drawled Nares, " there 's sixty pounds
of niggerhead on the quay, is n't there? and twenty
pounds of salts; and I never travel without some
painkiller in my gripsack."

As a matter of fact, we were richer. The captain had the usual sailor's provision of quack medicines, with which, in the usual sailor fashion, he
would daily drug himself, displaying an extreme
inconstancy, and flitting from Kennedy's Red Discovery to Kennedy's White, and from Hood's Sar-
saparilla to Mother Seigel's Syrup. And there
were, besides, some mildewed and half-empty bottles, the lables obliterated, over which Nares would
sometimes sniff and speculate. " Seems to smell
like diarrhœa stuff," he would remark. " I wish 't
I knew, and I would try it." But the slop-chest
was indeed represented by the plugs of nigger-

head, and nothing else. Thus paternal laws are made, thus they are evaded; and the schooner put to sea, like plenty of her neighbours, liable to a fine of six hundred dollars.

This characteristic scene, which has delayed me over-long, was but a moment in that day of exercise and agitation. To fit out a schooner for sea, and improvise a marriage between dawn and dusk, involves heroic effort. All day Jim and I ran, and tramped, and laughed, and came near crying, and fell in sudden anxious consultations, and were sped (with a prepared sarcasm on our lips) to some fallacious milliner, and made dashes to the schooner and John Smith's, and at every second corner were reminded (by our own huge posters) of our desperate estate. Between whiles, I had found the time to hover at some half-a-dozen jewellers' windows; and my present, thus intemperately chosen, was graciously accepted. I believe, indeed, that was the last (though not the least) of my concerns, before the old minister, shabby and benign, was routed from his house and led to the office like a performing poodle; and there, in the growing dusk, under the cold glitter of Thirteen Star, two hundred strong, and beside the garish glories of the agricultural engine, Mamie and Jim were made one. The scene was incongruous, but the business pretty, whimsical, and affecting: the typewriters with such kindly faces and fine posies, Mamie so demure, and Jim — how shall I describe that poor, transfigured Jim? He began by taking the minister aside to the far end of the

office. I knew not what he said, but I have reason to believe he was protesting his unfitness; for
he wept as he said it: and the old minister, himself genuinely moved, was heard to console and
encourage him, and at one time to use this expression: " I assure you, Mr. Pinkerton, there are
not many who can say so much "— from which
I gathered that my friend had tempered his self-
accusations with at least one legitimate boast.
From this ghostly counselling, Jim turned to me;
and though he never got beyond the explosive utterance of my name and one fierce handgrip, communicated some of his own emotion, like a charge
of electricity, to his best man. We stood up to
the ceremony at last, in a general and kindly dis-
composure. Jim was all abroad; and the divine
himself betrayed his sympathy in voice and demeanour, and concluded with a fatherly allocution,
in which he congratulated Mamie (calling her " my
dear ") upon the fortune of an excellent husband,
and protested he had rarely married a more interesting couple. At this stage, like a glory descending, there was handed in, *ex machina*, the card of
Douglas B. Longhurst, with congratulations and
four dozen Perrier-Jouet. A bottle was opened;
and the minister pledged the bride, and the brides-
maids simpered and tasted, and I made a speech
with airy bacchanalianism, glass in hand. But
poor Jim must leave the wine untasted. " Don't
touch it," I had found the opportunity to whisper; " in your state, it will make you as drunk
as a fiddler." And Jim had wrung my hand,

with a " God bless you, Loudon! — saved me again! "

Hard following upon this, the supper passed off at Frank's with somewhat tremulous gaiety. And thence, with one-half of the Perrier-Jouet — I would accept no more — we voyaged in a hack to the *Norah Creina.*

" What a dear little ship! " cried Mamie, as our miniature craft was pointed out to her. And then, on second thought, she turned to the best man. " And how brave you must be, Mr. Dodd," she cried, " to go in that tiny thing so far upon the ocean! " And I perceived I had risen in the lady's estimation.

The dear little ship presented a horrid picture of confusion, and its occupants of weariness and ill-humour. From the cabin the cook was storing tins into the lazarette, and the four hands, sweaty and sullen, were passing them from one to another from the waist. Johnson was three parts asleep over the table; and in his bunk, in his own cabin, the captain sourly chewed and puffed at a cigar.

" See here," he said, rising; " you 'll be sorry you came. We can't stop work if we 're to get away to-morrow. A ship getting ready for sea is no place for people, anyway. You 'll only interrupt my men."

I was on the point of answering something tart; but Jim, who was acquainted with the breed, as he was with most things that had a bearing on affairs, made haste to pour in oil.

"Captain," he said, "I know we're a nuisance here, and that you've had a rough time. But all we want is that you should drink one glass of wine with us, Perrier-Jouet, from Longhurst, on the occasion of my marriage, and Loudon's — Mr. Dodd's — departure."

"Well, it's your lookout," said Nares. "I don't mind half an hour. Spell, O!" he added to the men; "go and kick your heels for half an hour, and then you can turn to again a trifle livelier. Johnson, see if you can't wipe off a chair for the lady."

His tone was no more gracious than his language; but when Mamie had turned upon him the soft fire of her eyes, and informed him that he was the first sea-captain she had ever met, "except captains of steamers, of course"— she so qualified the statement — and had expressed a lively sense of his courage, and perhaps implied (for I suppose the arts of ladies are the same as those of men) a modest consciousness of his good looks, our bear began insensibly to soften; and it was already part as an apology, though still with unaffected heat of temper, that he volunteered some sketch of his annoyances.

"A pretty mess we've had," said he. "Half the stores were wrong; I'll wring John Smith's neck for him some of these days. Then two newspaper beasts came down, and tried to raise copy out of me, till I threatened them with the first thing handy; and then some kind of missionary bug, wanting to work his passage to Raiatea or

somewhere. I told him I would take him off the
wharf with the butt-end of my boot, and he went
away cursing. This vessel's been depreciated by
the look of him."

While the captain spoke, with his strange, humourous, arrogant abruptness, I observed Jim to
be sizing him up, like a thing at once quaint and
familiar, and with a scrutiny that was both curious and knowing.

" One word, dear boy," he said, turning suddenly to me. And when he had drawn me on
deck, " That man," says he, " will carry sail till
your hair grows white; but never you let on,
never breathe a word. I know his line: he'll die
before he'll take advice; and if you get his back
up, he'll run you right under. I don't often jam
in my advice, Loudon; and when I do, it means
I'm thoroughly posted."

The little party in the cabin, so disastrously
begun, finished, under the mellowing influence of
wine and woman, in excellent feeling and with
some hilarity. Mamie, in a plush Gainsborough
hat and a gown of wine-coloured silk, sat, an
apparent queen, among her rude surroundings
and companions. The dusky litter of the cabin
set off her radiant trimness: tarry Johnson was
a foil to her fair beauty; she glowed in that poor
place, fair as a star; until even I, who was not
usually of her admirers, caught a spark of admiration; and even the captain, who was in no
courtly humour, proposed that the scene should
be commemorated by my pencil. It was the last

act of the evening. Hurriedly as I went about my task, the half-hour had lengthened out to more than three before it was completed: Mamie in full value, the rest of the party figuring in outline only, and the artist himself introduced in a back view, which was pronounced a likeness. But it was to Mamie that I devoted the best of my attention; and it was with her I made my chief success.

"O!" she cried, "am I really like that? No wonder Jim . . ." She paused. "Why it's just as lovely as he's good!" she cried: an epigram which was appreciated, and repeated as we made our salutations, and called out after the retreating couple as they passed away under the lamp-light on the wharf.

Thus it was that our farewells were smuggled through under an ambuscade of laughter, and the parting over ere I knew it was begun. The figures vanished, the steps died away along the silent city front; on board, the men had returned to their labours, the captain to his solitary cigar; and after that long and complex day of business and emotion, I was at last alone and free. It was, perhaps, chiefly fatigue that made my heart so heavy. I leaned at least upon the house, and stared at the foggy heaven, or over the rail at the wavering reflection of the lamps, like a man that was quite done with hope and would have welcomed the asylum of the grave. And all at once, as I thus stood, the *City of Pekin* flashed into my mind, racing her thirteen knots for Honolulu, with the

hated Trent — perhaps with the mysterious Goddedaal — on board; and with the thought, the
blood leaped and careered through all my body.
It seemed no chase at all; it seemed we had no
chance, as we lay there bound to iron pillars, and
fooling away the precious moments over tins of
beans. "Let them get there first!" I thought.
"Let them! We can't be long behind." And
from that moment, I date myself a man of a
rounded experience: nothing had lacked but this, ·
that I should entertain and welcome the grim
thought of bloodshed.

It was long before the toil remitted in the cabin,
and it was worth my while to get to bed; long
after that, before sleep favoured me; and scarce
a moment later (or so it seemed) when I was
recalled to consciousness by bawling men and the
jar of straining hawsers.

The schooner was cast off before I got on deck.
In the misty obscurity of the first dawn, I saw the
tug heading us with glowing fires and blowing
smoke, and heard her beat the roughened waters
of the bay. Beside us, on her flock of hills, the
lighted city towered up and stood swollen in the
raw fog. It was strange to see her burn on thus
wastefully, with half-quenched luminaries, when
the dawn was already grown strong enough to
show me, and to suffer me to recognise, a solitary
figure standing by the piles.

Or was it really the eye, and not rather the
heart, that identified that shadow in the dusk,
among the shore-side lamps? I know not. It was

Jim, at least; Jim, come for a last look; and we had but time to wave a valedictory gesture and exchange a wordless cry. This was our second parting, and our capacities were now reversed. It was mine to play the Argonaut, to speed affairs, to plan and to accomplish — if need were, at the price of life; it was his to sit at home, to study the calendar, and to wait. I knew besides another thing that gave me joy. I knew that my friend had succeeded in my education; that the romance of business, if our fantastic purchase merited the name, had at last stirred my dilettante nature; and, as we swept under cloudy Tamalpais and through the roaring narrows of the bay, the Yankee blood sang in my veins with suspense and exultation.

Outside the heads, as if to meet my desire, we found it blowing fresh from the north-east. No time had been lost. The sun was not yet up before the tug cast off the hawser, gave us a salute of three whistles, and turned homeward toward the coast, which now began to gleam along its margin with the earliest rays of day. There was no other ship in view when the *Norah Creina*, lying over under all plain sail, began her long and lonely voyage to the wreck.

CHAPTER XII

THE "NORAH CREINA"

I LOVE to recall the glad monotony of a
Pacific voyage, when the trades are not
stinted, and the ship, day after day, goes
free. The mountain scenery of trade-wind clouds,
watched (and in my case painted) under every
vicissitude of light — blotting stars, withering in
the moon's glory, barring the scarlet eve, lying
across the dawn collapsed into the unfeatured
morning bank, or at noon raising their snowy
summits between the blue roof of heaven and the
blue floor of sea; the small, busy, and deliberate
world of the schooner, with its unfamiliar scenes,
the spearing of dolphin from the bowsprit end, the
holy war on sharks, the cook making bread on
the main hatch; reefing down before a violent
squall, with the men hanging out on the foot-
ropes; the squall itself, the catch at the heart, the
opened sluices of the sky; and the relief, the renewed loveliness of life, when all is over, the sun
forth again, and our out-fought enemy only a blot
upon the leeward sea. I love to recall, and would
that I could reproduce that life, the unforgettable,
the unrememberable. The memory, which shows
so wise a backwardness in registering pain, is be-

sides an imperfect recorder of extended pleasures; and a long-continued wellbeing escapes (as it were, by its mass) our petty methods of commemoration. On a part of our life's map there lies a roseate, undecipherable haze, and that is all.

Of one thing, if I am at all to trust my own annals, I was delightedly conscious. Day after day, in the sun-gilded cabin, the whisky-dealer's thermometer stood at 84. Day after day, the air had the same indescribable liveliness and sweetness, soft and nimble, and cool as the cheek of health. Day after day the sun flamed; night after night the moon beaconed, or the stars paraded their lustrous regiment. I was aware of a spiritual change, or, perhaps, rather a molecular reconstitution. My bones were sweeter to me. I had come home to my own climate, and looked back with pity on those damp and wintry zones, miscalled the temperate.

" Two years of this, and comfortable quarters to live in, kind of shake the grit out of a man," the captain remarked; " can't make out to be happy anywhere else. A townie of mine was lost down this way, in a coal-ship that took fire at sea. He struck the beach somewhere in the Navigators; and he wrote to me that when he left the place, it would be feet first. He 's well off, too, and his father owns some coasting-craft Down East; but Billy prefers the beach, and hot rolls off the breadfruit trees."

A voice told me I was on the same track as Billy. But when was this? Our outward track

in the *Norah Creina* lay well to the northward;
and perhaps it is but the impression of a few pet
days which I have unconsciously spread longer,
or perhaps the feeling grew upon me later, in the
run to Honolulu. One thing I am sure: it was
before I had ever seen an island worthy of the
name that I must date my loyalty to the South
Seas. The blank sea itself grew desirable under
such skies: and wherever the trade-wind blows, I
know no better country than a schooner's deck.

But for the tugging anxiety as to the journey's
end, the journey itself must thus have counted for
the best of holidays. My physical wellbeing was
over-proof; effects of sea and sky kept me for
ever busy with my pencil; and I had no lack of
intellectual exercise of a different order in the
study of my inconsistent friend, the captain. I
call him friend, here on the threshold; but that
is to look well ahead. At first, I was too much
horrified by what I considered his barbarities, too
much puzzled by his shifting humours, and too
frequently annoyed by his small vanities, to regard him otherwise than as the cross of my existence. It was only by degrees, in his rare hours
of pleasantness, when he forgot (and made me
forget) the weaknesses to which he was so prone,
that he won me to a kind of unconsenting fondness. Lastly, the faults were all embraced in a
more generous view: I saw them in their place,
like discords in a musical progression; and accepted them and found them picturesque, as we
accept and admire, in the habitable face of nature,

the smoky head of the volcano or the pernicious
thicket of the swamp.

He was come of good people Down East, and
had the beginnings of a thorough education. His
temper had been ungovernable from the first; and
it is likely the defect was inherited, and the blame
of the rupture not entirely his. He ran away at
least to sea; suffered horrible maltreatment, which
seemed to have rather hardened than enlightened
him; ran away again to shore in a South American port; proved his capacity and made money,
although still a child; fell among thieves and
was robbed; worked back a passage to the States,
.and knocked one morning at the door of an old
lady whose orchard he had often robbed. The
introduction appears insufficient; but Nares knew
what he was doing. The sight of her old neigh-
bourly depredator shivering at the door in tatters,
the very oddity of his appeal, touched a soft spot
in the spinster's heart. " I always had a fancy
for the old lady," Nares said, " even when she
used to stampede me out of the orchard, and shake
her thimble. and her old curls at me out of the
window as I was going by; I always thought she
was a kind of pleasant old girl. Well, when she
came to the door that morning, I told her so, and
that I was stone-broke; and she took me right
in, and fetched out the pie." She clothed him,
taught him, had him to sea again in better shape,
welcomed him to her hearth on his return from
every cruise, and when she died, bequeathed him
her possessions. " She was a good old girl," he

would say. " I tell you, Mr. Dodd, it was a queer thing to see me and the old lady talking a *pasear* in the garden, and the old man scowling at us over the pickets. She lived right next door to the old man, and I guess that's just what took me there. I wanted him to know that I was badly beat, you see, and would rather go to the devil than to him. What made the dig harder, he had quarrelled with the old lady about me and the orchard: I guess that made him rage. Yes, I was a beast when I was young. But I was always pretty good to the old lady." Since then he had prospered, not uneventfully, in his profession; the old lady's money had fallen in during the voyage of the *Gleaner,* and he was now, as soon as the smoke of that engagement cleared away, secure of his ship. I suppose he was about thirty: a powerful, active man, with a blue eye, a thick head of hair, about the colour of oakum and growing low over the brow; clean-shaved and lean about the jaw; a good singer; a good performer on that sea-instrument, the accordion; a quick observer, a close reasoner; when he pleased, of a really elegant address; and when he chose, the greatest brute upon the seas.

His usage of the men, his hazing, his bullying, his perpetual fault-finding for no cause, his perpetual and brutal sarcasm, might have raised a mutiny in a slave galley. Suppose the steerman's eye to have wandered: " You ——, ——, little, mutton-faced Dutchman," Nares would bawl; " you want a booting to keep you on your

course! I know a little city-front slush when I
see one. Just you glue your eye to that compass, or I'll show you round the vessel at the
butt-end of my boot." Or suppose a hand to
linger aft, whither he had perhaps been summoned
not a minute before. "Mr. Daniells, will you
oblige me by stepping clear of that main sheet?"
the captain might begin, with truculent courtesy.
"Thank you. And perhaps you'll be so kind as
to tell me what the hell you're doing on my
quarter-deck? I want no dirt of your sort here.
Is there nothing for you to do? Where's the
mate? Don't you set *me* to find work for you,
or I'll find you some that will keep you on your
back a fortnight.'" Such allocutions, conceived
with a perfect knowledge of his audience, so that
every insult carried home, were delivered with a
mien so menacing and an eye so fiercely cruel,
that his unhappy subordinates shrank and quailed.
Too often violence followed; too often I have
heard and seen, and boiled at the cowardly ag-
gression; and the victim, his hands bound by law,
has risen again from deck and crawled forward
stupefied — I know not what passion of revenge
in his wronged heart.

It seems strange I should have grown to like
this tyrant. It may even seem strange that I
should have stood by and suffered his excesses
to proceed. But I was not quite such a chicken
as to interfere in public; for I would rather have
a man or two mishandled than one-half of us
butchered in a mutiny and the rest suffer on the

gallows. And in private, I was unceasing in my protests.

"Captain," I once said to him, appealing to his patriotism, which was of a hardy quality, "this is no way to treat American seamen. You don't call it American to treat men like dogs?"

"Americans?" he said grimly. "Do you call these Dutchmen and Scattermouches [1] Americans? I 've been fourteen years to sea, all but one trip under American colours, and I 've never laid eye on an American foremast hand. There used to be such things in the old days, when thirty-five dollars were the wages out of Boston; and then you could see ships handled and run the way they want to be. But that 's all past and gone; and nowadays the only thing that flies in an American ship is a belaying-pin. You don't know; you have n't a guess. How would you like to go on deck for your middle watch, fourteen months on end, with all your duty to do and every one's life depending on you, and expect to get a knife ripped into you as you come out of your stateroom, or be sand-bagged as you pass the boat, or get tripped into the hold, if the hatches are off in fine weather? That kind of shakes the starch out of the brotherly love and New Jerusalem business. You go through the mill, and you 'll have a bigger grudge against every old shellback that dirties his plate in the three oceans, than the Bank of California could settle up.

[1] In sea-lingo (Pacific) *Dutchman* includes all Teutons and folk from the basin of the Baltic; *Scattermouch*, all Latins and Levantines.

No; it has an ugly look to it, but the only way to run a ship is to make yourself a terror."

"Come, Captain," said I, "there are degrees in everything. You know American ships have a bad name; you know perfectly well if it was n't for the high wage and the good food, there's not a man would ship in one if he could help; and even as it is, some prefer a British ship, beastly food and all."

"O, the lime-juicers?" said he. "There's plenty booting in lime-juicers, I guess; though I don't deny but what some of them are soft." And with that he smiled like a man recalling something. "Look here, that brings a yarn in my head," he resumed; "and for the sake of the joke, I'll give myself away. It was in 1874, I shipped mate in the British ship *Maria*, from 'Frisco for Melbourne. She was the queerest craft in some ways that ever I was aboard of. The food was a caution; there was nothing fit to put your lips to — but the lime-juice, which was from the end bin no doubt: it used to make me sick to see the men's dinners, and sorry to see my own. The old man was good enough, I guess; Green was his name; a mild, fatherly old galoot. But the hands were the lowest gang I ever handled; and whenever I tried to knock a little spirit into them, the old man took their part! It was Gilbert and Sullivan on the high seas; but you bet I would n't let any man dictate to me. ' You give me your orders, Captain Green,' I said, ' and you 'll find I 'll carry them out; that 's all you 've got

to say. You 'll find I do my duty,' I said; ' how
I do it is my lookout; and there 's no man born
that 's going to give me lessons.' Well, there was
plenty dirt on board that *Maria* first and last. Of
course, the old man put my back up, and, of course,
he put up the crew's; and I had to regular fight
my way through every watch. The men got to
hate me, so 's I would hear them grit their teeth
when I came up. At last, one day, I saw a big
hulking beast of a Dutchman booting the ship's
boy. I made one shoot of it off the house and laid
that Dutchman out. Up he came, and I laid him
out again. ' Now,' I said, ' if there 's a kick left
in you, just mention it, and I 'll stamp your ribs
in like a packing-case.' He thought better of it,
and never let on; lay there as mild as a deacon
at a funeral; and they took him below to reflect
on his native Dutchland. One night we got caught
in rather a dirty thing about 25 south. I guess
we were all asleep; for the first thing I knew
there was the fore-royal gone. I ran forward,
bawling blue hell; and just as I came by the
foremast, something struck me right through the
forearm and stuck there. I put my other hand
up, and by George! it was the grain; the beasts
had speared me like a porpoise. ' Cap'n!' I cried.
— ' What 's wrong?' says he. — ' They 've grained
me,' says I. — ' Grained you?' says he. ' Well,
I 've been looking for that.' — ' And by God,' I
cried, ' I want to have some of these beasts murdered for it!' — ' Now, Mr. Nares,' says he, ' you
better go below. If I had been one of the men,

you 'd have got more than this. And I want no
more of your language on deck. You 've cost
me my fore-royal already,' says he; 'and if you
carry on, you 'll have the three sticks out of her.'
That was old man Green's idea of supporting officers. But you wait a bit; the cream 's coming.
We made Melbourne right enough, and the old
man said: 'Mr. Nares, you and me don't draw
together. You 're a first-rate seaman, no mistake
of that; but you 're the most disagreeable man I
ever sailed with; and your language and your
conduct to the crew I cannot stomach. I guess
we 'll separate.' I did n't care about the berth,
you may be sure; but I felt kind of mean; and
if he made one kind of stink, I thought I could
make another. So I said I would go ashore and
see how things stood; went, found I was all right,
and came aboard again on the top rail. — 'Are
you getting your traps together, Mr. Nares?' says
the old man. — 'No,' says I; 'I don't know as
we 'll separate much before 'Frisco; at least,' I
said, 'it 's a point for your consideration. I 'm
very willing to say good-bye to the *Maria,* but
I don't know whether you 'll care to start me
out with three months' wages.' He got his
money-box right away. 'My son,' says he,
'I think it cheap at the money.' He had me
there."

It was a singular tale for a man to tell of himself; above all, in the midst of our discussion;
but it was quite in character for Nares. I never
made a good hit in our disputes, I never justly

resented any act or speech of his, but what I
found it long after carefully posted in his day-
book and reckoned (here was the man's oddity)
to my credit.   It was the same with his father,
whom he had hated; he would give a sketch of
the old fellow, frank and credible, and yet so
honestly touched that it was charming.   I have
never met a man so strangely constituted: to possess a reason of the most equal justice, to have
his nerves at the same time quivering with petty
spite, and to act upon the nerves and not the
reason.

A kindred wonder in my eyes was the nature
of his courage.   There was never a braver man:
he went out to welcome danger; an emergency
(came it never so sudden) strung him like a tonic.
And yet, upon the other hand, I have known none
so nervous, so oppressed with possibilities, looking
upon the world at large, and the life of a sailor in
particular, with so constant and haggard a consideration of the ugly chances.   All his courage
was in blood, not merely cold, but icy with reasoned apprehension.   He would lay our little craft
rail under, and " hang on " in a squall, until I gave
myself up for lost, and the men were rushing to
their stations of their own accord.   " There," he
would say, " I guess there's not a man on board
would have hung on as long as I did that time;
they'll have to give up thinking me no schooner
sailor.   I guess I can shave just as near capsizing
as any other captain of this vessel, drunk or sober."
And then he would fall to repining and wishing

himself well out of the enterprise, and dilate on the peril of the seas, the particular dangers of the schooner rig, which he abhorred, the various ways in which we might go to the bottom, and the prodigious fleet of ships that have sailed out in the course of history, dwindled from the eyes of watchers, and returned no more. " Well," he would wind up, " I guess it don't much matter. I can't see what any one wants to live for, anyway. If I could get into some one else's apple-tree, and be about twelve years old, and just stick the way I was, eating stolen apples, I won't say. But there 's no sense to this grown-up business — sail-orising, politics, the piety mill, and all the rest of it. Good clean drowning is good enough for me." It is hard to imagine any more depressing talk for a poor landsman on a dirty night; it is hard to imagine anything less sailor-like (as sailors are supposed to be and generally are) than this persistent harping on the minor.

But I was to see more of the man's gloomy constancy ere the cruise was at an end.

On the morning of the seventeenth day I came on deck, to find the schooner under double reefs, and flying rather wild before a heavy run of sea. Snoring trades and humming sails had been our portion hitherto. We were already nearing the island. My restrained excitement had begun again to overmaster me; and for some time my only book had been the patent log that trailed over the taffrail, and my chief interest the daily observation and our caterpillar progress across the chart. My

first glance which was at the compass, and my
second, which was at the log, were all that I could
wish. We lay our course; we had been doing over
eight since nine the night before; and I drew a
heavy breath of satisfaction. And then I know not
what odd and wintry appearance of the sea and
sky knocked suddenly at my heart. I observed the
schooner to look more than usually small, the men
silent and studious of the weather. Nares, in one
of his rusty humours, afforded me no shadow of
a morning salutation. He, too, seemed to observe
the behaviour of the ship with an intent and
anxious scrutiny. What I liked still less, Johnson
himself was at the wheel, which he span busily,
often with a visible effort; and as the seas ranged
up behind us, black and imminent, he kept casting
behind him eyes of animal swiftness, and drawing
in his neck between his shoulders, like a man dodg-
ing a blow. From these signs, I gathered that all
was not exactly for the best; and I would have
given a good handful of dollars for a plain answer
to the questions which I dared not put. Had I
dared, with the present danger signal in the captain's face, I should only have been reminded
of my position as supercargo — an office never
touched upon in kindness — and advised, in a very
indigestible manner, to go below. There was nothing for it, therefore, but to entertain my vague
apprehensions as best I should be able, until it
pleased the captain to enlighten me of his own accord. This he did sooner than I had expected; as
soon, indeed, as the Chinaman had summoned us

to breakfast, and we sat face to face across the narrow board.

"See here, Mr. Dodd," he began, looking at me rather queerly, "here is a business point arisen. This sea's been running up for the last two days, and now it's too high for comfort. The glass is falling, the wind is breezing up, and I won't say but what there's dirt in it. If I lay her to, we may have to ride out a gale of wind and drift God knows where — on these French Frigate Shoals, for instance. If I keep her as she goes, we'll make that island to-morrow afternoon, and have the lee of it to lie under, if we can't make out to run in. The point you have to figure on, is whether you'll take the big chances of that Captain Trent making the place before you, or take the risk of something happening. I'm to run this ship to your satisfaction," he added, with an ugly sneer. "Well, here's a point for the supercargo."

"Captain," I returned, with my heart in my mouth, "risk is better than certain failure."

"Life is all risk, Mr. Dodd," he remarked. "But there's one thing: it's now or never; in half an hour, Archdeacon Gabriel couldn't lay her to, if he came down-stairs on purpose."

"All right," said I. "Let's run."

"Run goes," said he; and with that he fell to breakfast, and passed half an hour in stowing away pie and devoutly wishing himself back in San Francisco. When we came on deck again, he took the wheel from Johnson — it appears they could trust none among the hands — and I stood close beside him, feeling safe in this proximity, and tasting a fearful joy from our surroundings and the consciousness of my decision. The breeze had already risen, and as it tore over our heads, it uttered at times a long hooting note that sent my heart into my boots. The sea pursued us without remission, leaping to the assault of the low rail. The quarter-deck was all awash, and we must close the companion doors.

"And all this, if you please, for Mr. Pinkerton's dollars!" the captain suddenly exclaimed, "There's many a fine fellow gone under, Mr. Dodd, because of drivers like your friend. What do they care for a ship or two? Insured, I guess, What do they care for sailors' lives alongside of a few thousand dollars? What they want is speed between ports, and a damned fool of a captain that'll drive a ship under as I'm doing this one. You can put in the morning, asking why I do it."

I sheered off to another part of the vessel as fast as civility permitted. This was not at all the talk that I desired, nor was the train of reflection which it started anyway welcome. Here I was, running some hazard of my life, and perilling the lives of seven others; exactly for what end, I was now at liberty to ask myself. For a very large amount of a very deadly poison, was the obvious answer; and I thought if all tales were true, and I were soon to be subjected to cross-examination at the bar of Eternal Justice, it was one which would not increase my popularity with the court. "Well, never mind, Jim," thought I. "I'm doing it for you."

Before eleven, a third reef was taken in the main-sail; and Johnson filled the cabin with a storm-sail of No. 1 duck and sat cross-legged on the streaming floor, vigorously putting it to rights with a couple of the hands. By dinner I had fled the deck, and sat in the bench corner, giddy, dumb, and stupefied with terror. The frightened leaps of the poor *Norah Creina,* spanking like a stag for bare existence, bruised me between the table and the berths. Overhead, the wild huntsman of the storm passed continuously in one blare of mingled noises; screaming wind, straining timber, lashing rope's end, pounding block and bursting sea contributed; and I could have thought there was at times another, a more piercing, a more human note, that dominated all, like the wailing of an angel; I could have thought I knew the angel's name, and that his wings were black. It seemed incredible that any creature of man's art could long endure the barbarous mishandling of the seas, kicked as the schooner was from mountain-side to mountain-side, beaten and blown upon and wrenched in every joint and sinew, like a child upon the rack. There was not a plank of her that did not cry aloud for mercy; and as she continued to hold together, I became conscious of a growing sympathy with her endeavours, a growing admiration for her gallant staunchness, that amused and at times obliterated my terrors for myself. God bless every man that swung a mallet on that tiny and strong hull! It was not for wages only that he laboured, but to save men's lives.

All the rest of the day, and all the following night, I sat in the corner or lay wakeful in my bunk; and it was only with the return of morning that a new phase of my alarms drove me once more on deck. A gloomier interval I never passed. Johnson and Nares steadily relieved each other at the wheel and came below. The first glance of each was at the glass, which he repeatedly knuckled and frowned upon; for it was sagging lower all the time. Then, if Johnson were the visitor, he would pick a snack out of the cupboard, and stand, braced against the table, eating it, and perhaps obliging me with a word or two of his hee-haw conversation: how it was "a son of a gun of a cold night on deck, Mr. Dodd" (with a grin): how "it was n't no night for panjammers, he could tell me": having transacted all which, he would throw himself down in his bunk and sleep his two hours with compunction. But the captain neither ate nor slept. "You there, Mr. Dodd?" he would say, after the obligatory visit to the glass. "Well, my son, we 're one hundred and four miles" (or whatever it was) "off the island, and scudding for all we 're worth. We 'll make it to-morrow about four, or not, as the case may be. That 's the news. And now, Mr. Dodd, I 've stretched a point for you; you can see I 'm dead tired; so just you stretch away back to your bunk again." And with this attempt at geniality, his teeth would settle hard down on his cigar, and he would pass his spell below staring and blinking at the cabin lamp through a cloud of tobacco smoke.

He has told me since that he was happy, which I should never have divined. "You see," he said, "the wind we had was never anything out of the way; but the sea was really nasty, the schooner wanted a lot of humouring, and it was clear from the glass that we were close to some dirt. We might be running out of it or we might be running right crack into it. Well, there's always something sublime about a big deal like that; and it kind of raises a man in his own liking. We're a queer kind of beasts, Mr. Dodd."

The morning broke with sinister brightness; the air alarmingly transparent, the sky pure, the rim of the horizon clear and strong against the heavens. The wind and the wild seas, now vastly swollen, indefatigably hunted us. I stood on deck, choking with fear; I seemed to lose all power upon my limbs; my knees were as paper when she plunged into the murderous valleys; my heart collapsed when some black mountain fell in avalanche beside her counter, and the water, that was more than spray, swept round my ankles like a torrent. I was conscious of but one strong desire, to bear myself decently in my terrors, and whatever should happen to my life, preserve my character: as the captain said, we are a queer kind of beasts. Breakfast time came, and I made shift to swallow some hot tea. Then I must stagger below to take the time, reading the chronometer with dizzy eyes, and marvelling the while what value there could be in observations taken in a ship launched (as ours then was) like a missile among flying seas. The fore-

noon dragged on in a grinding monotony of peril;
every spoke of the wheel a rash, but an obliged
experiment — rash as a forlorn hope, needful as
the leap that lands a fireman from a burning stair-
case. Noon was made; the captain dined on his
day's work, and I on watching him; and our place
was entered on the chart with a meticulous precision which seemed to me half pitiful and half
absurd, since the next eye to behold that sheet of
paper might be the eye of an exploring fish. One
o'clock came, then two; the captain gloomed and
chafed, as he held to the coaming of the house,
and if ever I saw dormant murder in man's eye,
it was in his. God help the hand that should have
disobeyed him.

Of a sudden, he turned towards the mate, who
was doing his trick at the wheel.

"Two points on the port bow," I heard him say.
And he took the wheel himself.

Johnson nodded, wiped his eyes with the back
of his wet hand, watched a chance as the vessel
lunged up-hill, and got to the main rigging, where
he swarmed aloft. Up and up, I watched him go,
hanging on at every ugly plunge, gaining with
every lull of the schooner's movement, until, clambering into the cross-trees and clinging with one
arm around the masts, I could see him take one
comprehensive sweep of the southwesterly horizon.
The next moment, he had slid down the backstay
and stood on deck, with a grin, a nod, and a gesture of the finger that said, " yes "; the next again,
and he was back sweating and squirming at the

wheel, his tired face streaming and smiling, and
his hair and the rags and corners of his clothes
lashing round him in the wind.

Nares went below, fetched up his binocular, and
fell into a silent perusal of the sea-line; I also,
with my unaided eyesight. Little by little, in that
white waste of water, I began to make out a
quarter where the whiteness appeared more condensed: the sky above was whitish likewise, and
misty like a squall; and little by little there
thrilled upon my ears a note deeper and more
terrible than the yelling of the gale — the long,
thundering roll of breakers. Nares wiped his
night glass on his sleeve and passed it to me,
motioning, as he did so, with his hand. An
endless wilderness of ranging billows came and
went and danced in the circle of the glass; now
and then a pale corner of sky, or the strong line
of the horizon rugged with the heads of waves;
and then of a sudden — come and gone ere I could
fix it, with a swallow's swiftness — one glimpse
of what we had come so far and paid so dear to
see: the masts and rigging of a brig pencilled on
heaven, with an ensign streaming at the main, and
the ragged ribbons of a topsail thrashing from the
yard. Again and again, with toilful searching, I
recalled that apparition. There was no sign of
any land; the wreck stood between sea and sky,
a thing the most isolated I had ever viewed; but
as we drew nearer, I perceived her to be defended
by a line of breakers which drew off on either
hand and marked, indeed, the nearest segment of

the reef. Heavy spray hung over them like a smoke, some hundred feet into the air; and the sound of their consecutive explosions rolled like a cannonade.

In half an hour we were close in; for perhaps as long again, we skirted that formidable barrier towards its farther side; and presently the sea began insensibly to moderate and the ship to go more sweetly. We had gained the lee of the island as (for form's sake) I may call that ring of foam and haze and thunder; and shaking out a reef, wore ship and headed for the passage.

CHAPTER XIII

THE ISLAND AND THE WRECK

ALL hands were filled with joy. It was betrayed in their alacrity and easy faces: Johnson smiling broadly at the wheel, Nares studying the sketch chart of the island with an eye at peace, and the hands clustered forward, eagerly talking and pointing: so manifest was our escape, so wonderful the attraction of a single foot of earth after so many suns had set and risen on an empty sea. To add to the relief, besides, by one of those malicious coincidences which suggest for fate the image of an underbred and grinning schooboy, we had no sooner worn ship than the wind began to abate.

For myself, however, I did but exchange anxieties. I was no sooner out of one fear than I fell upon another; no sooner secure that I should myself make the intended haven, than I began to be convinced that Trent was there before me. I climbed into the rigging, stood on the board, and eagerly scanned that ring of coral reef and bursting breaker, and the blue lagoon which they enclosed. The two islets within began to show plainly — Middle Brooks and Lower Brooks Island, the Directory named them: two low, bush-covered, rolling strips of sand, each with glittering beaches, each perhaps a mile or a mile and a half in length, running east and west, and divided by a narrow channel. Over these, innumerable as maggots, there hovered, chattered, screamed and clanged, millions of twinkling sea-birds: white and black; the black by far the largest. With singular scintillations, this vortex of winged life swayed to and fro in the strong sunshine, whirled continually through itself, and would now and again burst asunder and scatter as wide as the lagoon: so that I was irresistibly reminded of what I had read of nebular convulsions. A thin cloud overspread the area of the reef and the adjacent sea — the dust, as I could not but fancy, of earlier explosions. And a little apart, there was yet another focus of centrifugal and centripetal flight, where, hard by the deafening line of breakers, her sails (all but the tattered topsail) snugly furled down, and the red rag that marks Old England on the seas beating, union down, at the main — the *Flying Scud*, the fruit of so many toilers, a recollection in so many lives of men, whose tall spars had been mirrored in the remotest corners of the sea — lay stationary at last and for ever, in the first stage of naval dissolution. Towards her, the taut *Norah Creina*, vulture-wise, wriggled to windward: come from so far to pick her bones. And, look as I pleased, there was no other presence of man or of man's handiwork; no Honolulu schooner lay there crowded with armed rivals, no smoke rose from the fire at which I fancied Trent cooking a meal of sea-birds. It seemed, after all, we were in time, and I drew a mighty breath.

I had not arrived at this reviving certainty before the breakers were already close aboard, the leadsman at his station, and the captain posted in the fore cross-trees to con us through the coral lumps of the lagoon. All circumstances were in our favour, the light behind, the sun low, the wind still fresh and steady, and the tide about the turn. A moment later we shot at racing speed betwixt two pier-heads of broken water; the lead began to be cast, the captain to bawl down his anxious directions, the schooner to tack and dodge among the scattered dangers of the lagoon; and at one bell in the first dog watch, we had come to our anchor off the north-east end of Middle Brooks Island, in five fathoms water. The sails were gasketted and covered, the boats emptied of the miscellaneous stores and odds and ends of sea-furniture, that accumulate in the course of a voyage, the kedge sent ashore, and the decks tidied down: a good three-quarters of an hour's work, during which I raged about the deck like a man with a strong toothache. The transition from the wild sea to the comparative immobility of the lagoon had wrought strange distress among my nerves: I could not hold still whether in hand or foot; the slowness of the men, tired as dogs after our rough experience outside, irritated me like something personal; and the irrational screaming of the sea-birds saddened me like a dirge. It was a relief when, with Nares, and a couple of hands, I might drop into the boat and move off at last for the *Flying Scud*.

" She looks kind of pitiful, don't she? " observed the captain, nodding towards the wreck, from which we were separated by some half a mile. " Looks as if she did n't like her berth, and Captain Trent had used her badly. Give her ginger, boys ! " he added to the hands, " and you can all have shore liberty to-night to see the birds and paint the town red."

We all laughed at the pleasantry, and the boat skimmed the faster over the rippling face of the lagoon. The *Flying Scud* would have seemed small enough beside the wharves of San Francisco, but she was some thrice the size of the *Norah Creina*, which had been so long our continent ; and as we craned up at her wall-sides, she impressed us with a mountain magnitude. She lay head to the reef, where the huge blue wall of the rollers was for ever ranging up and crumbling down ; and to gain her starboard side, we must pass below the stern. The rudder was hard aport, and we could read the legend :

FLYING SCUD

HULL

On the other side, about the break of the poop, some half a fathom of rope ladder trailed over the rail, and by this we made our entrance.

She was a roomy ship inside, with a raised poop standing some three feet higher than the deck, and a small forward house, for the men's bunks and the galley, just abaft the foremast. There was one boat on the house, and another and larger one, in beds on deck, on either hand of it. She had been painted white, with tropical economy, outside and in; and we found, later on, that the stanchions of the rail, hoops of the scuttle-butt, etc., were picked out with green. At that time, however, when we first stepped aboard, all was hidden under the droppings of innumerable sea-birds.

The birds themselves gyrated and screamed meanwhile among the rigging; and when we looked into the galley, their outrush drove us back. Savage-looking fowl they were, savagely beaked, and some of the black ones great as eagles. Half buried in the slush, we were aware of a litter of kegs in the waist; and these, on being somewhat cleaned, proved to be water beakers and quarter casks of mess beef with some colonial brand, doubtless collected there before the *Tempest* hove in sight, and while Trent and his men had no better expectation than to strike for Honolulu in the boats. Nothing else was notable on deck, save where the loose topsail had played some havoc with the rigging, and there hung, and swayed, and sang in the declining wind, a raffle of intorted cordage.

With a shyness that was almost awe, Nares and I descended the companion. The stair turned upon

itself and landed us just forward of a thwart-ship
bulkhead that cut the poop in two. The fore part
formed a kind of miscellaneous storeroom, with
a double-bunked division for the cook (as Nares
supposed) and second mate. The after part contained, in the midst, the main cabin, running in
a kind of bow into the curvature of the stern; on
the port side, a pantry opening forward and a
stateroom for the mate; and on the starboard,
the captain's berth and water-closet. Into these
we did but glance: the main cabin holding us.
It was dark, for the sea-birds had obscured the
skylight with their droppings; it smelt rank and
fusty; and it was beset with a loud swarm of
flies that beat continually in our faces. Supposing them close attendants upon man and his broken
meat, I marvelled how they had found their way to
Midway reef; it was sure at least some vessel must
have brought them, and that long ago, for they
had multiplied exceedingly. Part of the floor was
strewn with a confusion of clothes, books, nautical
instruments, odds and ends of finery, and such
trash as might be expected from the turning out
of several seaman's chests, upon a sudden emergency and after a long cruise. It was strange in
that dim cabin, quivering with the near thunder
of the breakers and pierced with the screaming of
the fowls, to turn over so many things that other
men had coveted, and prized, and worn on their
warm bodies — frayed old underclothing, pajamas
of strange design, duck suits in every stage of
rustiness, oil skins, pilot coats, bottles of scent,

embroidered shirts, jackets of Ponjee silk — clothes
for the night watch at sea or the day ashore in the
hotel veranda; and mingled among these, books,
cigars, fancy pipes, quantities of tobacco, many
keys, a rusty pistol, and a sprinkling of cheap
curiosities — Benares brass, Chinese jars and pictures, and bottles of odd shells in cotton, each
designed no doubt for somebody at home — perhaps in Hull, of which Trent had been a native
and his ship a citizen.

Thence we turned our attention to the table,
which stood spread, as if for a meal, with stout
ship's crockery and the remains of food — a pot
of marmalade, dregs of coffee in the mugs, unrecognisable remains of foods, bread, some toast,
and a tin of condensed milk. The tablecloth,
originally of a red colour, was stained a dark
brown at the captain's end, apparently with coffee;
at the other end, it had been folded back, and a
pen and ink-pot stood on the bare table. Stools
were here and there about the table, irregularly
placed, as though the meal had been finished and
the men smoking and chatting; and one of the
stools lay on the floor, broken.

"See! they were writing up the log," said
Nares, pointing to the ink-bottle. "Caught nap-
ping, as usual. I wonder if there ever was a
captain yet, that lost a ship with his log-book up
to date? He generally has about a month to fill
up on a clean break, like Charles Dickens and
his serial novels. — What a regular, lime-juicer
spread!" he added contemptuously. "Marmalade

—and toast for the old man! Nasty, slovenly pigs!"

There was something in this criticism of the absent that jarred upon my feelings. I had no love indeed for Captain Trent or any of his vanished gang; but the desertion and decay of this, once habitable cabin struck me hard: the death of man's handiwork is melancholy like the death of man himself; and I was impressed with an involuntary and irrational sense of tragedy in my surroundings.

"This sickens me," I said. "Let's go on deck and breathe."

The captain nodded. "It *is* kind of lonely, is n't it?" he said. "But I can't go up till I get the code signals. I want to run up 'Got Left' or something, just to brighten up this island home. Captain Trent has n't been here yet, but he 'll drop in before long; and it 'll cheer him up to see a signal on the brig."

"Is n't there some official expression we could use?" I asked, vastly taken by the fancy. " 'Sold for the benefit of the underwriters: for further particulars, apply to J. Pinkerton, Montana Block, S. F.' "

"Well," returned Nares, "I won't say but what an old navy quartermaster might telegraph all that, if you gave him a day to do it in and a pound of tobacco for himself. But it 's above my register. I must try something short and sweet: KB, urgent signal, 'Heave all aback'; or LM, urgent, 'The berth you 're now in is not safe'; or what

do you say to PQH? — ' Tell my owners the ship
answers remarkably well.' "

" It 's premature," I replied; " but it seems calculated to give pain to Trent. PQH for me."

The flags were found in Trent's cabin, neatly
stored behind a lettered grating; Nares chose what
he required and (I following) returned on deck,
where the sun had already dipped, and the dusk
was coming.

" Here! don't touch that, you fool! " shouted
the captain to one of the hands, who was drinking
from the scuttle-butt. " That water 's rotten! "

" Beg pardon, sir," replied the man. " Tastes
quite sweet."

" Let me see," returned Nares, and he took the
dipper and held it to his lips. " Yes, it 's all
right," he said. " Must have rotted and come
sweet again. Queer, is n't it, Mr. Dodd? Though
I 've known the same on a Cape-Horner."

There was something in his intonation that made
me look him in the face; he stood a little on tiptoe
to look right and left about the ship, like a man
filled with curiosity, and his whole expression and
bearing testified to some suppressed excitement.

" You don't believe what you 're saying! " I
broke out.

" O, I don't know but what I do! " he replied,
laying a hand upon me soothingly. " The thing 's
very possible. Only, I 'm bothered about something
else."

And with that he called a hand, gave him the
code flags, and stepped himself to the main signal

halliards, which vibrated under the weight of the ensign overhead. A minute later, the American colours, which we had brought in the boat, replaced the English red, and PQH was fluttering at the fore.

"Now, then," said Nares, who had watched the breaking out of his signal with the old-maidish particularity of an American sailor, "out with those handspikes, and let's see what water there is in the lagoon."

The bars were shoved home; the barbarous cacophony of the clanking pump rose in the waist; and streams of ill-smelling water gushed on deck and made valleys in the slab guano. Nares leaned on the rail, watching the steady stream of bilge as though he found some interest in it.

"What is it that bothers you?" I asked.

"Well, I'll tell you one thing shortly," he replied. "But here's another. Do you see those boats there, one on the house and two on the beds? Well, where is the boat Trent lowered when he lost the hands?"

"Got it aboard again, I suppose," said I.

"Well, if you'll tell me why!" returned the captain.

"Then it must have been another," I suggested.

"She might have carried another on the main hatch, I won't deny," admitted Nares; "but I can't see what she wanted with it, unless it was for the old man to go out and play the accordion in, on moonlight nights."

"It can't much matter, anyway," I reflected.

"O, I don't suppose it does," said he, glancing over his shoulder at the spouting of the scuppers.

"And how long are we to keep up this racket?" I asked. "We 're simply pumping up the lagoon. Captain Trent himself said she had settled down and was full forward."

"Did he?" said Nares, with a significant dryness. And almost as he spoke the pumps sucked, and sucked again, and the men threw down their bars. "There, what do you make of that?" he asked. "Now, I 'll tell, Mr. Dodd," he went on, lowering his voice, but not shifting from his easy attitude against the rail, "this ship is as sound as the *Norah Creina*. I had a guess of it before we came aboard, and now I know."

"It 's not possible!" I cried. "What do you make of Trent?"

"I don't make anything of Trent; I don't know whether he 's a liar or only an old wife; I simply tell you what 's the fact," said Nares. "And I 'll tell you something more," he added: "I 've taken the ground myself in deep-water vessels; I know what I 'm saying; and I say that, when she first struck and before she bedded down, seven or eight hours' work would have got this hooker off, and there 's no man that ever went two years to sea but must have known it."

I could only utter an exclamation.

Nares raised his finger warningly. "Don't let *them* get hold of it," said he. "Think what you like, but say nothing."

I glanced round; the dusk was melting into

early night; the twinkle of a lantern marked the schooner's position in the distance; and our men, free from further labour, stood grouped together in the waist, their faces illuminated by their glowing pipes.

"Why didn't Trent get her off?" inquired the captain. "Why did he want to buy her back in 'Frisco for these fabulous sums, when he might have sailed her into the bay himself?"

"Perhaps he never knew her value until then," I suggested.

"I wish we knew her value now," exclaimed Nares. "However, I don't want to depress you; I'm sorry for you, Mr. Dodd; I know how bothering it must be to you; and the best I can say's this: I haven't taken much time getting down, and now I'm here I mean to work this thing in proper style. I just want to put your mind at rest: you shall have no trouble with me."

There was something trusty and friendly in his voice; and I found myself gripping hands with him, in that hard, short shake that means so much with English-speaking people.

"We'll do, old fellow," said he. "We've shaken down into pretty good friends, you and me; and you won't find me working the business any the less hard for that. And now let's scoot for supper."

After supper, with the idle curiosity of the seafarer, we pulled ashore in a fine moonlight, and landed on Middle Brooks Island. A flat beach surrounded it upon all sides; and the midst was

occupied by a thicket of bushes, the highest of them
scarcely five feet high, in which the sea-fowl lived.
Through this we tried at first to strike; but it were
easier to cross Trafalgar Square upon a day of
demonstration than to invade these haunts of sleeping sea-birds; the nests sank, and the eggs burst
under footing; wings beat in our faces, beaks menaced our eyes, our minds were confounded with the
screeching, and the coil spread over the island and
mounted high into the air.

" I guess we 'll saunter round the beach," said
Nares, when we had made good our retreat.

The hands were all busy after sea-birds' eggs,
so there were none to follow us. Our way lay on
the crisp sand by the margin of the water : on one
side, the thicket from which we had been dislodged ;
on the other, the face of the lagoon, barred with
a broad path of moonlight, and beyond that, the
line, alternately dark and shining, alternately hove
high and fallen prone, of the external breakers.
The beach was strewn with bits of wreck and drift :
some redwood and spruce logs, no less than two
lower masts of junks, and the stern-post of a European ship; all of which we looked on with a shade
of serious concern, speaking of the dangers of the
sea and the hard case of castaways. In this sober
vein we made the greater part of the circuit of the
island; had a near view of its neighbour from
the southern end; walked the whole length of the
westerly side in the shadow of the thicket; and
came forth again into the moonlight at the opposite extremity.

On our right, at the distance of about half a mile, the schooner lay faintly heaving at her anchors. About half a mile down the beach, at a spot still hidden from us by the thicket, an upboiling of the birds showed where the men were still (with sailor-like insatiability) collecting eggs. And right be-fore us, in a small indentation of the sand, we were aware of a boat lying high and dry, and right side up.

Nares crouched back into the shadow of the bushes.

"What the devil's this?" he whispered.

"Trent," I suggested, with a beating heart.

"We were damned fools to come ashore un-armed," said he. "But I've got to know where I stand." In the shadow, his face looked con-spicuously white, and his voice betrayed a strong excitement. He took his boat's whistle from his pocket. "In case I might want to play a tune," said he, grimly, and thrusting it between his teeth, advanced into the moonlit open; which we crossed with rapid steps, looking guiltily about us as we went. Not a leaf stirred; and the boat, when we came up to it, offered convincing proof of long desertion. She was an eighteen-foot whale-boat of the ordinary type, equipped with oars and thole-pins. Two or three quarter-casks lay on the bilge amidships, one of which must have been broached, and now stank horribly; and these, upon examination, proved to bear the same New Zealand brand as the beef on board the wreck.

"Well, here's the boat," said I. "Here's one of your difficulties cleared away."

"H'm," said he. There was a little water in the bilge, and here he stooped and tasted it.

"Fresh," he said. "Only rain-water."

"You don't object to that?" I asked.

"No," said he.

"Well, then, what ails you?" I cried.

"In plain United States, Mr. Dodd," he returned, "a whale-boat, five ash sweeps, and a barrel of stinking pork."

"Or, in other words, the whole thing?" I commented.

"Well, it's this way," he condescended to explain. "I've no use for a fourth boat at all; but a boat of this model tops the business. I don't say the type's not common in these waters; it's as common as dirt; the traders carry them for surf-boats. But the *Flying Scud?* a deep-water tramp, who was lime-juicing around between big ports, Calcutta and Rangoon and 'Frisco and the Canton River? No; I don't see it."

We were leaning over the gunwale of the boat as we spoke. The captain stood nearest the bow, and he was idly playing with the trailing painter, when a thought arrested him. He hauled the line in hand over hand, and stared, and remained staring, at the end.

"Anything wrong with it?" I asked.

"Do you know, Mr. Dodd," said he, in a queer voice, "this painter's been cut? A sailor always seizes a rope's end, but this is sliced short off with the cold steel. This won't do at all for the men," he added. "Just stand by till I fix it up more natural."

"Any guess what it all means?" I asked.

"Well, it means one thing," said he. "It means Trent was a liar. I guess the story of the *Flying Scud* was a sight more picturesque than he gave out."

Half an hour later, the whale-boat was lying astern of the *Norah Creina;* and Nares and I sought our bunks, silent and half bewildered by our late discoveries.

CHAPTER XIV

THE CABIN OF THE "FLYING SCUD"

THE sun of the morrow had not cleared the morning bank: the lake of the lagoon, the islets, and the wall of breakers now beginning to subside, still lay clearly pictured in the flushed obscurity of early day, when we stepped again upon the deck of the *Flying Scud:* Nares, myself, the mate, two of the hands, and one dozen bright, virgin axes, in war against that massive structure. I think we all drew pleasurable breath; so profound in man is the instinct of destruction, so engaging is the interest of the chase. For we were now about to taste, in a supreme degree, the double joys of demolishing a toy and playing "Hide the handkerchief": sports from which we had all perhaps desisted since the days of infancy. And the toy we were to burst in pieces was a deep-sea ship; and the hidden good for which we were to hunt was a prodigious fortune.

The decks were washed down, the main hatch removed, and a gun-tackle purchase rigged, before the boat arrived with breakfast. I had grown so suspicious of the wreck, that it was a positive relief to me to look down into the hold, and see it full, or nearly full, of undeniable rice packed in the

Chinese fashion in boluses of matting. Breakfast
over, Johnson and the hands turned to upon the
cargo; while Nares and I, having smashed open
the skylight and rigged up a windsail on deck,
began the work of rummaging the cabins.

I must not be expected to describe our first day's
work, or (for that matter) any of the rest, in order
and detail as it occurred. Such particularity might
have been possible for several officers and a draft
of men from a ship of war, accompanied by an
experienced secretary with a knowledge of short-
hand. For two plain human beings, unaccustomed
to the use of the broad-axe and consumed with an
impatient greed of the result, the whole business
melts, in the retrospect, into a nightmare of exertion, heat, hurry, and bewilderment; sweat pouring from the face like rain, the scurry of rats, the
choking exhalations of the bilge, and the throbs
and splinterings of the toiling axes. I shall content
myself with giving the cream of our discoveries in
a logical rather than a temporal order; though the
two indeed practically coincided, and we had finished our exploration of the cabin, before we could
be certain of the nature of the cargo.

Nares and I began operations by tossing up
pell-mell through the companion, and piling in a
squalid heap about the wheel, all clothes, personal
effects, the crockery, the carpet, stale victuals, tins
of meat, and in a word, all movables from the main
cabin. Thence, we transferred our attention to the
captain's quarters on the starboard side. Using
the blankets for a basket, we sent up the books,

instruments, and clothes to swell our growing midden on the deck; and then Nares, going on hands and knees, began to forage underneath the bed. Box after box of Manilla cigars rewarded his search. I took occasion to smash some of these boxes open, and even to guillotine the bundles of cigars; but quite in vain — no secret *cache* of opium encouraged me to continue.

"I guess I've got hold of the dicky now!" exclaimed Nares, and turning round from my perquisitions, I found he had drawn forth a heavy iron box, secured to the bulkhead by chain and padlock. On this he was now gazing, not with the triumph that instantly inflamed my own bosom, but with a somewhat foolish appearance of surprise.

"By George, we have it now!" I cried, and would have shaken hands with my companion; but he did not see, or would not accept, the salutation.

"Let's see what's in it first," he remarked, drily. And he adjusted the box upon its side, and with some blows of an axe burst the lock open. I threw myself beside him, as he replaced the box on its bottom and removed the lid. I cannot tell what I expected; a million's worth of diamonds might perhaps have pleased me; my cheeks burned, my heart throbbed to bursting; and lo! there was disclosed but a trayful of papers, neatly taped, and a cheque-book of the customary pattern. I made a snatch at the tray to see what was beneath; but the captain's hand fell on mine, heavy and hard.

"Now, boss!" he cried, not unkindly, "is this to be run shipshape? or is it a Dutch grab-racket?"

And he proceeded to untie and run over the contents of the papers, with a serious face and what seemed an ostentation of delay. Me and my impatience it would appear he had forgotten; for when he was quite done, he sat awhile thinking, whistled a bar or two, refolded the papers, tied them up again; and then, and not before, deliberately raised the tray.

I saw a cigar-box, tied with a piece of fishing-line, and four fat canvas-bags. Nares whipped out his knife, cut the line, and opened the box. It was about half full of sovereigns.

"And the bags?" I whispered.

The captain ripped them open one by one, and a flood of mixed silver coin burst forth and rattled in the rusty bottom of the box. Without a word, he set to work to count the gold.

"What is this?" I asked.

"It's the ship's money," he returned, doggedly continuing his work.

"The ship's money?" I repeated. "That's the money Trent tramped and traded with? And there's his cheque-book to draw upon his owners? And he has left it?"

"I guess he has," said Nares, austerely, jotting down a note of the gold; and I was abashed into silence till his task should be completed.

It came, I think, to three hundred and seventy-eight pounds sterling; some nineteen pounds of

it in silver: all of which we turned again into
the chest.

"And what do you think of that?" I asked.

"Mr. Dodd," he replied, "you see something
of the rumness of this job, but not the whole.
The specie bothers you, but what gets me is the
papers. Are you aware that the master of a ship
has charge of all the cash in hand, pays the men
advances, receives freight and passage money, and
runs up bills in every port? All this he does as
the owner's confidential agent, and his integrity
is proved by his receipted bills. I tell you, the
captain of a ship is more likely to forget his
pants than these bills which guarantee his character. I 've known men drown to save them: bad
men, too; but this is the shipmaster's honour.
And here this Captain Trent — not hurried, not
threatened with anything but a free passage in a
British man-of-war — has left them all behind!
I don't want to express myself too strongly, because the facts appear against me, but the thing
is impossible."

Dinner came to us not long after, and we ate
it on deck, in a grim silence, each privately racking his brain for some solution of the mysteries.
I was indeed so swallowed up in these considerations, that the wreck, the lagoon, the islets, and
the strident sea-fowl, the strong sun then beating
on my head, and even the gloomy countenance of
the captain at my elbow, all vanished from the
field of consciousness. My mind was a blackboard,
on which I scrawled and blotted out hypotheses;

comparing each with the pictorial records in my memory: cyphering with pictures. In the course of this tense mental exercise I recalled and studied the faces of one memorial masterpiece, the scene of the saloon; and here I found myself, on a sudden, looking in the eyes of the Kanaka.

"There's one thing I can put beyond doubt, at all events," I cried, relinquishing my dinner and getting briskly afoot. "There was that Kanaka I saw in the bar with Captain Trent, the fellow the newspapers and ship's articles made out to be a Chinaman. I mean to rout his quarters out and settle that."

"All right," said Nares. "I'll lazy off a bit longer, Mr. Dodd; I feel pretty rocky and mean."

We had thoroughly cleared out the three after-compartments of the ship: all the stuff from the main cabin and the mate's and captain's quarters lay piled about the wheel; but in the forward stateroom with the two bunks, where Nares had said the mate and cook most likely berthed, we had as yet done nothing. Thither I went; it was very bare; a few photographs were tacked on the bulkhead, one of them indecent; a single chest stood open, and like all we had yet found, it had been partly rifled. An armful of two-shilling novels proved to me beyond a doubt it was a European's: no Chinaman would have possessed any, and the most literate Kanaka conceivable in a ship's galley was not likely to have gone beyond one. It was plain, then, that the cook had not berthed aft, and I must look elsewhere.

The men had stamped down the nests and driven the birds from the galley, so that I could now enter without contest. One door had been already blocked with rice; the place was in part darkness, full of a foul stale smell and a cloud of nasty flies; it had been left, besides, in some disorder, or else the birds, during their time of tenancy, had knocked the things about; and the floor, like the deck before we washed it, was spread with pasty filth. Against the wall, in the far corner, I found a handsome chest of camphor wood bound with brass, such as Chinamen and sailors love, and indeed all of mankind that plies in the Pacific. From its outside view I could thus make no deduction; and strange to say, the interior was concealed. All the other chests, as I have said already, we had found gaping open and their contents scattered abroad; the same remark we found to apply afterwards in the quarters of the seamen; only this camphor-wood chest, a singular exception, was both closed and locked.

I took an axe to it, readily forced the paltry Chinese fastening, and, like a custom-house officer, plunged my hands among the contents. For some while I groped among linen and cotton. Then my teeth were set on edge with silk, of which I drew forth several strips covered with mysterious characters. And these settled the business, for I recognised them as a kind of bed-hanging popular with the commoner class of the Chinese. Nor were farther evidences wanting, such as night-clothes of an extraordinary design, a three-stringed

Chinese fiddle, a silk handkerchief full of roots and herbs, and a neat apparatus for smoking opium with a liberal provision of the drug. Plainly, then, the cook had been a Chinaman; and if so, who was Jos. Amalu? Or had Jos. stolen the chest before he proceeded to ship under a false name and domicile? It was possible, as anything was possible in such a welter; but regarded as a solution, it only led and left me deeper in the bog. For why should this chest have been deserted and neglected, when the others were rummaged or removed? and where had Jos. come by that second chest, with which (according to the clerk at the What Cheer) he had started for Honolulu?

"And how have *you* fared?" inquired the captain, whom I found luxuriously reclining in our mound of litter. And the accent on the pronoun, the heightened colour of the speaker's face, and the contained excitement in his tones, advertised me at once that I had not been alone to make discoveries.

"I have found a Chinaman's chest in the galley," said I, "and John (if there was any John) was not so much as at the pains to take his opium."

Nares seemed to take it mighty quietly. "That so?" said he. "Now, cast your eyes on that and own you 're beaten!" And with a formidable clap of his open hand, he flattened out before me, on the deck, a pair of newspapers.

I gazed upon them dully, being in no mood for fresh discoveries.

"Look at them, Mr. Dodd," cried the captain,

sharply. " Can't you look at them? " And he ran a dirty thumb along the title. " ' *Sydney Morning Herald,* November 26th,' can't you make that out? " he cried, with rising energy. " And don't you know, sir, that not thirteen days after this paper appeared in New South Pole, this ship we 're standing in heaved her blessed anchors out of China? How did the *Sydney Morning Herald* get to Hong Kong in thirteen days? Trent made no land, he spoke no ship, till he got here. Then he either got it here or in Hong Kong. I give you your choice, my son! " he cried, and fell back among the clothes like a man weary of life.

" Where did you find them? " I asked. " In that black bag? "

" Guess so," he said. " You need n't fool with it. There 's nothing else but a lead-pencil and a kind of worked-out knife."

I looked in the bag, however, and was well rewarded.

" Every man to his trade, Captain," said I. " You 're a sailor, and you 've given me plenty of points; but I am an artist, and allow me to inform you this is quite as strange as all the rest. The knife is a palette knife; the pencil, a Windsor and Newton, and a B B B at that. A palette knife and a B B B on a tramp brig! It 's against the laws of nature."

" It would sicken a dog, would n't it? " said Nares.

" Yes," I continued, " it 's been used by an artist, too: see how it 's sharpened — not for writing —

no man could write with that. An artist, and
straight from Sydney? How can he come in?"

" O, that's natural enough," sneered Nares.
" They cabled him to come up and illustrate this
dime novel."

We fell awhile silent.

" Captain," I said at last, " there is something
deuced underhand about this brig. You tell me
you've been to sea a good part of your life. You
must have seen shady things done on ships, and
heard of more. Well, what is this? is it insurance? is it piracy? what is it *about?* what can
it be *for?*"

" Mr. Dodd," returned Nares, " you're right
about me having been to sea the bigger part of
my life. And you're right again, when you think
I know a good many ways in which a dishonest
captain may n't be on the square, nor do exactly
the right thing by his owners, and altogether be
just a little too smart by ninety-nine and three-
quarters. There's a good many ways, but not
so many as you'd think; and not one that has
any mortal thing to do with Trent. Trent and
his whole racket has got to do with nothing —
that's the bed-rock fact; there's no sense to it,
and no use in it, and no story to it: it's a beastly
dream. And don't you run away with that notion that landsmen take about ships. A society
actress don't go around more publicly than what
a ship does, nor is more interviewed, nor more
humbugged, nor more run after by all sorts of
little fussinesses in brass buttons. And more than

an actress, a ship has a deal to lose; she's capital,
and the actress only character — if she's that. The
ports of the world are thick with people ready to
kick a captain into the penitentiary, if he's not
as bright as a dollar and as honest as the morning
star; and what with Lloyd keeping watch and
watch in every corner of the three oceans, and the
insurance leeches, and the consuls, and the cus-
toms bugs, and the medicos, you can only get the
idea by thinking of a landsman watched by a
hundred and fifty detectives, or a stranger in a
village Down East."

"Well, but at sea?" I said.

"You make me tired," retorted the captain.
"What's the use — at sea? Everything's got to
come to bearings at some port, has n't it? You
can't stop at sea for ever, can you? — No; the
Flying Scud is rubbish; if it meant anything, it
would have to mean something so almighty intri-
cate that James G. Blaine has n't got the brains
to engineer it; and I vote for more axeing, pio-
neering, and opening up the resources of this phe-
nomenal brig, and less general fuss," he added,
arising. "The dime-museum symptoms will drop
in of themselves, I guess, to keep us cheery."

But it appeared we were at the end of discoveries
for the day; and we left the brig about sundown,
without being further puzzled or further enlightened. The best of the cabin spoils — books, instruments, papers, silks, and curiosities — we carried
along with us in a blanket, however, to divert
the evening hours; and when supper was over,

and the table cleared, and Johnson set down to a
dreary game of cribbage between his right hand
and his left, the captain and I turned out our
blanket on the floor, and sat side by side to examine and appraise the spoils.

The books were the first to engage our notice.
These were rather numerous (as Nares contemptuously put it) " for a lime-juicer." Scorn of the
British mercantile marine glows in the breast of
every Yankee merchant captain; as the scorn is
not reciprocated, I can only suppose it justified in
fact; and certainly the old country mariner appears of a less studious disposition. The more
credit to the officers of the *Flying Scud*, who had
quite a library, both literary and professional.
There were Findlay's five directories of the world
— all broken-backed, as is usual with Findlay, and
all marked and scribbled over with corrections and
additions — several books of navigation, a signal
code, and an Admiralty book of a sort of orange
hue, called *Islands of the Eastern Pacific Ocean,
Vol. III.*, which appeared from its imprint to be
the latest authority, and showed marks of frequent consultation in the passages about the
French Frigate Shoals, the Harman, Cure, Pearl,
and Hermes reefs, Lisiansky Island, Ocean Island,
and the place where we then lay — Brooks or
Midway. A volume of Macaulay's *Essays* and a
shilling Shakespeare led the van of the *belles
lettres;* the rest were novels: several Miss Brad-
dons — of course, *Aurora Floyd*, which has pene-
trated to every isle of the Pacific, a good many

cheap detective books, *Rob Roy*, Auerbach's *Auf
der Höhe* in the German, and a prize temperance
story, pillaged (to judge by the stamp) from an
Anglo-Indian circulating library.

"The admiralty man gives a fine picture of our
island," remarked Nares, who had turned up Midway Island. "He draws the dreariness rather mild,
but you can make out he knows the place."

"Captain," I cried, "you 've struck another point
in this mad business. See here," I went on eagerly,
drawing from my pocket a crumpled fragment of
the *Daily Occidental* which I had inherited from
Jim: "'misled by Hoyt's Pacific Directory'?
Where 's Hoyt?"

"Let 's look into that," said Nares. "I got that
book on purpose for this cruise." Therewith he
fetched it from the shelf in his berth, turned to
Midway Island, and read the account aloud. It
stated with precision that the Pacific Mail Company were about to form a depot there, in preference to Honolulu, and that they had already a
station on the island.

"I wonder who gives these Directory men
their information," Nares reflected. "Nobody can
blame Trent after that. I never got in company
with squarer lying; it reminds a man of a presi-
dential campaign."

"All very well," said I. "That 's your Hoyt,
and a fine, tall copy. But what I want to know
is, where is Trent's Hoyt?"

"Took it with him," chuckled Nares. "He had
left everything else, bills and money and all the

rest; he was bound to take something, or it would have aroused attention on the *Tempest:* 'Happy thought,' says he; 'let's take Hoyt.'"

"And has it not occurred to you," I went on, "that all the Hoyts in creation could n't have misled Trent, since he had in his hand that red admiralty book, an official publication, later in date, and particularly full on Midway Island?"

"That's a fact!" cried Nares; "and I bet the first Hoyt he ever saw was out of the mercantile library in San Francisco. Looks as if he'd brought her here on purpose, don't it? But then that's inconsistent with the steam-crusher of the sale. That's the trouble with this brig racket; any one can make half-a-dozen theories for sixty or seventy per cent of it; but when they're made, there's always a fathom or two of slack hanging out of the other end."

I believe our attention fell next on the papers, of which we had altogether a considerable bulk. I had hoped to find among these matter for a full-length character of Captain Trent, but here I was doomed, on the whole, to disappointment. We could make out he was an orderly man, for all his bills were docketed and preserved. That he was convivial, and inclined to be frugal even in conviviality, several documents proclaimed. Such letters as we found were, with one exception, arid notes from tradesmen. The exception, signed Hannah Trent, was a somewhat fervid appeal for a loan. "You know what misfortunes I have had to bear," wrote Hannah, "and how much I

am disappointed in George. The landlady appeared a true friend when I first came here, and
I thought her a perfect lady. But she has come out
since then in her *true colours;* and if you will not
be softened by this last appeal, I can't think what
is to become of your affectionate — " and then the
signature. This document was without place or
date, and a voice told me that it had gone likewise without answer. On the whole, there were
few letters anywhere in the ship; but we found
one before we were finished, in a seaman's chest,
of which I must transcribe some sentences. It was
dated from some place on the Clyde. " My dearist
son," it ran, " this is to tell you your dearist father
passed away, Jan twelft, in the peace of the Lord.
He had your photo and dear David's lade upon his
bed, made me sit by him. Let 's be a'thegither, he
said, and gave you all his blessing. O my dear
laddie, why were nae you and Davie here? He
would have had a happier passage. He spok of
both of ye all night most beautiful, and how ye
used to stravaig on the Saturday afternoons, and
of *auld Kelvinside.* Sooth the tune to me, he said,
though it was the Sabbath, and I had to sooth
him Kelvin Grove, and he looked at his fiddle, the
dear man. I cannae bear the sight of it, he 'll never
play it mair. O my lamb, come home to me, I 'm
all by my lane now." The rest was in a religious
vein and quite conventional. I have never seen
any one more put out than Nares, when I handed
him this letter; he had read but a few words, before he cast it down; it was perhaps a minute ere

he picked it up again, and the performance was repeated the third time before he reached the end.

"It's touching, isn't it?" said I.

For all answer, Nares exploded in a brutal oath; and it was some half an hour later that he vouchsafed an explanation. "I'll tell you what broke me up about that letter," said he. "My old man played the fiddle, played it all out of tune: one of the things he played was *Martyrdom*, I remember — it was all martyrdom to me. He was a pig of a father, and I was a pig of a son; but it sort of came over me I would like to hear that fiddle squeak again. Natural," he added; "I guess we're all beasts."

"All sons are, I guess," said I. "I have the same trouble on my conscience: we can shake hands on that." Which (oddly enough, perhaps) we did.

Amongst the papers we found a considerable sprinkling of photographs; for the most part either of very debonair-looking young ladies or old women of the lodging-house persuasion. But one among them was the means of our crowning discovery.

"They're not pretty, are they, Mr. Dodd?" said Nares, as he passed it over.

"Who?" I asked, mechanically taking the card (it was a quarter-plate) in hand, and smothering a yawn; for the hour was late, the day had been laborious, and I was wearying for bed.

"Trent and Company," said he. "That's a historic picture of the gang."

I held it to the light, my curiosity at a low ebb:
I had seen Captain Trent once, and had no delight
in viewing him again. It was a photograph of the
deck of the brig, taken from forward: all in apple-
pie order; the hands gathered in the waist, the
officers on the poop. At the foot of the card was
written, " Brig Flying Scud, Rangoon," and a
date; and above or below each individual figure
the name had been carefully noted.

As I continued to gaze, a shock went through
me; the dimness of sleep and fatigue lifted from
my eyes, as fog lifts in the channel; and I beheld
with startled clearness, the photographic present-
ment of a crowd of strangers. " I. Trent, Master "
at the top of the card directed me to a smallish,
weazened man, with bushy eyebrows and full white
beard, dressed in a frock-coat and white trousers;
a flower stuck in his button-hole, his bearded chin
set forward, his mouth clenched with habitual determination. There was not much of the sailor in
his looks, but plenty of the martinet: a dry, precise
man, who might pass for a preacher in some rigid
sect; and whatever he was, not the Captain Trent
of San Francisco. The men, too, were all new to
me: the cook, an unmistakable Chinaman, in his
characteristic dress, standing apart on the poop
steps. But perhaps I turned on the whole with the
greatest curiosity to the figure labelled " E. Goddedaal, 1st off." He whom I had never seen, he might ·
be the identical; he might be the clue and spring
of all this mystery; and I scanned his features
with the eye of a detective. He was of great stat-

ure, seemingly blond as a viking, his hair clustering
round his head in frowsy curls, and two enormous
whiskers, like the tusks of some strange animal,
jutting from his cheeks. With these virile appen-
dages and the defiant attitude in which he stood,
the expression of his face only imperfectly har-
monised. It was wild, heroic, and womanish looking; and I felt I was prepared to hear he was a
sentimentalist, and to see him weep.

For some while I digested my discovery in private, reflecting how best, and how with most of
drama, I might share it with the captain. Then
my sketch-book came in my head; and I fished it
out from where it lay, with other miscellaneous
possessions, at the foot of my bunk and turned to
my sketch of Captain Trent and the survivors of
the British brig *Flying Scud* in the San Francisco
bar-room.

"Nares," said I, "I've told you how I first saw
Captain Trent in that saloon in 'Frisco? how he
came with his men, one of them a Kanaka with
a canary-bird in a cage? and how I saw him
afterwards at the auction, frightened to death, and
as much surprised at how the figures skipped up
as anybody there? Well," said I, "there's the
man I saw " — and I laid the sketch before him
— "there's Trent of 'Frisco and there are his
three hands. Find one of them in the photograph,
and I'll be obliged."

Nares compared the two in silence. "Well,"
he said at last, "I call this rather a relief: seems
to clear the horizon. We might have guessed at

something of the kind from the double ration of chests that figured."

"Does it explain anything?" I asked.

"It would explain everything," Nares replied, "but for the steam-crusher. It 'll all tally as neat as a patent puzzle, if you leave out the way these people bid the wreck up. And there we come to a stone wall. But whatever it is, Mr. Dodd, it 's on the crook."

"And looks like piracy," I added.

"Looks like blind hookey!" cried the captain. "No, don't you deceive yourself; neither your head nor mine is big enough to put a name on this business."

CHAPTER XV

THE CARGO OF THE "FLYING SCUD"

IN my early days I was a man, the most wedded to his idols of my generation. I was a dweller under roofs: the gull of that which we call civilisation; a superstitious votary of the plastic arts: a cit; and a prop of restaurants. I had a comrade in those days, somewhat of an outsider, though he moved in the company of artists, and a man famous in our small world for gallantry, knee breeches, and dry and pregnant sayings. He, look·· ing on the long meals and waxing bellies of the French, whom I confess I somewhat imitated, branded me as "a cultivator of restaurant fat." And I believe he had his finger on the dangerous spot; I believe, if things had gone smooth with me, I should be now swollen like a prize-ox in body, and fallen in mind to a thing perhaps as low as many types of *bourgeois* — the implicit or exclusive artist. That was a home word of Pinkerton's, deserving to be writ in letters of gold on the portico of every school of art: " What I can't see is why you should want to do nothing else." The dull man is made, not by the nature, but by the degree of his immersion in a single business. And all the more if that be sedentary, uneventful, and ingloriously safe. More than one-half of him will then remain unexercised and undeveloped; the rest will be distended and deformed by over-nutrition, over-cerebration, and the heat of rooms. And I have often marvelled at the impudence of gentlemen, who describe and pass judgments on the life of man, in almost perfect ignorance of all its necessary elements and natural careers. Those who dwell in clubs and studios may paint excellent pictures or write enchanting novels. There is one thing that they should not do: they should pass no judgment on man's destiny, for it is a thing with which they are unacquainted. Their own life is an excrescence of the moment, doomed, in the vicissitude of history, to pass and disappear: the eternal life of man, spent under sun and rain and in rude physical effort, lies upon one side, scarce changed since the beginning.

I would I could have carried along with me to Midway Island all the writers and the prating artists of my time. Day after day of hope deferred, of heat, of unremitting toil; night after night of aching limbs, bruised hands, and a mind obscured with the grateful vacancy of physical fatigue: the scene, the nature of my employment; the rugged speech and faces of my fellow-toilers, the glare of the day on deck, the stinking twilight in the bilge, the shrill myriads of the ocean-fowl: above all, the sense of our immitigable isolation from the world and from the current epoch; — keeping another time, some eras old; the new day heralded by no daily paper, only by the rising sun; and the State, the ·churches, the peopled empires, war, and the rumours of war, and the voices of the arts, all gone silent as in the days ere they were yet invented. ·Such were the conditions of my new experience in life, of which (if I had been able) I would have had all my confrères and contemporaries to partake: forgetting, for that while, the orthodoxies of the moment, and devoted to a single and material purpose under the eye of heaven.

Of the nature of our task, I must continue to give some summary idea. The forecastle was lumbered with ship's chandlery, the hold nigh full of rice, the lazarette crowded with the teas and silks. These must all be dug out; and that made but a fraction of our task. The hold was ceiled throughout; a part, where perhaps some delicate cargo was once stored, had been lined, in addition, with inch boards; and between every beam there was a movable panel into the bilge. Any of these, the bulkheads of the cabins, the very timbers of the hull itself, might be the place of hiding. It was therefore necessary to demolish, as we proceeded, a great part of the ship's inner skin and fittings, and to auscultate what remained, like a doctor sounding for a lung disease. Upon the return, from any beam or bulkhead, of a flat or doubtful sound, we must up axe and hew into the timber: a violent and — from the amount of dry rot in the wreck — a mortifying exercise. Every night saw a deeper inroad into the bones of the *Flying Scud* — more beams tapped and hewn in splinters, more planking peeled away and tossed aside — and every

night saw us as far as ever from the end and object
of our arduous devastation. In this perpetual disappointment, my courage did not fail me, but my
spirits dwindled; and Nares himself grew silent
and morose. At night, when supper was done, we
passed an hour in the cabin, mostly without speech :
I, sometimes dozing over a book; Nares,. sullenly
but busily drilling sea-shells with the instrument
called a Yankee Fiddle. A stranger might have
supposed we were estranged; as a matter of fact,
in this silent comradeship of labour, our intimacy
grew.

I had been struck, at the first beginning of our
enterprise upon the wreck, to find the men so ready
at the captain's lightest word. I dare not say they
liked, but I can never deny that they admired him
thoroughly. A mild word from his mouth was
more valued than flattery and half a dollar from
myself; if he relaxed at all from his habitual attitude of censure, smiling alacrity surrounded him;
and I was led to think his theory of captainship,
even if pushed to excess, reposed upon some ground
of reason. But even terror and admiration of the
captain failed us before the end. The men wearied
of the hopeless, unremunerative quest and the long
strain of labour. They began to shirk and grumble.
Retribution fell on them at once, and retribution
multiplied the grumblings. With every day it took
harder driving to keep them to the daily drudge;
and we, in our narrow boundaries, were kept conscious every moment of the ill-will of our assistants.

In spite of the best care, the object of our search

was perfectly well known to all on board; and there had leaked out besides some knowledge of those inconsistencies that had so greatly amazed the captain and myself. I could overhear the men debate the character of Captain Trent, and set forth competing theories of where the opium was stowed; and as they seemed to have been eavesdropping on ourselves, I thought little shame to prick up my ears when I had the return chance of spying upon them, in this way. I could diagnose their temper and judge how far they were informed upon the mystery of the *Flying Scud*. It was after having thus overheard some almost mutinous speeches, that a fortunate idea crossed my mind. At night, I matured it in my bed, and the first thing the next morning, broached it to the captain.

"Suppose I spirit up the hands a bit," I asked, "by the offer of a reward?"

"If you think you're getting your month's wages out of them the way it is, I don't," was his reply. "However, they are all the men you've got, and you're the supercargo."

This, from a person of the captain's character, might be regarded as complete adhesion; and the crew were accordingly called aft. Never had the captain worn a front more menacing. It was supposed by all that some misdeed had been discovered, and some surprising punishment was to be announced.

"See here, you!" he threw at them over his shoulder as he walked the deck, "Mr. Dodd, here, is going to offer a reward to the first man who

strikes the opium in that wreck. There 's two ways
of making a donkey go; both good, I guess: the
one 's kicks and the other 's carrots. Mr. Dodd 's
going to try the carrots. Well, my sons," — and
here he faced the men for the first time with
his hands behind him — " if that opium 's not
found in five days, you can come to me for the
kicks."

He nodded to the present narrator, who took up
the tale. " Here is what I propose, men," said I:
" I put up one hundred and fifty dollars. If any
man can lay hands on the stuff right away, and off
his own club, he shall have the hundred and fifty
down. If any one can put us on the scent of where
to look, he shall have a hundred and twenty-five,
and the balance shall be for the lucky one who
actually picks it up. We 'll call it the Pinkerton
Stakes, Captain," I added, with a smile.

" Call it the Grand Combination Sweep, then,"
cries he. " For I go you better. Look here, men,
I make up this jack-pot to two hundred and fifty
dollars, American gold coin."

" Thank you, Captain Nares," said I; " that was
handsomely done."

" It was kindly meant," he returned.

The offer was not made in vain; the hands had
scarce yet realised the magnitude of the reward,
they had scarce begun to buzz aloud in the extremity of hope and wonder, ere the Chinese cook
stepped forward with gracious gestures and ex-
planatory smiles.

" Captain," he began, " I serv-um two year

Melican navy; serv-um six year mail-boat steward. Savvy plenty."

"Oho!" cried Nares, "you savvy plenty, do you? (Beggar's seen this trick in the mail-boats, I guess.) Well, why you no savvy a little sooner, sonny?"

"I think bimeby make-um reward," replied the cook, with smiling dignity.

"Well, you can't say fairer than that," the captain admitted, "and now the reward's offered, you'll talk? Speak up, then. Suppose you speak true, you get reward. See?"

"I think long time," replied the Chinaman. "See plenty litty mat lice; too-muchy plenty litty mat lice; sixty ton, litty mat lice. I think all-e-time: perhaps plenty opium plenty litty mat lice?"

"Well, Mr. Dodd, how does that strike you?" asked the captain. "He may be right, he may be wrong. He's likely to be right: for if he isn't, where can the stuff be? On the other hand, if he's wrong, we destroy a hundred and fifty tons of good rice for nothing. It's a point to be considered."

"I don't hesitate," said I. "Let's get to the bottom of the thing. The rice is nothing; the rice will neither make nor break us."

"That's how I expected you to see it," returned Nares.

And we called the boat away and set forth on our new quest.

The hold was now almost entirely emptied; the mats (of which there went forty to the short ton) had been stacked on deck, and now crowded the ship's waist and forecastle. It was our task to disembowel and explore six thousand individual mats, and incidentally to destroy a hundred and fifty tons of valuable food. Nor were the circumstances of the day's business less strange than its essential nature. Each man of us, armed with a great knife, attacked the pile from his own quarter, slashed into the nearest mat, burrowed in it with his hands, and shed forth the rice upon the deck, where it heaped up, overflowed, and was trodden down, poured at last into the scuppers, and occasionally spouted from the vents. About the wreck, thus transformed into an overflowing granary, the seafowl swarmed in myriads and with surprising insolence. The sight of so much food confounded them; they deafened us with their shrill tongues, swooped in our midst, dashed in our faces, and snatched the grain from between our fingers. The men — their hands bleeding from these assaults — turned savagely on the offensive, drove their knives into the birds, drew them out crimsoned, and turned again to dig among the rice, unmindful of the gawking creatures that struggled and died among their feet. We made a singular picture: the hovering and diving birds; the bodies of the dead discolouring the rice with blood; the scuppers vomiting breadstuff; the men, frenzied by the gold hunt, toiling, slaying, and shouting aloud: over all, the lofty intricacy of rigging and the radiant heaven of the Pacific. Every man there toiled in the immediate hope of fifty dollars; and I, of fifty thousand. Small wonder if we waded callously in blood and food.

It was perhaps about ten in the forenoon when the scene was interrupted. Nares, who had just ripped open a fresh mat, drew forth, and slung at his feet, among the rice, a papered tin box.

"How's that?" he shouted.

A cry broke from all hands: the next moment, forgetting their own disappointment, in that contagious sentiment of success, they gave three cheers that scared the sea-birds; and the next, they had crowded round the captain, and were jostling together and groping with emulous hands in the new-opened mat. Box after box rewarded them, six in all; wrapped, as I have said, in a paper envelope, and the paper printed on, in Chinese characters.

Nares turned to me and shook my hand. "I began to think we should never see this day," said he. "I congratulate you, Mr. Dodd, on having pulled it through."

The captain's tones affected me profoundly; and when Johnson and the men pressed round me in turn with congratulations, the tears came in my eyes.

"These are five-tael boxes, more than two pounds," said Nares, weighing one in his hand. "Say two hundred and fifty dollars to the mat. Lay into it, boys! we'll make Mr. Dodd a millionaire before dark."

It was strange to see with what a fury we fell to. The men had now nothing to expect; the mere idea of great sums inspired them with disinterested ardour. Mats were slashed and disembowelled, the rice flowed to our knees in the ship's waist, the sweat ran in our eyes and blinded us, our arms ached to agony; and yet our fire abated not. Dinner came; we were too weary to eat, too hoarse for conversation; and yet dinner was scarce done, before we were afoot again and delving in the rice. Before nightfall not a mat was unexplored, and we were face to face with the astonishing result.

For of all the inexplicable things in the story of the *Flying Scud,* here was the most inexplicable. Out of the six thousand mats, only twenty were found to have been sugared; in each we found the same amount, about twelve pounds of drug; making a grand total of two hundred and forty pounds. By the last San Francisco quotation, opium was selling for a fraction over twenty dollars a pound; but it had been known not long before to bring as much as forty in Honolulu, where it was contraband.

Taking, then, this high Honolulu figure, the value of the opium on board the *Flying Scud* fell considerably short of ten thousand dollars, while at the San Francisco rate, it lacked a trifle of five thousand. And fifty thousand was the price that Jim and I had paid for it. And Bellairs had been eager to go higher! There is no language to express the stupor with which I contemplated this result.

It may be argued we were not yet sure; there might be yet another *cache;* and you may be cer-

tain in that hour of my distress the argument was
not forgotten. There was never a ship more ar-
dently perquested; no stone was left unturned, and
no expedient untried; day after day of growing
despair, we punched and dug in the brig's vitals,
exciting the men with promises and presents; evening after evening Nares and I sat face to face in
the narrow cabin, racking our minds for some
neglected possibility of search. I could stake my
salvation on the certainty of the result: in all
that ship there was nothing left of value but the
timber and the copper nails. So that our case was
lamentably plain; we had paid fifty thousand dollars, borne the charges of the schooner, and paid
fancy interest on money; and if things went well
with us, we might realise fifteen per cent of the
first outlay. We were not merely bankrupt, we
were comic bankrupts: a fair butt for jeering in
the streets. I hope I bore the blow with a good
countenance; indeed, my mind had long been quite
made up, and since the day we found the opium I
had known the result. But the thought of Jim
and Mamie ached in me like a physical pain, and
I shrank from speech and companionship.

I was in this frame of mind when the captain
proposed that we should land upon the island. I
saw he had something to say, and only feared it
might be consolation; for I could just bear my
grief, not bungling sympathy; and yet I had no
choice but to accede to his proposal.

We walked awhile along the beach in silence.
The sun overhead reverberated rays of heat; the

staring sand, the glaring lagoon, tortured our eyes;
and the birds and the boom of the far-away
breakers made a savage symphony.

"I don't require to tell you the game's up?"
Nares asked.

"No," said I.

"I was thinking of getting to sea to-morrow,"
he pursued.

"The best thing you can do," said I.

"Shall we say Honolulu?" he inquired.

"O yes; let's stick to the programme," I cried.
"Honolulu be it!"

There was another silence, and then Nares
cleared his throat.

"We've been pretty good friends, you and
me, Mr. Dodd," he resumed. "We've been going
through the kind of thing that tries a man.
We've had the hardest kind of work, we've been
badly backed, and now we're badly beaten. And
we've fetched through without a word of disagree-
ment. I don't say this to praise myself: it's my
trade; it's what I'm paid for, and trained for,
and brought up to. But it was another thing for
you; it was all new to you; and it did me good
to see you stand right up to it and swing right
into it, day in, day out. And then see how you've
taken this disappointment, when everybody knows
you must have been taughtened up to shying-point!
I wish you'd let me tell you, Mr. Dodd, that you've
stood out mighty manly and handsomely in all this
business, and made every one like you and admire
you. And I wish you'd let me tell you, besides,

that I 've taken this wreck business as much to
heart as you have; something kind of rises in my
throat when I think we 're beaten; and if I thought
waiting would do it, I would stick on this reef until
we starved."

I tried in vain to thank him for these generous words, but he was beforehand with me in a
moment.

"I did n't bring you ashore to sound my
praises," he interrupted. "We understand one
another now, that 's all; and I guess you can
trust me. What I wished to speak about is
more important, and it 's got to be faced. What
are we to do about the Flying Scud and the
dime novel?"

"I really have thought nothing about that," I
replied. "But I expect I mean to get at the bottom of it; and if the bogus Captain Trent is to
be found on the earth's surface, I guess I mean
to find him."

"All you 've got to do is talk," said Nares;
"you can make the biggest kind of boom; it is n't
often the reporters have a chance at such a yarn
as this; and I can tell you how it will go. It will
go by telegraph, Mr. Dodd; it 'll be telegraphed
by the column, and head-lined, and frothed up, and
denied by authority; and it 'll hit bogus Captain
Trent in a Mexican bar-room, and knock over
bogus Goddedaal in a slum somewhere up the
Baltic, and bowl down Hardy and Brown in
sailors' music halls round Greenock. O, there 's
no doubt you can have a regular domestic Judg-

ment Day. The only point is whether you deliberately want to."

"Well," said I, " I deliberately don't want one thing: I deliberately don't want to make a public exhibition of myself and Pinkerton: so moral — smuggling opium; such damned fools — paying fifty thousand for a ' dead horse '! "

" No doubt it might damage you in a business sense," the captain agreed. " And I 'm pleased you take that view; for I 've turned kind of soft upon the job. There 's been some crookedness about, no doubt of it; but, Law bless you! if we dropped upon the troupe, all the premier artists would slip right out with the boodle in their gripsacks, and you 'd only collar a lot of old muttonheaded shell-backs that did n't know the back of the business from the front. I don't take much stock in Mercantile Jack, you know that; but, poor devil, he 's got to go where he 's told; and if you make trouble, ten to one it 'll make you sick to see the innocents who have to stand the racket. It would be different if we understood the operation; but we don't, you see: there 's a lot of queer corners in life; and my vote is to let the blame' thing lie."

" You speak as if we had that in our power," I objected.

" And so we have," said he.

" What about the men? " I asked. " They know too much by half; and you can't keep them from talking."

" Can't I? " returned Nares. " I bet a boarding-master can! They can be all half-seas over, when they get ashore, blind drunk by dark, and cruising out of the Golden Gate in different deep-sea ships by the next morning. Can't keep them from talking, can't I? Well, I can make them talk separate, leastways. If a whole crew came talking, parties would listen; but if it 's only one lone old shellback, it 's the usual yarn. And at least, they need n't talk before six months, or — if we have luck, and there 's a whaler handy — three years. And by that time, Mr. Dodd, it 's ancient history."

" That 's what they call shanghaiing, is n't it? " I asked. " I thought it belonged to the dime novel."

" O, dime novels are right enough," returned the captain. " Nothing wrong with the dime novel, only that things happen thicker than they do in life, and the practical seamanship is off colour."

" So we can keep the business to ourselves," I mused. .

" There 's one other person that might blab," said the captain. " Though I don't believe she has anything left to tell."

" And who is *she?* " I asked.

" The old girl there," he answered, pointing to the wreck. " I know there 's nothing in her; but somehow I 'm afraid of some one else — it 's the last thing you 'd expect, so it 's just the first that 'll happen — some one dropping into this God-forgotten island where nobody drops in, waltzing into that wreck that we 've grown old with searching, stooping straight down, and picking right up the very thing that tells the story. What 's that to me?

you may ask, and why am I gone Soft Tommy
on this Museum of Crooks? They 've smashed
up you and Mr. Pinkerton; they 've turned my
hair grey with conundrums; they 've been up
to larks, no doubt; and that 's all I know of
them — you say. Well, and that 's just where it
is. I don't know enough; I don't know what 's
uppermost; it 's just such a lot of miscellaneous
eventualities as I don't care to go stirring up; and
I ask you to let me deal with the old girl after
a patent of my own."

"Certainly — what you please," said I, scarce
with attention, for a new thought now occupied
my brain. "Captain," I broke out, "you are
wrong; we cannot hush this up. There is one
thing you have forgotten."

"What is that?" he asked.

"A bogus Captain Trent, a bogus Goddedaal, a
whole bogus crew, have all started home," said I.
"If we are right, not one of them will reach his
journey's end. And do you mean to say that such
a circumstance as that can pass without remark?"

"Sailors," said the captain, "only sailors! If
they were all bound for one place, in a body, I
don't say so; but they 're all going separate — to
Hull, to Sweden, to the Clyde, to the Thames.
Well, at each place, what is it? Nothing new.
Only one sailor man missing: got drunk, or got
drowned, or got left: the proper sailor's end."

Something bitter in the thought and in the
speaker's tones struck me hard. "Here is one
that has got left!" I cried, getting sharply to my

feet; for we had been some time seated. " I wish
it were the other. I don't — don't relish going
home to Jim with this!"

" See here," said Nares, with ready tact, " I
must be getting aboard. Johnson's in the brig
annexing chandlery and canvas, and there's some
things in the *Norah* that want fixing against we
go to sea. Would you like to be left here in the
chicken-ranch? I'll send for you to supper."

I embraced the proposal with delight. Solitude,
in my frame of mind, was not too dearly pur-
chased at the risk of sunstroke or sand-blindness;
and soon I was alone on the ill-omened islet. I
should find it hard to tell of what I thought —
of Jim, of Mamie, of our lost fortune, of my lost
hopes, of the doom before me: to turn to at some
mechanical occupation in some subaltern rank, and
to toil there, unremarked and unamused, until the
hour of the last deliverance. I was, at least, so
sunk in sadness, that I scarce remarked where I
was going; and chance (or some finer sense that
lives in us, and only guides us when the mind is
in abeyance) conducted my steps into a quarter of
the island where the birds were few. By some
devious route, which I was unable to retrace for
my return, I was thus able to mount, without interruption, to the highest point of land. And here
I was recalled to consciousness by a last discovery.

The spot on which I stood was level, and commanded a wide view of the lagoon, the bound-
ing reef, the round horizon. Nearer hand I saw
the sister islet, the wreck, the *Norah Creina*, and the

Norah's boat already moving shoreward. For the sun was now low, flaming on the sea's verge; and the galley chimney smoked on board the schooner.

It thus befell that though my discovery was both affecting and suggestive, I had no leisure to examine further. What I saw was the blackened embers of fire of wreck. By all the signs, it must have blazed to a good height and burned for days; from the scantling of a spar that lay upon the margin only half consumed, it must have been the work of more than one; and I received at once the image of a forlorn troop of castaways, houseless in that lost corner of the earth, and feeding there their fire of signal. The next moment a hail reached me from the boat; and bursting through the bushes and the rising sea-fowl, I said farewell (I trust for ever) to that desert isle.

CHAPTER XVI

IN WHICH I TURN SMUGGLER, AND THE CAPTAIN CASUIST

THE last night at Midway, I had little sleep; the next morning, after the sun was risen, and the clatter of departure had begun to reign on deck, I lay a long while dozing; and when at last I stepped from the companion, the schooner was already leaping through the pass into the open sea. Close on her board, the huge scroll of a breaker unfurled itself along the reef with a prodigious clamour; and behind I saw the wreck vomiting into the morning air a coil of smoke. The wreaths already blew out far to leeward; flames already glittered in the cabin skylight; and the sea-fowl were scattered in surprise as wide as the lagoon. As we drew further off, the conflagration of the *Flying Scud* flamed higher; and long after we had dropped all signs of Midway Island, the smoke still hung in the horizon like that of a distant steamer. With the fading out of that last vestige, the *Norah Creina* passed again into the empty world of cloud and water by which she had approached; and the next features that appeared, eleven days later, to break the line of sky, were the arid mountains of Oahu.

It has often since been a comfortable thought to me that we had thus destroyed the tell-tale remnants of the *Flying Scud;* and often a strange one that my last sight and reminiscence of that fatal ship should be a pillar of smoke on the horizon. To so many others besides myself the same appearance had played a part in the various stages of that business: luring some to what they little imagined, filling some with unimaginable terrors. But ours was the last smoke raised in the story; and with its dying away the secret of the *Flying Scud* became a private property.

It was by the first light of dawn that we saw, close on board, the metropolitan island of Hawaii. We held along the coast, as near as we could venture, with a fresh breeze and under an unclouded heaven; beholding, as we went, the arid mountainsides and scrubby cocoa-palms of that somewhat melancholy archipelago. About four of the afternoon we turned Waimanolo Point, the westerly headland of the great bight of Honolulu; showed ourselves for twenty minutes in full view; and then fell again to leeward, and put in the rest of daylight, plying under shortened sail under the lee of Waimanolo.

A little after dark we beat once more about the point, and crept cautiously toward the mouth of the Pearl Lochs, where Jim and I had arranged I was to meet the smugglers. The night was happily obscure, the water smooth. We showed, according to instructions, no light on deck: only a red lantern dropped from either cathead to within a couple of feet of the water. A look-out was stationed on the bowsprit end, another in the cross-trees; and the whole ship's company crowded forward, scouting for enemies or friends. It was now the crucial moment of our enterprise; we were now risking liberty and credit; and that for a sum so small to a man in my bankrupt situation, that I could have laughed aloud in bitterness. But the piece had been arranged, and we must play it to the finish.

For some while, we saw nothing but the dark mountain outline of the island, the torches of native fishermen glittering here and there along the foreshore, and right in the midst, that cluster of brave lights with which the town of Honolulu advertises itself to the seaward. Presently a ruddy star appeared inshore of us, and seemed to draw near unsteadily. This was the anticipated signal; and we made haste to show the countersign, lowering a white light from the quarter, extinguishing the two others, and laying the schooner incontinently to. The star approached slowly; the sounds of oars and of men's speech came to us across the water; and then a voice hailed us.

" Is that Mr. Dodd?"

" Yes," I returned. " Is Jim Pinkerton there?"

" No, sir," replied the voice. " But there's one of his crowd here; name of Speedy."

"I'm here, Mr. Dodd," added Speedy himself. "I have letters for you."

"All right," I replied. "Come aboard, gentlemen, and let me see my mail."

A whale-boat accordingly ranged alongside, and three men boarded us: my old San Francisco friend, the stock-gambler Speedy, a little wizened person of the name of Sharpe, and a big, flourishing, dissipated-looking man called Fowler. The two last (I learned afterward) were frequent partners; Sharpe supplied the capital, and Fowler, who was quite a character in the islands and occupied a considerable station, brought activity, daring, and a private influence, highly necessary in the case. Both seemed to approach the business with a keen sense of romance; and I believe this was the chief attraction, at least with Fowler — for whom I early conceived a sentiment of liking. But in that first moment I had something else to think of than to judge my new acquaintances; and before Speedy had fished out the letters, the full extent of our misfortune was revealed.

"We've rather bad news for you, Mr. Dodd," said Fowler. "Your firm's gone up."

"Already!" I exclaimed.

"Well, it was thought rather a wonder Pinkerton held on as long as he did," was the reply. "The wreck deal was too big for your credit; you were doing a big business, no doubt, but you were doing it on precious little capital; and when the strain came, you were bound to go. Pinkerton's through all right: seven cents dividend; some

remarks made, but nothing to hurt: the press let
you down easy — I guess Jim had relations there.
The only trouble is, that all this *Flying Scud* affair
got in the papers with the rest; everybody's wide
awake in Honolulu; and the sooner we get the
stuff in and the dollars out, the better for all
concerned."

"Gentlemen," said I, "you must excuse me.
My friend, the captain here, will drink a glass of
champagne with you to give you patience; but as
for myself, I am unfit even for ordinary conversation till I have read these letters."

They demurred a little: and indeed the danger
of delay seemed obvious; but the sight of my distress, which I was unable entirely to control, appealed strongly to their good-nature; and I was
suffered at last to get by myself on deck, where,
by the light of a lantern smuggled under shelter
of the low rail, I read the following wretched
correspondence.

"My dear Loudon," ran the first, "this will be handed
you by your friend Speedy of the *Catamount*. His sterling
character and loyal devotion to yourself pointed him out as
the best man for our purposes in Honolulu — the parties on
the spot being difficult to manipulate. A man called Billy
Fowler (you must have heard of Billy) is the boss; he is in
politics some, and squares the officers. I have hard times
before me in the city, but I feel as bright as a dollar and as
strong as John L. Sullivan. What with Mamie here, and my
partner speeding over the seas, and the bonanza in the wreck,
I feel like I could juggle with the Pyramids of Egypt, same
as conjurers do with aluminium balls. My earnest prayers
follow you, Loudon, that you may feel the way I do — just
inspired ! My feet don't touch the ground; I kind of swim.

Mamie is like Moses and Aaron that held up the other individual's arms. She carries me along like a horse and
buggy. I am beating the record.

> " Your true partner,
>
> " J. PINKERTON."

Number two was in a different style:

" My dearest Loudon, how am I to prepare you for this
dire intelligence? O dear me, it will strike you to the earth.
The Fiat has gone forth; our firm went bust at a quarter
before twelve. It was a bill of Bradley's (for $200) that
brought these vast operations to a close, and evolved liabilities
of upwards of two hundred and fifty thousand. O, the shame
and pity of it! and you but three weeks gone! Loudon,
don't blame your partner: if human hands and brains could
have sufficed, I would have held the thing together. But it
just slowly crumbled; Bradley was the last kick, but the
blamed business just *melted*. I give the liabilities; it's supposed they're all in; for the cowards were waiting, and the
claims were filed like taking tickets to hear Patti. I don't
quite have the hang of the assets yet. our interests were so
extended; but I am at it day and night, and I guess will
make a creditable dividend. If the wreck pans out only half
the way it ought, we'll turn the laugh still. I am as full of
grit and work as ever, and just tower above our troubles.
Mamie is a host in herself. Somehow I feel like it was only
me that had gone bust, and you and she soared clear of it.
Hurry up. That's all you have to do.

> " Yours ever,
>
> " J. PINKERTON."

The third was yet more altered:

" My poor Loudon," it began, " I labour far into the night
getting our affairs in order; you could not believe their vast-
ness and complexity. Douglas B. Longhurst said humorously that the receiver's work would be cut out for him. I
cannot deny that some of them have a speculative look.
God forbid a sensitive, refined spirit like yours should ever

come face to face with a Commissioner in Bankruptcy;
these men get all the sweetness knocked right out of them.
But I could bear up better if it were n't for press comments.
Often and often, Loudon, I recall to mind your most legitimate
critiques of the press system. They published an interview
with me, not the least like what I said, and with *jeering*
comments; it would make your blood boil, it was literally
inhumane; I would n't have written it about a yellow dog
that was in trouble like what I am. Mamie just winced, the
first time she has turned a hair right through the whole
catastrophe. How wonderfully true was what you said long
ago in Paris, about touching on people's personal appearance!
The fellow said —— "

And then these words had been scored through;
and my distressed friend turned to another subject.

"I cannot bear to dwell upon our assets. They simply
don't show up. Even *Thirteen Star*, as sound a line as can
be produced upon this coast, goes begging. The wreck has
thrown a blight on all we ever touched. And where 's the
use? God never made a wreck big enough to fill our deficit.
I am haunted by the thought that you may blame me ; I
know how I despised your remonstrances. O, Loudon, don't
be hard on your miserable partner. The funny-dog business
is what kills. I fear your stern rectitude of mind like the eye
of God. I cannot think but what some of my books seem
mixed up; otherwise, I don't seem to see my way as plain as
I could wish to. Or else my brain is gone soft. Loudon, if
there should be any unpleasantness, you can trust me to
do the right thing and keep you clear. I 've been telling
them already, how you had no business grip and never saw
the books. O, I trust I have done right in this ! I knew
it was a liberty; I know you may justly complain ; but it was
some things that were said. And mind you, all legitimate
business ! Not even your shrinking sensitiveness could find
fault with the first look of one of them, if they had panned
out right. And you know, the *Flying Scud* was the biggest
gamble of the crowd, and that was your own idea. Mamie

says she never could bear to look you in the face, if that idea had been mine ; she is *so* conscientious !

"Your broken-hearted
" Jim."

The last began without formality :

"This is the end of me commercially. I give up ; my nerve is gone. I suppose I ought to be glad ; for we 're through the court. I don't know as ever I knew how, and I 'm sure I don't remember. If it pans out — the wreck, I mean — we 'll go to Europe, and live on the interest of our money. No more work for me. I shake when people speak to me. I have gone on, hoping and hoping, and working and working, and the lead has pinched right out. I want to lie on my back in a garden, and read Shakespeare and E. P. Roe. Don't suppose it 's cowardice, Loudon. I 'm a sick man. Rest is what I must have. I 've worked hard all my life ; I never spared myself ; every dollar I ever made, I 've coined my brains for it. I 've never done a mean thing ; I 've lived respectable, and given to the poor. Who has a better right to a holiday than I have ? And I mean to have a year of it straight out ; and if I don't, I shall lie right down here in my tracks, and die of worry and brain trouble. Don't mistake. That 's so. If there are any pickings at all, *trust Speedy ;* don't let the creditors get wind of what there is. I helped you when you were down ; help me now. Don't deceive yourself ; you 've got to help me right now, or never. I am clerking, and *not fit to cypher.* Mamie 's typewriting at the Phœnix Guano Exchange down town. The light is right out of my life. I know you 'll not like to do what I propose. Think only of this ; that it 's life or death for

" Jim Pinkerton.

"P. S. Our figure was seven per cent. O, what a fall was there ! Well, well, it 's past mending ; I don't want to whine. But, Loudon, I do want to live. No more ambition ; all I ask is life. I have so much to make it sweet to me ! I am clerking, and *useless at that.* I know I would have fired such a clerk inside of forty minutes, in *my* time. But my time 's over. I can only cling on to you. Don't fail.

" Jim Pinkerton."

There was yet one more postscript, yet one more outburst of self-pity and pathetic adjuration; and a doctor's opinion, unpromising enough, was besides enclosed. I pass them both in silence. I think shame to have shown, at so great length, the half-baked virtues of my friend dissolving in the crucible of sickness and distress; and the effect upon my spirits can be judged already. I got to my feet, when I had done, drew a deep breath, and stared hard at Honolulu. One moment the world seemed at an end; the next, I was conscious of a rush of independent energy. On Jim I could rely no longer; I must now take hold myself. I must decide and act on my own better thoughts.

The word was easy to say; the thing, at the first blush, was undiscoverable. I was overwhelmed with miserable, womanish pity for my broken friend; his outcries grieved my spirit; I saw him then and now — then, so invincible; now, brought so low — and knew neither how to refuse, nor how to consent to his proposal. The remembrance of my father, who had fallen in the same field unstained, the image of his monument incongruously rising, a fear of the law, a chill air that seemed to blow upon my fancy from the doors of prisons, and the imaginary clank of fetters, recalled me to a different resolve. And then again, the wails of my sick partner intervened. So I stood hesitating, and yet with a strong sense of capacity behind: sure, if I could but choose my path, that I should walk in it with resolution.

Then I remembered that I had a friend on board, and stepped to the companion.

"Gentlemen," said I, "only a few moments more: but these, I regret to say, I must make more tedious still by removing your companion. It is indispensable that I should have a word or two with Captain Nares."

Both the smugglers were afoot at once, protesting. The business, they declared, must be despatched at once; they had run risk enough, with a conscience; and they must either finish now, or go.

"The choice is yours, gentlemen," said I, "and, I believe, the eagerness. I am not yet sure that I have anything in your way; even if I have, there are a hundred things to be considered; and I assure you it is not at all my habit to do business with a pistol to my head."

"That is all very proper, Mr. Dodd; there is no wish to coerce you, believe me," said Fowler; "only, please consider our position. It is really dangerous; we were not the only people to see your schooner off Waimanolo."

"Mr. Fowler," I replied, "I was not born yesterday. Will you allow me to express an opinion, in which I may be quite wrong, but to which I am entirely wedded? If the custom-house officers had been coming, they would have been here now. In other words, somebody is working the oracle, and (for a good guess) his name is Fowler."

Both men laughed loud and long; and being supplied with another bottle of Longhurst's champagne, suffered the captain and myself to leave them without further word.

I gave Nares the correspondence, and he skimmed it through.

"Now, Captain," said I, "I want a fresh mind on this. What does it mean?"

"It's large enough text," replied the captain. "It means you're to stake your pile on Speedy, hand him over all you can, and hold your tongue. I almost wish you had n't shown it me," he added, wearily. "What with the specie from the wreck and the opium money, it comes to a biggish deal."

"That's supposing that I do it?" said I.

"Exactly," said he, "supposing you do it."

"And there are pros and cons to that," I observed.

"There's San Quentin, to start in with," said the captain; "and suppose you clear the penitentiary, there's the nasty taste in the mouth. The figure's big enough to make bad trouble, but it's not big enough to be picturesque; and I should guess a man always feels kind of small who has sold himself under six cyphers. That would be my way, at least; there's an excitement about a million that might carry me on; but the other way, I should feel kind of lonely when I woke in bed. Then there's Speedy. Do you know him well?"

"No, I do not," said I.

"Well, of course he can vamoose with the entire speculation, if he chooses," pursued the captain, "and if he don't I can't see but what you've got to support and bed and board with him to the end of time. I guess it would weary me. Then there's Mr. Pinkerton, of course. He's been a good friend to you, has n't he? Stood by you, and all that? and pulled you through for all he was worth?"

"That he has," I cried; "I could never begin telling you my debt to him!"

"Well, and that's a consideration," said the captain. "As a matter of principle, I would n't look at this business at the money. 'Not good enough,' would be my word. But even principle goes under when it comes to friends — the right sort, I mean. This Pinkerton is frightened, and he seems sick; the medico don't seem to care a cent about his state of health; and you 've got to figure how you would like it, if he came to die. Remember, the risk of this little swindle is all yours; it 's no sort of risk to Mr. Pinkerton. Well, you 've got to put it that way plainly, and see how you like the sound of it: my friend Pinkerton is in danger of the New Jerusalem, I am in danger of San Quentin; which risk do I propose to run?"

"That's an ugly way to put it," I objected, "and perhaps hardly fair. There's right and wrong to be considered."

"Don't know the parties," replied Nares; "and I 'm coming to them, anyway. For it strikes me, when it came to smuggling opium, you walked right up?"

"So I did," I said; "sick I am to have to say it!"

"All the same," continued Nares, "you went into the opium-smuggling with your head down; and a good deal of fussing I've listened to, that you had n't more of it to smuggle. Now, maybe your partner's not quite fixed the same as you are; maybe he sees precious little difference between the one thing and the other."

"You could not say truer: he sees none, I do believe," cried I; "and though I see one, I could never tell you how."

"We never can," said the oracular Nares; "taste is all a matter of opinion. But the point is, how will your friend take it? You refuse a favour, and you take the high horse at the same time; you disappoint him, and you rap him over the knuckles. It won't do, Mr. Dodd; no friendship can stand that. You must be as good as your friend, or as bad as your friend, or start on a fresh deal without him."

"I don't see it!" said I. "You don't know Jim!"

"Well, you *will* see," said Nares. "And now, here's another point. This bit of money looks mighty big to Mr. Pinkerton; it may spell life or health to him; but among all your creditors, I don't see that it amounts to a hill of beans — I don't believe it'll pay their car-fares all round. And don't you think you'll ever get thanked. You were known to pay a long price for the chance of rummaging that wreck; you do the rummaging, you come home, and you hand over ten thousand — or twenty, if you like — a part of which

you 'll have to own up you made by smuggling;
and, mind! you 'll never get Billy Fowler to stick
his name to a receipt. Now, just glance at the
transaction from the outside, and see what a clear
case it makes. Your ten thousand is a sop; and
people will only wonder you were so damned im-
pudent as to offer such a small one! Whichever
way you take it, Mr. Dodd, the bottom 's out of
your character; so there 's one thing less to be
considered."

"I dare say you 'll scarce believe me," said I,
"but I feel that a positive relief."

"You must be made some way different from
me, then," returned Nares. "And, talking about
me, I might just mention how I stand. You 'll
have no trouble from me — you 've trouble enough
of your own; and I 'm friend enough, when a
friend 's in need, to shut my eyes and go right
where he tells me. All the same, I 'm rather
queerly fixed. My owners 'll have to rank with
the rest on their charter-party. Here am I, their
representative! and I have to look over the ship's
side while the bankrupt walks his assets ashore in
Mr. Speedy 's hat-box. It 's a thing I would n't do
for James G. Blaine; but I 'll do it for you, Mr.
Dodd, and only sorry I can't do more."

"Thank you, Captain; my mind is made up,"
said I. "I 'll go straight, *ruat cælum!* I never
understood that old tag before to-night."

"I hope it is n't my business that decides you?"
asked the captain.

"I 'll never deny it was an element," said I.

"I hope, I hope I'm not cowardly; I hope I could steal for Jim myself; but when it comes to dragging in you and Speedy, and this one and the other, why, Jim has got to die, and there's an end. I'll try and work for him when I get to 'Frisco, I suppose; and I suppose I'll fail, and look on at his death, and kick myself: it can't be helped — I'll fight it on this line."

"I don't say as you're wrong," replied Nares, "and I'll be hanged if I know if you're right. It suits me anyway. And look here — hadn't you better just show our friends over the side?" he added; "no good of being at the risk and worry of smuggling for the benefit of creditors."

"I don't think of the creditors," said I. "But I've kept this pair so long, I haven't got the brass to fire them now."

Indeed, I believe that was my only reason for entering upon a transaction which was now outside my interest, but which (as it chanced) repaid me fifty-fold in entertainment. Fowler and Sharpe were both preternaturally sharp; they did me the honour in the beginning to attribute to myself their proper vices; and before we were done had grown to regard me with an esteem akin to worship. This proud position I attained by no more recondite arts, than telling the mere truth and unaffectedly displaying my indifference to the result. I have doubtless stated the essentials of all good diplomacy, which may be rather regarded, therefore, as a grace of state, than the effect of management. For to tell the truth is not

in itself diplomatic, and to have no care for the
result a thing involuntary. When I mentioned,
for instance, that I had but two hundred and forty
pound of drug, my smugglers exchanged meaning
glances, as who should say, " Here is a foeman
worthy of our steel!" But when I carelessly proposed thirty-five dollars a pound, as an amendment
to their offered twenty, and wound up with the
remark: " The whole thing is a matter of moon-
shine to me, gentlemen. Take it or want it, and
fill your glasses " — I had the indescribable gratification to see Sharpe nudge Fowler warningly,
and Fowler choke down the jovial acceptance that
stood ready on his lips, and lamely substitute a
" No — no more wine, please, Mr. Dodd!" Nor
was this all: for when the affair was settled at fifty
dollars a pound — a shrewd stroke of business for
my creditors — and our friends had got on board
their whale-boat and shoved off, it appeared they
were imperfectly acquainted with the conveyance
of sound upon still water, and I had the joy to
overhear the following testimonial.

" Deep man, that Dodd," said Sharpe.

And the bass-toned Fowler echoed, "Damned
if I understand his game."

Thus we were left once more alone upon the
Norah Creina; and the news of the night, and the
lamentations of Pinkerton, and the thought of my
own harsh decision, returned and besieged me in
the dark. According to all the rubbish I had read,
I should have been sustained by the warm consciousness of virtue. Alas, I had but the one

feeling: that I had sacrificed my sick friend to the fear of prison-cells and stupid starers. And no moralist has yet advanced so far as to number cowardice amongst the things that are their own reward.

CHAPTER XVII

LIGHT FROM THE MAN OF WAR

IN the early sunlight of the next day, we tossed close off the buoy and saw the city sparkle in its groves about the foot of the Punch-bowl, and the masts clustering thick in the small harbour. A good breeze, which had risen with the sea, carried us triumphantly through the intricacies of the passage; and we had soon brought up not far from the landing-stairs. I remember to have remarked an ugly horned reptile of a modern war-ship in the usual moorings across the port, but my mind was so profoundly plunged in melancholy that I paid no heed.

Indeed, I had little time at my disposal. Messieurs Sharpe and Fowler had left the night before in the persuasion that I was a liar of the first magnitude; the genial belief brought them aboard again with the earliest opportunity, proffering help to one who had proved how little he required it, and hospitality to so respectable a character. I had business to mind, I had some need both of assistance and diversion; I liked Fowler—I don't know why; and in short, I let them do with me as they desired. No creditor intervening, I spent the first half of the day inquiring into the conditions of the tea

and silk market under the auspices of Sharpe;
lunched with him in a private apartment at the
Hawaiian Hotel — for Sharpe was a teetotaller in
public; and about four in the afternoon was delivered into the hands of Fowler. This gentleman
owned a bungalow on the Waikiki beach; and there
in company with certain young bloods of Honolulu, I was entertained to a sea-bathe, indiscrimi-
nate cocktails, a dinner, a *hula-hula,* and (to round
off the night) poker and assorted liquors. To lose
money in the small hours to pale, intoxicated youth,
has always appeared to me a pleasure overrated.
In my then frame of mind, I confess I found it
even delightful; put up my money (or rather my
creditors'), and put down Fowler's champagne
with equal avidity and success; and awoke the
next morning to a mild headache and the rather
agreeable lees of the last night's excitement. The
young bloods, many of whom were still far from
sober, had taken the kitchen into their own hands,
vice the Chinaman deposed; and since each was
engaged upon a dish of his own, and none had
the least scruple in demolishing his neighbour's
handiwork, I became early convinced that many
eggs would be broken and few omelets made. The
discovery of a jug of milk and a crust of bread
enabled me to stay my appetite; and since it was
Sunday, when no business could be done, and the
festivities were to be renewed that night in the
abode of Fowler, it occurred to me to slip silently
away and enjoy some air and solitude.

I turned seaward under the dead crater known

as Diamond Head. My way was for some time
under the shade of certain thickets of green, thorny
trees, dotted with houses. Here I enjoyed some
pictures of the native life: wide-eyed, naked children, mingled with pigs; a youth asleep under a
tree; an old gentleman spelling through glasses
his Hawaiian Bible; the somewhat embarrassing
spectacle of a lady at her bath in a spring; and
the glimpse of gaudy-coloured gowns in the deep
shade of the houses. Thence I found a road along
the beach itself, wading in sand, opposed and buf-
feted by the whole weight of the trade: on one
hand, the glittering and sounding surf, and the bay
lively with many sails; on the other, precipitous,
arid gullies and sheer cliffs, mounting towards the
crater and the blue sky. For all the companionship of skimming vessels, the place struck me with
a sense of solitude. There came in my head what
I had been told the day before at dinner, of a
cavern above in the bowels of the volcano, a place
only to be visited with the light of torches, a
treasure-house of the bones of priests and war-
riors, and clamorous with the voice of an unseen
river pouring seaward through the crannies of the
mountain. At the thought, it was revealed to me
suddenly, how the bungalows, and the Fowlers,
and the bright, busy town and crowding ships,
were all children of yesterday; and for centuries
before, the obscure life of the natives, with its
glories and ambitions, its joys and crimes and
agonies, had rolled unseen, like the mountain river,
in that sea-girt place. Not Chaldea appeared more

ancient, nor the Pyramids of Egypt more abstruse;
and I heard time measured by "the drums and
tramplings" of immemorial conquests, and saw
myself the creature of an hour. Over the bankruptcy of Pinkerton and Dodd of Montana Block,
S. F., and the conscientious troubles of the junior
partner, the spirit of eternity was seen to smile.

To this mood of philosophic sadness, my excesses of the night before no doubt contributed;
for more things than virtue are at times their own
reward: but I was greatly healed at least of my
distresses. And while I was yet enjoying my abstracted humour, a turn of the beach brought me
in view of the signal station, with its watch-house
and flag-staff, perched on the immediate margin
of a cliff. The house was new and clean and bald,
and stood naked to the trades. The wind beat
about it in loud squalls; the seaward windows rattled without mercy; the breach of the surf below
contributed its increment of noise; and the fall
of my foot in the narrow veranda passed unheard
by those within.

They were two on whom I thus entered unexpectedly: the look-out man, with grizzled beard,
keen seaman's eyes, and that brand on his countenance that comes of solitary living; and a visitor,
an oldish oratorical fellow, in the smart tropical
array of the British man-o'-war's man, perched on
a table, and smoking a cigar. I was made pleasantly welcome, and was soon listening with amusement to the sea-lawyer.

"No, if I had n't have been born an English-

man," was one of his sentiments, "damn me! I 'd
rather 'a' been born a Frenchy! I 'd like to see
another nation fit to black their boots." Presently
after, he developed his views on home politics with
similar trenchancy. "I 'd rather be a brute beast
than what I 'd be a liberal," he said. "Carrying
banners and that! a pig 's got more sense. Why,
look at our chief engineer — they do say he carried a banner with his own 'ands: 'Hooroar for
Gladstone!' I suppose, or 'Down with the Aristocracy!' What 'arm does the aristocracy do?
Show me a country any good without one! Not
the States; why, it 's the 'ome of corruption! I
knew a man — he was a good man, 'ome born —
who was signal quartermaster in the *Wyandotte*.
He told me he could never have got there, if he
had n't have ' run with the boys ' — told it me as
I 'm telling you. Now we 're all British subjects
here —— " he was going on.

"I am afraid I am an American," I said
apologetically.

He seemed the least bit taken aback, but recovered himself; and with the ready tact of his betters,
paid me the usual British compliment on the ri-
poste. "You don't say so!" he exclaimed. "Well,
I give you my word of honour, I 'd never have
guessed it. Nobody could tell it on you," said he,
as though it were some form of liquor.

I thanked him, as I always do, at this particular
stage, with his compatriots: not so much perhaps
for the compliment to myself and my poor country,
as for the revelation (which is ever fresh to me)

22

of Britannic self-sufficiency and taste. And he was so far softened by my gratitude, as to add a word of praise on the American method of lacing sails. "You 're ahead of us in lacing sails," he said. "You can say that with a clear conscience."

"Thank you," I replied. "I shall certainly do so."

At this rate, we got along swimmingly; and when I rose to retrace my steps to the Fowlery, he at once started to his feet and offered me the welcome solace of his company for the return. I believe I discovered much alacrity at the idea: for the creature (who seemed to be unique, or to represent a type like that of the dodo) entertained me hugely. But when he had produced his hat, I found I was in the way of more than entertainment; for on the ribbon I could read the legend: "H. M. S. Tempest."

"I say," I began, when our adieus were paid, and we were scrambling down the path from the look-out, "it was your ship that picked up the men on board the *Flying Scud,* was n't it?"

"You may say so," said he. "And a blessed good job for the Flying-Scuds. It 's a God-forsaken spot, that Midway Island."

"I 've just come from there," said I. "It was I who bought the wreck."

"Beg your pardon, sir," cried the sailor: "gen'-lem'n in the white schooner?"

"The same," said I.

My friend saluted, as though we were now, for the first time, formally introduced.

"Of course," I continued, "I am rather taken up with the whole story; and I wish you would tell me what you can of how the men were saved."

"It was like this," said he. "We had orders to call at Midway after castaways, and had our distance pretty nigh run down the day before. We steamed half-speed all night, looking to make it about noon; for old Tootles — beg your pardon, sir — the captain — was precious scared of the place at night. Well, there 's nasty, filthy currents round that Midway; *you* know, as has been there; and one on 'em must have set us down. Leastways, about six bells, when we had ought to been miles away, some one sees a sail, and lo and be'old, there was the spars of a full-rigged brig! We raised her pretty fast, and the island after her; and made out she was hard aground, canted on her bilge, and had her ens'n flying, union down. It was breaking 'igh on the reef, and we laid well out, and sent a couple of boats. I did n't go in neither; only stood and looked on; but it seems they was all badly scared and muddled, and did n't know which end was uppermost. One on 'em kep' snivelling and wringing of his 'ands; he come on board all of a sop like a monthly nurse. That Trent, he come first, with his 'and in a bloody rag. I was near 'em as I am to you; and I could make out he was all to bits — 'eard his breath rattle in his blooming lungs as he come down the ladder. Yes, they was a scared lot, small blame to 'em, *I* say! The next after Trent, come him as was mate."

"Goddedaal!" I exclaimed.

"And a good name for him, too," chuckled the man-o'-war's man, who probably confounded the word with a familiar oath. "A good name, too; only it were n't his. He was a gen'lem'n born, sir, as had gone maskewerading. One of our officers knowed him at 'ome, reckonises him, steps up, 'olds out his 'and right off, and says he: ''Ullo, Norrie, old chappie!' he says. The other was coming up, as bold as look at it; did n't seem put out — that's where blood tells, sir! Well, no sooner does he 'ear his born name given him, than he turns as white as the Day of Judgment, stares at Mr. Sebright like he was looking at a ghost, and then (I give you my word of honour) turned to, and doubled up in a dead faint. 'Take him down to my berth,' says Mr. Sebright. ''T is poor old Norrie Carthew,' he says."

"And what — what sort of a gentleman was this Mr. Carthew?" I gasped.

"The ward-room steward told me he was come of the best blood in England," was my friend's reply: "Eton and 'Arrow bred; — and might have been a bar'net!"

"No, but to look at?" I corrected him.

"The same as you or me," was the uncompromising answer: "not much to look at. *I* did n't know he was a gen'lem'n; but then, I never see him cleaned up."

"How was that?" I cried. "O, yes, I remember: he was sick all the way to 'Frisco, was he not?"

" Sick, or sorry, or something," returned my
informant. " My belief, he did n't hanker after
showing up. He kep' close; the ward-room steward, what took his meals in, told me he ate nex'
to nothing; and he was fetched ashore at 'Frisco
on the quiet. Here was how it was. It seems
his brother had took and died, him as had the
estate. This one had gone in for his beer, by
what I could make out; the old folks at 'ome had
turned rusty; no one knew where he had gone to.
Here he was, slaving in a merchant brig, ship-
wrecked on Midway, and packing up his duds
for a long voyage in a open boat. He comes on
board our ship, and by God, here he is a landed
proprietor, and may be in Parliament to-morrow!
It 's no less than natural he should keep dark: so
would you and me, in the same box."

" I dare say," said I. " But you saw more of
the others? "

" To be sure," says he: " no 'arm in them from
what I see. There was one 'Ardy there: colonial
born he was, and had been through a power of
money. There was no nonsense about 'Ardy; he
had been up, and he had come down, and took it
so. His 'eart was in the right place; and he was
well informed, and knew French; and Latin, I
believe, like a native! I liked that 'Ardy; he was
a good-looking boy, too."

" Did they say much about the wreck? " I
asked.

" There was n't much to say, I reckon," replied
the man-o'-war's man. " It was all in the papers.

'Ardy used to yarn most about the coins he had gone through; he had lived with book-makers, and jockeys, and pugs, and actors, and all that: a precious low lot!" added this judicious person. "But it's about here my 'orse is moored, and by your leave I'll be getting ahead."

"One moment," said I. "Is Mr. Sebright on board?"

"No, sir, he's ashore to-day," said the sailor. "I took up a bag for him to the 'otel."

With that we parted. Presently after my friend overtook and passed me on a hired steed which seemed to scorn its cavalier; and I was left in the dust of his passage, a prey to whirling thoughts. For I now stood, or seemed to stand, on the immediate threshold of these mysteries. I knew the name of the man Dickson — his name was Carthew; I knew where the money came from that opposed us at the sale — it was part of Carthew's inheritance; and in my gallery of illustrations to the history of the wreck, one more picture hung; perhaps the most dramatic of the series. It showed me the deck of a war-ship in that distant part of the great ocean, the officers and seamen looking curiously on; and a man of birth and education, who had been sailing under an alias on a trading-brig, and was now rescued from desperate peril, felled like an ox by the bare sound of his own name. I could not fail to be reminded of my own experience at the Occidental telephone. The hero of three styles, Dickson, Goddedaal, or Carthew, must be the owner of a lively — or a

loaded — conscience, and the reflection recalled to
me the photograph found on board the *Flying
Scud;* just such a man, I reasoned, would be capable of just such starts and crises; and I inclined
to think that Goddedaal (or Carthew) was the
mainspring of the mystery.

One thing was plain: as long as the *Tempest*
was in reach, I must make the acquaintance of
both Sebright and the doctor. To this end, I
excused myself with Mr. Fowler, returned to
Honolulu, and passed the remainder of the day
hanging vainly round the cool verandas of the
hotel. It was near nine o'clock at night before
I was rewarded.

"That is the gentleman you were asking for,"
said the clerk.

I beheld a man in tweeds, of an incomparable
languor of demeanour, and carrying a cane with
genteel effort. From the name, I had looked to
find a sort of viking and young ruler of the battle
and the tempest; and I was the more disappointed,
and not a little alarmed, to come face to face with
this impracticable type.

"I believe I have the pleasure of addressing
Lieutenant Sebright," said I, stepping forward.

"Aw, yes," replied the hero; "but, aw! I dawn't
knaw you, do I?" (He spoke for all the world
like Lord Foppington in the old play — a proof
of the perennial nature of man's affectations.
But his limping dialect, I scorn to continue to
reproduce.)

"It was with the intention of making myself

known, that I have taken this step," said I, entirely unabashed (for impudence begets in me its like — perhaps my only martial attribute). " We have a common subject of interest, to me very lively; and I believe I may be in a position to be of some service to a friend of yours — to give him, at least, some very welcome information."

The last clause was a sop to my conscience: I could not pretend, even to myself, either the power or the will to serve Mr. Carthew; but I felt sure he would like to hear the *Flying Scud* was burned.

" I don't know — I — I don't understand you," stammered my victim. " I don't have any friends in Honolulu, don't you know?"

" The friend to whom I refer is English," I replied. " It is Mr. Carthew, whom you picked up at Midway. My firm has bought the wreck; I am just returned from breaking her up; and — to make my business quite clear to you — I have a communication it is necessary I should make; and have to trouble you for Mr. Carthew's address."

It will be seen how rapidly I had dropped all hope of interesting the frigid British bear. He, on his side, was plainly on thorns at my insistence; I judged he was suffering torments of alarm lest I should prove an undesirable acquaintance; diagnosed him for a shy, dull, vain, unamiable animal, without adequate defence — a sort of dishoused snail; and concluded, rightly enough, that he would consent to anything to bring our interview

to a conclusion. A moment later, he had fled,
leaving with me a sheet of paper, thus inscribed:

Norris Carthew,

  Stallbridge-le-Carthew,

.   *Dorset.*

I might have cried victory, the field of battle
and some of the enemy's baggage remaining in
my occupation. As a matter of fact, my moral
sufferings during the engagement had rivalled
those of Mr. Sebright; I was left incapable of fresh
hostilities; I owned that the navy of old England
was (for me) invincible as of yore; and giving
up all thought of the doctor, inclined to salute her
veteran flag, in the future, from a prudent distance. Such was my inclination, when I retired
to rest; and my first experience the next morning
strengthened it to certainty. For I had the
pleasure of encountering my fair antagonist on
his way on board; and he honoured me with a
recognition so disgustingly dry, that my impatience overflowed, and (recalling the tactics of
Nelson) I neglected to perceive or to return it.

Judge of my astonishment, some half-hour later,
to receive a note of invitation from the *Tempest.*

" Dear Sir," it began, " we are all naturally
very much interested in the wreck of the *Flying
Scud,* and as soon as I mentioned that I had the
pleasure of making your acquaintance, a very general wish was expressed that you would come and
dine on board. It will give us all the greatest

pleasure to see you to-night, or in case you should be otherwise engaged, to luncheon either to-morrow or to-day." A note of the hours followed, and the document wound up with the name of " J. Lascelles Sebright," under an undeniable statement that he was sincerely mine.

" No, Mr. Lascelles Sebright," I reflected, " you are not, but I begin to suspect that (like the lady in the song) you are another's. You have mentioned your adventure, my friend; you have been blown up; you have got your orders; this note has been dictated; and I am asked on board (in spite of your melancholy protests) not to meet the men, and not to talk about the *Flying Scud*, but to undergo the scrutiny of some one interested in Carthew: the doctor, for a wager. And for a second wager, all this springs from your facility in giving the address." I lost no time in answering the billet, electing for the earliest occasion; and at the appointed hour, a somewhat blackguard-looking boat's crew from the *Norah Creina* conveyed me under the guns of the *Tempest*.

The ward-room appeared pleased to see me; Sebright's brother officers, in contrast to himself, took a boyish interest in my cruise; and much was talked of the *Flying Scud;* of how she had been lost, of how I had found her, and of the weather, the anchorage, and the currents about Midway Island. Carthew was referred to more than once without embarrassment; the parallel case of a late Earl of Aberdeen, who died mate on board a Yankee schooner, was adduced. If they told

me little of the man, it was because they had not
much to tell, and only felt an interest in his recognition and pity for his prolonged ill-health.   I
could never think the subject was avoided; and
it was clear that the officers, far from practising
concealment, had nothing to conceal.

So far, then, all seemed natural, and yet the
doctor troubled me. This was a tall, rugged, plain
man, on the wrong side of fifty, already grey, and
with a restless mouth and bushy eyebrows: he
spoke seldom, but then with gaiety; and his great,
quaking, silent laughter was infectious. I could
make out that he was at once the quiz of the ward-
room and perfectly respected; and I made sure that
he observed me covertly. It is certain I returned
the compliment. If Carthew had feigned sickness
— and all seemed to point in that direction — here
was the man who knew all — or certainly knew
much. His strong, sterling face progressively and
silently persuaded of his full knowledge. That
was not the mouth, these were not the eyes of one
who would act in ignorance, or could be led at
random. Nor again was it the face of a man
squeamish in the case of malefactors; there was
even a touch of Brutus there, and something of
the hanging judge. In short, he seemed the last
character for the part assigned him in my theories;
and wonder and curiosity contended in my mind.

Luncheon was over, and an adjournment to
the smoking-room proposed, when (upon a sudden impulse) I burned my ships, and pleading
indisposition, requested to consult the doctor.

"There is nothing the matter with my body, Dr. Urquart," said I, as soon as we were alone.

He hummed, his mouth worked, he regarded me steadily with his grey eyes, but resolutely held his peace.

"I want to talk to you about the *Flying Scud* and Mr. Carthew," I resumed. "Come: you must have expected this. I am sure you know all; you are shrewd, and must have a guess that I know much. How are we to stand to one another? and how am I to stand to Mr. Carthew?"

"I do not fully understand you," he replied, after a pause; and then, after another: "It is the spirit I refer to, Mr. Dodd."

"The spirit of my inquiries?" I asked.

He nodded.

"I think we are at cross-purposes," said I. "The spirit is precisely what I came in quest of. I bought the *Flying Scud* at a ruinous figure, run up by Mr. Carthew through an agent; and I am, in consequence, a bankrupt. But if I have found no fortune in the wreck, I have found unmistakable evidences of foul play. Conceive my position: I am ruined through this man, whom I never saw; I might very well desire revenge or compensation; and I think you will admit I have the means to extort either."

He made no sign in answer to this challenge.

"Can you not understand, then," I resumed, "the spirit in which I come to one who is surely in the secret, and ask him, honestly and plainly: How do I stand to Mr. Carthew?"

"I must ask you to be more explicit," said he.

"You do not help me much," I retorted. "But see if you can understand: my conscience is not very fine spun; still, I have one. Now, there are degrees of foul play, to some of which I have no particular objection. I am sure with Mr. Carthew, I am not at all the person to forego an advantage; and I have much curiosity. But on the other hand, I have no taste for persecution; and I ask you to believe that I am not the man to make bad worse, or heap trouble on the unfortunate."

"Yes; I think I understand," said he. "Suppose I pass you my word that, whatever may have occurred, there were excuses — great excuses — I may say, very great?"

"It would have weight with me, doctor," I replied.

"I may go further," he pursued. "Suppose I had been there or you had been there: after a certain event had taken place, it's a grave question what we might have done — it's even a question what we could have done — ourselves. Or take me. I will be plain with you, and own that I am in possession of the facts. You have a shrewd guess how I have acted in that knowledge. May I ask you to judge from the character of my action, something of the nature of that knowledge, which I have no call, nor yet no title, to share with you?"

I cannot convey a sense of the rugged conviction and judicial emphasis of Dr. Urquart's speech: to those who did not hear him. it may appear as if he fed me on enigmas; to myself, who heard, I seemed to have received a lesson and a compliment.

"I thank you," I said. "I feel you have said as much as possible, and more than I had any right to ask. I take that as a mark of confidence, which I will try to deserve. I hope, sir, you will let me regard you as a friend."

He evaded my proffered friendship with a blunt proposal to rejoin the mess; and yet a moment later, contrived to alleviate the snub. For, as we entered the smoking-room, he laid his hand on my shoulder with a kind familiarity.

"I have just prescribed for Mr. Dodd," says he, "a glass of our Madeira."

I have never again met Dr. Urquart; but he wrote himself so clear upon my memory that I think I see him still. And indeed I had cause to remember the man for the sake of his communication. It was hard enough to make a theory fit the circumstances of the *Flying Scud;* but one in which the chief actor should stand the least excused, and might retain the esteem or at least the pity of a man like Dr. Urquart, failed me utterly. Here at least was the end of my discoveries; I learned no more, till I learned all; and my reader has the evidence complete. Is he more astute than I was? or, like me, does he give it up?

CHAPTER XVIII

CROSS-QUESTIONS AND CROOKED ANSWERS

I HAVE said hard words of San Francisco;
they must scarce be literally understood (one
cannot suppose the Israelites did justice to
the land of Pharaoh); and the city took a fine
revenge of me on my return. She had never
worn a more becoming guise; the sun shone, the
air was lively, the people had flowers in their but-
tonholes and smiles upon their faces; and as I
made my way towards Jim's place of employment,
with some very black anxieties at heart, I seemed
to myself a blot on the surrounding gaiety.

My destination was in a by-street, in a mean,
rickety building; "The Franklin H. Dodge Steam
Printing Company" appeared upon its front, and
in characters of greater freshness, so as to suggest recent conversion, the watch-cry, "White
Labor Only." In the office, in a dusty pen, Jim
sat alone before a table. A wretched change had
overtaken him in clothes, body, and bearing; he
looked sick and shabby; he who had once rejoiced
in his day's employment, like a horse among pas-
tures, now sat staring on a column of accounts,
idly chewing a pen, at times heavily sighing, the
picture of inefficiency and inattention. He was

sunk deep in a painful reverie; he neither saw
nor heard me; and I stood and watched him unobserved. I had a sudden vain relenting. Re-
pentance bludgeoned me. As I had predicted to
Nares, I stood and kicked myself. Here was I
come home again, my honour saved; there was
my friend in want of rest, nursing, and a generous diet; and I asked myself with Falstaff, " What
is in that word honour? what is that honour? "
and, like Falstaff, I told myself that it was
air.

" Jim! " said I.

" Loudon! " he gasped, and jumped from his
chair and stood shaking.

The next moment I was over the barrier, and
we were hand in hand.

" My poor old man! " I cried.

" Thank God you 're home at last! " he gulped,
and kept patting my shoulder with his hand.

" I 've no good news for you, Jim! " said I.

" You 've come — that 's the good news that I
want," he replied. " O, how I 've longed for you,
Loudon! "

" I could n't do what you wrote me," I said,
lowering my voice. " The creditors have it all.
I could n't do it."

" Ssh! " returned Jim. " I was crazy when I
wrote. I could never have looked Mamie in the
face if we 'd have done it. O, Loudon, what a
gift that woman is! You think you know something of life: you just don't know anything. It 's
the *goodness* of the woman, it 's a revelation! "

"That's all right," said I. "That's how I hoped to hear you, Jim."

"And so the *Flying Scud* was a fraud," he resumed. "I didn't quite understand your letter, but I made out that."

"Fraud is a mild term for it," said I. "The creditors will never believe what fools we were. And that reminds me," I continued, rejoicing in the transition, "how about the bankruptcy?"

"You were lucky to be out of that," answered Jim, shaking his head; "you were lucky not to see the papers. The *Occidental* called me a fifth-rate Kerbstone broker with water on the brain; another said I was a tree-frog that had got into the same meadow with Longhurst, and had blown myself out till I went pop. It was rough on a man in his honeymoon; so was what they said about my looks, and what I had on, and the way I perspired. But I braced myself up with the *Flying Scud*. How did it exactly figure out anyway? I don't seem to catch on to that story, Loudon."

"The devil you don't!" thinks I to myself; and then aloud: "You see we had neither one of us good luck. I didn't do much more than cover current expenses; and you got floored immediately. How did we come to go so soon?"

"Well, we'll have to have a talk over all this," said Jim with a sudden start. "I should be getting to my books; and I guess you had better go up right away to Mamie. She's at Speedy's. She expects you with impatience. She regards you in the light of a favourite brother, Loudon."

Any scheme was welcome which allowed me to postpone the hour of explanation, and avoid (were it only for a breathing space) the topic of the *Flying Scud*. I hastened accordingly to Bush Street. Mrs. Speedy, already rejoicing in the return of a spouse, hailed me with acclamation. "And it's beautiful you're looking, Mr. Dodd, my dear," she was kind enough to say. "And a miracle they naygur waheenies let ye lave the oilands. I have my suspicions of Shpeedy," she added, roguishly. "Did ye see him after the naygresses now?"

I gave Speedy an unblemished character.

"The one of ye will niver bethray the other," said the playful dame, and ushered me into a bare room, where Mamie sat working a type-writer.

I was touched by the cordiality of her greeting. With the prettiest gesture in the world she gave me both her hands; wheeled forth a chair; and produced, from a cupboard, a tin of my favourite tobacco and a book of my exclusive cigarette papers.

"There!" she cried, "you see, Mr. Loudon, we were all prepared for you; the things were bought the very day you sailed."

I imagine she had always intended me a pleasant welcome; but the certain fervour of sincerity, which I could not help remarking, flowed from an unexpected source. Captain Nares, with a kindness for which I can never be sufficiently grateful, had stolen a moment from his occupations, driven to call on Mamie, and drawn her a generous picture of my prowess at the wreck. She was careful not to breathe a word of this interview, till she had led me on to tell my adventures for myself.

"Ah! Captain Nares was better," she cried, when I had done. "From your account, I have only learned one new thing, that you are modest as well as brave."

I cannot tell with what sort of disclamation I sought to reply.

"It is of no use," said Mamie. "I know a hero. And when I heard of you working all day like a common labourer, with your hands bleeding and your nails broken — and how you told the captain to 'crack on' (I think he said) in the storm, when he was terrified himself — and the danger of that horrid mutiny" — (Nares had been obligingly dipping his brush in earthquake and eclipse) — "and how it was all done, in part at least, for Jim and me — I felt we could never say how we admired and thanked you."

"Mamie," I cried, "don't talk of thanks; it is not a word to be used between friends. Jim and I have been prosperous together; now we shall be poor together. We've done our best, and that's all that need be said. The next thing is for me to find a situation, and send you and Jim up country for a long holiday in the redwoods — for a holiday Jim has got to have."

"Jim can't take your money, Mr. Loudon," said Mamie.

"Jim?" cried I. "He's got to. Did n't I take his?"

Presently after, Jim himself arrived, and before he had yet done mopping his brow, he was at me with the accursed subject. "Now, Loudon," said he, "here we are all together, the day's work done and the evening before us; just start in with the whole story."

"One word on business first," said I, speaking from the lips outward, and meanwhile (in the private apartments of my brain) trying for the thousandth time to find some plausible arrangement of my story. "I want to have a notion how we stand about the bankruptcy."

"O, that's ancient history," cried Jim. "We paid seven cents, and a wonder we did as well. The receiver — "(methought a spasm seized him at the name of this official, and he broke off). "But it's all past and done with anyway; and what I want to get at is the facts about the wreck. I don't seem to understand it: appears to me like as there was something underneath."

"There was nothing *in* it anyway," I said, with a forced laugh.

"That's what I want to judge of," returned Jim.

"How the mischief is it I can never keep you to that bankruptcy? It looks as if you avoided it," said I — for a man in my situation, with unpardonable folly.

"Don't it look a little as if you were trying to avoid the wreck?" asked Jim.

It was my own doing; there was no retreat.

"My dear fellow, if you make a point of it, here goes!" said I, and launched with spurious gaiety into the current of my tale. I told it with point and spirit; described the island and the wreck, mimicked Anderson and the Chinese, maintained the suspense. . . . My pen has stumbled on the fatal word. I maintained the suspense so well that it was never relieved; and when I stopped — I dare not say concluded, where there was no conclusion — I found Jim and Mamie regarding me with surprise.

"Well?" said Jim.

"Well, that 's all," said I.

"But how do you explain it?" he asked.

"I can't explain it," said I.

Mamie wagged her head ominously.

"But, great Cæsar's ghost! the money was offered!" cried Jim. "It won't do, Loudon; it 's nonsense, on the face of it! I don't say but what you and Nares did your best; I 'm sure, of course, you did; but I do say, you got fooled. I say the stuff is in that ship to-day, and I say I mean to get it."

"There is nothing in the ship, I tell you, but old wood and iron!" said I.

"You 'll see," said Jim. "Next time I go myself. I 'll take Mamie for the trip; Longhurst won't refuse me the expense of a schooner. You wait till I get the searching of her."

"But you can't search her!" cried I. "She 's burned."

"Burned!" cried Mamie, starting a little from

the attitude of quiescent capacity in which she had hitherto sat to hear me, her hands folded in her lap.

There was an appreciable pause.

" I beg your pardon, Loudon," began Jim at last, " but why in snakes did you burn her?"

" It was an idea of Nares's," said I.

" This is certainly the strangest circumstance of all," observed Mamie.

" I must say, Loudon, it does seem kind of unexpected," added Jim. " It seems kind of crazy even. What did you — what did Nares expect to gain by burning her?"

" I don't know; it did n't seem to matter; we had got all there was to get," said I.

" That 's the very point," cried Jim. " It was quite plain you had n't."

" What made you so sure?" asked Mamie.

" How can I tell you?" I cried. " We had been all through her. We *were* sure; that 's all that I can say."

" I begin to think you were," she returned, with a significant emphasis.

Jim hurriedly intervened. " What I don't quite make out, Loudon, is that you don't seem to appreciate the peculiarities of the thing," said he. " It does n't seem to have struck you same as it does me."

" Pshaw! why go on with this?" cried Mamie, suddenly rising. " Mr. Dodd is not telling us either what he thinks or what he knows."

" Mamie!" cried Jim.

"You need not be concerned for his feelings, James; he is not concerned for yours," returned the lady. "He dare not deny it, besides. And this is not the first time he has practised reticence. Have you forgotten that he knew the address, and did not tell it you until that man had escaped?"

Jim turned to me pleadingly; we were all on our feet. "Loudon," he said, "you see Mamie has some fancy; and I must say there's just a sort of a shadow of an excuse; for it *is* bewildering — even to me, Loudon, with my trained business intelligence. For God's sake, clear it up."

"This serves me right," said I. "I should not have tried to keep you in the dark; I should have told you at first that I was pledged to secrecy; I should have asked you to trust me in the beginning. It is all I can do now. There is more of the story, but it concerns none of us, and my tongue is tied. I have given my word of honour. You must trust me and try to forgive me."

"I dare say I am very stupid, Mr. Dodd," begun Mamie, with an alarming sweetness, "but I thought you went upon this trip as my husband's representative and with my husband's money? You tell us now that you are pledged, but I should have thought you were pledged first of all to James. You say it does not concern us; we are poor people, and my husband is sick, and it concerns us a great deal to understand how we come to have lost our money, and why our representative comes back to us with nothing. You ask that we should trust you; you do not seem to under-

stand; the question we are asking ourselves is
whether we have not trusted you too much."

"I do not ask you to trust me," I replied. "I
ask Jim. He knows me."

"You think you can do what you please with
James; you trust to his affection, do you not?
And me, I suppose, you do not consider," said
Mamie. "But it was perhaps an unfortunate day
for you when we were married, for I at least am
not blind. The crew run away, the ship is sold for
a great deal of money, you know that man's address
and you conceal it, you do not find what you were
sent to look for, and yet you burn the ship; and
now, when we ask explanations, you are pledged
to secrecy! But I am pledged to no such thing;
I will not stand by in silence and see my sick and
ruined husband betrayed by his condescending
friend. I will give you the truth for once. Mr.
Dodd, you have been bought and sold."

"Mamie," cried Jim, "no more of this! It's
me you're striking; it's only me you hurt. You
don't know, you cannot understand these things.
Why, to-day, if it had n't been for Loudon, I
could n't have looked you in the face. He saved
my honesty."

"I have heard plenty of this talk before," she
replied. "You are a sweet-hearted fool, and I
love you for it. But I am a clear-headed woman;
my eyes are open, and I understand this man's
hypocrisy. Did he not come here to-day and pretend he would take a situation — pretend he would
share his hard-earned wages with us until you were

well? Pretend! It makes me furious! His wages!
a share of his wages! That would have been your
pittance, that would have been your share of the
Flying Scud — you who worked and toiled for him
when he was a beggar in the streets of Paris. But
we do not want your charity; thank God, I can
work for my own husband! See what it is to have
obliged a gentleman. He would let you pick him
up when he was begging; he would stand and look
on, and let you black his shoes, and sneer at you.
For you were always sneering at my James; you
always looked down upon him in your heart, you
know it!" She turned back to Jim. "And now
when he is rich," she began, and then swooped
again on me. "For you are rich, I dare you to
deny it; I defy you to look me in the face and try
to deny that you are rich — rich with our money
— my husband's money —— "

Heaven knows to what a height she might have
risen, being, by this time, bodily whirled away in
her own hurricane of words. Heart-sickness, a
black depression, a treacherous sympathy with my
assailant, pity unutterable for poor Jim, already
filled, divided, and abashed my spirit. Flight
seemed the only remedy; and making a private
sign to Jim, as if to ask permission, I slunk from
the unequal field.

I was but a little way down the street, when I
was arrested by the sound of some one running,
and Jim's voice calling me by name. He had followed me with a letter which had been long awaiting my return.

I took it in a dream. " This has been a devil of
a business," said I.

" Don't think hard of Mamie," he pleaded.
" It 's the way she 's made; it 's her high-toned
loyalty. And of course I know it 's all right. I
know your sterling character; but you did n't,
somehow, make out to give us the thing straight,
Loudon. Anybody might have — I mean it —
I mean —— "

" Never mind what you mean, my poor Jim,"
said I. " She 's a gallant little woman and a loyal
wife: and I thought her splendid. My story was
as fishy as the devil. I 'll never think the less of
either her or you."

" It 'll blow over, it must blow over," said he.

" It never can," I returned, sighing: " and don't
you try to make it! Don't name me, unless it 's
with an oath. And get home to her right away.
Good-bye, my best of friends. Good-bye, and God
bless you. We shall never meet again."

" O Loudon, that we should live to say such
words! " he cried.

I had no views on life, beyond an occasional
impulse to commit suicide, or to get drunk, and
drifted down the street, semi-conscious, walking
apparently on air, in the light-headedness of grief.
I had money in my pocket, whether mine or my
creditors' I had no means of guessing; and, the
Poodle Dog lying in my path, I went mechanically
in and took a table. A waiter attended me, and I
suppose I gave my orders; for presently I found
myself, with a sudden return of consciousness, be-

ginning dinner. On the white cloth at my elbow
lay the letter, addressed in a clerk's hand, and bearing an English stamp and the Edinburgh postmark.
A bowl of bouillon and a glass of wine awakened
in one corner of my brain (where all the rest was
in mourning, the blinds down as for a funeral) a
faint stir of curiosity; and while I waited the next
course, wondering the while what I had ordered,
I opened and began to read the epoch-making
document.

"DEAR SIR: I am charged with the melancholy duty of
announcing to you the death of your excellent grandfather,
Mr. Alexander Loudon, on the 17th ult. On Sunday the
13th, he went to church as usual in the forenoon, and stopped
on his way home, at the corner of Princes Street, in one of
our seasonable east winds, to talk with an old friend. The
same evening acute bronchitis declared itself; from the first,
Dr. M'Combie anticipated a fatal result, and the old gentleman appeared to have no illusion as to his own state. He
repeatedly assured me it was 'by' with him now; 'and high
time, too,' he once added with characteristic asperity. He
was not in the least changed on the approach of death : only
(what I am sure must be very grateful to your feelings) he
seemed to think and speak even more kindly than usual of
yourself: referring to you as 'Jeannie's yin,' with strong expressions of regard. 'He was the only one I ever liket of
the hale jing-bang,' was one of his expressions ; and you will
be glad to know that he dwelt particularly on the dutiful
respect you had always displayed in your relations. The
small codicil, by which he bequeaths you his Molesworth and
other professional works, was added (you will observe) on the
day before his death; so that you were in his thoughts until
the end. I should say that, though rather a trying patient,
he was most tenderly nursed by your uncle, and your cousin,
Miss Euphemia. I enclose a copy of the testament, by which
you will see that you share equally with Mr. Adam, and that

I hold at your disposal a sum nearly approaching seventeen
thousand pounds. I beg to congratulate you on this considerable acquisition, and expect your orders, to which I shall
hasten to give my best attention. Thinking that you might
desire to return at once to this country, and not knowing how
you may be placed, I enclose a credit for six hundred pounds.
Please sign the accompanying slip, and let me have it at your
earliest convenience.

"I am, dear sir, yours truly,

"W. RUTHERFORD GREGG."

"God bless the old gentleman!" I thought;
"and for that matter God bless Uncle Adam! and
my cousin Euphemia! and Mr. Gregg!" I had a
vision of that grey old life now brought to an
end — "and high time too" — a vision of those
Sabbath streets alternately vacant and filled with
silent people; of the babel of the bells, the long-
drawn psalmody, the shrewd sting of the east
wind, the hollow, echoing, dreary house to which
"Ecky" had returned with the hand of death
already on his shoulder; a vision, too, of the
long, rough country lad, perhaps a serious courtier
of the lasses in the hawthorn den, perhaps a rustic
dancer on the green, who had first earned and
answered to that harsh diminutive. And I asked
myself if, on the whole, poor Ecky had succeeded
in life; if the last state of that man were not on
the whole worse than the first; and the house in
Randolph Crescent a less admirable dwelling than
the hamlet where he saw the day and grew to
manhood. Here was a consolatory thought for
one who was himself a failure.

Yes, I declare the word came in my mind; and

all the while, in another partition of the brain, I was glowing and singing for my new-found opulence. The pile of gold — four thousand two hundred and fifty double eagles, seventeen thousand ugly sovereigns, twenty-one thousand two hundred and fifty Napoleons — danced, and rang and ran molten, and lit up life with their effulgence, in the eye of fancy. Here were all things made plain to me: Paradise — Paris, I mean — Regained, Carthew protected, Jim restored, the creditors . . .

"The creditors!" I repeated, and sank back benumbed. It was all theirs to the last farthing: my grandfather had died too soon to save me.

I must have somewhere a rare vein of decision. In that revolutionary moment, I found myself prepared for all extremes except the one: ready to do anything, or to go anywhere, so long as I might save my money. At the worst, there was flight, flight to some of those blest countries where the serpent, extradition, has not yet entered in.

> On no condition is extradition
> Allowed in Callao!

— the old lawless words haunted me; and I saw myself hugging my gold in the company of such men as had once made and sung them, in the rude and bloody wharf-side drinking-shops of Chili and Peru. The run of my ill-luck, the breach of my old friendship, this bubble fortune flaunted for a moment in my eyes and snatched again, had made me desperate and (in the expressive vulgarism) ugly. To drink vile spirits among vile companions by the flare of a pine-torch; to go burthened with my furtive treasure in a belt; to fight for it knife in hand, rolling on a clay floor; to flee perpetually in fresh ships and to be chased through the sea from isle to isle, seemed, in my then frame of mind, a welcome series of events.

That was for the worst; but it began to dawn slowly on my mind that there was yet a possible better. Once escaped, once safe in Callao, I might approach my creditors with a good grace; and properly handled by a cunning agent, it was just possible they might accept some easy composition. The hope recalled me to the bankruptcy. It was strange, I reflected: often as I had questioned Jim, he had never obliged me with an answer. In his haste for news about the wreck, my own no less legitimate curiosity had gone disappointed. Hateful as the thought was to me, I must return at once and find out where I stood.

I left my dinner still unfinished, paying for the whole of course, and tossing the waiter a gold piece. I was reckless; I knew not what was mine and cared not: I must take what I could get and give as I was able; to rob and to squander seemed the complementary parts of my new destiny. I walked up Bush Street, whistling, brazening myself to confront Mamie in the first place, and the world at large and a certain visionary judge upon a bench in the second. Just outside, I stopped and lighted a cigar to give me greater countenance; and puffing this and wearing what (I am sure) was a wretched assumption of braggadocio, I reappeared on the scene of my disgrace.

My friend and his wife were finishing a poor meal — rags of old mutton, the remainder cakes from breakfast eaten cold, and a starveling pot of coffee.

" I beg your pardon, Mrs. Pinkerton," said I. " Sorry to inflict my presence where it cannot be desired; but there is a piece of business necessary to be discussed."

" Pray do not consider me," said Mamie, rising, and she sailed into the adjoining bedroom.

Jim watched her go and shook his head; he looked miserably old and ill.

" What is it, now? " he asked.

" Perhaps you remember you answered none of my questions," said I.

" Your questions? " faltered Jim.

" Even so, Jim. My questions," I repeated. " I put questions as well as yourself; and however little I may have satisfied Mamie with my answers, I beg to remind you that you gave me none at all."

" You mean about the bankruptcy? " asked Jim.

I nodded.

He writhed in his chair. " The straight truth is, I was ashamed," he said. " I was trying to dodge you. I 've been playing fast and loose with you, Loudon; I 've deceived you from the first, I blush to own it. And here you came home and put the very question I was fearing. Why did

we bust so soon? Your keen business eye had
not deceived you. That's the point, that's my
shame; that's what killed me this afternoon when
Mamie was treating you so, and my conscience
was telling me all the time, Thou art the man."

"What was it, Jim?" I asked.

"What I had been at all the time, Loudon,"
he wailed; "and I don't know how I'm to look
you in the face and say it, after my duplicity. It
was stocks," he added in a whisper.

"And you were afraid to tell me that!" I cried.
"You poor, old, cheerless dreamer! what would
it matter what you did or did n't? Can't you see
we 're doomed? And anyway, that's not my point.
It's how I stand that I want to know. There is
a particular reason. Am I clear? Have I a certificate, or what have I to do to get one? And
when will it be dated? You can't think what
hangs by it!"

"That's the worst of all," said Jim, like a
man in a dream, "I can't see how to tell him!"

"What do you mean?" I cried, a small pang
of terror at my heart.

"I'm afraid I sacrificed you, Loudon," he said,
looking at me pitifully.

"Sacrificed me?" I repeated. "How? What
do you mean by sacrifice?"

"I know it'll shock your delicate self-respect,"
he said; "but what was I to do? Things looked
so bad. The receiver —" (as usual, the name
stuck in his throat, and he began afresh). "There
was a lot of talk; the reporters were after me

already; there was the trouble and all about the
Mexican business; and I got scared right out,
and I guess I lost my head. You were n't there,
you see, and that was my temptation."

I did not know how long he might thus beat
about the bush with dreadful hintings, and I was
already beside myself with terror. What had he
done? I saw he had been tempted; I knew from
his letters that he was in no condition to resist.
How had he sacrificed the absent?

"Jim," I said, "you must speak right out. I 've
got all that I can carry."

"Well," he said — " I know it was a liberty —
I made it out you were no business man, only a
stone-broke painter; that half the time you did n't
know anything anyway, particularly money and
accounts. I said you never could be got to understand whose was whose. I had to say that
because of some entries in the books ——— "

"For God's sake," I cried, "put me out of this
agony! What did you accuse me of?"

"Accused you of?" repeated Jim. "Of what
I 'm telling you. And there being no deed of
partnership, I made out you were only a kind of
clerk that I called a partner just to give you taffy;
and so I got you ranked a creditor on the estate
for your wages and the money you had lent.
And ——— "

I believe I reeled. "A creditor!" I roared; "a
creditor! I 'm not in the bankruptcy at all?"

"No," said Jim. "I know it was a liberty ——— "

24

"O damn your liberty! read that," I cried, dashing the letter before him on the table, "and call in your wife, and be done with eating this truck"—as I spoke, I slung the cold mutton in the empty grate—"and let's all go and have a champagne supper. I've dined—I'm sure I don't remember what I had; I'd dine again ten scores of times upon a night like this. Read it, you blaying ass! I'm not insane. Here, Mamie," I continued, opening the bedroom door, "come out and make it up with me, and go and kiss your husband; and I'll tell you what, after the supper, let's go to some place where there's a band, and I'll waltz with you till sunrise."

"What does it all mean?" cried Jim.

"It means we have a champagne supper to-night, and all go to Napa Valley or to Monterey to-morrow," said I. "Mamie, go and get your things on; and you, Jim, sit down right where you are, take a sheet of paper, and tell Franklin Dodge to go to Texas. Mamie, you were right, my dear; I was rich all the time, and did n't know it."

CHAPTER XIX

TRAVELS WITH A SHYSTER

THE absorbing and disastrous adventure of the *Flying Scud* was now quite ended; we had dashed into these deep waters and we had escaped again to starve, we had been ruined and were saved, had quarrelled and made up; there remained nothing but to sing *Te Deum*, draw a line, and begin on a fresh page of my unwritten diary. I do not pretend that I recovered all I had lost with Mamie; it would have been more than I had merited; and I had certainly been more uncommunicative than became either the partner or the friend. But she accepted the position handsomely; and during the week that I now passed with them, both she and Jim had the grace to spare me questions. It was to Calistoga that we went; there was some rumour of a Napa land-boom at the moment, the possibility of stir attracted Jim, and he informed me he would find a certain joy in looking on, much as Napoleon on St. Helena took a pleasure to read military works. The field of his ambition was quite closed; he was done with action; and looked forward to a ranch in a mountain dingle, a patch of corn, a pair of kine, a leisurely and contemplative age in the green shade of forests. "Just let me get down on my back in a hay-field," said he, "and you'll find there's no more snap to me than that much putty."

And for two days the perfervid being actually rested. The third, he was observed in consultation with the local editor, and owned he was in two minds about purchasing the press and paper. "It's a kind of a hold for an idle man," he said, pleadingly; "and if the section was to open up the way it ought to, there might be dollars in the thing." On the fourth day he was gone till dinner-time alone; on the fifth we made a long picnic drive to the fresh field of enterprise; and the sixth was passed entirely in the preparation of prospectuses. The pioneer of McBride City was already upright and self-reliant as of yore; the fire rekindled in his eye, the ring restored to his voice; a charger sniffing battle and saying ha-ha, among the spears. On the seventh morning we signed a deed of partnership, for Jim would not accept a dollar of my money otherwise; and having once more engaged myself — or that mortal part of me, my purse — among the wheels of his machinery, I returned alone to San Francisco and took quarters in the Palace Hotel.

The same night I had Nares to dinner. His sunburnt face, his queer and personal strain of talk, recalled days that were scarce over and that seemed already distant. Through the music of the band outside, and the chink and clatter of the dining-room, it seemed to me as if I heard the foaming of the surf and the voices of the sea-birds about Midway Island. The bruises on our hands were not yet healed; and there we sat, waited on by elaborate darkies, eating pompino and drinking iced champagne.

"Think of our dinners on the *Norah*, Captain, and then oblige me by looking round the room for contrast."

He took the scene in slowly. "Yes, it is like a dream," he said: "like as if the darkies were really about as big as dimes; and a great big scuttle might open up there, and Johnson stick in a great big head and shoulders, and cry, 'Eight bells!' — and the whole thing vanish."

"Well, it's the other thing that has done that," I replied. "It's all bygone now, all dead and buried. Amen! say I."

"I don't know that, Mr. Dodd; and to tell you the fact, I don't believe it," said Nares. "There's more *Flying Scud* in the oven; and the baker's name, I take it, is Bellairs. He tackled me the day we came in: sort of a razee of poor old humanity — jury clothes — full new suit of pimples: knew him at once from your description. I let him pump me till I saw his game. He knows a good deal that we don't know, a good deal that we do, and suspects the balance. There's trouble brewing for somebody."

I was surprised I had not thought of this before. Bellairs had been behind the scenes; he had known Dickson; he knew the flight of the crew; it was hardly possible but what he should suspect; it was certain if he suspected, that he would seek to trade on the suspicion. And sure enough, I was not yet dressed the next morning ere the lawyer was knocking at my door. I let him in, for I was curious; and he, after some ambiguous prolegomena, roundly proposed I should go shares with him.

"Shares in what?" I inquired.

"If you will allow me to clothe my idea in a somewhat vulgar form," said he, "I might ask you, did you go to Midway for your health?"

"I don't know that I did," I replied.

"Similarly, Mr. Dodd, you may be sure I would never have taken the present step without influential grounds," pursued the lawyer. "Intrusion is foreign to my character. But you and I, sir, are engaged on the same ends. If we can continue to work the thing in company, I place at your disposal my knowledge of the law and a considerable practice in delicate negotiations similar to this. Should you refuse to consent, you might find in me a formidable and " — he hesitated — " and to my own regret, perhaps a dangerous competitor."

"Did you get this by heart?" I asked, genially.

"I advise *you* to!" he said, with a sudden sparkle of temper and menace, instantly gone, instantly succeeded by fresh cringing. "I assure you, sir, I arrive in the character of a friend; and I believe you underestimate my information. If I may instance an example, I am acquainted to the last dime with what you made (or rather lost),

and I know you have since cashed a considerable
draft on London."

"What do you infer?" I asked.

"I know where that draft came from," he cried,
wincing back like one who has greatly dared, and
instantly regrets the venture.

"So?" said I.

"You forget I was Mr. Dickson's confidential
agent," he explained. "You had his address, Mr.
Dodd. We were the only two that he communicated with in San Francisco. You see my deductions are quite obvious: you see how open and
frank I deal with you; as I should wish to do with
any gentleman with whom I was conjoined in
business. You see how much I know; and it can
scarcely escape your strong common-sense, how
much better it would be if I knew all. You cannot
hope to get rid of me at this time of day, I have
my place in the affair, I cannot be shaken off;
I am, if you will excuse a rather technical pleasantry, an encumbrance on the estate. The actual
harm I can do, I leave you to valuate for yourself.
But without going so far, Mr. Dodd, and without
in any way inconveniencing myself, I could make
things very uncomfortable. For instance, Mr.
Pinkerton's liquidation. You and I know, sir —
and you better than I — on what a large fund you
draw. Is Mr. Pinkerton in the thing at all? It
was you only who knew the address, and you were
concealing it. Suppose I should communicate with
Mr. Pinkerton —— "

"Look here!" I interrupted, "communicate

with him (if you will permit me to clothe my idea in a vulgar shape) till you are blue in the face. There is only one person with whom I refuse to allow you to communicate farther, and that is myself. Good-morning."

He could not conceal his rage, disappointment, and surprise; and in the passage (I have no doubt) was shaken by St. Vitus.

I was disgusted by this interview; it struck me hard to be suspected on all hands, and to hear again from this trafficker what I had heard already from Jim's wife; and yet my strongest impression was different and might rather be described as an impersonal fear. There was something against nature in the man's craven impudence; it was as though a lamb had butted me; such daring at the hands of such a dastard, implied unchangeable resolve, a great pressure of necessity, and powerful means. I thought of the unknown Carthew, and it sickened me to see this ferret on his trail.

Upon inquiry I found the lawyer was but just disbarred for some malpractice; and the discovery added excessively to my disquiet. Here was a rascal without money or the means of making it, thrust out of the doors of his own trade, publicly shamed, and doubtless in a deuce of a bad temper with the universe. Here, on the other hand, was a man with a secret; rich, terrified, practically in hiding; who had been willing to pay ten thousand pounds for the bones of the *Flying Scud*. I slipped insensibly into a mental alliance with the victim; the business weighed on me; all day long, I was wondering how much the lawyer knew, how much he guessed, and when he would open his attack.

Some of these problems are unsolved to this day; others were soon made clear. Where he got Carthew's name is still a mystery; perhaps some sailor on the *Tempest,* perhaps my own sea-lawyer served him for a tool; but I was actually at his elbow when he learned the address. It fell so. One evening, when I had an engagement and was killing time until the hour, I chanced to walk in the court of the hotel while the band played. The place was bright as day with the electric light; and I recognised, at some distance among the loiterers, the person of Bellairs in talk with a gentleman, whose face appeared familiar. It was certainly some one I had seen, and seen recently; but who or where, I knew not. A porter standing hard by, gave me the necessary hint. The stranger was an English navy man, invalided home from Honolulu, where he had left his ship; indeed it was only from the change of clothes and the effects of sickness, that I had not immediately recognised my friend and correspondent, Lieutenant Sebright.

The conjunction of these planets seeming ominous, I drew near; but it seemed Bellairs had done his business; he vanished in the crowd, and I found my officer alone.

" Do you know whom you have been talking to, Mr. Sebright? " I began.

" No," said he. " I don't know him from Adam. Anything wrong? "

" He is a disreputable lawyer, recently dis-

barred," said I. "I wish I had seen you in time.
I trust you told him nothing about Carthew?"

He flushed to his ears. "I'm awfully sorry,"
he said. "He seemed civil, and I wanted to get
rid of him. It was only the address he asked."

"And you gave it?" I cried.

"I'm really awfully sorry," said Sebright.
"I'm afraid I did."

"God forgive you!" was my only comment,
and I turned my back upon the blunderer.

The fat was in the fire now: Bellairs had the
address, and I was the more deceived or Carthew
would have news of him. So strong was this impression, and so painful, that the next morning
I had the curiosity to pay the lawyer's den a visit.
An old woman was scrubbing the stair, and the
board was down.

"Lawyer Bellairs?" said the old woman.
"Gone East this morning. There's Lawyer
Dean next block up."

I did not trouble Lawyer Dean, but walked
slowly back to my hotel, ruminating as I went.
The image of the old woman washing that dese-
crated stair had struck my fancy; it seemed that all
the water-supply of the city and all the soap in the
State would scarce suffice to cleanse it, it had been
so long a clearing-house of dingy secrets and a
factory of sordid fraud. And now the corner was
untenanted; some judge, like a careful housewife,
had knocked down the web, and the bloated spider
was scuttling elsewhere after new victims. I had
of late (as I have said) insensibly taken sides with

Carthew; now when his enemy was at his heels, my interest grew more warm; and I began to wonder if I could not help. The drama of the *Flying Scud* was entering on a new phase. It had been singular from the first: it promised an extraordinary conclusion; and I who had paid so much to learn the beginning, might pay a little more and see the end. I lingered in San Francisco, indemnifying myself after the hardships of the cruise, spending money, regretting it, continually promising departure for the morrow. Why not go indeed, and keep a watch upon Bellairs? If I missed him, there was no harm done, I was the nearer Paris. If I found and kept his trail, it was hard if I could not put some stick in his machinery, and at the worst I could promise myself interesting scenes and revelations.

In such a mixed humour, I made up what it pleases me to call my mind, and once more involved myself in the story of Carthew and the *Flying Scud*. The same night I wrote a letter of farewell to Jim, and one of anxious warning to Dr. Urquart begging him to set Carthew on his guard; the morrow saw me in the ferry-boat; and ten days later, I was walking the hurricane deck on the *City of Denver*. By that time my mind was pretty much made down again, its natural condition: I told myself that I was bound for Paris or Fontainebleau to resume the study of the arts; and I thought no more of Carthew or Bellairs, or only to smile at my own fondness. The one I could not serve, even if I wanted; the other I had no means of finding,

even if I could have at all influenced him after he
was found.

And for all that, I was close on the heels of an
absurd adventure. My neighbour at table that
evening was a 'Frisco man whom I knew slightly.
I found he had crossed the plains two days in front
of me, and this was the first steamer that had left
New York for Europe since his arrival. Two days
before me, meant a day before Bellairs; and dinner
was scarce done before I was closeted with the
purser.

" Bellairs? " he repeated. " Not in the saloon,
I am sure. He may be in the second class. The
lists are not made out, but — Hullo! ' Harry D.
Bellairs '? That the name? He 's there right
enough."

And the next morning I saw him on the forward
deck, sitting in a chair, a book in his hand, a shabby
puma skin rug about his knees: the picture of respectable decay. Off and on, I kept him in my eye.
He read a good deal, he stood and looked upon the
sea, he talked occasionally with his neighbours,
and once when a child fell he picked it up and
soothed it. I damned him in my heart; the book,
which I was sure he did not read — the sea, to
which I was ready to take oath he was indifferent
— the child, whom I was certain he would as lieve
have tossed overboard — all seemed to me elements in a theatrical performance; and I made
no doubt he was already nosing after the secrets of
his fellow-passengers. I took no pains to conceal
myself, my scorn for the creature being as strong

as my disgust. But he never looked my way, and
it was night before I learned he had observed me.

I was smoking by the engine-room door, for the
air was a little sharp, when a voice rose close
beside me in the darkness.

"I beg your pardon, Mr. Dodd?" it said.

"That you, Bellairs?" I replied.

"A single word, sir. Your presence on this
ship has no connection with our interview?" he
asked. "You have no idea, Mr. Dodd, of returning upon your determination?"

"None," said I; and then, seeing he still lingered, I was polite enough to add "Good-evening;" at which he sighed and went away.

The next day, he was there again with the chair
and the puma skin; read his book and looked at
the sea with the same constancy; and though
there was no child to be picked up, I observed
him to attend repeatedly on a sick woman. Nothing fosters suspicion like the act of watching; a
man spied upon can hardly blow his nose but
we accuse him of designs; and I took an early
opportunity to go forward and see the woman for
myself. She was poor, elderly, and painfully
plain; I stood abashed at the sight, felt I owed
Bellairs amends for the injustice of my thoughts,
and seeing him standing by the rail in his usual
attitude of contemplation, walked up and addressed
him by name.

"You seem very fond of the sea," said I.

"I may really call it a passion, Mr. Dodd," he
replied. "*And the tall cataract haunted me like*

a passion," he quoted. " I never weary of the sea, sir. This is my first ocean voyage. I find it a glorious experience." And once more my disbarred lawyer dropped into poetry : " *Roll on, thou deep and dark blue ocean, roll!* "

Though I had learned the piece in my reading-book at school, I came into the world a little too late on the one hand — and I dare say a little too early on the other — to think much of Byron; and the sonorous verse, prodigiously well delivered, struck me with surprise.

" You are fond of poetry, too ? " I asked.

" I am a great reader," he replied. " At one time I had begun to amass quite a small but well-selected library; and when that was scattered, I still managed to preserve a few volumes — chiefly of pieces designed for recitation — which have been my travelling companions."

" Is that one of them ? " I asked, pointing to the volume in his hand.

" No, sir," he replied, showing me a translation of the *Sorrows of Werther,* " that is a novel I picked up some time ago. It has afforded me great pleasure, though immoral."

" O, immoral ! " cried I, indignant as usual at any implication of art and ethics.

" Surely you cannot deny that, sir — if you know the book," he said. " The passion is illicit, although certainly drawn with a good deal of pathos. It is not a work one could possibly put into the hands of a lady; which is to be regretted on all accounts, for I do not know how it may strike you; but it seems to me — as a depiction, if I make myself clear — to rise high above its compeers, even famous compeers. Even in Scott, Dickens, Thackeray, or Hawthorne, the sentiment of love appears to me to be frequently done less justice to."

"You are expressing a very general opinion," said I.

"Is that so, indeed, sir?" he exclaimed, with unmistakable excitement. "Is the book well known? and who was *Go-eath?* I am interested in that, because upon the title-page the usual initials are omitted, and it runs simply 'by *Go-eath.*' Was he an author of distinction? Has he written other works?"

Such was our first interview, the first of many; and in all he showed the same attractive qualities and defects. His taste for literature was native and unaffected; his sentimentality, although extreme and a thought ridiculous, was plainly genuine. I wondered at my own innocent wonder. I knew that Homer nodded, that Cæsar had compiled a jest-book, that Turner lived by preference the life of Puggy Booth, that Shelley made paper boats, and Wordsworth wore green spectacles! and with all this mass of evidence before me, I had expected Bellairs to be entirely of one piece, subdued to what he worked in, a spy all through. As I abominated the man's trade, so I had expected to detest the man himself; and behold, I liked him. Poor devil! he was essentially a man on wires, all sensibility and tremor, brimful of a cheap poetry, not without parts, quite without courage. His boldness was despair; the gulf behind him thrust him on; he was one of those who might commit a murder rather than confess the theft of a postage-stamp. I was sure that his coming interview with Carthew rode his imagination like a nightmare; when the thought crossed his mind, I used to think I knew of it, and that the qualm appeared in his face visibly. Yet he would never flinch: necessity stalking at his back, famine (his old pursuer) talking in his ear; and I used to wonder whether I most admired, or most despised, this quivering heroism for evil. The image that occurred to me after his visit was just; I had been butted by a lamb; and the phase of life that I was now studying might be called the Revolt of a Sheep.

It could be said of him that he had learned in sorrow what he taught in song — or wrong; and his life was that of one of his victims. He was born in the back parts of the State of New York; his father a farmer, who became subsequently bankrupt and went West. The lawyer and money-lender who had ruined this poor family seems to have conceived in the end a feeling of remorse; he turned the father out indeed, but he offered, in compensation, to charge himself with one of the sons: and Harry, the fifth child and already sickly, was chosen to be left behind. He made himself useful in the office; picked up the scattered rudiments of an education; read right and left; attended and debated at the Young Men's

Christian Association; and in all his early years, was the model for a good story-book. His landlady's daughter was his bane. He showed me her photograph; she was a big, handsome, dashing, dressy, vulgar hussy, without character, without tenderness, without mind, and (as the result proved) without virtue. The sickly and timid boy was in the house; he was handy; when she was otherwise unoccupied, she used and played with him: Romeo and Cressida; till in that dreary life of a poor boy in a country town, she grew to be the light of his days and the subject of his dreams. He worked hard, like Jacob, for a wife; he surpassed his patron in sharp practice; he was made head clerk; and the same night, encouraged by a hundred freedoms, depressed by the sense of his youth and his infirmities, he offered marriage and was received with laughter. Not a year had passed, before his master, conscious of growing infirmities, took him for a partner; he proposed again; he was accepted; led two years of troubled married life; and awoke one morning to find his wife had run away with a dashing drummer, and had left him heavily in debt. The debt, and not the drummer, was supposed to be the cause of the hegira; she had concealed her liabilities, they were on the point of bursting forth, she was weary of Bellairs; and she took the drummer as she might have taken a cab. The blow disabled her husband; his partner was dead; he was now alone in the business, for which he was no longer fit; the debts hampered him; bank-

ruptcy followed; and he fled from city to city,
falling daily into lower practice. It is to be considered that he had been taught, and had learned
as a delightful duty, a kind of business whose
highest merit is to escape the commentaries of the
bench: that of the usurious lawyer in a county
town. With this training, he was now shot, a
penniless stranger, into the deeper gulfs of cities;
and the result is scarce a thing to be surprised at.

"Have you heard of your wife again?" I asked.

He displayed a pitiful agitation. "I am afraid
you will think ill of me," he said.

"Have you taken her back?" I asked.

"No, sir. I trust I have too much self-respect,"
he answered, "and, at least, I was never tempted.
She won't come, she dislikes, she seems to have
conceived a positive distaste for me, and yet I
was considered an indulgent husband."

"You are still in relations, then?" I asked.

"I place myself in your hands, Mr. Dodd," he
replied. "The world is very hard; I have found
it bitter hard myself — bitter hard to live. How
much worse for a woman, and one who has placed
herself (by her own misconduct, I am far from
denying that) in so unfortunate a position!"

"In short, you support her?" I suggested.

"I cannot deny it. I practically do," he admitted. "It has been a mill-stone round my neck.
But I think she is grateful. You can see for
yourself."

He handed me a letter in a sprawling, ignorant
hand, but written with violet ink on fine, pink

paper with a monogram. It was very foolishly
expressed, and I thought (except for a few obvious cajoleries) very heartless and greedy in
meaning. The writer said she had been sick,
which I disbelieved; declared the last remittance
was all gone in doctor's bills, for which I took
the liberty of substituting dress, drink, and mono-
grams; and prayed for an increase, which I could
only hope had been denied her.

"I think she is really grateful?" he asked, with
some eagerness, as I returned it.

"I dare say," said I. "Has she any claim on
you?"

"O, no, sir. I divorced her," he replied. "I
have a very strong sense of self-respect in such
matters, and I divorced her immediately."

"What sort of life is she leading now?" I
asked.

"I will not deceive you, Mr. Dodd. I do not
know, I make a point of not knowing; it appears
more dignified. I have been very harshly criticised," he added, sighing.

It will be seen that I had fallen into an ignominious intimacy with the man I had gone out
to thwart. My pity for the creature, his admiration for myself, his pleasure in my society, which
was clearly unassumed, were the bonds with which
I was fettered; perhaps I should add, in honesty,
my own ill-regulated interest in the phases of life
and human character. The fact is (at least) that
we spent hours together daily, and that I was
nearly as much on the forward deck as in the

saloon. Yet all the while I could never forget
he was a shabby trickster, embarked that very
moment in a dirty enterprise. I used to tell myself at first that our acquaintance was a stroke
of art, and that I was somehow fortifying Carthew. I told myself, I say; but I was no such
fool as to believe it, even then. In these circumstances I displayed the two chief qualities of my
character on the largest scale — my helplessness
and my instinctive love of procrastination — and
fell upon a course of action so ridiculous that I
blush when I recall it.

We reached Liverpool one forenoon, the rain
falling thickly and insidiously on the filthy town.
I had no plans, beyond a sensible unwillingness
to let my rascal escape; and I ended by going to
the same inn with him, dining with him, walking
with him in the wet streets, and hearing with him
in a penny gaff that venerable piece, *The Ticket-
of-Leave Man*. It was one of his first visits to
a theatre, against which places of entertainment
he had a strong prejudice; and his innocent,
pompous talk, innocent old quotations, and innocent reverence for the character of Hawkshaw
delighted me beyond relief. In charity to myself,
I dwell upon and perhaps exaggerate my pleasures. I have need of all conceivable excuses,
when I confess that I went to bed without one
word upon the matter of Carthew, but not without having covenanted with my rascal for a visit
to Chester the next day. At Chester we did the
cathedral, walked on the walls, discussed Shake-

speare and the musical glasses — and made a fresh engagement for the morrow. I do not know, and I am glad to have forgotten, how long these travels were continued. We visited at least, by singular zigzags, Stratford, Warwick, Coventry, Gloucester, Bristol, Bath, and Wells. At each stage we spoke dutifully of the scene and its associations; I sketched, the shyster spouted poetry and copied epitaphs. Who could doubt we were the usual Americans, travelling with a design of self-improvement? Who was to guess that one was a blackmailer, trembling to approach the scene of action — the other a helpless, amateur detective, waiting on events.

It is unnecessary to remark that none occurred, or none the least suitable with my design of protecting Carthew. Two trifles, indeed, completed though they scarcely changed my conception of the shyster. The first was observed in Gloucester, where we spent Sunday, and I proposed we should hear service in the cathedral. To my surprise, the creature had an *ism* of his own, to which he was loyal; and he left me to go alone to the cathedral — or perhaps not to go at all — and stole off down a deserted alley to some Bethel or Ebenezer of the proper shade. When we met again at lunch, I rallied him, and he grew restive.

"You need employ no circumlocutions with me, Mr. Dodd," he said, suddenly. "You regard my behaviour from an unfavourable point of view: you regard me, I much fear, as hypocritical."

I was somewhat confused by the attack. "You

know what I think of your trade," I replied, lamely and coarsely.

"Excuse me, if I seem to press the subject," he continued, "but if you think my life erroneous, would you have me neglect the means of grace? Because you consider me in the wrong on one point, would you have me place myself on the wrong in all? Surely, sir, the church is for the sinner."

"Did you ask a blessing on your present enterprise?" I sneered.

He had a bad attack of St. Vitus, his face was changed, and his eyes flashed. "I will tell you what I did!" he cried. "I prayed for an unfortunate man and a wretched woman whom he tries to support."

I cannot pretend that I found any repartee.

The second incident was at Bristol, where I lost sight of my gentleman some hours. From this eclipse, he returned to me with thick speech, wandering footsteps, and a back all whitened with plaster. I had half expected, yet I could have wept to see it. All disabilities were piled on that weak back — domestic misfortune, nervous disease, a displeasing exterior, empty pockets, and the slavery of vice.

I will never deny that our prolonged conjunction was the result of double cowardice. Each was afraid to leave the other, each was afraid to speak, or knew not what to say. Save for my ill-judged allusion at Gloucester, the subject uppermost in both our minds was buried. Carthew, Stall-

bridge-le-Carthew, Stallbridge-Minster—which we
had long since (and severally) identified to be the
nearest station — even the name of Dorsetshire
was studiously avoided. And yet we were making progress all the time, tacking across broad
England like an unweatherly vessel on a wind;
approaching our destination, not openly, but by a
sort of flying sap. And at length, I can scarce
tell how, we were set down by a dilatory butt-
end of local train on the untenanted platform of
Stallbridge-Minster.

The town was ancient and compact: a domino
of tiled houses and walled gardens, dwarfed by
the disproportionate bigness of the church. From
the midst of the thoroughfare which divided it
in half, fields and trees were visible at either end;
and through the sally-port of every street, there
flowed in from the country a silent invasion of
green grass. Bees and birds appeared to make
the majority of the inhabitants; every garden had
its row of hives, the eaves of every house were
plastered with the nests of swallows, and the pin-
nacles of the church were flickered about all day
long by a multitude of wings. The town was of
Roman foundation; and as I looked out that
afternoon from the low windows of the inn, I
should scarce have been surprised to see a cen-
turion coming up the street with a fatigue draft
of legionaries. In short, Stallbridge-Minster was
one of those towns which appear to be maintained by England for the instruction and delight
of the American rambler; to which he seems

guided by an instinct not less surprising than the
setter's; and which he visits and quits with equal
enthusiasm.

I was not at all in the humour of the tourist.
I had wasted weeks of time and accomplished
nothing; we were on the eve of the engagement,
and I had neither plans nor allies; I had thrust
myself into the trade of private providence and
amateur detective; I was spending money and
I was reaping disgrace. All the time, I kept telling myself that I must at least speak; that this
ignominious silence should have been broken long
ago, and must be broken now. I should have
broken it when he first proposed to come to
Stallbridge-Minster; I should have broken it in
the train; I should break it there and then, on
the inn doorstep, as the omnibus rolled off. I
turned toward him at the thought; he seemed
to wince, the words died on my lips, and I proposed instead that we should visit the Minster.

While we were engaged upon this duty, it came
on to rain in a manner worthy of the tropics.
The vault reverberated; every gargoyle instantly
poured its full discharge; we waded back to the
inn, ankle deep in impromptu brooks; and the
rest of the afternoon sat weatherbound, hearken-
ing to the sonorous deluge. For two hours I
talked of indifferent matters, laboriously feeding
the conversation; for two hours my mind was
quite made up to do my duty instantly — and at
each particular instant I postponed it till the next.
To screw up my faltering courage, I called at

dinner for some sparkling wine. It proved when it came to be detestable; I could not put it to my lips; and Bellairs, who had as much palate as a weevil, was left to finish it himself. Doubtless the wine flushed him; doubtless he may have observed my embarrassment of the afternoon; doubtless he was conscious that we were approaching a crisis, and that that evening, if I did not join with him, I must declare myself an open enemy. At least he fled. Dinner was done; this was the time when I had bound myself to break my silence; no more delays were to be allowed, no more excuses received. I went up-stairs after some tobacco; which I felt to be a mere necessity in the circumstances; and when I returned, the man was gone. The waiter told me he had left the house.

The rain still plumped, like a vast shower-bath, over the deserted town. The night was dark and windless: the street lit glimmeringly from end to end, lamps, house windows, and the reflections in the rain-pools all contributing. From a public-house on the other side of the way, I heard a harp twang and a doleful voice upraised in the "Larboard Watch," "The Anchor's Weighed," and other naval ditties. Where had my shyster wandered? In all likelihood to that lyrical tavern; there was no choice of diversion; in comparison with Stallbridge-Minster on a rainy night, a sheep-fold would seem gay.

Again I passed in review the points of my interview, on which I was always constantly

resolved so long as my adversary was absent from
the scene: and again they struck me as inade-
quate. From this dispiriting exercise I turned
to the native amusements of the inn coffee-room,
and studied for some time the mezzotints that
frowned upon the wall. The railway guide, after
showing me how soon I could leave Stallbridge
and how quickly I could reach Paris, failed to
hold my attention. An illustrated advertisement
book of hotels brought me very low indeed; and
when it came to the local paper, I could have
wept. At this point, I found a passing solace
in a copy of Whittaker's Almanac, and obtained
in fifty minutes more information than I have
yet been able to use.

Then a fresh apprehension assailed me. Suppose Bellairs had given me the slip? suppose he
was now rolling on the road to Stallbridge-le-
Carthew? or perhaps there already and laying before a very white-faced auditor his threats and
propositions? A hasty person might have instantly pursued. Whatever I am, I am not hasty,
and I was aware of three grave objections. In
the first place, I could not be certain that Bellairs was gone. In the second, I had no taste
whatever for a long drive at that hour of the
night and in so merciless a rain. In the third,
I had no idea how I was to get admitted if I
went, and no idea what I should say if I got
admitted. "In short," I concluded, "the whole
situation is the merest farce. You have thrust
yourself in where you had no business and have

no power. You would be quite as useful in San Francisco; far happier in Paris; and being (by the wrath of God) at Stallbridge-Minster, the wisest thing is to go quietly to bed." On the way to my room, I saw (in a flash) that which I ought to have done long ago, and which it was now too late to think of — written to Carthew, I mean, detailing the facts and describing Bellairs, letting him defend himself if he were able, and giving him time to flee if he were not. It was the last blow to my self-respect; and I flung myself into my bed with contumely.

I have no guess what hour it was, when I was wakened by the entrance of Bellairs carrying a candle. He had been drunk, for he was bedaubed with mire from head to foot; but he was now sober and under the empire of some violent emotion which he controlled with difficulty. He trembled visibly; and more than once, during the interview which followed, tears suddenly and silently overflowed his cheeks.

"I have to ask your pardon, sir, for this untimely visit," he said. "I make no defence, I have no excuse, I have disgraced myself, I am properly punished; I appear before you to appeal to you in mercy for the most trifling aid or, God help me! I fear I may go mad."

"What on earth is wrong?" I asked.

"I have been robbed," he said. "I have no defence to offer; it was of my own fault, I am properly punished."

" But, gracious goodness me ! " I cried, " who
is there to rob you in a place like this ? "

" I can form no opinion," he replied. " I have
no idea. I was lying in a ditch inanimate. This
is a degrading confession, sir; I can only say in
self-defence that perhaps (in your good-nature)
you have made yourself partly responsible for my
shame. I am not used to these rich wines."

" In what form was your money ? Perhaps it
may be traced," I suggested.

" It was in English sovereigns. I changed it
in New York; I got very good exchange," he
said, and then, with a momentary outbreak, " God
in heaven, how I toiled for it ! " he cried.

" That doesn't sound encouraging," said I.
" It may be worth while to apply to the police,
but it doesn't sound a hopeful case."

" And I have no hope in that direction," said
Bellairs. " My hopes, Mr. Dodd, are all fixed
upon yourself. I could easily convince you that
a small, a very small advance, would be in the
nature of an excellent investment; but I prefer
to rely on your humanity. Our acquaintance began
on an unusual footing; but you have now known
me for some time, we have been some time — I
was going to say we had been almost intimate.
Under the impulse of instinctive sympathy, I have
bared my heart to you, Mr. Dodd, as I have done
to few; and I believe — I trust — I may say that
I feel sure — you heard me with a kindly sentiment.
This is what brings me to your side at this most
inexcusable hour. But put yourself in my place

— how could I sleep — how could I dream of sleeping, in this blackness of remorse and despair? There was a friend at hand — so I ventured to think of you; it was instinctive; I fled to your side, as the drowning man clutches at a straw. These expressions are not exaggerated, they scarcely serve to express the agitation of my mind. And think, sir, how easily you can restore me to hope and, I may say, to reason. A small loan, which shall be faithfully repaid. Five hundred dollars would be ample." He watched me with burning eyes. " Four hundred would do. I believe, Mr. Dodd, that I could manage with economy on two."

" And then you will repay me out of Carthew's pocket? " I said. " I am much obliged. But I will tell you what I will do : I will see you on board a steamer, pay your fare through to San Francisco, and place fifty dollars in the purser's hands, to be given you in New York."

He drank in my words; his face represented an ecstasy of cunning thought. I could read there, plain as print, that he but thought to overreach me.

" And what am I to do in 'Frisco? " he asked. " I am disbarred, I have no trade, I cannot dig, to beg — " he paused in the citation. " And you know that I am not alone," he added, " others depend upon me."

" I will write to Pinkerton," I returned. " I feel sure he can help you to some employment, and in the meantime, and for three months after

your arrival, he shall pay to yourself personally, on the first and the fifteenth, twenty-five
dollars."

"Mr. Dodd, I scarce believe you can be serious
in this offer," he replied. "Have you forgotten
the circumstances of the case? Do you know these
people are the magnates of the section? They
were spoken of to-night in the saloon; their wealth
must amount to many millions of dollars in real
estate alone; their house is one of the sights of
the locality, and you offer me a bribe of a few
hundred!"

"I offer you no bribe, Mr. Bellairs, I give you
alms," I returned. "I will do nothing to forward
you in your hateful business; yet I would not willingly have you starve."

"Give me a hundred dollars then, and be done
with it," he cried.

"I will do what I have said, and neither more
nor less," said I.

"Take care," he cried. "You are playing a
fool's game; you are making an enemy for nothing; you will gain nothing by this, I warn you of
it!" And then with one of his changes, "Seventy
dollars — only seventy — in mercy, Mr. Dodd,
in common charity. Don't dash the bowl from
my lips! You have a kindly heart. Think of
my position, remember my unhappy wife."

"You should have thought of her before," said
I. "I have made my offer, and I wish to
sleep."

"Is that your last word, sir? Pray consider;

pray weigh both sides: my misery, your own
danger. I warn you — I beseech you; measure
it well before you answer," so he half pleaded,
half threatened me, with clasped hands.

" My first word, and my last," said I.

The change upon the man was shocking. In
the storm of anger that now shook him, the lees
of his intoxication rose again to the surface; his
face was deformed, his words insane with fury;
his pantomime, excessive in itself, was distorted
by an access of St. Vitus.

" You will perhaps allow me to inform you of
my cold opinion," he began, apparently self-pos-
sessed, truly bursting with rage: " when I am a
glorified saint, I shall see you howling for a drop
of water and exult to see you. That your last
word! Take it in your face, you spy, you false
friend, you fat hypocrite! I defy, I defy and
despise and spit upon you! I 'm on the trail, his
trail or yours, I smell blood, I 'll follow it on my
hands and knees, I 'll starve to follow it! I 'll
hunt you down, hunt you, hunt you down! If
I were strong, I 'd tear your vitals out, here in
this room — tear them out -- I 'd tear them out!
Damn, damn, damn! You think me weak? I
can bite, bite to the blood, bite you, hurt you,
disgrace you . . ."

He was thus incoherently raging, when the
scene was interrupted by the arrival of the landlord and inn servants in various degrees of desha-
bille, and to them I gave my temporary lunatic in
charge.

"Take him to his room," I said, "he's only drunk."

These were my words; but I knew better. After all my study of Mr. Bellairs, one discovery had been reserved for the last moment: that of his latent and essential madness.

CHAPTER XX

STALLBRIDGE-LE-CARTHEW

LONG before I was awake, the shyster had disappeared, leaving his bill unpaid. I did not need to inquire where he was gone, I knew too well, I knew there was nothing left me but to follow; and about ten in the morning, set forth in a gig for Stallbridge-le-Carthew.

The road, for the first quarter of the way, deserts the valley of the river, and crosses the summit of a chalk-down, grazed over by flocks of sheep and haunted by innumerable larks. It was a pleasant but a vacant scene, arousing but not holding the attention; and my mind returned to the violent passage of the night before. My thought of the man I was pursuing had been greatly changed. I conceived of him, somewhere in front of me, upon his dangerous errand, not to be turned aside, not to be stopped, by either fear or reason. I had called him a ferret; I conceived him now as a mad dog. Methought he would run, not walk; methought, as he ran, that he would bark and froth at the lips; methought, if the great wall of China were to rise across his path, he would attack it with his nails.

Presently the road left the down, returned by a precipitous descent into the valley of the Stall, and ran thenceforward among enclosed fields and under the continuous shade of trees. I was told we had now entered on the Carthew property. By and by, a battlemented wall appeared on the left hand, and a little after I had my first glimpse of the mansion. It stood in the hollow of a bosky park, crowded to a degree that surprised and even displeased me, with huge timber and dense shrubberies of laurel and rhododendron. Even from this low station and the thronging neighbourhood of the trees, the pile rose conspicuous like a cathedral. Behind, as we continued to skirt the park wall, I began to make out a straggling town of offices which became conjoined to the rear with those of the home farm. On the left was an ornamental water sailed in by many swans. On the right extended a flower garden, laid in the old manner, and at this season of the year, as brilliant as stained glass. The front of the house presented a façade of more than sixty windows, surmounted by a formal pediment and raised upon a terrace. A wide avenue, part in gravel, part in turf, and bordered by triple alleys, ran to the great double gateways. It was impossible to look without surprise on a place that had been prepared through so many generations, had cost so many tons of minted gold, and was maintained in order by so great a company of emulous servants. And yet of these there was no sign but the perfection of their work. The whole domain was drawn to the line and weeded like the front plot of some suburban amateur; and I looked in vain for any belated

gardener, and listened in vain for any sounds of
labour. Some lowing of cattle and much calling
of birds alone disturbed the stillness, and even
the little hamlet, which clustered at the gates, appeared to hold its breath in awe of its great neighbour, like a troop of children who should have
strayed into a king's anteroom.

The *Carthew Arms,* the small but very comfortable inn, was a mere appendage and outpost of
the family whose name it bore. Engraved portraits of by-gone Carthews adorned the walls;
Fielding Carthew, Recorder of the city of London;
Major-General John Carthew in uniform, commanding some military operations; the Right Honourable Bailley Carthew, Member of Parliament
for Stallbridge, standing by a table and brandish-
ing a document; Singleton Carthew, Esquire, represented in the foreground of a herd of cattle —
doubtless at the desire of his tenantry who had
made him a compliment of this work of art; and
the Venerable Archdeacon Carthew, D.D., LL.D.,
A.M., laying his hand on the head of a little child
in a manner highly frigid and ridiculous. So far
as my memory serves me, there were no other
pictures in this exclusive hostelry; and I was not
surprised to learn that the landlord was an ex-
butler, the landlady an ex-lady's-maid, from the
great house; and that the bar-parlour was a sort
of perquisite of former servants.

To an American, the sense of the domination
of this family over so considerable tract of earth
was even oppressive; and as I considered their

simple annals, gathered from the legends of the engravings, surprise began to mingle with my disgust. " Mr. Recorder " doubtless occupies an honourable post; but I thought that, in the course of so many generations, one Carthew might have clambered higher. The soldier had stuck at Major-General; the churchmen bloomed unremarked in an archdiaconate: and though the Right Honourable Bailley seemed to have sneaked into the privy council, I have still to learn what he did when he had got there. Such vast means, so long a start, and such a modest standard of achievement, struck in me a strong sense of the dulness of that race.

I found that to come to the hamlet and not visit the Hall, would be regarded as a slight. To feed the swans, to see the peacocks and the Raphaels — for these commonplace people actually possessed two Raphaels — to risk life and limb among a famous breed of cattle called the Carthew Chillinghams, and to do homage to the sire (still living) of Donibristle, a renowned winner of the Oaks: these, it seemed, were the inevitable stations of the pilgrimage. I was not so foolish as to resist, for I might have need before I was done of general good-will; and two pieces of news fell in which changed my resignation to alacrity. It appeared in the first place, that Mr. Norris was from home " travelling "; in the second, that a visitor had been before me and already made the tour of the Carthew curiosities. I thought I knew who this must be; I was anxious to learn what he

had done and seen; and fortune so far favoured
me that the under-gardener singled out to be my
guide had already performed the same function
for my predecessor.

" Yes, sir," he said, " an American gentleman
right enough. At least, I don't think he was quite
a gentleman, but a very civil person."

The person, it seems, had been civil enough to
be delighted with the Carthew Chillinghams, to
perform the whole pilgrimage with rising admiration, and to have almost prostrated himself before
the shrine of Donibristle's sire.

" He told me, sir," continued the gratified under-gardener, " that he had often read of ' the
stately 'omes of England,' but ours was the first
he had the chance to see. When he came to the
'ead of the long alley, he fetched his breath. ' This
is indeed a lordly domain!' he cries. And it was
natural he should be interested in the place, for
it seems Mr. Carthew had been kind to him in the
States. In fact, he seemed a grateful kind of person, and wonderful taken up with flowers."

I heard this story with amazement. The phrases
quoted told their own tale; they were plainly from
the shyster's mint. A few hours back I had seen
him a mere bedlamite and fit for a strait-waist-
coat; he was penniless in a strange country; it
was highly probable he had gone without breakfast; the absence of Norris must have been a
crushing blow; the man (by all reason) should
have been despairing. And now I heard of
him, clothed and in his right mind, deliberate,

insinuating, admiring vistas, smelling flowers, and talking like a book, The strength of character implied amazed and daunted me.

"This is curious," I said to the under-gardener. "I have had the pleasure of some acquaintance with Mr. Carthew myself; and I believe none of our western friends ever were in England. Who can this person be? He could n't — no, that 's impossible, he could never have had the impudence. His name was not Bellairs?"

"I did n't 'ear the name, sir. Do you know anything against him?" cried my guide.

"Well," said I, "he is certainly not the person Carthew would like to have here in his absence."

"Good gracious me!" exclaimed the gardener. "He was so pleasant spoken, too; I thought he was some form of a schoolmaster. Perhaps, sir, you would n't mind going right up to Mr. Denman? I recommended him to Mr. Denman, when he had done the grounds. Mr. Denman is our butler, sir," he added.

The proposal was welcome, particularly as affording me a graceful retreat from the neighbourhood of the Carthew Chillinghams; and, giving up our projected circuit, we took a short cut through the shrubbery and across the bowling green to the back quarters of the Hall.

The bowling green was surrounded by a great hedge of yew, and entered by an archway in the quick. As we were issuing from this passage, my conductor arrested me.

"The Honourable Lady Ann Carthew," he said,

in an august whisper. And looking over his
shoulder, I was aware of an old lady with a stick,
hobbling somewhat briskly along the garden path.
She must have been extremely handsome in her
youth; and even the limp with which she walked
could not deprive her of an unusual and almost
menacing dignity of bearing. Melancholy was
impressed besides on every feature, and her eyes,
as she looked straight before her, seemed to con-
template misfortune.

"She seems sad," said I, when she had hobbled
past and we had resumed our walk.

"She enjoy rather poor spirits, sir," responded
the under-gardener. "Mr. Carthew — the old
gentleman, I mean — died less than a year ago;
Lord Tillibody, her ladyship's brother, two months
after; and then there was the sad business about
the young gentleman. Killed in the 'unting-field,
sir; and her ladyship's favourite. The present Mr.
Norris has never been so equally."

"So I have understood," said I, persistently,
and (I think) gracefully pursuing my inquiries
and fortifying my position as a family friend.
"Dear, dear, how sad! And has this change —
poor Carthew's return, and all — has this not
mended matters?"

"Well, no, sir, not a sign of it," was the reply.
"Worse, we think, than ever."

"Dear, dear!" said I, again.

"When Mr. Norris arrived, she did seem glad
to see him," he pursued; "and we were all pleased,
I'm sure; for no one knows the young gentleman

but what likes him. Ah, sir, it did n't last long!
That very night they had a talk, and fell out or
something; her ladyship took on most painful; it
was like old days, but worse. And the next morning Mr. Norris was off again upon his travels.
'Denman,' he said to Mr. Denman, 'Denman, I 'll
never come back,' he said, and shook him by the
'and. I would n't be saying all this to a stranger,
sir," added my informant, overcome with a sudden fear lest he had gone too far.

He had indeed told me much, and much that
was unsuspected by himself. On that stormy
night of his return, Carthew had told his story;
the old lady had more upon her mind than mere
bereavements; and among the mental pictures
on which she looked, as she walked staring down
the path, was one of Midway Island and the
Flying Scud.

Mr. Denman heard my inquiries with discom-
posure, but informed me the shyster was already
gone.

"Gone?" cried I. "Then what can he have
come for? One thing I can tell you; it was not
to see the house."

"I don't see it could have been anything else,"
replied the butler.

"You may depend upon it it was," said I.
"And whatever it was, he has got· it. By the
way, where is Mr. Carthew at present? I was
sorry to find he was from home."

"He is engaged in travelling, sir," replied the
butler, drily.

"Ah, bravo!" cried I. "I laid a trap for you there, Mr. Denman. Now I need not ask you; I am sure you did not tell this prying stranger."

"To be sure not, sir," said the butler.

I went through the form of "shaking him by the 'and'"—like Mr. Norris—not, however, with genuine enthusiasm. For I had failed ingloriously to get the address for myself; and I felt a sure conviction that Bellairs had done better, or he had still been here and still cultivating Mr. Denman.

I had escaped the grounds and the cattle; I could not escape the house. A lady with silver hair, a slender silver voice, and a stream of insignificant information not to be diverted, led me through the picture gallery, the music-room, the great dining-room, the long drawing-room, the Indian room, the theatre, and every corner (as I thought) of that interminable mansion. There was but one place reserved; the garden-room, whither Lady Ann had now retired. I paused a moment on the outside of the door, and smiled to myself. The situation was indeed strange, and these thin boards divided the secret of the *Flying Scud*.

All the while, as I went to and fro, I was considering the visit and departure of Bellairs. That he had got the address, I was quite certain: that he had not got it by direct questioning, I was convinced; some ingenuity, some lucky accident, had served him. A similar chance, an equal ingenuity, was required; or I was left helpless, the ferret must run down his prey, the great oaks fall, the Raphaels be scattered, the house let to some stock-broker. suddenly made rich, and the name which now filled the mouths of five or six parishes dwindle to a memory. Strange that such great matters, so old a mansion, a family so ancient and so dull, should come to depend for perpetuity upon the intelligence, the discretion, and the cunning of a Latin-Quarter student! What Bellairs had done, I must do likewise. Chance or ingenuity, ingenuity or chance — so I continued to ring the changes as I walked away down the avenue, cast-ing back òccasional glances at the red brick façade and the twinkling windows of the house. How was I to command chance? where was I to find the ingenuity?

These reflections brought me to the door of the inn. And here, pursuant to my policy of keeping well with all men, I immediately smoothed my brow, and accepted (being the only guest in the house) an invitation to dine with the family in the bar-parlour. I sat down accordingly with Mr. Higgs the ex-butler, Mrs. Higgs the ex-lady's-maid, and Miss Agnes Higgs, their frowsy-headed little girl, the least promising and (as the event showed) the most useful of the lot. The talk ran endlessly on the great house and the great family; the roast beef, the Yorkshire pudding, the jam-roll, and the cheddar cheese came and went, and still the stream flowed on; near four generations of Carthews were touched upon without eliciting one point of interest; and we had killed Mr. Henry in " the 'unting field," with a vast elaboration of painful circumstance, and buried him in the midst of a whole sorrowing county, before I could so much as manage to bring upon the stage my intimate friend, Mr. Norris. At the name, the ex-butler grew diplomatic, and the ex-lady's-maid tender. He was the only person of the whole featureless series who seemed to have accomplished anything worth mention; and his achievements, poor dog, seemed to have been confined to going to the devil and leaving some regrets. He had been the image of the Right Honourable Bailley, one of the lights of that dim house, and a career of distinction had been predicted of him in consequence almost from the cradle. But before he was out of long clothes, the cloven foot began to show; he proved to be no Carthew, developed a taste for low pleasures and bad company, went birds-nesting with a stable-boy before he was eleven, and when he was near twenty, and might have been expected to display at least some rudiments of the family gravity, rambled the county over with a knapsack, making sketches and keeping company in wayside inns. He had no pride about him, I was told; he would sit down with any man; and it was somewhat woundingly implied that I was indebted to this peculiarity for my own acquaintance with the hero. Unhappily, Mr. Norris was not only eccentric, he was fast. His debts were still remembered at the University; still more, it appeared, the highly humourous circumstances attending his expulsion. " He was always fond of his jest," commented Mrs. Higgs.

"That he were!" observed her lord.

But it was after he went into the diplomatic service that the real trouble began.

"It seems, sir, that he went the pace extraordinary," said the ex-butler, with a solemn gusto.

"His debts were somethink awful," said the lady's-maid. "And as nice a young gentleman all the time as you would wish to see!"

"When word came to Mr. Carthew's ears, the turn up was 'orrible," continued Mr. Higgs. "I remember it as if it was yesterday. The bell was rung after her la'ship was gone, which I answered it myself, supposing it were the coffee. There was Mr. Carthew on his feet. ''Iggs,' he says, pointing with his stick, for he had a turn of the gout, 'order the dog-cart instantly for this son of mine which has disgraced hisself.' Mr. Norris say nothink: he sit there with his 'ead down, making belief to be looking at a walnut. You might have bowled me over with a straw," said Mr. Higgs.

"Had he done anything very bad?" I asked.

"Not he, Mr. Dodsley!" cried the lady — it was so she had conceived my name. "He never did anythink to all really wrong in his poor life. The 'ole affair was a disgrace. It was all rank favouritising."

"Mrs. 'Iggs! Mrs. 'Iggs!" cried the butler, warningly.

"Well, what do I care?" retorted the lady,

shaking her ringlets. " You know it was yourself, Mr. 'Iggs, and so did every member of the
staff."

While I was getting these facts and opinions,
I by no means neglected the child. She was not
attractive; but fortunately she had reached the
corrupt age of seven, when half a crown appears
about as large as a saucer and is fully as rare as
the dodo. For a shilling down, sixpence in her
money-box, and an American gold dollar which
I happened to find in my pocket, I bought the
creature soul and body. She declared her intention to accompany me to the ends of the earth;
and had to be chidden by her sire for drawing
comparisons between myself and her uncle William, highly damaging to the latter.

Dinner was scarce done, the cloth was not yet
removed, when Miss Agnes must needs climb into
my lap with her stamp album, a relic of the generosity of Uncle William. There are few things
I despise more than old stamps, unless perhaps it
be crests; for cattle (from the Carthew Chillinghams down to the old gate-keeper's milk cow in
the lane) contempt is far from being my first
sentiment. But it seemed I was doomed to pass
that day in viewing curiosities, and smothering a
yawn, I devoted myself once more to tread the
well-known round. I fancy Uncle William must
have begun the collection himself and tired of it,
for the book (to my surprise) was quite respecta-
bly filled. There were the varying shades of the
English penny, Russians with the coloured heart,

old undecipherable Thurn-und-Taxis, obsolete tri-
angular Cape of Good Hopes, Swan Rivers with
the Swan, and Guianas with the sailing ship.
Upon all these I looked with the eyes of a fish
and the spirit of a sheep; I think indeed I was
at times asleep; and it was probably in one of
these moments that I capsized the album, and there
fell from the end of it, upon the floor, a considerable number of what I believe to be called
" exchanges."

Here, against all probability, my chance had
come to me; for as I gallantly picked them up,
I was struck with the disproportionate amount of
five-sous French stamps. Some one, I reasoned,
must write very regularly from France to the
neighbourhood of Stallbridge-le-Carthew. Could
it be Norris? On one stamp I made out an
initial C; upon a second I got as far as C H;
beyond which point, the postmark used was in
every instance undecipherable. C H, when you
consider that about a quarter of the towns in
France begin with " chateau," was an insufficient
clue; and I promptly annexed the plainest of the
collection in order to consult the post-office.

The wretched infant took me in the fact.
" Naughty man, to 'teal my 'tamp!" she cried;
and when I would have brazened it off with a
denial, recovered and displayed the stolen article.

My position was now highly false: and I believe it was in mere pity that Mrs. Higgs came
to my rescue with a welcome proposition. If the
gentleman was really interested in stamps, she

said, probably supposing me a monomaniac on the point, he should see Mr. Denman's album. Mr. Denman had been collecting forty years, and his collection was said to be worth a mint of money. "Agnes," she went on, "if you were a kind little girl, you would run over to the 'All, tell Mr. Denman there's a connaisseer in the 'ouse, and ask him if one of the young gentlemen might bring the album down."

"I should like to see his exchanges too," I cried, rising to the occasion. "I may have some of mine in my pocket-book and we might trade."

Half an hour later, Mr. Denman arrived himself with a most unconscionable volume under his arm. "Ah, sir," he cried, "when I 'eard you was a collector, I dropped all. It's a saying of mine, Mr. Dodsley, that collecting stamps makes all collectors kin. It's a bond, sir; it creates a bond."

Upon the truth of this, I cannot say; but there is no doubt that the attempt to pass yourself off for a collector falsely creates a precarious situation.

"Ah, here's the second issue!" I would say, after consulting the legend at the side. "The pink — no, I mean the mauve — yes, that's the beauty of this lot. Though of course, as you say," I would hasten to add, "this yellow on the thin paper is more rare."

Indeed I must certainly have been detected, had I not plied Mr. Denman in self-defence with his favourite liquor — a port so excellent that it could never have ripened in the cellar of the *Carthew*

Arms, but must have been transported, under cloud of night, from the neighbouring vaults of the great house. At each threat of exposure, and in particular whenever I was directly challenged for an opinion, I made haste to fill the butler's glass, and by the time we had got to the exchanges, he was in a condition in which no stamp collector need be seriously feared. God forbid I should hint that he was drunk; he seemed incapable of the necessary liveliness; but the man's eyes were set, and so long as he was suffered to talk without interruption, he seemed careless of my heeding him.

In Mr. Denman's exchanges, as in those of little Agnes, the same peculiarity was to be remarked, an undue preponderance of that despicably common stamp, the French twenty-five centimes. And here joining them in stealthy review, I found the C and the C H; then something of an A just following; and then a terminal Y. Here was almost the whole name spelled out to me; it seemed familiar, too; and yet for some time I could not bridge the imperfection. Then I came upon another stamp, in which an L was legible before the Y, and in a moment the word leaped up complete. Chailly, that was the name; Chailly-en-Bière, the post town of Barbizon — ah, there was the very place for any man to hide himself — there was the very place for Mr. Norris, who had rambled over England making sketches — the very place for Goddedaal, who had left a palette knife on board the *Flying Scud*. Singular, indeed, that while I was drifting over England with the shyster, the man we were in quest of awaited me at my own ultimate destination.

Whether Mr. Denman had shown his album to Bellairs, whether, indeed, Bellairs could have caught (as I did) this hint from an obliterated postmark, I shall never know, and it mattered not. We were equal now; my task at Stallbridge-le-Carthew was accomplished; my interest in postage-stamps died shamelessly away; the astonished Denman was bowed out; and ordering the horse to be put in, I plunged into the study of the time-table.

.

27

CHAPTER XXI

FACE TO FACE

I FELL from the skies on Barbizon about two o'clock of a September afternoon. It is the dead hour of the day; all the workers have gone painting, all the idlers strolling, in the forest or the plain; the winding causeway street is solitary, and the inn deserted. I was the more pleased to find one of my old companions in the dining-room; his town clothes marked him for a man in the act of departure; and indeed his portmanteau lay beside him on the floor.

"Why, Stennis," I cried, "you 're the last man I expected to find here."

"You won't find me here long," he replied. "*King Pandion he is dead; all his friends are lapped in lead.* For men of our antiquity, the poor old shop is played out."

"*I have had playmates, I have had companions,*" I quoted in return. We were both moved, I think, to meet again in this scene of our old pleasure parties so unexpectedly, after so long an interval, and both already so much altered.

"That is the sentiment," he replied. "*All, all are gone, the old familiar faces.* I have been here a week, and the only living creature who seemed

to recollect me was the Pharaon. Bar the Sirons,
of course, and the perennial Bodmer."

" Is there no survivor?" I inquired.

" Of our geological epoch? not one," he replied.
" This is the city of Petra in Edom."

" And what sort of Bedouins encamp among
the ruins?" I asked.

" Youth, Dodd, youth; blooming, conscious
youth," he returned. " Such a gang, such rep-
tiles! to think we were like that! I wonder Siron
did n't sweep us from his premises."

" Perhaps we were n't so bad," I suggested.

" Don't let me depress you," said he. " We
were both Anglo-Saxons, anyway, and the only
redeeming feature to-day is another."

The thought of my quest, a moment driven out
by this rencounter, revived in my mind. " Who
is he?" I cried. " Tell me about him."

" What, the Redeeming Feature?" said he.
" Well, he 's a very pleasing creature, rather dim,
and dull, and genteel, but really pleasing. He
is very British, though, the artless Briton! Perhaps you 'll find him too much so for the trans-
atlantic nerves. Come to think of it, on the other
hand, you ought to get on famously. He is an
admirer of your great republic in one of its (excuse me) shoddiest features; he takes in and
sedulously reads a lot of American papers. I
warned you he was artless."

" What papers are they?" cried I.

" San Francisco papers," said he. " He gets a
bale of them about twice a week, and studies them

like the Bible. That's one of his weaknesses;
another is to be incalculably rich. He has taken
Masson's old studio — you remember? — at the
corner of the road; he has furnished it regardless
of expense, and lives there surrounded with *vins
fins* and works of art. When the youth of to-day
goes up to the Caverne des Brigands to make
punch — they do all that we did, like some nau-
seous form of ape (I never appreciated before what
a creature of tradition mankind is) — this Madden follows with a basket of champagne. I told
them he was wrong, and the punch tasted better;
but he thought the boys liked the style of the
thing, and I suppose they do. He is a very good-
natured soul, and very melancholy, and rather a
helpless. O, and he has a third weakness which
I came near forgetting. He paints. He has never
been taught, and he's past thirty, and he paints."

"How?" I asked.

"Rather well, I think," was the reply. "That's
the annoying part of it. See for yourself. That
panel is his."

I stepped toward the window. It was the old
familiar room, with the tables set like a Greek P,
and the sideboard, and the aphasiac piano, and
the panels on the wall. There were Romeo and
Juliet, Antwerp from the river, Enfield's ships
among the ice, and the huge huntsman winding
a huge horn; mingled with them a few new ones,
the thin crop of a succeeding generation, not better
and not worse. It was to one of these I was directed; a thing coarsely and wittily handled, mostly

with the palette knife, the colour in some parts
excellent, the canvas in others loaded with mere
clay. But it was the scene, and not the art or
want of it, that riveted my notice. The foreground was of sand and scrub and wreckwood;
in the middle distance the many-hued and smooth
expanse of a lagoon, enclosed by a wall of breakers; beyond, a blue strip of ocean. The sky was
cloudless, and I could hear the surf break. For
the place was Midway Island; the point of view
the very spot at which I had landed with the captain for the first time, and from which I had re-
embarked the day before we sailed. I had already
been gazing for some seconds, before my attention
was arrested by a blur on the sea-line; and stooping to look, I recognised the smoke of a steamer.

" Yes," said I, turning towards Stennis, " it has
merit. What is it?"

" A fancy piece," he returned. " That's what
pleased me. So few of the fellows in our time
had the imagination of a garden snail."

" Madden, you say his name is?" I pursued.

" Madden," he repeated.

" Has he travelled much?" I inquired.

" I have n't an idea. He is one of the least
autobiographical of men. He sits, and smokes,
and giggles, and sometimes he makes small jests;
but his contributions to the art of pleasing are
generally confined to looking like a gentleman
and being one. No," added Stennis, " he 'll never
suit you, Dodd; you like more head on your liquor.
You 'll find him as dull as ditch water."

"Has he big blond side-whiskers like tusks?"
I asked, mindful of the photograph of Goddedaal.

"Certainly not: why should he?" was the
reply.

"Does he write many letters?" I continued.

"God knows," says Stennis. "What is wrong
with you? I never saw you taken this way
before."

"The fact is, I think I know the man," said I.
"I think I'm looking for him. I rather think he
is my long-lost brother."

"Not twins, anyway," returned Stennis.

And about the same time, a carriage driving
up to the inn, he took his departure.

I walked till dinner-time in the plain, keeping
to the fields; for I instinctively shunned observation, and was racked by many incongruous and
impatient feelings. Here was a man whose voice
I had once heard, whose doings had filled so many
days of my life with interest and distress, whom
I had lain awake to dream of like a lover; and now
his hand was on the door; now we were to meet;
now I was to learn at last the mystery of the substituted crew. The sun went down over the plain
of the Angelus, and as the hour approached, my
courage lessened. I let the laggard peasants pass
me on the homeward way. The lamps were lit,
the soup was served, the company were all at table,
and the room sounded already with multitudi-
nous talk before I entered. I took my place and
found I was opposite to Madden. Over six feet
high and well set up, the hair dark and streaked

with silver, the eyes dark and kindly, the mouth
very good-natured, the teeth admirable; linen and
hands exquisite; English clothes, an English voice,
an English bearing: the man stood out conspicuous from the company. Yet he had made himself
at home, and seemed to enjoy a certain quiet popularity among the noisy boys of the table d'hôte.
He had an odd, silver giggle of a laugh, that
sounded nervous even when he was really amused,
and accorded ill with his big stature and manly,
melancholy face. This laugh fell in continually
all through dinner like the note of the triangle
in a piece of modern French music; and he had
at times a kind of pleasantry, rather of manner
than of words, with which he started or maintained the merriment. He took his share in these
diversions, not so much like a man in high spirits,
but like one of an approved good-nature, habit-
ually self-forgetful, accustomed to please and to
follow others. I have remarked in old soldiers
much the same smiling sadness and sociable self-
effacement.

I feared to look at him, lest my glances should
betray my deep excitement, and chance served me
so well that the soup was scarce removed before
we were naturally introduced. My first sip of
Château Siron, a vintage from which I had been
long estranged, startled me into speech.

" O, this 'll never do!" I cried, in English.

" Dreadful stuff, is n't it?" said Madden, in the
same language. " Do let me ask you to share my
bottle. They call it Chambertin, which it is n't;

but it's fairly palatable, and there's nothing in this house that a man can drink at all."

I accepted; anything would do that paved the way to better knowledge.

"Your name is Madden, I think," said I. "My old friend Stennis told me about you when I came."

"Yes: I am sorry he went; I feel such a Grandfather William, alone among all these lads," he replied.

"My name is Dodd," I resumed.

"Yes," said he, "so Madame Siron told me."

"Dodd, of San Francisco," I continued. "Late of Pinkerton and Dodd."

"Montana Block? I think," said he.

"The same," said I.

Neither of us looked at the other; but I could see his hand deliberately making bread pills.

"That's a nice thing of yours," I pursued, "that panel. The foreground is a little clayey, perhaps, but the lagoon is excellent."

"You ought to know," said he.

"Yes," returned I, "I'm rather a good judge of — that panel."

There was a considerable pause.

"You know a man by the name of Bellairs, don't you?" he resumed.

"Ah!" cried I, "you have heard from Dr. Urquart?"

"This very morning," he replied.

"Well, there is no hurry about Bellairs," said I. "It's rather a long story and rather a silly one. But I think we have a good deal to tell each other, and perhaps we had better wait till we are more alone."

"I think so," said he. "Not that any of these fellows know English, but we'll be more comfortable over at my place. Your health, Dodd."

And we took wine together across the table.

Thus had this singular introduction passed unperceived in the midst of more than thirty persons, art students, ladies in dressing-gowns and covered with rice powder, six foot of Siron whisking dishes over our head, and his noisy sons clattering in and out with fresh relays.

"One question more," said I. "Did you recognise my voice?"

"Your voice?" he repeated. "How should I? I had never heard it — we have never met."

"And yet, we have been in conversation before now," said I, "and I asked you a question which you never answered, and which I have since had many thousand better reasons for putting to myself."

He turned suddenly white. "Good God!" he cried, "are you the man in the telephone?"

I nodded.

"Well, well!" said he. "It would take a good deal of magnanimity to forgive you that. What nights I have passed! That little whisper has whistled in my ear ever since, like the wind in a keyhole. Who could it be? What could it mean? I suppose I have had more real, solid misery out of that . . ." He paused, and looked troubled.

"Though I had more to bother me, or ought to have," he added, and slowly emptied his glass.

"It seems we were born to drive each other crazy with conundrums," said I. "I have often thought my head would split."

Carthew burst into his foolish laugh. "And yet neither you nor I had the worst of the puzzle," he cried. "There were others deeper in."

"And who were they?" I asked.

"The underwriters," said he.

"Why, to be sure," cried I. "I never thought of that. What could they make of it?"

"Nothing," replied Carthew. "It could n't be explained. They were a crowd of small dealers at Lloyd's who took it up in syndicate; one of them has a carriage now; and people say he is a deuce of a deep fellow, and has the makings of a great financier. Another furnished a small villa on the profits. But they 're all hopelessly muddled; and when they meet each other, they don't know where to look, like the Augurs."

Dinner was no sooner at an end, than he carried me across the road to Masson's old studio. It was strangely changed. On the walls were tapestry, a few good etchings, and some amazing pictures — a Rousseau, a Corot, a really superb old Crome, a Whistler, and a piece which my host claimed (and I believe) to be a Titian. The room was furnished with comfortable English smoking-room chairs, some American rockers, and an elaborate business table; spirits and soda-water (with the mark of Schweppe, no less) stood ready

on a butler's tray, and in one corner, behind a
half-drawn curtain, I spied a camp-bed and a ca-
pacious tub. Such a room in Barbizon astonished
the beholder, like the glories of the cave of Monte
Cristo.

" Now," said he, " we are quiet. Sit down, if
you don't mind, and tell me your story all
through."

I did as he asked, beginning with the day when
Jim showed me the passage in the *Daily Occidental,* and winding up with the stamp album
and the Chailly postmark. It was a long business; and Carthew made it longer, for he was
insatiable of details; and it had struck midnight
on the old eight-day clock in the corner, before
I had made an end.

" And now," said he, " turn about: I must tell
you my side, much as I hate it. Mine is a beastly
story. You 'll wonder how I can sleep. I 've
told it once before, Mr. Dodd."

" To Lady Ann? " I asked.

" As you suppose," he answered; " and to say
the truth, I had sworn never to tell it again.
Only, you seem somehow entitled to the thing;
you have paid dear enough, God knows; and God
knows I hope you may like it, now you 've got it! "

With that he began his yarn. A new day had
dawned, the cocks crew in the village and the early
woodmen were afoot, when he concluded.

CHAPTER XXII

THE REMITTANCE MAN

SINGLETON CARTHEW, the father of
Norris, was heavily built and feebly vitalised, sensitive as a musician, dull as a
sheep, and conscientious as a dog. He took his
position with seriousness, even with pomp; the
long rooms, the silent servants, seemed in his eyes
like the observances of some religion of which he
was the mortal god. He had the stupid man's
intolerance of stupidity in others; the vain man's
exquisite alarm lest it should be detected in himself. And on both sides Norris irritated and
offended him. He thought his son a fool, and
he suspected that his son returned the compliment
with interest. The history of their relation was
simple; they met seldom, they quarrelled often.
To his mother, a fiery, pungent, practical woman,
already disappointed in her husband and her
elder son, Norris was only a fresh disappointment.

Yet the lad's faults were no great matter; he
was diffident, placable, passive, unambitious, un-
enterprising; life did not much attract him; he
watched it like a curious and dull exhibition, not
much amused, and not tempted in the least to

take a part. He beheld his father ponderously grinding sand, his mother fierily breaking butterflies, his brother labouring at the pleasures of the Hawbuck with the ardour of a soldier in a doubtful battle; and the vital sceptic looked on wondering. They were careful and troubled about many things; for him there seemed not even one thing needful. He was born disenchanted, the world's promises awoke no echo in his bosom, the world's activities and the world's distinctions seemed to him equally without a base in fact. He liked the open air; he liked comradeship, it mattered not with whom, his comrades were only a remedy for solitude. And he had a taste for painted art. An array of fine pictures looked upon his childhood and from these roods of jewelled canvas he received an indelible impression. The gallery at Stallbridge betokened generations of picture lovers; Norris was perhaps the first of his race to hold the pencil. The taste was genuine, it grew and strengthened with his growth; and yet he suffered it to be suppressed with scarce a struggle. Time came for him to go to Oxford, and he resisted faintly. He was stupid, he said; it was no good to put him through the mill; he wished to be a painter. The words fell on his father like a thunderbolt, and Norris made haste to give way. "It did n't really matter, don't you know?" said he. "And it seemed an awful shame to vex the old boy."

To Oxford he went obediently, hopelessly; and at Oxford became the hero of a certain circle.

He was active and adroit; when he was in the humour, he excelled in many sports; and his singular melancholy detachment gave him a place apart. He set a fashion in his clique; envious undergraduates sought to parody his unaffected lack of zeal and fear; it was a kind of new Byronism more composed and dignified. " Nothing really mattered "; among other things, this formula embraced the dons; and though he always meant to be civil, the effect on the college authorities was one of startling rudeness. His indifference cut like insolence; and in some outbreak of his constitutional levity (the complement of his melancholy) he was " sent down " in the middle of the second year.

The event was new in the annals of the Carthews, and Singleton was prepared to make the most of it. It had been long his practice to prophesy for his second son a career of ruin and disgrace. There is an advantage in this artless parental habit. Doubtless the father is interested in his son; but doubtless also the prophet grows to be interested in his prophecies. If the one goes wrong, the others come true. Old Carthew drew from this source esoteric consolations; he dwelt at length on his own foresight; he produced variations hitherto unheard from the old theme " I told you so," coupled his son's name with the gallows and the hulks, and spoke of his small handful of college debts as though he must raise money on a mortgage to discharge them.

" I don't think that is fair, sir," said Norris.

" I lived at college exactly as you told me. I am
sorry I was sent down, and you have a perfect
right to blame me for that; but you have no right
to pitch into me about these debts."

The effect upon a stupid man not unjustly incensed need scarcely be described. For awhile
Singleton raved.

" I 'll tell you what, father," said Norris at last,
" I don't think this is going to do. I think you
had better let me take to painting. It 's the only
thing I take a spark of interest in. I shall never
be steady as long as I 'm at anything else."

" When you stand here, sir, to the neck in disgrace," said the father, " I should have hoped you
would have had more good taste than to repeat
this levity."

The hint was taken; the levity was nevermore
obtruded on the father's notice, and Norris was
inexorably launched upon a backward voyage.
He went abroad to study foreign languages, which
he learned, at a very expensive rate; and a fresh
crop of debts fell soon to be paid, with similar
lamentations, which were in this case perfectly
justified, and to which Norris paid no regard.
He had been unfairly treated over the Oxford
affair; and with a spice of malice very surprising
in one so placable, and an obstinacy remarkable in
one so weak, refused from that day forward to
exercise the least captaincy on his expenses. He
wasted what he would; he allowed his servants
to despoil him at their pleasure; he sowed in-
solvency; and when the crop was ripe, notified

his father with exasperating calm. His own
capital was put in his hands, he was planted in
the diplomatic service and told he must depend
upon himself.

He did so till he was twenty-five; by· which
time he had spent his money, laid in a handsome
choice of debts, and acquired (like so many other
melancholic and uninterested persons) a habit
of gambling. An Austrian colonel — the same
who afterwards hanged himself at Monte Carlo —
gave him a lesson which lasted two-and-twenty
hours, and left him wrecked and helpless. Old
Singleton once more repurchased the honour of
his name, this time at a fancy figure; and Norris
was set afloat again on stern conditions. An
allowance of three hundred pounds in the year
was to be paid to him quarterly by a lawyer in
Sydney, New South Wales. He was not to write.
Should he fail on any quarter-day to be in Sydney,
he was to be held for dead and the allowance tacitly
withdrawn. Should he return to Europe, an advertisement publicly disowning him was to appear
in every paper of repute.

It was one of his most annoying features as a
son, that he was always polite, always just, and
in whatever whirlwind of domestic anger, always
calm. He expected trouble; when trouble came,
he was unmoved: he might have said with Singleton "*I told you so*"; he was content with thinking
"*just as I expected.*" On the fall of these last
thunderbolts, he bore himself like a person only
distantly interested in the event; pocketed the

money and the reproaches, obeyed orders punctually; took ship and came to Sydney. Some men are still lads at twenty-five; and so it was with Norris. Eighteen days after he landed, his quarter's allowance was all gone; and with the light-hearted hopefulness of strangers in what is called a new country, he began to besiege offices and apply for all manner of incongruous situations. Everywhere and last of all from his lodgings, he was bowed out; and found himself reduced, in a very elegant suit of summer tweeds, to herd and camp with the degraded outcasts of the city.

In this strait, he had recourse to the lawyer who paid him his allowance.

"Try to remember that my time is valuable, Mr. Carthew," said the lawyer. "It is quite unnecessary you should enlarge on the peculiar position in which you stand. *Remittance men,* as we call them here, are not so rare in my experience; and in such cases I act upon a system. I make you a present of a sovereign; here it is. Every day you choose to call, my clerk will advance you a shilling; on Saturday, since my office is closed on Sunday, he will advance you half a crown. My conditions are these: that you do not come to me, but to my clerk; that you do not come here the worse of liquor; and you go away the moment you are paid and have signed a receipt. I wish you a good-morning."

"I have to thank you, I suppose," said Carthew. "My position is so wretched that I cannot even refuse this starvation allowance."

"Starvation!" said the lawyer, smiling. "No man will starve here on a shilling a day. I have had on my hands another young gentleman, who remained continuously intoxicated for six years on the same allowance." And he once more busied himself with his papers.

In the time that followed, the image of the smiling lawyer haunted Carthew's memory. "That three minutes' talk was all the education I ever had worth talking of," says he. "It was all life in a nut-shell. Confound it! I thought, have I got to the point of envying that ancient fossil?"

Every morning for the next two or three weeks, the stroke of ten found Norris, unkempt and haggard, at the lawyer's door. The long day and longer night he spent in the Domain, now on a bench, now on the grass under a Norfolk Island pine, the companion of perhaps the lowest class on earth, the Larrikins of Sydney. Morning after morning, the dawn behind the lighthouse recalled him from slumber; and he would stand and gaze upon the changing east, the fading lenses, the smokeless city, and the many-armed and many-masted harbour growing slowly clear under his eyes. His bed-fellows (so to call them) were less active; they lay sprawled upon the grass and benches, the dingy men, the frowsy women, prolonging their late repose; and Carthew wandered among the sleeping bodies alone, and cursed the incurable stupidity of his behaviour. Day brought a new society of nursery-maids and children, and fresh-dressed and (I am sorry to say) tight-laced

maidens, and gay people in rich traps; upon the
skirts of which Carthew and "the other black-
guards" — his own bitter phrase — skulked, and
chewed grass, and looked on. Day passed, the
light died, the green and leafy precinct sparkled
with lamps or lay in shadow, and the round of
the night began again, the loitering women, the
lurking men, the sudden outburst of screams, the
sound of flying feet. "You may n't believe it,"
says Carthew, "but I got to that pitch that I
did n't care a hang. I have been wakened out of
my sleep to hear a woman screaming, and I have
only turned upon my other side. Yes, it 's a queer
place, where the dowagers and the kids walk all
day, and at night you can hear people bawling for
help as if it was the Forest of Bondy, with the
lights of a great town all round, and parties spinning through in cabs from Government House
and dinner with my lord!"

It was Norris's diversion, having none other, to
scrape acquaintance, where, how, and with whom
he could. Many a long dull talk he held upon the
benches or the grass; many a strange waif he
came to know; many strange things he heard,
and saw some that were abominable. It was to one
of these last that he owed his deliverance from
the Domain. For some time the rain had been
merciless; one night after another he had been
obliged to squander fourpence on a bed and re-
duce his board to the remaining eightpence: and
he sat one morning near the Macquarrie Street
entrance, hungry, for he had gone without break-

fast, and wet, as he had already been for several days, when the cries of an animal in distress attracted his attention. Some fifty yards away, in the extreme angle of the grass, a party of the chronically unemployed had got hold of a dog, whom they were torturing in a manner not to be described. The heart of Norris, which had grown indifferent to the cries of human anger or distress, woke at the appeal of the dumb creature. He ran amongst the Larrikins, scattered them, rescued the dog, and stood at bay. They were six in number, shambling gallowsbirds; but for once the proverb was right, cruelty was coupled with cowardice, and the wretches cursed him and made off. It chanced this act of prowess had not passed unwitnessed. On a bench near by there was seated a shopkeeper's assistant out of employ, a diminutive, cheerful, red-headed creature by the name of Hemstead. He was the last man to have interfered himself, for his discretion more than equalled his valour; but he made haste to congratulate Carthew, and to warn him he might not always be so fortunate.

"They're a dyngerous lot of people about this park. My word! it does n't do to ply with them!" he observed, in that *rycy Austrylian* English, which (as it has received the imprimatur of Mr. Froude) we should all make haste to imitate.

"Why, I'm one of that lot myself," returned Carthew.

Hemstead laughed and remarked that he knew a gentleman when he saw one.

"For all that, I am simply one of the unem-

ployed," said Carthew, seating himself beside his
new acquaintance, as he had sat (since this experience began) beside so many dozen others.

" I am out of a plyce myself," said Hemstead.

" You beat me all the way and back," says
Carthew. " My trouble is that I have never been
in one."

" I suppose you 've no tryde?" asked Hemstead.

" I know how to spend money," replied Carthew,
" and I really do know something of horses and
something of the sea. But the unions head me
off; if it were n't for them, I might have had a
dozen berths."

" My word!" cried the sympathetic listener.
" Ever try the mounted police?" he inquired.

" I did, and was bowled out," was the reply;
" could n't pass the doctors."

" Well, what do you think of the ryleways,
then?" asked Hemstead.

" What do *you* think of them, if you come to
that?" asked Carthew.

" O, *I* don't think of them; I don't go in for
manual labour," said the little man, proudly. " But
if a man don't mind that, he 's pretty sure of a
job there."

" By George, you tell me where to go!" cried
Carthew, rising.

The heavy rains continued, the country was
already overrun with floods; the railway system
daily required more hands, daily the superintend-
ent advertised; but " the unemployed " preferred .
the resources of charity and rapine, and a navvy,

even an amateur navvy, commanded money in the market. The same night, after a tedious journey, and a change of trains to pass a landslip, Norris found himself in a muddy cutting behind South Clifton, attacking his first shift of manual labour.

For weeks the rain scarce relented. The whole front of the mountain slipped seaward from above, avalanches of clay, rock, and uprooted forest spewed over the cliffs and fell upon the beach or in the breakers. Houses were carried bodily away and smashed like nuts; others were menaced and deserted, the door locked, the chimney cold, the dwellers fled elsewhere for safety. Night and day the fire blazed in the encampment; night and day hot coffee was served to the overdriven toilers in the shift; night and day the engineer of the section made his rounds with words of encouragement, hearty and rough and well suited to his men. Night and day, too, the telegraph clicked with disastrous news and anxious inquiry. Along the terraced line of rail, rare trains came creeping and signalling; and paused at the threatened corner, like living things conscious of peril. The commandant of the post would hastily review his labours, make (with a dry throat) the signal to advance; and the whole squad line the way and look on in a choking silence, or burst into a brief cheer as the train cleared the point of danger and shot on, perhaps through the thin sunshine between squalls, perhaps with blinking lamps into the gathering, rainy twilight.

One such scene Carthew will remember till he

dies. It blew great guns from the seaward; a huge surf bombarded, five hundred feet below him, the steep mountain's foot; close in was a vessel in distress, firing shots from a fowling-piece, if any help might come. So he saw and heard her the moment before the train appeared and paused, throwing up a Babylonian tower of smoke into the rain and oppressing men's hearts with the scream of her whistle. The engineer was there himself; he paled as he made the signal: the engine came at a foot's pace; but the whole bulk of mountain shook and seemed to nod seaward, and the watching navvies instinctively clutched at shrubs and trees: vain precautions, vain as the shots from the poor sailors. Once again fear was disappointed; the train passed unscathed; and Norris, drawing a long breath, remembered the labouring ship and glanced below. She was gone.

So the days and the nights passed: Homeric labour in Homeric circumstance. Carthew was sick with sleeplessness and coffee; his hands, softened by the wet, were cut to ribbons; yet he enjoyed a peace of mind and health of body hitherto unknown. Plenty of open air, plenty of physical exertion, a continual instancy of toil, here was what had been hitherto lacking in that misdirected life, and the true cure of vital scepticism. To get the train through: there was the recurrent problem; no time remained to ask if it were necessary. Carthew, the idler, the spendthrift, the drifting dilettante, was soon remarked, praised, and advanced. The engineer swore by him and pointed

him out for an example. " I 've a new chum, up
here," Norris overheard him saying, " a young
swell. He 's worth any two in the squad." The
words fell on the ears of the discarded son
like music; and from that moment, he not only
found an interest, he took a pride, in his plebeian
tasks.

. The press of work was still at its highest when
quarter-day approached. Norris was now raised
to a position of some trust; at his discretion, trains
were stopped or forwarded at the dangerous cor-
nice near North Clifton; and he found in this
responsibility both terror and delight. The thought
of the seventy-five pounds that would soon await
him at the lawyer's, and of his own obligation
to be present every quarter-day in Sydney, filled
him for a little with divided councils. Then he
made up his mind, walked in a slack moment to
the inn at Clifton, ordered a sheet of paper and a
bottle of beer, and wrote, explaining that he held
a good appointment which he would lose if he came
to Sydney, and asking the lawyer to accept this
letter as an evidence of his presence in the colony
and retain the money till next quarter-day. The
answer came in course of post, and was not merely
favourable but cordial. " Although what you propose is contrary to the terms of my instructions,"
it ran, "I willingly accept the responsibility of
granting your request. I should say I am agreeably disappointed in your behaviour. My experience has not led me to found much expectations on
gentlemen in your position."

The rains abated, and the temporary labour was discharged; not Norris, to whom the engineer clung as to found money; not Norris, who found himself a ganger on the line in the regular staff of navvies. His camp was pitched in a grey wilderness of rock and forest, far from any house; as he sat with his mates about the evening fire, the trains passing on the track were their next and indeed their only neighbours, except the wild things of the wood. Lovely weather, light and monotonous employment, long hours of somnolent campfire talk, long sleepless nights, when he reviewed his foolish and fruitless career as he rose and walked in the moonlit forest, an occasional paper of which he would read all, the advertisements with as much relish as the text: such was the tenor of an existence which soon began to weary and harass him. He lacked and regretted the fatigue, the furious hurry, the suspense, the fires, the midnight coffee, the rude and mud-bespattered poetry of the first toilful weeks. In the quietness of his new surroundings, a voice summoned him from this exorbital part of life, and about the middle of October he threw up his situation and bade farewell to the camp of tents and the shoulder of Bald Mountain.

Clad in his rough clothes, with a bundle on his shoulder and his accumulated wages in his pocket, he entered Sydney for the second time, and walked with pleasure and some bewilderment in the cheerful streets, like a man landed from a voyage. The sight of the people led him on. He forgot his necessary errands, he forgot to eat. He wandered in moving multitudes like a stick upon a river. Last he came to the Domain and strolled there, and remembered his shame and sufferings, and looked with poignant curiosity at his successors. Hemstead, not much shabbier and no less cheerful than before, he recognised and addressed like an old family friend.

"That was a good turn you did me," said he. "That railway was the making of me. I hope you 've had luck yourself."

"My word, no!" replied the little man. "I just sit here and read the *Dead Bird*. It 's the depression in tryde, you see. There 's no positions goin' that a man like me would care to look at." And he showed Norris his certificates and written characters, one from a grocer in Wooloomooloo, one from an ironmonger, and a third from a billiard saloon. "Yes," he said, "I tried bein' a billiard marker. It 's no account; these lyte hours are no use for a man's health. I won't be no man's slyve," he added firmly.

On the principle that he who is too proud to be a slave is usually not too modest to become a pensioner, Carthew gave him half a sovereign, and departed, being suddenly struck with hunger, in the direction of the Paris House. When he came to that quarter of the city, the barristers were trotting in the streets in wig and gown, and he stood to observe them with his bundle on his shoulder, and his mind full of curious recollections of the past.

" By George! " cried a voice, " it 's Mr. Carthew!"

And turning about, he found himself face to face with a handsome sunburnt youth, somewhat fatted, arrayed in the finest of fine raiment, and sporting about a sovereign's worth of flowers in his buttonhole. Norris had met him during his first days in Sydney at a farewell supper; had even escorted him on board a schooner full of cockroaches and black-boy sailors in which he was bound for six months among the islands; and had kept him ever since in entertained remembrance. Tom Hadden (known to the bulk of Sydney folk as *Tommy*) was heir to a considerable property, which a prophetic father had placed in the hands of rigorous trustees. The income supported Mr. Hadden in splendour for about three months out of twelve; the rest of the year he passed in retreat among the islands. He was now about a week returned from his eclipse, pervading Sydney in hansom cabs and airing the first bloom of six new suits of clothes; and yet the unaffected creature hailed Carthew in his working jeans and with the damning bundle on his shoulder, as he might have claimed acquaintance with a duke.

" Come and have a drink! " was his cheerful cry.

" I 'm just going to have lunch at the Paris House," returned Carthew. " It 's a long time since I have had a decent meal."

" Splendid scheme! " said Hadden. " I 've only had breakfast half an hour ago; but we 'll have a private room, and I 'll manage to pick something.

It 'll brace me up. I was on an awful tear last night, and I 've met no end of fellows this morning." To meet a fellow, and to stand and share a drink, were with Tom synonymous terms.

They were soon at table in the corner room upstairs, and paying due attention to the best fare in Sydney. The odd similarity of their positions drew them together, and they began soon to exchange confidences. Carthew related his privations in the Domain and his toils as a navvy; Hadden gave his experience as an amateur copra merchant in the South Seas, and drew a humourous picture of life in a coral island. Of the two plans of retirement, Carthew gathered that his own had been vastly the more lucrative; but Hadden's trading outfit had consisted largely of bottled stout and brown sherry for his own consumption.

" I had champagne too," said Hadden, " but I kept that in case of sickness, until I did n't seem to be going to be sick, and then I opened a pint every Sunday. Used to sleep all morning, then breakfast with my pint of fizz, and lie in a hammock and read Hallam's *Middle Ages*. Have you read that? I always take something solid to the islands. There 's no doubt I did the thing in rather a fine style; but if it was gone about a little cheaper, or there were two of us to bear the expense, it ought to pay hand over fist. I 've got the influence, you see. I 'm a chief now, and sit in the speak-house under my own strip of roof. I 'd like to see them taboo *me!* They dare n't try it; I 've a strong party, I can tell you. Why, I 've had upwards of thirty cowtops sitting in my front veranda eating tins of salmon."

"Cowtops?" asked Carthew, "what are they?"

"That's what Hallam would call feudal retainers," explained Hadden, not without vainglory. "They're My Followers. They belong to My Family. I tell you, they come expensive, though; you can't fill up all these retainers on tinned salmon for nothing; but whenever I could get it, I would give 'em squid. Squid's good for natives, but I don't care for it, do you? — or shark either. It's like the working classes at home. With copra at the price it is, they ought to be willing to bear their share of the loss; and so I've told them again and again. I think it's a man's duty to open their minds, and I try to, but you can't get political economy into them; it does n't seem to reach their intelligence."

There was an expression still sticking in Carthew's memory, and he returned upon it with a smile. "Talking of political economy," said he, "you said if there were two of us to bear the expense, the profits would increase. How do you make out that?"

"I'll show you! I'll figure it out for you!" cried Hadden, and with a pencil on the back of the bill of fare, proceeded to perform miracles. He was a man, or let us rather say a lad, of unusual projective power. Give him the faintest hint of any speculation, and the figures flowed from him by the page. A lively imagination and a ready though inaccurate memory supplied his data; he delivered himself with an inimitable heat that made him seem the picture of pugnacity; lavished contradiction; had a form of words, with or without significance, for every form of criticism; and the looker-on alternately smiled at his simplicity and fervour, or was amazed by his unexpected shrewdness. He was a kind of Pinkerton in play. I have called Jim's the romance of business; this was its Arabian tale.

"Have you any idea what this would cost?" he asked, pausing at an item.

"Not I," said Carthew.

"Ten pounds ought to be ample," concluded the projector.

"O, nonsense!" cried Carthew. "Fifty at the very least."

"You told me yourself this moment you knew nothing about it!" cried Tommy. "How can I make a calculation, if you blow hot and cold? You don't seem able to be serious!"

But he consented to raise his estimate to twenty; and a little after, the calculation coming out with a deficit, cut it down again to five pound ten, with the remark, "I told you it was nonsense. This sort of thing has to be done strictly, or where's the use?"

Some of these processes struck Carthew as unsound; and he was at times altogether thrown out by the capricious startings of the prophet's mind. These plunges seemed to be gone into for exercise and by the way, like the curvets of a willing horse. Gradually the thing took shape; the glittering if

baseless edifice arose; and the hare still ran on the
mountains, but the soup was already served in silver plate. Carthew in a few days could command
a hundred and fifty pounds; Hadden was ready
with five hundred; why should they not recruit
a fellow or two more, charter an old ship, and go
cruising on their own account? Carthew was an
experienced yachtsman; Hadden professed himself able to " work an approximate sight." Money
was undoubtedly to be made, or why should so
many vessels cruise about the islands? they, who
worked their own ship, were sure of a still higher
profit.

" And whatever else comes of it, you see," cried
Hadden, " we get our keep for nothing. Come,
buy some togs, that 's the first thing you have to
do of course; and then we 'll take a hansom and go
to the *Currency Lass.*"

" I 'm going to stick to the togs I have," said
Norris.

" Are you?" cried Hadden. " Well, I must say
I admire you. You 're a regular sage. It 's what
you call Pythagoreanism, is n't it? if I have n't
forgotten my philosophy."

" Well, I call it economy," returned Carthew.
" If we are going to try this thing on, I shall want
every sixpence."

" You 'll see if we 're going to try it!" cried
Tommy, rising radiant from table. " Only, mark
you, Carthew, it must be all in your name. I have
capital, you see; but you 're all right. You can
play *vacuus viator,* if the thing goes wrong."

"I thought we had just proved it was quite safe," said Carthew.

"There's nothing safe in business, my boy," replied the sage; "not even bookmaking."

The public house and tea garden called the *Currency Lass* represented a moderate fortune gained by its proprietor, Captain Bostock, during a long, active, and occasionally historic career among the islands. Anywhere from Tonga to the Admiralty Isles, he knew the ropes and could lie in the native dialect. He had seen the end of sandal wood, the end of oil, and the beginning of copra; and he was himself a commercial pioneer, the first that ever carried human teeth into the Gilberts. He was tried for his life in Fiji in Sir Arthur Gordon's time; and if ever he prayed at all, the name of Sir Arthur was certainly not forgotten. He was speared in seven places in New Ireland — the same time his mate was killed — the famous "outrage on the brig *Jolly Roger*"; but the treacherous savages made little by their wickedness, and Bostock, in spite of their teeth, got seventy-five head of volunteer labour on board, of whom not more than a dozen died of injuries. He had a hand, besides, in the amiable pleasantry which cost the life of Patteson; and when the sham bishop landed, prayed, and gave his benediction to the natives, Bostock, arrayed in a female chemise out of the traderoom, had stood at his right hand and boomed amens. This, when he was sure he was among good fellows, was his favourite yarn. "Two hundred head of labour for a hatful of amens," he used to

name the tale; and its sequel, the death of the real
bishop, struck him as a circumstance of extraordinary humour.

Many of these details were communicated in the
hansom, to the surprise of Carthew.

" Why do we want to visit this old ruffian? " he
asked.

" You wait till you hear him," replied Tommy.
" That man knows everything."

On descending from the hansom at the *Currency
Lass*, Hadden was struck with the appearance of
the cabman, a gross, salt-looking man, red-faced,
blue-eyed, short-handed and short-winded, perhaps
nearing forty.

" Surely I know you? " said he. " Have you
driven me before? "

" Many 's the time, Mr. Hadden," returned the
driver. " The last time you was back from the
islands, it was me that drove you to the races,
sir."

" All right: jump down and have a drink then,"
said Tom, and he turned and led the way into the
garden.

Captain Bostock met the party: he was a slow,
sour old man, with fishy eyes; greeted Tommy
offhand, and (as was afterwards remembered)
exchanged winks with the driver.

" A bottle of beer for the cabman there at that
table," said Tom. " Whatever you please from
shandygaff to champagne at this one here; and
you sit down with us. Let me make you acquainted with my friend, Mr. Carthew. I 've come

on business, Billy; I want to consult you as a friend; I'm going into the island trade upon my own account."

Doubtless the captain was a mine of counsel, but opportunity was denied him. He could not venture on a statement, he was scarce allowed to finish a phrase, before Hadden swept him from the field with a volley of protest and correction. That projector, his face blazing with inspiration, first laid before him at inordinate length a question, and as soon as he attempted to reply, leaped at his throat, called his facts in question, derided his policy, and at times thundered on him from the heights of moral indignation.

"I beg your pardon," he said once. "I am a gentleman, Mr. Carthew here is a gentleman, and we don't mean to do that class of business. Can't you see who you're talking to? Can't you talk sense? Can't you give us 'a dead bird' for a good traderoom?"

"No, I don't suppose I can," returned old Bostock; "not when I can't hear my own voice for two seconds together. It was gin and guns I did it with."

"Take your gin and guns to Putney!" cried Hadden. "It was the thing in your times, that's right enough; but you're old now, and the game's up. I'll tell you what's wanted nowadays, Bill Bostock," said he; and did, and took ten minutes to it.

Carthew could not refrain from smiling. He began to think less seriously of the scheme, Had-

den appearing too irresponsible a guide; but on
the other hand, he enjoyed himself amazingly. It
was far from being the same with Captain Bostock.

"You know a sight, don't you?" remarked that
gentleman, bitterly, when Tommy paused.

"I know a sight more than you, if that 's what
you mean," retorted Tom. "It stands to reason
I do. You 're not a man of any education; you 've
been all your life at sea or in the islands; you
don't suppose you can give points to a man like
me?"

"Here 's your health, Tommy," returned Bostock. "You 'll make an A 1 bake in the New
Hebrides."

"That 's what I call talking," cried Tom, not
perhaps grasping the spirit of this doubtful compliment. "Now you give me your attention. We
have the money and the enterprise, and I have the
experience: what we want is a cheap, smart boat,
a good captain, and an introduction to some house
that will give us credit for the trade."

"Well, I 'll tell you," said Captain Bostock.
"I seen men like you baked and eaten, and complained of afterwards. Some was tough, and
some had n't no flaviour," he added grimly.

"What do you mean by that?" cried Tom.

"I mean I don't care," said Bostock. "It ain't
any of my interests. I have n't underwrote your
life. Only I 'm blest if I 'm not sorry for the
cannibal as tries to eat your head. And what
I recommend is a cheap, smart coffin and a good
undertaker. See if you can find a house to give

you credit for a coffin! Look at your friend there; he 's got some sense; he 's laughing at you so as he can't stand."

The exact degree of ill-feeling in Mr. Bostock's mind was difficult to gauge; perhaps there was not much, perhaps he regarded his remarks as a form of courtly badinage. But there is little doubt that Hadden resented them. He had even risen from his place, and the conference was on the point of breaking up, when a new voice joined suddenly in the conversation.

The cabman sat with his back turned upon the party, smoking a meerschaum pipe. Not a word of Tommy's eloquence had missed him, and he now faced suddenly about with these amazing words:

"Excuse me, gentlemen; if you 'll buy me the ship I want, I 'll get you the trade on credit."

There was a pause.

" Well, what do you mean? " gasped Tommy.

" Better tell 'em who I am, Billy," said the cabman.

" Think it safe, Joe? " inquired Mr. Bostock.

" I 'll take my risk of it," returned the cabman.

" Gentlemen," said Bostock, rising solemnly, " let me make you acquainted with Captain Wicks of the *Grace Darling*."

" Yes, gentlemen, that is what I am," said the cabman. " You know I 've been in trouble; and I don't deny but what I struck the blow, and where was I to get evidence of my provocation?

So I turned to and took a cab, and I 've driven one for three year now and nobody the wiser."

"I beg your pardon," said Carthew, joining almost for the first time; "I am a new chum. What was the charge?"

"Murder," said Captain Wicks, "and I don't deny but what I struck the blow. And there 's no sense in my trying to deny I was afraid to go to trial, or why would I be here? But it 's a fact it was flat mutiny. Ask Billy here. He knows how it was."

Carthew breathed long; he had a strange, half-pleasurable sense of wading deeper in the tide of life. "Well?" said he, "you were going on to say?"

"I was going on to say this," said the captain, sturdily. "I 've overheard what Mr. Hadden has been saying, and I think he talks good sense. I like some of his ideas first chop. He 's sound on traderooms; he 's all there on the traderoom; and I see that he and I would pull together. Then you 're both gentlemen, and I like that," observed Captain Wicks. "And then I 'll tell you I 'm tired of this cabbing cruise, and I want to get to work again. Now here 's my offer. I 've a little money I can stake up, — all of a hundred anyway. Then my old firm will give me trade, and jump at the chance; they never lost by me; they know what I 'm worth as supercargo. And last of all, you want a good captain to sail your ship for you. Well, here I am. I 've sailed schooners for ten years. Ask Billy if I can handle a schooner."

"No man better," said Billy.

"And as for my character as a shipmate," concluded Wicks, "go and ask my old firm."

"But look here!" cried Hadden. "How do you mean to manage? You can whisk round in a hansom, and no questions asked. But if you try to come on a quarter-deck, my boy, you'll get nabbed."

"I'll have to keep back till the last," replied Wicks, "and take another name."

"But how about clearing? what other name?" asked Tommy, a little bewildered.

"I don't know yet," returned the captain, with a grin. "I'll see what the name is on my new certificate, and that'll be good enough for me. If I can't get one to buy, though I never heard of such a thing, there's old Kirkup, he's turned some sort of farmer down Bondy way; he'll hire me his."

"You seemed to speak as if you had a ship in view," said Carthew.

"So I have, too," said Captain Wicks, "and a beauty. Schooner yacht *Dream;* got lines you never saw the beat of; and a witch to go. She passed me once off Thursday Island, doing two knots to my one and laying a point and a half better; and the *Grace Darling* was a ship that I was proud of. I took and tore my hair. The *Dream*'s been *my* dream ever since. That was in her old days, when she carried a blue ens'n. Grant Sanderson was the party as owned her; he was rich and mad, and got a fever at last some-

where about the Fly River, and took and died.
The captain brought the body back to Sydney,
and paid off. Well, it turned out Grant Sanderson had left any quantity of wills and any quantity of widows, and no fellow could make out which
was the genuine article. All the widows brought
lawsuits against all the rest, and every will had
a firm of lawyers on the quarter-deck as long as
your arm. They tell me it was one of the biggest turns-to that ever was seen, bar Tichborne;
the Lord Chamberlain himself was floored, and
so was the Lord Chancellor; and all that time
the *Dream* lay rotting up by Glebe Point. Well,
it 's done now; they 've picked out a widow and
a will; tossed up for it, as like as not; and the
Dream 's for sale. She 'll go cheap; she 's had a
long turn-to at rotting."

" What size is she? "

" Well, big enough. We don't want her bigger. A hundred and ninety, going two hundred,"
replied the captain. " She 's fully big for us three;
it would be all the better if we had another hand,
though it 's a pity too, when you can pick up natives for half nothing. Then we must have a cook.
I can fix raw sailor-men, but there 's no going to
sea with a new-chum cook. I can lay hands on
the man we want for that: a Highway boy, an old
shipmate of mine, of the name of Amalu. Cooks
first-rate, and it 's always better to have a native;
he ain't fly, you can turn him to as you please, and
he don't know enough to stand out for his rights."

From the moment that Captain Wicks joined in

the conversation, Carthew recovered interest and
confidence; the man (whatever he might have
done) was plainly good-natured, and plainly capable; if he thought well of the enterprise, offered
to contribute money, brought experience, and could
thus solve at a word the problem of the trade,
Carthew was content to go ahead. As for Hadden, his cup was full; he and Bostock forgave
each other in champagne; toast followed toast; it
was proposed and carried amid acclamation to
change the name of the schooner (when she should
be bought) to the *Currency Lass;* and the *Currency Lass Island Trading Company* was practically founded before dusk.

Three days later, Carthew stood before the
lawyer, still in his jean suit, received his hundred and fifty pounds, and proceeded rather timidly
to ask for more indulgence.

"I have a chance to get on in the world," he
said. "By to-morrow evening I expect to be
part owner of a ship."

"Dangerous property, Mr. Carthew," said the
lawyer.

"Not if the partners work her themselves and
stand to go down along with her," was the reply.

"I conceive it possible you might make something of it that way," returned the other. "But
are you a seaman? I thought you had been in
the diplomatic service."

"I am an old yachtsman," said Norris. "And
I must do the best I can. A fellow can't live in
New South Wales upon diplomacy. But the point

I wish to prepare you for is this. It will be impossible I should present myself here next quarter-day; we expect to make a six-months' cruise of it among the islands."

"Sorry, Mr. Carthew: I can't hear of that," replied the lawyer.

"I mean upon the same conditions as the last," said Carthew.

"The conditions are exactly opposite," said the lawyer. "Last time I had reason to know you were in the colony; and even then I stretched a point. This time, by your own confession, you are contemplating a breach of the agreement; and I give you warning if you carry it out and I receive proof of it (for I will agree to regard this conversation as confidential) I shall have no choice but to do my duty. Be here on quarter-day, or your allowance ceases."

"This is very hard and, I think, rather silly," returned Carthew.

"It is not of my doing. I have my instructions," said the lawyer.

"And you so read these instructions, that I am to be prohibited from making an honest livelihood?" asked Carthew.

"Let us be frank," said the lawyer. "I find nothing in these instructions about an honest livelihood. I have no reason to suppose my clients care anything about that. I have reason to suppose only one thing, — that they mean you shall stay in this colony, and to guess another, Mr. Carthew. And to guess another."

"What do you mean by that?" asked Norris.

"I mean that I imagine, on very strong grounds, that your family desire to see no more of you," said the lawyer. "O, they may be very wrong; but that is the impression conveyed, that is what I suppose I am paid to bring about, and I have no choice but to try and earn my hire."

"I would scorn to deceive you," said Norris, with a strong flush, "you have guessed rightly. My family refuse to see me; but I am not going to England, I am going to the islands. How does that affect the islands?"

"Ah, but I don't know that you are going to the islands," said the lawyer, looking down, and spearing the blotting-paper with a pencil.

"I beg your pardon. I have the pleasure of informing you," said Norris.

"I am afraid, Mr. Carthew, that I cannot regard that communication as official," was the slow reply.

"I am not accustomed to have my word doubted!" cried Norris.

"Hush! I allow no one to raise his voice in my office," said the lawyer. "And for that matter — you seem to be a young gentleman of sense — consider what I know of you. You are a discarded son; your family pays money to be shut of you. What have you done? I don't know. But do you not see how foolish I should be, if I exposed my business reputation on the safeguard of the honour of a gentleman of whom I know just so much and no more? This interview is very disagreeable. Why prolong it? Write home, get my instructions changed, and I will change my behaviour. Not otherwise."

"I am very fond of three hundred a year," said Norris, "but I cannot pay the price required. I shall not have the pleasure of seeing you again."

"You must please yourself," said the lawyer. "Fail to be here next quarter-day, and the thing stops. But I warn you, and I mean the warning in a friendly spirit. Three months later you will be here begging, and I shall have no choice but to show you in the street."

"I wish you a good-evening," said Norris.

"The same to you, Mr. Carthew," retorted the lawyer, and rang for his clerk.

So it befell that Norris, during what remained to him of arduous days in Sydney, saw not again the face of his legal adviser; and he was already at sea, and land was out of sight, when Hadden brought him a Sydney paper, over which he had been dozing in the shadow of the galley, and showed him an advertisement.

"Mr. Norris Carthew is earnestly entreated to call without delay at the office of Mr. ——, where important intelligence awaits him."

"It must manage to wait for me six months," said Norris, lightly enough, but yet conscious of a pang of curiosity.

CHAPTER XXIII

THE BUDGET OF THE " CURRENCY LASS "

BEFORE noon on the 26th November, there cleared from the port of Sydney the schooner, *Currency Lass.* The owner, Norris Carthew, was on board in the somewhat unusual position of mate; the master's name purported to be William Kirkup; the cook was a Hawaiian boy, Joseph Amalu; and there were two hands before the mast, Thomas Hadden and Richard Hemstead, the latter chosen partly because of his humble character, partly because he had an odd-job-man's handiness with tools. The *Currency Lass* was bound for the South Sea Islands, and first of all for Butaritari in the Gilberts, on a register; but it was understood about the harbour that her cruise was more than half a pleasure trip. A friend of the late Grant Sanderson (of Auchentroon and Kilclarty) might have recognised in that tall-masted ship, the transformed and rechristened *Dream;* and a Lloyd's surveyor, had the services of such an one been called in requisition, must have found abundant subject of remark.

For time, during her three years' inaction, had eaten deep into the *Dream* and her fittings; she had sold in consequence a shade above her value as old junk; and the three adventurers had scarce been able to afford even the most vital repairs. The rigging, indeed, had been partly renewed, and the rest set up; all Grant Sanderson's old canvas had been patched together into one decently serviceable suit of sails; Grant Sanderson's masts still stood, and might have wondered at themselves. "I have n't the heart to tap them," Captain Wicks used to observe, as he squinted up their height or patted their rotundity; and "as rotten as our foremast" was an accepted metaphor in the ship's company. The sequel rather suggests it may have been sounder than was thought; but no one knew for certain, just as no one except the captain appreciated the dangers of the cruise. The captain, indeed, saw with clear eyes and spoke his mind aloud; and though a man of an astonishing hot-blooded courage, following life and taking its dangers in the spirit of a hound upon the slot, he had made a point of a big whale-boat. "Take your choice," he had said; "either new masts and rigging or that boat. I simply ain't going to sea without the one or the other. Chicken coops are good enough, no doubt, and so is a dinghy; but they ain't for Joe." And his partners had been forced to consent, and saw six and thirty pounds of their small capital vanish in the turn of a hand.

All four had toiled the best part of six weeks getting ready; and though Captain Wicks was of course not seen or heard of, a fifth was there to

help them, a fellow in a bushy red beard, which
he would sometimes lay aside when he was below,
and who strikingly resembled Captain Wicks in
voice and character. As for Captain Kirkup, he
did not appear till the last moment, when he
proved to be a burly mariner, bearded like Abou
Ben Adhem. All the way down the harbour and
through the Heads, his milk-white whiskers blew
in the wind and were conspicuous from shore; but
the *Currency Lass* had no sooner turned her back
upon the lighthouse, than he went below for the
inside of five seconds and reappeared clean shaven.
So many doublings and devices were required to
get to sea with an unseaworthy ship and a captain
that was " wanted." Nor might even these have
sufficed, but for the fact that Hadden was a public
character, and the whole cruise regarded with an
eye of indulgence as one of Tom's engaging eccentricities. The ship, besides, had been a yacht before; and it came the more natural to allow her
still some of the dangerous liberties of her old
employment.

A strange ship they had made of it, her lofty
spars disfigured with patched canvas, her panelled
cabin fitted for a traderoom with rude shelves.
And the life they led in that anomalous schooner
was no less curious than herself. Amalu alone
berthed forward; the rest occupied staterooms,
camped upon the satin divans, and sat down in
Grant Sanderson's parquetry smoking-room to
meals of junk and potatoes, bad of their kind
and often scant in quantity. Hemstead grumbled;

Tommy had occasional moments of revolt and increased the ordinary by a few haphazard tins or a bottle of his own brown sherry. But Hemstead grumbled from habit, Tommy revolted only for the moment, and there was underneath a real and general acquiescence in these hardships. For besides onions and potatoes, the *Currency Lass* may be said to have gone to sea without stores. She carried two thousand pounds' worth of assorted trade, advanced on credit, their whole hope and fortune. It was upon this that they subsisted — mice in their own granary. They dined upon their future profits; and every scanty meal was so much in the savings bank.

Republican ·as were their manners, there was no practical, at least no dangerous, lack of discipline. Wicks was the only sailor on board, there was none to criticise; and besides, he was so easy-going, and so merry-minded, that none could bear to disappoint him. Carthew did his best, partly for the love of doing it, partly for love of the captain; Amalu was a willing drudge, and even Hemstead and Hadden turned to upon occasion with a will. Tommy's department was the trade and traderoom; he would work down in the hold or over the shelves of the cabin, till the Sydney dandy was unrecognisable; come up at last, draw a bucket of sea-water, bathe, change, and lie down on deck over a big sheaf of Sydney *Heralds* and *Dead Birds,* or perhaps with a volume of Buckle's *History of Civilisation*, the standard work selected for that cruise. In the latter case, a smile went round the ship, for Buckle almost invariably laid his student out, and when Tom awoke again he was almost always in the humour for brown sherry. The connection was so well established that "a glass of Buckle" or "a bottle of civilisation" became current pleasantries on board the *Currency Lass.*

Hemstead's province was that of the repairs, and he had his hands full. Nothing on board but was decayed in a proportion; the lamps leaked; so did the decks; door-knobs came off in the hand, mouldings parted company with the panels, the pump declined to suck, and the defective bathroom came near to swamp the ship. Wicks insisted that all the nails were long ago consumed, and that she was only glued together by the rust. "You should n't make me laugh so much, Tommy," he would say. "I 'm afraid I 'll shake the sternpost out of her." And, as Hemstead went to and fro with his tool basket on an endless round of tinkering, Wicks lost no opportunity of chaffing him upon his duties. "If you 'd turn to at sailoring or washing paint or something useful, now," he would say, "I could see the fun of it. But to be mending things that have n't no insides to them, appears to me the height of foolishness." And doubtless these continual pleasantries helped to reassure the landsmen, who went to and fro unmoved, under circumstances that might have daunted Nelson.

The weather was from the outset splendid, and the wind fair and steady. The ship sailed like a witch. "This *Currency Lass* is a powerful old girl, and has more complaints than I would care to put a name on," the captain would say, as he pricked the chart; " but she could show her blooming heels to anything of her size in the Western Pacific." To wash decks, relieve the wheel, do the day's work after dinner on the smoking-room table, and take in kites at night — such was the easy routine of their life. In the evening — above all, if Tommy had produced some of his civilisation — yarns and music were the rule. Amalu had a sweet Hawaiian voice; and Hemstead, a great hand upon the banjo, accompanied his own quavering tenor with effect. There was a sense in which the little man could sing. It was great to hear him deliver *My Boy Tammie* in Austrylian; and the words (some of the worst of the ruffian Macneil's) were hailed in his version with inextinguishable mirth.

Where hye ye been a' dye?

he would ask, and answer himself:

> I 've been by burn and flowery brye
> Meadow green an' mountain grye,
> Courtin' o' this young thing,
> Just come frye her mammie.

It was the accepted jest for all hands to greet the conclusion of this song with the simultaneous cry: " My word!" thus winging the arrow of ridicule with a feather from the singer's wing. But he had his revenge with *Home, Sweet Home*, and

30

Where is my Wandering Boy To-night? — ditties
into which he threw the most intolerable pathos.
It appeared he had no home, nor had ever had
one, nor yet any vestige of a family, except a
truculent uncle, a baker in Newcastle, N. S. W.
His domestic sentiment was therefore wholly in
the air, and expressed an unrealised ideal. Or
perhaps, of all his experiences, this of the *Currency Lass,* with its kindly, playful, and tolerant
society, approached it the most nearly.

It is perhaps because I know the sequel, but I
can never think upon this voyage without a profound sense of pity and mystery; of the ship
(once the whim of a rich blackguard) faring with
her battered fineries and upon her homely errand,
across the plains of ocean, and past the gorgeous
scenery of dawn and sunset; and the ship's company, so strangely assembled, so Britishly chuckle-
headed, filling their days with chaff in place of
conversation; no human book on board with them
except Hadden's Buckle, and not a creature fit
either to read or to understand it; and the one
mark of any civilised interest, being when Carthew filled in his spare hours with the pencil and
the brush: the whole unconscious crew of them
posting in the meanwhile towards so tragic a
disaster.

Twenty-eight days out of Sydney, on Christmas
eve, they fetched up to the entrance of the lagoon,
and plied all that night outside, keeping their position by the lights of fishers on the reef and the
outlines of the palms against the cloudy sky. With

the break of day, the schooner was hove to, and the signal for a pilot shown. But it was plain her lights must have been observed in the darkness by the native fishermen, and word carried to the settlement, for a boat was already under way. She came towards them across the lagoon under a great press of sail, lying dangerously down, so that at times, in the heavier puffs, they thought she would turn turtle; covered the distance in fine style, luffed up smartly alongside, and emitted a haggard looking white man in pajamas.

"Good-mornin', Cap'n," said he, when he had made good his entrance. "I was taking you for a Fiji man-of-war, what with your flush decks and them spars. Well, gen'lemen all, here 's wishing you a Merry Christmas and a Happy New Year," he added, and lurched against a stay.

"Why, you 're never the pilot?" exclaimed Wicks, studying him with a profound disfavour. "You 've never taken a ship in — don't tell me!"

"Well, I should guess I have," returned the pilot. "I 'm Captain Dobbs, I am; and when I take charge, the captain of that ship can go below and shave."

"But, man alive! you 're drunk, man!" cried the captain.

"Drunk!" repeated Dobbs. "You can't have seen much life if you call me drunk. I 'm only just beginning. Come night, I won't say; I guess I 'll be properly full by then. But now I 'm the soberest man in all Big Muggin."

"It won't do," retorted Wicks. "Not for Joseph, sir. I can't have you piling up my schooner."

"All right," said Dobbs, "lay and rot where you are, or take and go in and pile her up for yourself like the captain of the *Leslie*. That's business, I guess; grudged me twenty dollars' pilotage, and lost twenty thousand in trade and a brand new schooner; ripped the keel right off of her, and she went down in the inside of four minutes, and lies in twenty fathom, trade and all."

"What's all this?" cried Wicks. "Trade? What vessel was this *Leslie*, anyhow?"

"Consigned to Cohen and Co., from 'Frisco," returned the pilot, "and badly wanted. There's a barque inside filling up for Hamburg — you see her spars over there; and there's two more ships due, all the way from Germany, one in two months, they say, and one in three; and Cohen and Co.'s agent (that's Mr. Topelius) has taken and lain down with the jaundice on the strength of it. I guess most people would, in his shoes; no trade, no copra, and twenty hundred ton of shipping due. If you've any copra on board, Cap'n, here's your chance. Topelius will buy, gold down, and give three cents. It's all found money to him, the way it is, whatever he pays for it. And that's what come of going back on the pilot."

"Excuse me one moment, Captain Dobbs. I wish to speak with my mate," said the captain, whose face had begun to shine and his eyes to sparkle.

"Please yourself," replied the pilot. "You

could n't think of offering a man a nip, could you?
just to brace him up. This kind of thing looks
damned inhospitable, and gives a schooner a bad
name."

"I 'll talk about that after the anchor 's down,"
returned Wicks, and he drew Carthew forward.
"I say," he whispered, "here 's a fortune."

"How much do you call that?" asked Carthew.

"I can't put a figure on it yet — I dare n't!"
said the captain. "We might cruise twenty years
and not find the match of it. And suppose another
ship came in to-night? Everything 's possible!
And the difficulty is this Dobbs. He 's as drunk
as a marine. How can we trust him? We ain't
insured, worse luck!"

"Suppose you took him aloft and got him to
point out the channel?" suggested Carthew. "If
he tallied at all with the chart, and did n't fall out
of the rigging, perhaps we might risk it."

"Well, all 's risk here," returned the captain.
"Take the wheel yourself, and stand by. Mind,
if there 's two orders, follow mine, not his. Set
the cook for'ard with the heads'ls, and the two
others at the main sheet, and see they don't sit on
it." With that he called the pilot; they swarmed
aloft in the fore rigging, and presently after there
was bawled down the welcome order to ease sheets
and fill away.

At a quarter before nine o'clock on Christmas
morning, the anchor was let go.

The first cruise of the *Currency Lass* had thus
ended in a stroke of fortune almost beyond hope.

She had brought two thousand pounds' worth of trade, straight as a homing pigeon, to the place where it was most required. And Captain Wicks (or, rather, Captain Kirkup) showed himself the man to make the best of his advantage. For hard upon two days he walked a veranda with Topelius; for hard upon two days his partners watched from the neighbouring public house the field of battle; and the lamps were not yet lighted on the evening of the second before the enemy surrendered. Wicks came across to the *Sans Souci,* as the saloon was called, his face nigh black, his eyes almost closed and all bloodshot, and yet bright as lighted matches.

"Come out here, boys," he said; and when they were some way off among the palms, "I hold twenty-four," he added, in a voice scarce recognisable, and doubtless referring to the venerable game of cribbage.

"What do you mean?" asked Tommy.

"I 've sold the trade," answered Wicks; "or, rather, I 've sold only some of it, for I kept back all the mess beef and half the flour and biscuit; and, by God, we 're still provisioned for four months! By God, it 's as good as stolen!"

"My word!" cried Hemstead.

"But what have you sold it for?" gasped Carthew, the captain's almost insane excitement shaking his nerve.

"Let me tell it my own way," cried Wicks, loosening his neck. "Let me get at it gradual, or I 'll explode. I 've not only sold it, boys, I 've wrung

out a charter on my own terms to 'Frisco and back;
on my own terms. I made a point of it. I fooled
him first by making believe I wanted copra, which
of course I knew he would n't hear of — could n't,
in fact; and whenever he showed fight, I trotted out
the copra, and that man dived! I would take nothing but copra, you see; and so I 've got the blooming lot in specie — all but two short bills on 'Frisco.
And the sum? Well, this whole adventure, including two thousand pounds of credit, cost us two
thousand seven hundred and some odd. That 's all
paid back; in thirty days' cruise we 've paid for the
schooner and the trade. Heard ever any man the
match of that? And it 's not all! For besides
that," said the captain, hammering his words,
" we 've got Thirteen Blooming Hundred Pounds
of profit to divide. I bled him in four Thou.!" he
cried, in a voice that broke like a schoolboy's.

For a moment the partners looked upon their
chief with stupefaction, incredulous surprise their
only feeling. Tommy was the first to grasp the
consequences.

" Here!" he said, in a hard, business tone.
" Come back to that saloon. I 've got to get
drunk."

" You must please excuse me, boys," said the
captain, earnestly. " I dare n't taste nothing. If
I was to drink one glass of beer, it 's my belief I 'd
have the apoplexy. The last scrimmage, and the
blooming triumph, pretty nigh hand done me."

" Well, then, three cheers for the captain!" proposed Tommy.

But Wicks held up a shaking hand. "Not that either, boys," he pleaded. "Think of the other buffer, and let him down easy. If I'm like this, just fancy what Topelius is! If he heard us singing out, he'd have the staggers."

As a matter of fact, Topelius accepted his defeat with a good grace; but the crew of the wrecked *Leslie*, who were in the same employment and loyal to their firm, took the thing more bitterly. Rough words and ugly looks were common. Once even they hooted Captain Wicks from the saloon veranda; the Currency-Lasses drew out on the other side; for some minutes there had like to have been a battle in Butaritari; and though the occasion passed off without blows, it left on either side an increase of ill-feeling.

No such small matter could affect the happiness of the successful traders. Five days more the ship lay in the lagoon, with little employment for any one but Tommy and the captain — for Topelius's natives discharged cargo and brought ballast; the time passed like a pleasant dream; the adventurers sat up half the night debating and praising their good fortune, or strayed by day in the narrow isle, gaping like Cockney tourists; and on the first of the new year, the *Currency Lass* weighed anchor for the second time and set sail for 'Frisco, attended by the same fine weather and good luck. She crossed the doldrums with but small delay; on a wind and in ballast of broken coral, she outdid expectations; and what added to the happiness of the ship's company, the small amount of work that fell on them to do, was now lessened by the presence of another hand. This was the boatswain of the *Leslie;* he had been on bad terms with his own captain, had already spent his wages in the saloons of Butaritari, had wearied of the place, and while all his shipmates coldly refused to set foot on board the *Currency Lass,* he had offered to work his passage to the coast. He was a north of Ireland man, between Scotch and Irish, rough, loud, humourous, and emotional, not without sterling qualities, and an expert and careful sailor. His frame of mind was different indeed from that of his new shipmates; instead of making an unexpected fortune, he had lost a berth; and he was besides disgusted with the rations, and really appalled at the condition of the schooner. A stateroom door had stuck, the first day at sea, and Mac (as they called him) laid his strength to it and plucked it from the hinges.

" Glory ! " said he, " this ship 's rotten."

" I believe you, my boy," said Captain Wicks.

The next day the sailor was observed with his nose aloft.

" Don't you get looking at these sticks," the captain said, " or you 'll have a fit and fall overboard."

Mac turned towards the speaker with rather a wild eye. " Why, I see what looks like a patch of dry rot up yonder, that I bet I could stick my fist into," said he.

" Looks as if a fellow could stick his head into it, don't it? " returned Wicks. " But there 's no good prying into things that can't be mended."

" I think I was a *Currency Ass* to come on board of her ! " reflected Mac.

" Well, I never said she was seaworthy," replied the captain: " I only said she could show her blooming heels to anything afloat. And besides, I don't know that it 's dry rot; I kind of sometimes hope it is n't. Here; turn to and heave the log; that 'll cheer you up."

" Well, there 's no denying it, you 're a holy captain," said Mac.

And from that day on, he made but the one reference to the ship's condition; and that was whenever Tommy drew upon his cellar. " Here 's to the junk trade ! " he would say, as he held out his can of sherry.

" Why do you always say that ? " asked Tommy.

" I had an uncle in the business," replied Mac, and launched at once into a yarn, in which an incredible number of the characters were " laid out as nice as you would want to see," and the oaths made up about two-fifths of every conversation.

Only once he gave them a taste of his violence; he talked of it, indeed, often; " I 'm rather a voilent man," he would say, not without pride; but this was the only specimen. Of a sudden, he turned on Hemstead in the ship's waist, knocked him against the foresail boom, then knocked him under it, and had set him up and knocked him down once more, before any one had drawn a breath.

" Here ! Belay that ! " roared Wicks, leaping to his feet. " I won't have none of this."

Mac turned to the captain with ready civility.

"I only want to learn him manners," said he. "He took and called me Irishman."

"Did he?" said Wicks. "O, that's a different story! What made you do it, you tomfool? You ain't big enough to call any man that."

"I didn't call him it," spluttered Hemstead, through his blood and tears. "I only mentioned-like he was."

"Well, let's have no more of it," said Wicks.

"But you *are* Irish, ain't you?" Carthew asked of his new shipmate shortly after.

"I may be," replied Mac, "but I'll allow no Sydney duck to call me so. No," he added, with a sudden heated countenance, "nor any Britisher that walks! Why, look here," he went on, "you're a young swell, aren't you? Suppose I called you that! 'I'll show you,' you would say, and turn to and take it out of me straight."

On the 28th of January, when in lat. 27° 20′ N., long. 177° W., the wind chopped suddenly into the west, not very strong, but puffy and with flaws of rain. The captain, eager for easting, made a fair wind of it and guyed the booms out wing and wing. It was Tommy's trick at the wheel, and as it was within half an hour of the relief (seven thirty in the morning), the captain judged it not worth while to change him.

The puffs were heavy but short; there was nothing to be called a squall, no danger to the ship, and scarce more than usual to the doubtful spars. All hands were on deck in their oilskins, expecting breakfast; the galley smoked, the ship smelt of coffee, all were in good-humour to be speeding eastward a full nine; when the rotten foresail tore suddenly between two cloths and then split to either hand. It was for all the world as though some archangel with a huge sword had slashed it with the figure of a cross; all hands ran to secure the slatting canvas; and in the sudden uproar and alert, Tommy Hadden lost his head. Many of his days have been passed since then in explaining how the thing happened; of these explanations it will be sufficient to say that they were all different and none satisfactory; and the gross fact remains that the main boom gybed, carried away the tackle, broke the mainmast some three feet above the deck and whipped it overboard. For near a minute the suspected foremast gallantly resisted; then followed its companion; and by the time the wreck was cleared, of the whole beautiful fabric that enabled them to skim the seas, two ragged stumps remained.

In these vast and solitary waters, to be dismasted is perhaps the worst calamity. Let the ship turn turtle and go down, and at least the pang is over. But men chained on a hulk may pass months scanning the empty sea-line and counting the steps of death's invisible approach. There is no help but in the boats, and what a help is that! There heaved the *Currency Lass*, for instance, a wingless lump, and the nearest human coast (that of Kauai in the Sandwiches) lay about a thousand miles to south and east of her. Over the way there, to men contemplating that passage in an open boat, all kinds of misery, and the fear of death and of madness, brooded.

A serious company sat down to breakfast; but the captain helped his neighbours with a smile.

"Now, boys," he said, after a pull at the hot coffee, "we 're done with this *Currency Lass*, and no mistake. One good job: we made her pay while she lasted, and she paid first-rate; and if we care to try our hand again, we can try in style. Another good job: we have a fine, stiff, roomy boat, and you know who you have to thank for that. We 've got six lives to save, and a pot of money; and the point is, where are we to take 'em?"

"It 's all two thousand miles to the nearest of the Sandwiches, I fancy," observed Mac.

"No, not so bad as that," returned the captain. "But it 's bad enough: rather better 'n a thousand."

"I know a man who once did twelve hundred in a boat," said Mac, "and he had all he wanted. He fetched ashore in the *Marquesas*, and never set a foot on anything floating from that day to this. He said he would rather put a pistol to his head and knock his brains out."

"Ay, ay!" said Wicks. "Well I remember a boat's crew that made this very island of Kauai, and from just about where we lie, or a bit further. When they got up with the land, they were clean crazy. There was an iron-bound coast and an Old Bob Ridley of a surf on. The natives hailed 'em from fishing-boats, and sung out it

could n't be done at the money. Much they cared!
there was the land, that was all they knew; and
they turned to and drove the boat slap ashore
in the thick of it, and was all drowned but one.
No; boat trips are my eye," concluded the captain, gloomily.

The tone was surprising in a man of his indomitable temper. " Come, Captain," said Carthew, " you have something else up your sleeve;
out with it."

" It 's a fact," admitted Wicks. " You see
there 's a raft of little bally reefs about here, kind
of chicken-pox on the chart. Well, I looked 'em
all up, and there 's one — Midway or Brooks they
call it, not forty mile from our assigned position
— that I got news of. It turns out it 's a coaling-
station of the Pacific Mail," he said, simply.

" Well, and I know it ain't no such a thing,"
said Mac. " I been quartermaster in that line
myself."

" All right," returned Wicks. " There 's the
book. Read what Hoyt says — read it aloud and
let the others hear."

Hoyt's falsehood (as readers know) was explicit; incredulity was impossible, and the news
itself delightful beyond hope. Each saw in his
mind's eye the boat draw in to a trim island with
a wharf, coal-sheds, gardens, the Stars and Stripes
and the white cottage of the keeper; saw themselves idle a few weeks in tolerable quarters, and
then step on board the China mail, romantic waifs,
and yet with pocketsful of money, calling for

champagne and waited on by troops of stewards. Breakfast, that had begun so dully, ended amid sober jubilation, and all hands turned immediately to prepare the boat.

Now that all spars were gone, it was no easy job to get her launched. Some of the necessary cargo was first stowed on board; the specie, in particular, being packed in a strong chest and secured with lashings to the afterthwart in case of a capsize. Then a piece of the bulwark was razed to the level of the deck, and the boat swung thwart-ship, made fast with a slack-line to either stump, and successfully run out. For a voyage of forty miles to hospitable quarters, not much food or water was required; but they took both in superfluity. Amalu and Mac, both ingrained sailor-men, had chests which were the headquarters of their lives; two more chests with hand-bags, oilskins, and blankets supplied the others; Hadden, amid general applause, added the last case of the brown sherry; the captain brought the log, instruments, and chronometer; nor did Hemstead forget the banjo or a pinned handkerchief of Butaritari shells.

It was about three P. M. when they pushed off, and (the wind being still westerly) fell to the oars. "Well, we 've got the guts out of *you!*" was the captain's nodded farewell to the hulk of the *Currency Lass*, which presently shrank and faded in the sea. A little after a calm succeeded with much rain; and the first meal was eaten, and the watch below lay down to their uneasy

slumber on the bilge under a roaring shower-
bath. The twenty-ninth dawned overhead from
out of ragged clouds; there is no moment when
a boat at sea appears so trenchantly black and
so conspicuously little; and the crew looked about
them at the sky and water with a thrill of loneli-
ness and fear. With sunrise the trade set in,
lusty and true to the point; sail was made; the
boat flew; and by about four of the afternoon,
they were well up with the closed part of the
reef, and the captain standing on the thwart, and
holding by the mast, was studying the island
through the binoculars.

"Well, and where's your station?" cried Mac.

"I don't someway pick it up," replied the
captain.

"No, nor never will!" retorted Mac, with a
clang of despair and triumph in his tones.

The truth was soon plain to all. No buoys, no
beacons, no lights, no coal, no station; the castaways pulled through a lagoon and landed on an
isle, where was no mark of man but wreckwood,
and no sound but of the sea. For the sea-fowl
that harboured and lived there at the epoch of my
visit were then scattered into the uttermost parts
of the ocean, and had left no traces of their sojourn besides dropped feathers and addled eggs.
It was to this they had been sent, for this they
had stooped all night over the dripping oars,
hourly moving further from relief. The boat, for
as small as it was, was yet eloquent of the hands
of men, a thing alone indeed upon the sea but yet

in itself all human, and the isle, for which they
had exchanged it, was ingloriously savage, a place
of distress, solitude, and hunger unrelieved. There
was a strong glare and shadow of the evening
over all; in which they sat or lay, not speaking,
careless even to eat, men swindled out of life and
riches by a lying book. In the great good-nature
of the whole party, no word of reproach had been
addressed to Hadden, the author of these disas-
ters. But the new blow was less magnanimously
borne, and many angry glances rested on the
captain.

Yet it was himself who roused them from their
lethargy. Grudgingly they obeyed, drew the boat
beyond tide-mark, and followed him to the top
of the miserable islet, whence a view was commanded of the whole wheel of the horizon, then
part darkened under the coming night, part dyed
with the hues of the sunset and populous with
the sunset clouds. Here the camp was pitched
and a tent run up with the oars, sails, and mast.
And here Amalu, at no man's bidding, from the
mere instinct of habitual service, built a fire and
cooked a meal. Night was come, and the stars
and the silver sickle of the new moon beamed
overhead before the meal was ready. The cold
sea shone about them, and the fire glowed in their
faces, as they ate. Tommy had opened his case,
and the brown sherry went the round; but it was
long before they came to conversation.

" Well, is it to be Kauai after all? " asked Mac
suddenly.

"This is bad enough for me," said Tommy.
"Let 's stick it out where we are."

"Well, I can tell ye one thing," said Mac, "if
ye care to hear it. When I was in the China mail,
we once made this island. It 's in the course from
Honolulu."

"Deuce it is!" cried Carthew. "That settles
it, then. Let 's stay. We must keep good fires
going; and there 's plenty wreck."

"Lashings of wreck!" said the Irishman.
"There 's nothing here but wreck and coffin
boards."

"But we 'll have to make a proper blyze," objected Hemstead. "You can't see a fire like this,
not any wye awye, I mean."

"Can't you?" said Carthew. "Look round."

They did, and saw the hollow of the night, the
bare bright face of the sea, and the stars regarding them; and the voices died in their bosoms
at the spectacle. In that huge isolation, it seemed
they must be visible from China on the one hand
and California on the other.

"My God, it 's dreary!" whispered Hemstead.

"Dreary?" cried Mac, and fell suddenly silent.

"It 's better than a boat, anyway," said Hadden.
"I 've had my bellyful of boat."

"What kills me is that specie!" the captain
broke out. "Think of all that riches, — four
thousand in gold, bad silver, and short bills —
all found money, too! — and no more use than
that much dung!"

"I 'll tell you one thing," said Tommy. "I

don't like it being in the boat — I don't care to
have it so far away."

"Why, who's to take it?" cried Mac, with a
guffaw of evil laughter.

But this was not at all the feeling of the partners, who rose, clambered down the isle, brought
back the inestimable treasure-chest slung upon two
oars, and set it conspicuous in the shining of the
fire.

"There's my beauty!" cried Wicks, viewing
it with a cocked head. "That's better than a
bonfire. What! we have a chest here, and bills
for close upon two thousand pounds; there's no
show to that, — it would go in your vest pocket,
— but the rest! upwards of forty pounds avoir-
dupois of coined gold, and close on two hundredweight of Chile silver! What! ain't that good
enough to fetch a fleet? Do you mean to say
that won't affect a ship's compass? Do you mean
to tell me the look-out won't turn to and *smell*
it?" he cried.

Mac, who had no part nor lot in the bills, the
forty pounds of gold, or the two hundredweight
of silver, heard this with impatience, and fell into
a bitter, choking laughter. "You'll see!" he
said, harshly. "You'll be glad to feed them bills
into the fire before you're through with ut!" And
he turned, passed by himself out of the ring of
the firelight, and stood gazing seaward.

His speech and his departure extinguished instantly those sparks of better humour kindled by
the dinner and the chest. The group fell again

to an ill-favoured silence, and Hemstead began to touch the banjo, as was his habit of an evening. His repertory was small: the chords of *Home, Sweet Home* fell under his fingers; and when he had played the symphony, he instinctively raised up his voice. " Be it never so 'umble, there's no plyce like 'ome," he sang. The last word was still upon his lips, when the instrument was snatched from him and dashed into the fire; and he turned with a cry to look into the furious countenance of Mac.

" I 'll be damned if I stand this! " cried the captain, leaping up belligerent.

" I told ye I was a voilent man," said Mac, with a movement of deprecation very surprising in one of his character. " Why don't he give me a chance, then? Have n't we enough to bear the way we are? " And to the wonder and dismay of all, the man choked upon a sob. " It 's ashamed of meself I am," he said presently, his Irish accent twenty-fold increased. " I ask all your pardons for me voilence; and especially the little man's, who is a harmless crayture, and here 's me hand to 'm, if he 'll condescind to take me by 't."

So this scene of barbarity and sentimentalism passed off, leaving behind strange and incongruous impressions. True, every one was perhaps glad when silence succeeded that all too appropriate music; true, Mac's apology and subsequent be-haviour rather raised him in the opinion of his fellow-castaways. But the discordant note had been struck, and its harmonics tingled in the brain.

In that savage, houseless isle, the passions of man had sounded, if only for the moment, and all men trembled at the possibilities of horror.

It was determined to stand watch and watch in case of passing vessels; and Tommy, on fire with an idea, volunteered to stand the first. The rest crawled under the tent, and were soon enjoying that comfortable gift of sleep, which comes everywhere and to all men, quenching anxieties and speeding time. And no sooner were all settled, no sooner had the drone of many snorers begun to mingle with and overcome the surf, than Tommy stole from his post with the case of sherry, and dropped it in a quiet cove in a fathom of water. But the stormy inconstancy of Mac's behaviour had no connection with a gill or two of wine; his passions, angry and otherwise, were on a different sail plan from his neighbours'; and there were possibilities of good and evil in that hybrid Celt beyond their prophecy.

About two in the morning, the starry sky — or so it seemed, for the drowsy watchman had not observed the approach of any cloud — brimmed over in a deluge; and for three days it rained without remission. The islet was a sponge, the castaways sops; the view all gone, even the reef concealed behind the curtain of the falling water. The fire was soon drowned out; after a couple of boxes of matches had been scratched in vain, it was decided to wait for better weather; and the party lived in wretchedness on raw tins and a ration of hard bread.

By the 2d February, in the dark hours of the
morning watch, the clouds were all blown by; the
sun rose glorious; and once more the castaways sat
by a quick fire, and drank hot coffee with the greed
of brutes and sufferers. Thenceforward their
affairs moved in a routine. A fire was constantly
maintained; and this occupied one hand continuously, and the others for an hour or so in the day.
Twice a day, all hands bathed in the lagoon, their
chief, almost their only pleasure. Often they fished
in the lagoon with good success. And the rest was
passed in lolling, strolling, yarns, and disputation.
The time of the China steamers was calculated to
a nicety; which done, the thought was rejected
and ignored. It was one that would not bear consideration. The boat voyage having been tacitly
set aside, the desperate part chosen to wait there
for the coming of help or of starvation, no man had
courage left to look his bargain in the face, far less
to discuss it with his neighbours. But the un-
uttered terror haunted them; in every hour of idle-
ness, at every moment of silence, it returned, and
breathed a chill about the circle, and carried men's
eyes to the horizon. Then, in a panic of self-
defence, they would rally to some other subject.
And, in that lone spot, what else was to be found
to speak of but the treasure?

That was indeed the chief singularity, the one
thing conspicuous in their island life; the presence
of that chest of bills and specie dominated the mind
like a cathedral; and there were besides connected
with it, certain irking problems well fitted to occupy

the idle. Two thousand pounds were due to the
Sydney firm: two thousand pounds were clear
profit, and fell to be divided in varying proportions
among five. It had been agreed how the partners
were to range; every pound of capital subscribed,
every pound that fell due in wages, was to count
for one "lay." Of these, Tommy could claim five
hundred and ten, Carthew one hundred and seventy, Wicks one hundred and forty, and Hemstead
and Amalu ten apiece: eight hundred and forty
" lays " in all. What was the value of a lay? This
was at first debated in the air and chiefly by the
strength of Tommy's lungs. Then followed a
series of incorrect calculations; from which they
issued, arithmetically foiled, but agreed from
weariness upon an approximate value of £2 7s.
7¼d. The figures were admittedly incorrect; the
sum of the shares came not to £2000, but to £1996
6s.: £3 14s. being thus left unclaimed. But it was
the nearest they had yet found, and the highest as
well, so that the partners were made the less critical by the contemplation of their splendid dividends. Wicks put in £100 and stood to draw
captain's wages for two months; his taking was
£333 3s. 6¾d. Carthew had put in £150: he was
to take out £401 18s. 6½d. Tommy's £500 had
grown to be £1213 12s. 9¾d.; and Amalu and
Hemstead, ranking for wages only, had £22 16s.
0½d., each.

From talking and brooding on these figures, it
was but a step to opening the chest; and once the
chest open, the glamour of the cash was irresistible.

Each felt that he must see his treasure separate with the eye of flesh, handle it in the hard coin, mark it for his own, and stand forth to himself the approved owner. And here an insurmountable difficulty barred the way. There were some seventeen shillings in English silver: the rest was Chile; and the Chile dollar, which had been taken at the rate of six to the pound sterling, was practically their smallest coin. It was decided, therefore, to divide the pounds only, and to throw the shillings, pence, and fractions in a common fund. This, with the three pound fourteen already in the heel, made a total of seven pounds one shilling.

"I'll tell you," said Wicks. "Let Carthew and Tommy and me take one pound apiece, and Hemstead and Amalu split the other four, and toss up for the odd bob."

"O, rot!" said Carthew. "Tommy and I are bursting already. We can take half a sov' each, and let the other three have forty shillings."

"I'll tell you now — it's not worth splitting," broke in Mac. "I've cards in my chest. Why don't you play for the slump sum?"

In that idle place, the proposal was accepted with delight. Mac, as the owner of the cards, was given a stake; the sum was played for in five games of cribbage; and when Amalu, the last survivor in the tournament, was beaten by Mac, it was found the dinner hour was past. After a hasty meal, they fell again immediately to cards, this time (on Carthew's proposal) to Van John. It was then probably two P.M. of the 9th February; and they played with varying chances for twelve hours, slept heavily, and rose late on the morrow to resume the game. All day of the 10th, with grudging intervals for food, and with one long absence on the part of Tommy from which he returned dripping with the case of sherry, they continued to deal and stake. Night fell: they drew the closer to the fire. It was maybe two in the morning, and Tommy was selling his deal by auction, as usual with that timid player; when Carthew, who did n't intend to bid, had a moment of leisure and looked round him. He beheld the moonlight on the sea, the money piled and scattered in that incongruous place, the perturbed faces of the players; he felt in his own breast the familiar tumult; and it seemed as if there rose in his ears a sound of music, and the moon seemed still to shine upon a sea, but the sea was changed, and the Casino towered from among lamplit gardens, and the money clinked on the green board. "Good God!" he thought, "am I gambling again?" He looked the more curiously about the sandy table. He and Mac had played and won like gamblers; the mingled gold and silver lay by their places in the heap. Amalu and Hemstead had each more than held their own: but Tommy was cruel far to leeward, and the captain was reduced to perhaps fifty pounds.

"I say, let's knock off," said Carthew.

"Give that man a glass of Buckle," said some one, and a fresh bottle was opened, and the game went inexorably on.

Carthew was himself too heavy a winner to
withdraw or to say more; and all the rest of the
night he must look on at the progress of this folly,
and make gallant attempts to lose with the not
uncommon consequence of winning more. The
first dawn of the 11th February found him well-
nigh desperate. It chanced he was then dealer,
and still winning. He had just dealt a round of
many tens; every one had staked heavily; the captain had put up all that remained to him, twelve
pounds in gold and a few dollars; and Carthew,
looking privately at his cards before he showed
them, found he held a natural.

"See here, you fellows," he broke out, "this
is a sickening business, and I'm done with it for
one." So saying, he showed his cards, tore them
across, and rose from the ground.

The company stared and murmured in mere
amazement; but Mac stepped gallantly to his
support.

"We've had enough of it, I do believe," said
he. "But of course it was all fun, and here's
my counters back. All counters in, boys!" and
he began to pour his winnings into the chest,
which stood fortunately near him.

Carthew stepped across and wrung him by the
hand. "I'll never forget this," he said.

"And what are ye going to do with the Highway boy and the plumber?" inquired Mac, in
a low tone of voice. "They've both wan, ye
see."

"That's true!" said Carthew aloud. "Amalu

and Hemstead, count your winnings; Tommy and I pay that."

It was carried without speech: the pair glad enough to receive their winnings, it mattered not from whence; and Tommy, who had lost about five hundred pounds, delighted with the compromise.

"And how about Mac?" asked Hemstead. "Is he to lose all?"

"I beg your pardon, plumber. I'm sure ye mean well," returned the Irishman, "but you'd better shut your face, for I'm not that kind of a man. If I t'ought I had wan that money fair, there's never a soul here could get it from me. But I t'ought it was in fun; that was my mistake, ye see; and there's no man big enough upon this island to give a present to my mother's son. So there's my opinion to ye, plumber, and you can put it in your pockut till required."

"Well, I will say, Mac, you're a gentleman," said Carthew, as he helped him to shovel back his winnings into the treasure chest.

"Divil a fear of it, sir! a drunken sailor-man," said Mac.

The captain had sat somewhile with his face in his hands: now he rose mechanically, shaking and stumbling like a drunkard after a debauch. But as he rose, his face was altered, and his voice rang out over the isle, "Sail, ho!"

All turned at the cry, and there, in the wild light of the morning, heading straight for Midway Reef, was the brig *Flying Scud* of Hull.

CHAPTER XXIV

A HARD BARGAIN

THE ship which thus appeared before the castaways had long "tramped" the ocean, wandering from one port to another as freights offered. She was two years out from London, by the Cape of Good Hope, India, and the Archipelago; and was now bound for San Francisco in the hope of working homeward round the Horn. Her captain was one Jacob Trent. He had retired some five years before to a suburban cottage, a patch of cabbages, a gig, and the conduct of what he called a Bank. The name appears to have been misleading. Borrowers were accustomed to choose works of art and utility in the front shop; loaves of sugar and bolts of broadcloth were deposited in pledge; and it was a part of the manager's duty to dash in his gig on Saturday evenings from one small retailer's to another, and to annex in each the bulk of the week's takings. His was thus an active life, and to a man of the type of a rat, filled with recondite joys. An unexpected loss, a law suit, and the unintelligent commentary of the judge upon the bench, combined to disgust him of the business. I was so extraordinarily fortunate as to find, in an old newspaper, a report of the proceedings in *Lyall* v. *The Cardiff Mutual Accommodation Banking Co.* " I confess I fail entirely to understand the nature of the business," the judge had remarked, while Trent was being examined in chief ; a little after, on fuller information — " They call it a bank," he had opined, " but it seems to me to be an unlicensed pawnshop " ; and he wound up with this appalling allocution: " Mr. Trent, I must put you on your guard; you must be very careful, or we shall see you here again." In the inside of a week the captain disposed of the bank, the cottage, and the gig and horse ; and to sea again in the *Flying Scud*, where he did well and gave high satisfaction to his owners. But the glory clung to him; he was a plain sailor-man, he said, but he could never long allow you to forget that he had been a banker.

His mate, Elias Goddedaal, was a huge viking of a man, six feet three and of proportionate mass, strong, sober, industrious, musical, and sentimental. He ran continually over into Swedish melodies, chiefly in the minor. He had paid nine dollars to hear Patti; to hear Nilsson, he had deserted a ship and two months' wages; and he was ready at any time to walk ten miles for a good concert or seven to a reasonable play. On board he had three treasures: a canary bird, a concertina, and a blinding copy of the works of Shakespeare. He had a gift, peculiarly Scandinavian, of making friends at sight: an elemental innocence commended him; he was without fear, without reproach, and without money or the hope of making it.

Holdorsen was second mate, and berthed aft, but messed usually with the hands.

Of one more of the crew, some image lives. This was a foremost hand out of the Clyde, of the name of Brown. A small, dark, thickset creature, with dog's eyes, of a disposition incomparably mild and harmless, he knocked about seas and cities, the uncomplaining whiptop of one vice. "The drink is my trouble, ye see," he said to Carthew shyly; "and it 's the more shame to me because I 'm come of very good people at Bowling down the wa'er." The letter that so much affected Nares, in case the reader should remember it, was addressed to this man Brown.

Such was the ship that now carried joy into the bosoms of the castaways. After the fatigue and the bestial emotions of their night of play, the approach of salvation shook them from all self-control. Their hands trembled, their eyes shone, they laughed and shouted like children as they cleared their camp: and some one beginning to whistle *Marching through Georgia,* the remainder of the packing was conducted, amidst a thousand interruptions, to these martial strains. But the strong head of Wicks was only partly turned.

"Boys," he said, "easy all! We 're going aboard of a ship of which we don't know nothing; we 've got a chest of specie, and seeing the weight, we can't turn to and deny it. Now, suppose she was fishy; suppose it was some kind of a Bully

Hayes business! It's my opinion we'd better be on hand with the pistols."

Every man of the party but Hemstead had some kind of a revolver; these were accordingly loaded and disposed about the persons of the castaways, and the packing was resumed and finished in the same rapturous spirit as it was begun. The sun was not yet ten degrees above the eastern sea, but the brig was already close in and hove to, before they had launched the boat and sped, shouting at the oars, towards the passage.

It was blowing fresh outside with a strong send of sea. The spray flew in the oarsmen's faces. They saw the union jack blow abroad from the *Flying Scud,* the men clustered at the rail, the cook in the galley door, the captain on the quarter-deck with a pith helmet and binoculars. And the whole familiar business, the comfort, company, and safety of a ship, heaving nearer at each stroke, maddened them with joy.

Wicks was the first to catch the line, and swam on board, helping hands grabbing him as he came and hauling him across the rail.

" Captain, sir, I suppose? " he said, turning to the hard old man in the pith helmet.

" Captain Trent, sir," returned the old gentleman.

" Well, I'm Captain Kirkup, and this is the crew of the Sydney schooner, *Currency Lass,* dismasted at sea January 28th."

" Ay, ay," said Trent. " Well, you're all right now. Lucky for you I saw your signal. I didn't know I was so near this beastly island, there must be a drift to the south'ard here; and when I came on deck this morning at eight bells, I thought it was a ship afire."

It had been agreed that, while Wicks was to board the ship and do the civil, the rest were to remain in the whale-boat and see the treasure safe. A tackle was passed down to them; to this they made fast the invaluable chest, and gave the word to heave. But the unexpected weight brought the hand at the tackle to a stand; two others ran to tail on and help him; and the thing caught the eye of Trent.

"'Vast heaving!" he cried sharply; and then to Wicks: "What's that? I don't ever remember to have seen a chest weigh like that."

"It's money," said Wicks.

"It's what?" cried Trent.

"Specie," said Wicks; "saved from the wreck."

Trent looked at him sharply. "Here, let go that chest again, Mr. Goddedaal," he commanded, "shove the boat off, and stream her with a line astern."

"Ay, ay, sir!" from Goddedaal.

"What the devil's wrong?" asked Wicks.

"Nothing, I dare say," returned Trent. "But you'll allow it's a queer thing when a boat turns up in mid-ocean with half a ton of specie, — and everybody armed," he added, pointing to Wicks's pocket. "Your boat will lay comfortably astern, while you come below and make yourself satisfactory."

" O, if that's all! " said Wicks. " My log and
papers are as right as the mail; nothing fishy
about us." And he hailed his friends in the boat,
bidding them have patience, and turned to follow
Captain Trent.

" This way, Captain Kirkup," said the latter.
" And don't blame a man for too much caution;
no offence intended; and these China rivers shake
a fellow's nerve. All I want is just to see you're
what you say you are; it's only my duty, sir, and
what you would do yourself in the circumstances.
I've not always been a ship-captain: I was a
banker once, and I tell you that's the trade to
learn caution in. You have to keep your weather-
eye lifting Saturday nights." And with a dry,
businesslike cordiality, he produced a bottle of
gin.

The captains pledged each other; the papers
were overhauled; the tale of Topelius and the
trade was told in appreciative ears and cemented
their acquaintance. Trent's suspicions, thus finally
disposed of, were succeeded by a fit of profound
thought, during which he sat lethargic and stern,
looking at and drumming on the table.

" Anything more? " asked Wicks.

" What sort of a place is it inside? " inquired
Trent, sudden as though Wicks had touched a
spring.

" It's a good enough lagoon — a few horses'
heads, but nothing to mention," answered Wicks.

" I've a good mind to go in," said Trent. " I
was new rigged in China; it's given very bad,

and I'm getting frightened for my sticks. We could set it up as good as new in a day. For I dare say your lot would turn to and give us a hand?"

"You see if we don't!" said Wicks.

"So be it then," concluded Trent. "A stitch in time saves nine."

They returned on deck; Wicks cried the news to the Currency-Lasses; the foretopsail was filled again, and the brig ran into the lagoon lively, the whale-boat dancing in her wake, and came to single anchor off Middle Brooks Island before eight. She was boarded by the castaways, breakfast was served, the baggage slung on board and piled in the waist, and all hands turned to upon the rigging. All day the work continued, the two crews rivalling each other in expense of strength. Dinner was served on deck, the officers messing aft under the slack of the spanker, the men fraternising forward. Trent appeared in excellent spirits, served out grog to all hands, opened a bottle of Cape wine for the after-table, and obliged his guests with many details of the life of a financier in Cardiff. He had been forty years at sea, had five times suffered shipwreck, was once nine months the prisoner of a pepper rajah, and had seen service under fire in Chinese rivers; but the only thing he cared to talk of, the only thing of which he was vain, or with which he thought it possible to interest a stranger, was his career as a money-lender in the slums of a seaport town.

The afternoon spell told cruelly on the Currency-Lasses. Already exhausted as they were with sleeplessness and excitement, they did the last hours of this violent employment on bare nerves; and when Trent was at last satisfied with the condition of his rigging, expected eagerly the word to put to sea. But the captain seemed in no hurry. He went and walked by himself softly, like a man in thought. Presently he hailed Wicks.

" You 're a kind of company, ain't you, Captain Kirkup? " he inquired.

" Yes, we 're all on board on lays," was the reply.

" Well, then, you won't mind if I ask the lot of you down to tea in the cabin? " asked Trent.

Wicks was amazed, but he naturally ventured no remark; and a little after, the six Currency-Lasses sat down with Trent and Goddedaal to a spread of marmalade, butter, toast, sardines, tinned tongue, and steaming tea. The food was not very good, and I have no doubt Nares would have reviled it, but it was manna to the castaways. Goddedaal waited on them with a kindness far before courtesy, a kindness like that of some old, honest countrywoman in her farm. It was remembered afterwards that Trent took little share in these attentions, but sat much absorbed in thought, and seemed to remember and forget the presence of his guests alternately.

Presently he addressed the Chinaman.

" Clear out! " said he, and watched him till he had disappeared in the stair. " Now, gentle-

men," he went on, " I understand you 're a joint-
stock sort of crew, and that 's why I 've had you
all down; for there 's a point I want made clear.
You see what sort of a ship this is — a good ship,
though I say it, and you see what the rations are
— good enough for sailor-men."

There was a hurried murmur of approval, but
curiosity for what was coming next prevented an
articulate reply.

" Well," continued Trent, making bread pills
and looking hard at the middle of the table, " I 'm
glad of course to be able to give you a passage
to 'Frisco; one sailor-man should help another,
that 's my motto. But when you want a thing in
this world, you generally always have to pay for
it." He laughed a brief, joyless laugh. " I have
no idea of losing by my kindness."

" We have no idea you should, Captain," said
Wicks.

" We are ready to pay anything in reason,"
added Carthew.

At the words, Goddedaal, who sat next to him,
touched him with his elbow, and the two mates
exchanged a significant look. The character of
Captain Trent was given and taken in that silent
second.

" In reason? " repeated the captain of the brig.
" I was waiting for that. Reason 's between two
people, and there 's only one here. I 'm the judge;
I 'm reason. If you want an advance you have to
pay for it " — he hastily corrected himself — " If
you want a passage in my ship, you have to pay

my price," he substituted. "That's business, I believe. I don't want you; you want me."

"Well, sir," said Carthew, "and what *is* your price?"

The captain made bread pills. "If I were like you," he said, "when you got hold of that merchant in the Gilberts, I might surprise you. You had your chance then; seems to me it's mine now. Turn about's fair play. What kind of mercy did you have on that Gilbert merchant?" he cried, with a sudden stridency. "Not that I blame you. All's fair in love and business," and he laughed again, a little frosty giggle.

"Well, sir?" said Carthew, gravely.

"Well, this ship's mine, I think?" he asked sharply.

"Well, I'm of that way of thinking meself," observed Mac.

"I say it's mine, sir!" reiterated Trent, like a man trying to be angry. "And I tell you all, if I was a driver like what you are, I would take the lot. But there's two thousand pounds there that don't belong to you, and I'm an honest man. Give me the two thousand that's yours, and I'll give you a passage to the coast, and land every man-jack of you in 'Frisco with fifteen pounds in his pocket, and the captain here with twenty-five."

Goddedaal laid down his head on the table like a man ashamed.

"You're joking," cried Wicks, purple in the face.

"Am I?" said Trent. "Please yourselves.
You're under no compulsion. This ship's mine,
but there's that Brooks Island don't belong to
me, and you can lay there till you die for what I
care."

"It's more than your blooming brig's worth!"
cried Wicks.

"It's my price anyway," returned Trent.

"And do you mean to say you would land us
there to starve?" cried Tommy.

Captain Trent laughed the third time. "Starve?
I defy you to," said he. "I'll sell you all the
provisions you want at a fair profit."

"I beg your pardon, sir," said Mac, "but my
case is by itself. I'm working me passage; I got
no share in that two thousand pounds nor nothing
in my pockut; and I'll be glad to know what you
have to say to me?"

"I ain't a hard man," said Trent. "That shall
make no difference. I'll take you with the rest,
only of course you get no fifteen pound."

The impudence was so extreme and startling,
that all breathed deep, and Goddedaal raised up
his face and looked his superior sternly in the
eye.

But Mac was more articulate. "And you're
what ye call a British sayman, I suppose? the
sorrow in your guts!" he cried.

"One more such word, and I clap you in
irons!" said Trent, rising gleefully at the face
of opposition.

"And where would I be while you were doin'

ut?" asked Mac. "After you and your rigging, too! Ye ould puggy, ye have n't the civility of a bug, and I 'll learn ye some."

His voice did not even rise as he uttered the threat; no man present, Trent least of all, expected that which followed. The Irishman's hand rose suddenly from below the table, an open clasp-knife balanced on the palm; there was a movement swift as conjuring; Trent started half to his feet, turning a little as he rose so as to escape the table, and the movement was his bane. The missile struck him in the jugular; he fell forward, and his blood flowed among the dishes on the cloth.

The suddenness of the attack and the catastrophe, the instant change from peace to war and from life to death, held all men spellbound. Yet a moment they sat about the table staring open-mouthed upon the prostrate captain and the flowing blood. The next, Goddedaal had leaped to his feet, caught up the stool on which he had been sitting, and swung it high in air, a man transfigured, roaring (as he stood) so that men's ears were stunned with it. There was no thought of battle in the Currency-Lasses; none drew his weapon; all huddled helplessly from before the face of the baresark Scandinavian. His first blow sent Mac to ground with a broken arm. His second dashed out the brains of Hemstead. He turned from one to another, menacing and trumpeting like a wounded elephant, exulting in his rage. But there was no council, no light of reason, in that ecstasy of battle; and he shied from the pursuit of victory to hail fresh blows upon the supine Hemstead, so that the stool was shattered and the cabin rang with their violence. The sight of that post-mortem cruelty recalled Carthew to the life of instinct, and his revolver was in hand and he had aimed and fired before he knew. The ear-bursting sound of the report was accompanied by a yell of pain; the colossus paused, swayed, tottered, and fell headlong on the body of his victim.

In the instant silence that succeeded, the sound of feet pounding on the deck and in the companion leaped into hearing; and a face, that of the sailor Holdorsen, appeared below the bulkheads in the cabin doorway. Carthew shattered it with a second shot, for he was a marksman.

"Pistols!" he cried, and charged at the companion, Wicks at his heels, Tommy and Amalu following. They trod the body of Holdorsen underfoot, and flew up-stairs and forth into the dusky blaze of a sunset red as blood. The numbers were still equal, but the Flying-Scuds dreamed not of defence, and fled with one accord for the forecastle scuttle. Brown was first in flight; he disappeared below unscathed; the Chinaman followed head-foremost with a ball in his side; and the others shinned into the rigging.

A fierce composure settled upon Wicks and Carthew, their fighting second wind. They posted Tommy at the fore and Amalu at the main to guard the masts and shrouds, and going themselves into the waist, poured out a box of cartridges on deck and filled the chambers. The poor devils aloft bleated aloud for mercy. But the hour of any mercy was gone by; the cup was brewed and must be drunken to the dregs; since so many had fallen, all must fall. The light was bad, the cheap revolvers fouled and carried wild, the screaming wretches were swift to flatten themselves against the masts and yards or find a momentary refuge in the hanging sails. The fell business took long, but it was done at last. Hardy the Londoner was shot on the foreroyal yard, and hung horribly suspended in the brails. Wallen, the other, had his jaw broken on the main topgallant cross-trees, and exposed himself, shrieking, till a second shot dropped him on the deck.

This had been bad enough, but worse remained behind. There was still Brown in the forepeak. Tommy, with a sudden clamour of weeping, begged for his life. " One man can't hurt us," he sobbed. " We can't go on with this. I spoke to him at dinner. He's an awful decent little cad. It can't be done. Nobody can go into that place and murder him. It's too damned wicked."

The sound of his supplications was perhaps audible to the unfortunate below.

" One left, and we all hang," said Wicks. " Brown must go the same road." The big man was deadly white and trembled like an aspen; and he had no sooner finished speaking, than he went to the ship's side and vomited.

"We can never do it if we wait," said Carthew. "Now or never," and he marched towards the scuttle.

"No, no, no!" wailed Tommy, clutching at his jacket.

But Carthew flung him off, and stepped down the ladder, his heart rising with disgust and shame. The Chinaman lay on the floor, still groaning; the place was pitch dark.

"Brown!" cried Carthew, "Brown, where are you?"

His heart smote him for the treacherous apostrophe, but no answer came.

He groped in the bunks: they were all empty. Then he moved towards the forepeak, which was hampered with coils of rope and spare chandlery in general.

"Brown!" he said again.

"Here, sir," answered a shaking voice; and the poor invisible caitiff called on him by name, and poured forth out of the darkness an endless, garrulous appeal for mercy. A sense of danger, of daring, had alone nerved Carthew to enter the forecastle; and here was the enemy crying and pleading like a frightened child. His obsequious "Here, sir," his horrid fluency of obtestation, made the murder tenfold more revolting. Twice Carthew raised the pistol, once he pressed the trigger (or thought he did) with all his might, but no explosion followed; and with that the lees of his courage ran quite out, and he turned and fled from before his victim.

Wicks sat on the fore hatch, raised the face of
a man of seventy, and looked a wordless question.
Carthew shook his head. With such composure
as a man displays marching towards the gallows.
Wicks arose, walked to the scuttle, and went down.
Brown thought it was Carthew returning, and discovered himself, half crawling from his shelter,
with another incoherent burst of pleading. Wicks
emptied his revolver at the voice, which broke into
mouse-like whimperings and groans. Silence succeeded, and the murderer ran on deck like one
possessed.

The other three were now all gathered on the
fore hatch, and Wicks took his place beside them
without question asked or answered. They sat
close, like children in the dark, and shook each
other with their shaking. The dusk continued to
fall; and there was no sound but the beating of
the surf and the occasional hiccup of a sob from
Tommy Hadden.

" God, if there was another ship!" cried Carthew of a sudden.

Wicks started and looked aloft with the trick
of all seamen, and shuddered as he saw the hanging figure on the royal yard.

" If I went aloft, I 'd fall," he said simply.
" I 'm done up."

It was Amalu who volunteered, climbed to the
very truck, swept the fading horizon, and announced nothing within sight.

" No odds," said Wicks. " We can't sleep . . ."

" Sleep!" echoed Carthew; and it seemed as

if the whole of Shakespeare's *Macbeth* thundered
at the gallop through his mind.

"Well, then, we can't sit and chitter here," said
Wicks, "till we've cleaned ship; and I can't turn
to till I've had gin, and the gin's in the cabin,
and who's to fetch it?"

"I will," said Carthew, "if any one has
matches."

Amalu passed him a box, and he went aft and
down the companion and into the cabin, stumbling
upon bodies. Then he struck a match, and his
looks fell upon two living eyes.

"Well?" asked Mac, for it was he who still
survived in that shambles of a cabin.

"It's done; they're all dead," answered Carthew.

"Christ!" said the Irishman, and fainted.

The gin was found in the dead captain's cabin;
it was brought on deck, and all hands had a
dram, and attacked their farther task. The night
was come, the moon would not be up for hours;
a lamp was set on the main hatch to light Amalu
as he washed down decks; and the galley lantern
was taken to guide the others in their grave-
yard business. Holdorsen, Hemstead, Trent, and
Goddedaal were first disposed of, the last still
breathing as he went over the side; Wallen followed; and then Wicks, steadied by the gin, went
aloft with a boathook and succeeded in dislodging
Hardy. The Chinaman was their last task; he
seemed to be light-headed, talked aloud in his unknown language as they brought him up, and it

was only with the splash of his sinking body that the gibberish ceased. Brown, by common consent, was left alone. Flesh and blood could go no farther.

All this time they had been drinking undiluted gin like water; three bottles stood broached in different quarters; and none passed without a gulp. Tommy collapsed against the mainmast; Wicks fell on his face on the poop ladder and moved no more; Amalu had vanished unobserved. Carthew was the last afoot: he stood swaying at the break of the poop, and the lantern, which he still carried, swung with his movement. His head hummed; it swarmed with broken thoughts; memory of that day's abominations flared up and died down within him, like the light of a lamp in a strong draught. And then he had a drunkard's inspiration.

"There must be no more of this," he thought, and stumbled once more below.

The absence of Holdorsen's body brought him to a stand. He stood and stared at the empty floor, and then remembered and smiled. From the captain's room he took the open case with one dozen and three bottles of gin, put the lantern inside, and walked precariously forth. Mac was once more conscious; his eyes haggard, his face drawn with pain and flushed with fever; and Carthew remembered he had never been seen to, had lain there helpless, and was so to lie all night, injured, perhaps dying. But it was now too late; reason had now fled from that silent ship. If

Carthew could get on deck again, it was as much
as he could hope; and casting on the unfortunate
a glance of pity, the tragic drunkard shouldered
his way up the companion, dropped the case overboard, and fell in the scuppers helpless.

CHAPTER XXV

A BAD BARGAIN

WITH the first colour in the east, Carthew awoke and sat up. Awhile he gazed at the scroll of the morning bank and the spars and hanging canvas of the brig, like a man who wakes in a strange bed, with a child's simplicity of wonder. He wondered above all what ailed him, what he had lost, what disfavour had been done him, which he knew he should resent, yet had forgotten. And then, like a river bursting through a dam, the truth rolled on him its instantaneous volume: his memory teemed with speech and pictures that he should never again forget; and he sprang to his feet, stood a moment hand to brow, and began to walk violently to and fro by the companion. As he walked, he wrung his hands. "God — God — God," he kept saying, with no thought of prayer, uttering a mere voice of agony.

The time may have been long or short, it was perhaps minutes, perhaps only seconds, ere he awoke to find himself observed, and saw the captain sitting up and watching him over the break of the poop, a strange blindness as of fever in his eyes, a haggard knot of corrugations on his

brow. Cain saw himself in a mirror. For a
flash they looked upon each other, and then
glanced guiltily aside; and Carthew fled from the
eye of his accomplice, and stood leaning on the
taffrail.

An hour went by, while the day came brighter,
and the sun rose and drank up the clouds: an
hour of silence in the ship, an hour of agony beyond narration for the sufferers. Brown's gab-
bling prayers, the cries of the sailors in the rigging,
strains of the dead Hemstead's minstrelsy, ran
together in Carthew's mind, with sickening itera-
tion. He neither acquitted nor condemned himself: he did not think, he suffered. In the bright
water into which he stared, the pictures changed
and were repeated: the baresark rage of Goddedaal; the blood-red light of the sunset into which
they had run forth; the face of the babbling
Chinaman as they cast him over; the face of the
captain, seen a moment since, as he awoke from
drunkenness into remorse. And time passed, and
the sun swam higher, and his torment was not
abated.

Then were fulfilled many sayings, and the weak-
est of these condemned brought relief and healing
to the others. Amalu the drudge awoke (like
the rest) to sickness of body and distress of mind;
but the habit of obedience ruled in that simple
spirit, and appalled to be so late, he went direct
into the galley, kindled the fire, and began to
get breakfast. At the rattle of dishes, the snap-
ping of the fire, and the thin smoke that went

up straight into the air, the spell was lifted. The condemned felt once more the good dry land of habit underfoot; they touched again the familiar guide-ropes of sanity; they were restored to a sense of the blessed revolution and return of all things earthly. The captain drew a bucket of water and began to bathe. Tommy sat up, watched him awhile, and slowly followed his example; and Carthew, remembering his last thoughts of the night before, hastened to the cabin.

Mac was awake; perhaps had not slept. Over his head Goddedaal's canary twittered shrilly from its cage.

"How are you?" asked Carthew.

"Me arrum's broke," returned Mac; "but I can stand that. It's this place I can't abide. I was coming on deck anyway."

"Stay where you are, though," said Carthew. "It's deadly hot above, and there's no wind. I'll wash out this — " and he paused, seeking a word and not finding one for the grisly foulness of the cabin.

"Faith, I'll be obliged to ye, then," replied the Irishman. He spoke mild and meek, like a sick child with its mother. There was now no violence in the violent man; and as Carthew fetched a bucket and swab and the steward's sponge, and began to cleanse the field of battle, he alternately watched him or shut his eyes and sighed like a man near fainting. "I have to ask all your pardons," he began again presently, "and the more shame to me as I got ye into the trouble and

33

could n't do nothing when it came. Ye saved me life, sir; ye 're a clane shot."

" For God's sake, don't talk of it!" cried Carthew. " It can't be talked of; you don't know what it was. It was nothing down here; they fought. On deck — O, my God!" And Carthew, with the bloody sponge pressed to his face, struggled a moment with hysteria.

" Kape cool, Mr. Cart'ew. It 's done now," said Mac; " and ye may bless God ye 're not in pain and helpless in the bargain."

There was no more said by one or other, and the cabin was pretty well cleansed when a stroke on the ship's bell summoned Carthew to breakfast. Tommy had been busy in the meanwhile; he had hauled the whale-boat close aboard, and already lowered into it a small keg of beef that he found ready broached beside the galley door; it was plain he had but the one idea — to escape.

" We have a shipful of stores to draw upon," he said. " Well, what are we staying for? Let 's get off at once for Hawaii. I 've begun preparing already."

" Mac has his arm broken," observed Carthew; " how would he stand the voyage?"

" A broken arm?" repeated the captain. " That all? I 'll set it after breakfast. I thought he was dead like the rest. That madman hit out like —— " and there, at the evocation of the battle, his voice ceased and the talk died with it.

After breakfast, the three white men went down into the cabin.

"I 've come to set your arm," said the captain.

"I beg your pardon, Captain," replied Mac; "but the firrst thing ye got to do is to get this ship to sea. We 'll talk of me arrum after that."

"O, there 's no such blooming hurry," returned Wicks.

"When the next ship sails in, ye 'll tell me stories!" retorted Mac.

"But there 's nothing so unlikely in the world," objected Carthew.

"Don't be deceivin' yourself," said Mac. "If ye want a ship, divil a one 'll look near ye in six year; but if ye don't, ye may take my word for ut, we 'll have a squadron layin' here."

"That 's what I say," cried Tommy; "that 's what I call sense! Let 's stock that whale-boat and be off."

"And what will Captain Wicks be thinking of the whale-boat?" asked the Irishman.

"I don't think of it at all," said Wicks. "We 've a smart-looking brig underfoot; that 's all the whale-boat I want."

"Excuse me!" cried Tommy. "That 's childish talk. You 've got a brig, to be sure, and what use is she? You dare n't go anywhere in her. What port are you to sail for?"

"For the port of Davy Jones's Locker, my son," replied the captain. "This brig 's going to be lost at sea. I 'll tell you where, too, and that 's about forty miles to windward of Kauai. We 're going to stay by her till she 's down; and once the masts are under, she 's the *Flying Scud* no more, and we never heard of such a brig; and it's the crew of the schooner *Currency Lass* that comes ashore in the boat, and takes the first chance to Sydney."

"Captain dear, that's the first Christian word I've heard of ut!" cried Mac. "And now, just let me arrum be, jewel, and get the brig outside."

"I'm as anxious as yourself, Mac," returned Wicks; "but there's not wind enough to swear by. So let's see your arm, and no more talk."

The arm was set and splinted; the body of Brown fetched from the forepeak, where it lay stiff and cold, and committed to the waters of the lagoon; and the washing of the cabin rudely finished. All these were done ere midday; and it was past three when the first cat's-paw ruffled the lagoon, and the wind came in a dry squall, which presently sobered to a steady breeze.

The interval was passed by all in feverish impatience, and by one of the party in secret and extreme concern of mind. Captain Wicks was a fore-and-aft sailor; he could take a schooner through a Scotch reel, felt her mouth and divined her temper like a rider with a horse; she, on her side, recognising her master and following his wishes like a dog. But by a not very unusual train of circumstance, the man's dexterity was partial and circumscribed. On a schooner's deck he was Rembrandt or (at the least) Mr. Whistler; on board a brig he was Pierre Grassou. Again and again in the course of the morning, he had reasoned out his policy and rehearsed his orders;

and ever with the same depression and weariness. It was guess-work; it was chance; the ship might behave as he expected, and might not; suppose she failed him, he stood there helpless, beggared of all the proved resources of experience. Had not all hands been so weary, had he not feared to communicate his own misgivings, he could have towed her out. But these reasons sufficed, and the most he could do was to take all possible precautions. Accordingly he had Carthew aft, explained what was to be done with anxious patience, and visited along with him the various sheets and braces.

"I hope I'll remember," said Carthew. "It seems awfully muddled."

"It's the rottenest kind of rig," the captain admitted: "all blooming pocket-handkerchiefs! And not one sailor-man on deck! Ah, if she'd only been a brigantine, now! But it's lucky the passage is so plain; there's no manoeuvring to mention. We get under way before the wind, and run right so till we begin to get foul of the island; then we haul our wind and lie as near south-east as may be till we're on that line; 'bout ship there and stand straight out on the port tack. Catch the idea?"

"Yes, I see the idea," replied Carthew rather dismally, and the two incompetents studied for a long time in silence the complicated gear above their heads.

But the time came when these rehearsals must be put in practice. The sails were lowered, and all hands heaved the anchor short. The whale-boat was then cut adrift, the upper topsails and the spanker set, the yards braced up, and the spanker sheet hauled out to starboard.

"Heave away on your anchor, Mr. Carthew."

"Anchor's gone, sir."

"Set jibs."

It was done, and the brig still hung enchanted. Wicks, his head full of a schooner's mainsail, turned his mind to the spanker. First he hauled in the sheet, and then he hauled it out, with no result.

"Brail the damned thing up!" he bawled at last, with a red face. "There ain't no sense in it."

It was the last stroke of bewilderment for the poor captain, that he had no sooner brailed up the spanker, than the brig came before the wind. The laws of nature seemed to him to be suspended; he was like a man in a world of pantomime tricks; the cause of any result, and the probable result of any action, equally concealed from him. He was the more careful not to shake the nerve of his amateur assistants. He stood there with a face like a torch; but he gave his orders with aplomb; and indeed, now the ship was under way, supposed his difficulties over.

The lower topsails and courses were then set, and the brig began to walk the water like a thing of life, her forefoot discoursing music, the birds flying and crying over her spars. Bit by bit the passage began to open and the blue sea to show between the flanking breakers on the reef; bit by

bit, on the starboard bow, the low land of the
islet began to heave closer aboard. The yards were
braced up, the spanker sheet hauled aft again;
the brig was close hauled, lay down to her work
like a thing in earnest, and had soon drawn near
to the point of advantage, where she might stay
and lie out of the lagoon in a single tack.

Wicks took the wheel himself, swelling with
success. He kept the brig full to give her heels,
and began to bark his orders: " Ready about.
Helm 's a-lee. Tacks and sheets. Mainsail haul."
And then the fatal words: " That 'll do your
main-sail; jump forrard and haul round your
foreyards."

To stay a square-rigged ship is an affair of
knowledge and swift sight; and a man used to the
succinct evolutions of a schooner will always tend
to be too hasty with a brig. It was so now. The
order came too soon; the topsails set flat aback;
the ship was in irons. Even yet, had the helm been
reversed, they might have saved her. But to think
of a stern-board at all, far more to think of
profiting by one, were foreign to the schooner-
sailor's mind. Wicks made haste instead to wear
ship, a manœuvre for which room was wanting,
and the *Flying Scud* took ground on a bank of
sand and coral about twenty minutes before five.

Wicks was no hand with a square-rigger, and
he had shown it. But he was a sailor and a born
captain of men for all homely purposes, where
intellect is not required and an eye in a man's
head and a heart under his jacket will suffice.

Before the others had time to understand the misfortune, he was bawling fresh orders, and had the
sails clewed up, and took soundings round the
ship.

"She lies lovely," he remarked, and ordered
out a boat with the starboard anchor.

"Here! steady!" cried Tommy. "You ain't
going to turn us to, to warp her off?"

"I am though," replied Wicks.

"I won't set a hand to such tomfoolery for
one," replied Tommy. "I 'm dead beat." He
went and sat down doggedly on the main hatch.
"You got us on; get us off again," he added.

Carthew and Wicks turned to each other.

"Perhaps you don't know how tired we are,"
said Carthew.

"The tide 's flowing!" cried the captain. "You
would n't have me miss a rising tide?"

"O gammon! there 's tides to-morrow!" retorted Tommy.

"And I 'll tell you what," added Carthew, "the
breeze is failing fast, and the sun will soon be
down. We may get into all kinds of fresh mess
in the dark and with nothing but light airs."

"I don't deny it," answered Wicks, and stood
awhile as if in thought. "But what I can't make
out," he began again, with agitation, "what I
can't make out is what you 're made of! To stay
in this place is beyond me. There 's the bloody
sun going down — and to stay here is beyond
me."

The others looked upon him with horrified surprise. This fall of their chief pillar — this irrational passion in the practical man, suddenly barred out of his true sphere, the sphere of action — shocked and daunted them. But it gave to another and unseen hearer the chance for which he had been waiting. Mac, on the striking of the brig, had crawled up the companion, and he now showed himself and spoke up.

"Captain Wicks," he said, "it's me that brought this trouble on the lot of ye. I'm sorry for ut, I ask all your pardons, and if there's any one can say 'I forgive ye,' it'll make my soul the lighter."

Wicks stared upon the man in amaze; then his self-control returned to him. "We're all in glass houses here," he said; "we ain't going to turn to and throw stones. I forgive you, sure enough; and much good may it do you!"

The others spoke to the same purpose.

"I thank ye for ut, and 't is done like gentlemen," said Mac. "But there's another thing I have upon my mind. I hope we're all Prodestan's here?"

It appeared they were; it seemed a small thing for the Protestant religion to rejoice in!

"Well, that's as it should be," continued Mac. "And why shouldn't we say the Lord's Prayer? There can't be no hurt in ut."

He had the same quiet, pleading, childlike way with him as in the morning; and the others accepted his proposal, and knelt down without a word.

"Knale if ye like!" said he. "I stand." And he covered his eyes.

So the prayer was said to the accompaniment of the surf and sea-birds, and all rose refreshed and felt lightened of a load. Up to then, they had cherished their guilty memories in private, or only referred to them in the heat of a moment and fallen immediately silent. Now they had faced their remorse in company, and the worst seemed over. Nor was it only that. But the petition "Forgive us our trespasses," falling in so apposite after they had themselves forgiven the immediate author of their miseries, sounded like an absolution.

Tea was taken on deck in the time of the sunset, and not long after the five castaways — castaways once more — lay down to sleep.

Day dawned windless and hot. Their slumbers had been too profound to be refreshing, and they woke listless, and sat up, and stared about them with dull eyes. Only Wicks, smelling a hard day's work ahead, was more alert. He went first to the well, sounded it once and then a second time, and stood awhile with a grim look, so that all could see he was dissatisfied. Then he shook himself, stripped to the buff, clambered on the rail, drew himself up and raised his arms to plunge. The dive was never taken. He stood instead transfixed, his eyes on the horizon.

"Hand up that glass," he said.

In a trice they were all swarming aloft, the nude captain leading with the glass.

On the northern horizon was a finger of grey smoke, straight in the windless air like a point of admiration.

"What do you make it?" they asked of Wicks.

"She's truck down," he replied; "no telling yet. By the way the smoke builds, she must be heading right here."

"What can she be?"

"She might be the China mail," returned Wicks, "and she might be a blooming man-of-war, come to look for castaways. Here! This ain't the time to stand staring. On deck, boys!"

He was the first on deck, as he had been the first aloft, handed down the ensign, bent it again to the signal halliards, and ran it up union down.

"Now hear me," he said, jumping into his trousers, "and everything I say you grip on to. If that's a man-of-war, she'll be in a tearing hurry; all these ships are what don't do nothing and have their expenses paid. That's our chance; for we'll go with them, and they won't take the time to look twice or to ask a question. I'm Captain Trent; Carthew, you're Goddedaal; Tommy, you're Hardy; Mac's Brown; Amalu — Hold hard! we can't make a Chinaman of him! Ah Wing must have deserted; Amalu stowed away; and I turned him to as cook, and was never at the bother to sign him. Catch the idea? Say your names."

And that pale company recited their lesson earnestly.

"What were the names of the other two?" he

asked. "Him Carthew shot in the companion, and the one I caught in the jaw on the main topgallant?"

"Holdorsen and Wallen," said some one.

"Well, they're drowned," continued Wicks; "drowned alongside trying to lower a boat. We had a bit of a squall last night: that's how we got ashore." He ran and squinted at the compass. "Squall out of nor'-nor'-west-half-west; blew hard; every one in a mess, falls jammed, and Holdorsen and Wallen spilt overboard. See? Clear your blooming heads!" He was in his jacket now, and spoke with a feverish impatience and contention that rang like anger.

"But is it safe?" asked Tommy.

"Safe?" bellowed the captain. "We're standing on the drop, you moon-calf! If that ship's bound for China (which she don't look to be), we're lost as soon as we arrive; if she's bound the other way, she comes from China, don't she? Well, if there's a man on board of her that ever clapped eyes on Trent or any blooming hand out of this brig, we'll all be in irons in two hours. Safe! no, it ain't safe; it's a beggarly last chance to shave the gallows, and that's what it is."

At this convincing picture, fear took hold on all.

"Hadn't we a hundred times better stay by the brig?" cried Carthew. "They would give us a hand to float her off."

"You'll make me waste this holy day in chattering!" cried Wicks. "Look here, when I sounded the well this morning, there was two

foot of water there against eight inches last night.
What 's wrong? I don't know; might be nothing;
might be the worst kind of smash. And then,
there we are in for a thousand miles in an open
boat, if that 's your taste!"

"But it may be nothing, and anyway their car-
penters are bound to help us repair her," argued
Carthew.

"Moses Murphy!" cried the captain. "How
did she strike? Bows on, I believe. And she 's
down by the head now. If any carpenter comes
tinkering here, where 'll he go first? Down in
the forepeak, I suppose! And then, how about
all that blood among the chandlery? You would
think you were a lot of members of Parliament
discussing Plimsoll; and you 're just a pack of
murderers with the halter round your neck. Any
other ass got any time to waste? No? Thank
God for that! Now, all hands! I 'm going below,
and I leave you here on deck. You get the boat
cover off that boat; then you turn to and open
the specie chest. There are five of us; get five
chests, and divide the specie equal among the five
— put it at the bottom — and go at it like
tigers. Get blankets, or canvas, or clothes, so it
won't rattle. It 'll make five pretty heavy chests,
but we can't help that. You, Carthew — dash
me! — You Mr. Goddedaal, come below. We 've
our share before us."   .

And he cast another glance at the smoke, and
hurried below with Carthew at his heels.

The logs were found in the main cabin behind

the canary's cage; two of them, one kept by Trent, one by Goddedaal. Wicks looked first at one, then at the other, and his lips stuck out.

"Can you forge hand of write?" he asked.

"No," said Carthew.

"There's luck for you — no more can I!" cried the captain. "Hullo! here's worse yet, here's this Goddedaal up to date; he must have filled it in before supper. See for yourself: 'Smoke observed. — Captain Kirkup and five hands of the schooner *Currency Lass*.' Ah! this is better," he added, turning to the other log. "The old man ain't written anything for a clear fortnight. We'll dispose of your log altogether, Mr. Goddedaal, and stick to the old man's — to mine, I mean; only I ain't going to write it up, for reasons of my own. You are. You're going to sit down right here and fill it in the way I tell you."

"How to explain the loss of mine?" asked Carthew.

"You never kept one," replied the captain. "Gross neglect of duty. You'll catch it."

"And the change of writing?" resumed Carthew. "You began; why do you stop and why do I come in? And you'll have to sign anyway."

"O! I've met with an accident and can't write," replied Wicks.

"An accident?" repeated Carthew. "It don't sound natural. What kind of an accident?"

Wicks spread his hand face-up on the table, and drove a knife through his palm.

"That kind of an accident," said he. "There's

a way to draw to windward of most difficulties, if
you 've a head on your shoulders." He began to
bind up his hand with a handkerchief, glancing the
while over Goddedaal's log. "Hullo!" he said,
"this 'll never do for us — this is an impossible
kind of a yarn. Here, to begin with, is this Captain Trent trying some fancy course, leastways he 's
a thousand miles to south'ard of the great circle.
And here, it seems, he was close up with this island
on the sixth, sails all these days, and is close up
with it again by daylight on the eleventh."

"Goddedaal said they had the deuce's luck,"
said Carthew.

"Well, it don't look like real life — that 's all
I can say," returned Wicks.

"It 's the way it was, though," argued Carthew.

"So it is; and what the better are we for that,
if it don't look so?" cried the captain, sounding
unwonted depths of art criticism. "Here! try and
see if you can't tie this bandage; I 'm bleeding like
a pig."

As Carthew sought to adjust the handkerchief,
his patient seemed sunk in a deep muse, his eye
veiled, his mouth partly open. The job was yet
scarce done, when he sprang to his feet.

"I have it," he broke out, and ran on deck.
"Here, boys!" he cried, "we did n't come here
on the eleventh; we came in here on the evening
of the sixth, and lay here ever since becalmed.
As soon as you 're done with these chests," he
added, "you can turn to and roll out beef
and water breakers; it 'll look more shipshape

— like as if we were getting ready for the boat voyage."

And he was back again in a moment, cooking the new log. Goddedaal's was then carefully destroyed, and a hunt began for the ship's papers. Of all the agonies of that breathless morning, this was perhaps the most poignant. Here and there the two men searched, cursing, cannoning together, streaming with heat, freezing with terror. News was bawled down to them that the ship was indeed a man-of-war, that she was close up, that she was lowering a boat; and still they sought in vain. By what accident they missed the iron box with the money and accounts, is hard to fancy; but they did. And the vital documents were found at last in the pocket of Trent's shore-going coat, where he had left them when last he came on board.

Wicks smiled for the first time that morning. "None too soon," said he. "And now for it! Take these others for me; I 'm afraid I 'll get them mixed if I keep both."

" What are they ? " Carthew asked.

" They 're the Kirkup and *Currency Lass* papers," he replied. " Pray God we need 'em again ! "

" Boat 's inside the lagoon, sir," hailed down Mac, who sat by the skylight doing sentry while the others worked.

" Time we were on deck, then, Mr. Goddedaal," said Wicks.

As they turned to leave the cabin, the canary burst into piercing song.

"My God!" cried Carthew, with a gulp, "we can't leave that wretched bird to starve. It was poor Goddedaal's."

"Bring the bally thing along!" cried the captain.

And they went on deck.

An ugly brute of a modern man-of-war lay just without the reef, now quite inert, now giving a flap or two with her propeller. Nearer hand, and just within, a big white boat came skimming to the stroke of many oars, her ensign blowing at the stern.

"One word more," said Wicks, after he had taken in the scene. "Mac, you 've been in China ports? All right; then you can speak for yourself. The rest of you I kept on board all the time we were in Hong Kong, hoping you would desert; but you fooled me and stuck to the brig. That 'll make your lying come easier."

The boat was now close at hand; a boy in the stern sheets was the only officer, and a poor one plainly, for the men were talking as they pulled.

"Thank God, they 've only sent a kind of a middy!" ejaculated Wicks. "Here you, Hardy, stand for'ard! I 'll have no deck hands on my quarter-deck," he cried, and the reproof braced the whole crew like a cold douche.

The boat came alongside with perfect neatness, and the boy officer stepped on board, where he was respectfully greeted by Wicks.

"You the master of this ship?" he asked.

"Yes, sir," said Wicks. "Trent is my name, and this is the *Flying Scud* of Hull."

"You seem to have got into a mess," said the officer.

"If you 'll step aft with me here, I 'll tell you all there is of it," said Wicks.

"Why, man, you 're shaking!" cried the officer.

"So would you, perhaps, if you had been in the same berth," returned Wicks; and he told the whole story of the rotten water, the long calm, the squall, the seamen drowned; glibly and hotly; talking, with his head in the lion's mouth, like one pleading in the dock. I heard the same tale from the same narrator in the saloon in San Francisco; and even then his bearing filled me with suspicion. But the officer was no observer.

"Well, the captain is in no end of a hurry," said he; "but I was instructed to give you all the assistance in my power, and signal back for another boat if more hands were necessary. What can I do for you?"

"O, we won't keep you no time," replied Wicks, cheerily. "We 're all ready, bless you — men's chests, chronometer, papers and all."

"Do you mean to leave her?" cried the officer. "She seems to me to lie nicely; can't we get your ship off?"

"So we could, and no mistake; but how we 're to keep her afloat 's another question. Her bows is stove in," replied Wicks.

The officer coloured to the eyes. He was incompetent and knew he was; thought he was already detected, and feared to expose himself again. There was nothing further from his mind than that the captain should deceive him; if the captain was pleased, why, so was he. "All right," he said. " Tell your men to get their chests aboard."

"Mr. Goddedaal, turn the hands to to get the chests aboard," said Wicks.

The four Currency-Lasses had waited the while on tenter-hooks. This welcome news broke upon them like the sun at midnight; and Hadden burst into a storm of tears, sobbing aloud as he heaved upon the tackle. But the work went none the less briskly forward; chests, men, and bundles were got over the side with alacrity; the boat was shoved off; it moved out of the long shadow of the *Flying Scud,* and its bows were pointed at the passage.

So much, then, was accomplished. The sham wreck had passed muster; they were clear of her, they were safe away; and the water widened between them and her damning evidences. On the other hand, they were drawing nearer to the ship of war, which might very well prove to be their prison and a hangman's cart to bear them to the gallows — of which they had not yet learned either whence she came or whither she was bound; and the doubt weighed upon their heart like mountains.

It was Wicks who did the talking. The sound was small in Carthew's ears, like the voices of men miles away, but the meaning of each word struck home to him like a bullet. "What did you say your ship was?" inquired Wicks.

"*Tempest,* don't you know?" returned the officer.

Don't you know? What could that mean? Perhaps nothing: perhaps that the ships had met already. Wicks took his courage in both hands. "Where is she bound?" he asked.

"O, we 're just looking in at all these miserable islands here," said the officer. "Then we bear up for San Francisco."

"O, yes, you 're from China ways, like us?" pursued Wicks.

"Hong Kong," said the officer, and spat over the side.

Hong Kong. Then the game was up; as soon as they set foot on board, they would be seized; the wreck would be examined, the blood found, the lagoon perhaps dredged, and the bodies of the dead would reappear to testify. An impulse almost incontrollable bade Carthew rise from the thwart, shriek out aloud, and leap overboard; it seemed so vain a thing to dissemble longer, to dally with the inevitable, to spin out some hundred seconds more of agonised suspense, with shame and death thus visibly approaching. But the indomitable Wicks persevered. His face was like a skull, his voice scarce recognisable; the dullest of men and officers (it seemed) must have remarked that telltale countenance and broken utterance. And still he persevered, bent upon certitude.

"Nice place, Hong Kong?" he said.

"I 'm sure I don't know," said the officer. "Only a day and a half there; called for orders and came straight on here. Never heard of such a beastly cruise." And he went on describing and lamenting the untoward fortunes of the *Tempest*.

But Wicks and Carthew heeded him no longer. They lay back on the gunnel, breathing deep, sunk in a stupor of the body: the mind within still nimbly and agreeably at work, measuring the past danger, exulting in the present relief, numbering with ecstasy their ultimate chances of escape. For the voyage in the man-of-war they were now safe; yet a few more days of peril, activity, and presence of mind in San Francisco, and the whole horrid tale was blotted out; and Wicks again became Kirkup, and Goddedaal became Carthew — men beyond all shot of possible suspicion, men who had never heard of the *Flying Scud,* who had never been in sight of Midway Reef.

So they came alongside, under many craning heads of seamen and projecting mouths of guns; so they climbed on board somnambulous, and looked blindly about them at the tall spars, the white decks, and the crowding ship's company, and heard men as from far away, and answered them at random.

And then a hand fell softly on Carthew's shoulder.

" Why, Norrie, old chappie, where have you dropped from? All the world 's been looking for you. Don't you know you 've come into your kingdom? "

He turned, beheld the face of his old schoolmate Sebright, and fell unconscious at his feet.

The doctor was attending him, awhile later, in Lieutenant Sebright's cabin, when he came to himself. He opened his eyes, looked hard in the strange face, and spoke with a kind of solemn vigour.

"Brown must go the same road," he said; "now or never." And then paused, and his reason coming to him with more clearness, spoke again: "What was I saying? Where am I? Who are you?"

"I am the doctor of the *Tempest*," was the reply. "You are in Lieutenant Sebright's berth, and you may dismiss all concern from your mind. Your troubles are over, Mr. Carthew."

"Why do you call me that?" he asked. "Ah, I remember — Sebright knew me! O!" and he groaned and shook. "Send down Wicks to me; I must see Wicks at once!" he cried, and seized the doctor's wrist with unconscious violence.

"All right," said the doctor. "Let's make a bargain. You swallow down this draught, and I'll go and fetch Wicks."

And he gave the wretched man an opiate that laid him out within ten minutes and in all likelihood preserved his reason.

It was the doctor's next business to attend to Mac; and he found occasion, while engaged upon his arm, to make the man repeat the names of the rescued crew. It was now the turn of the captain, and there is no doubt he was no longer the man that we have seen; sudden relief, the sense of perfect safety, a square meal and a good glass of grog, had all combined to relax his vigilance and depress his energy.

"When was this done?" asked the doctor, looking at the wound.

"More than a week ago," replied Wicks, thinking singly of his log.

"Hey?" cried the doctor, and he raised his head and looked the captain in the eyes.

"I don't remember exactly," faltered Wicks.

And at this remarkable falsehood, the suspicions of the doctor were at once quadrupled.

"By the way, which of you is called Wicks?" he asked easily.

"What's that?" snapped the captain, falling white as paper.

"Wicks," repeated the doctor; "which of you is he? that's surely a plain question."

Wicks stared upon his questioner in silence.

"Which is Brown, then?" pursued the doctor.

"What are you talking of? what do you mean by this?" cried Wicks, snatching his half-bandaged hand away, so that the blood sprinkled in the surgeon's face.

He did not trouble to remove it. Looking straight at his victim, he pursued his questions. "Why must Brown go the same way?" he asked.

Wicks fell trembling on a locker. "Carthew's told you," he cried.

"No," replied the doctor, "he has not. But he 'and you between you have set me thinking, and I think there 's something wrong."

"Give me some grog," said Wicks. "I 'd rather tell than have you find out. I 'm damned if it 's half as bad as what any one would think."

And with the help of a couple of strong grogs, the tragedy of the *Flying Scud* was told for the first time.

It was a fortunate series of accidents that brought the story to the doctor. He understood and pitied the position of these wretched men, and came whole-heartedly to their assistance. He and Wicks and Carthew (so soon as he was recovered) held a hundred councils and prepared a policy for San Francisco. It was he who certified "Goddedaal" unfit to be moved and smuggled Carthew ashore under cloud of night; it was he who kept Wicks's wound open that he might sign with his left hand; he who took all their Chile silver and (in the course of the first day) got it converted for them into portable gold. He used his influence in the wardroom to keep the tongues of the young officers in order, so that Carthew's identification was kept out of the papers. And he rendered another service yet more important. He had a friend in San Francisco, a millionaire; to this man he privately presented Carthew as a young gentleman come newly into a huge estate, but troubled with Jew debts which he was trying to settle on the quiet. The millionaire came readily to help; and it was with his money that the wrecker gang was to be fought. What was his name, out of a thousand guesses? It was Douglas Longhurst.'

As long as the Currency-Lasses could all disappear under fresh names, it did not greatly matter if the brig were bought, or any small discrepancies should be discovered in the wrecking. The identification of one of their number had changed all that. The smallest scandal must now direct attention to the movements of Norris. It would be asked how he, who had sailed in a schooner from Sydney, had turned up so shortly after in a brig out of Hong Kong; and from one question to another all his original shipmates were pretty sure to be involved. Hence arose naturally the idea of preventing danger, profiting by Carthew's new-found wealth, and buying the brig under an alias; and it was put in hand with equal energy and caution. Carthew took lodgings alone under a false name, picked up Bellairs at random, and commissioned him to buy the wreck.

" What figure, if you please? " the lawyer asked.

" I want it bought," replied Carthew. " I don't mind about the price."

" Any price is no price," said Bellairs. " Put a name upon it."

" Call it ten thousand pounds then, if you like! " said Carthew.

In the meanwhile, the captain had to walk the streets, appear in the consulate, be cross-examined by Lloyd's agent, be badgered about his lost accounts, sign papers with his left hand, and repeat his lies to every skipper in San Francisco: not knowing at what moment he might run into the arms of some old friend who should hail him by the name of Wicks, or some new enemy who should be in a position to deny him that of Trent. And the latter incident did actually befall him, but was transformed by his stout countenance into

an element of strength. It was in the consulate
(of all untoward places) that he suddenly heard a
big voice inquiring for Captain Trent. He turned
with the customary sinking at his heart.

" *You* ain't Captain Trent! " said the stranger,
falling back. " Why, what 's all this? They tell
me you 're passing off as Captain Trent — Captain
Jacob Trent — a man I knew since I was that
high."

" O, you 're thinking of my uncle as had the
bank in Cardiff," replied Wicks, with desperate
aplomb.

" I declare I never knew he had a nevvy! " said
the stranger.

" Well, you see he has! " says Wicks.

" And how is the old man? " asked the other.

" Fit as a fiddle," answered Wicks, and was op-
portunely summoned by the clerk.

This alert was the only one until the morning
of the sale, when he was once more alarmed by
his interview with Jim; and it was with some
anxiety that he attended the sale, knowing only
that Carthew was to be represented, but neither
who was to represent him nor what were the instructions given. I suppose Captain Wicks is a
good life. In spite of his personal appearance and
his own known uneasiness, I suppose he is secure
from apoplexy, or it must have struck him there
and then, as he looked on at the stages of that
insane sale and saw the old brig and her not very
valuable cargo knocked down at last to a total
stranger for ten thousand pounds.

It had been agreed that he was to avoid Carthew, and above all Carthew's lodging, so that no connection might be traced between the crew and the pseudonymous purchaser. But the hour for caution was gone by, and he caught a tram and made all speed to Mission Street.

Carthew met him in the door.

" Come away, come away from here," said Carthew; and when they were clear of the house, " All 's up! " he added.

" O, you 've heard of the sale then? " said Wicks.

" The sale! " cried Carthew. " I declare I had forgotten it." And he told of the voice in the telephone, and the maddening question: Why did you want to buy the *Flying Scud?*

This circumstance, coming on the back of the monstrous improbabilities of the sale, was enough to have shaken the reason of Immanuel Kant. The earth seemed banded together to defeat them; the stones and the boys on the street appeared to be in possession of their guilty secret. Flight was their one thought. The treasure of the *Currency Lass* they packed in waist-belts, expressed their chests to an imaginary address in British Columbia, and left San Francisco the same afternoon, booked for Los Angeles.

The next day they pursued their retreat by the Southern Pacific route, which Carthew followed on his way to England; but the other three branched off for Mexico.

EPILOGUE

TO WILL H. LOW

DEAR LOW: The other day (at Manihiki of all places) I had the pleàsure to meet Dodd. We sat some two hours in the neat, little, toy-like church, set with pews after the manner of Europe, and inlaid with mother-of-pearl in the style (I suppose) of the New Jerusalem. The natives, who are decidedly the most attractive inhabitants of this planet, crowded round us in the pew, and fawned upon and patted us; and here it was I put my questions, and Dodd answered me.

I first carried him back to the night in Barbizon when Carthew told his story, and asked him what was done about Bellairs. It seemed he had put the matter to his friend at once, and that Carthew took it with an inimitable lightness. " He 's poor, and I 'm rich," he had said. " I can afford to smile at him. I go somewhere else, that 's all — somewhere that 's far away and dear to get to. Persia would be found to answer, I fancy. No end of a place, Persia. Why not come with me? " And they had left the next afternoon for Constantinople, on their way to Teheran. Of the shyster, it is only known (by a newspaper paragraph) that he returned somehow to San Francisco and died in the hospital.

"Now there's another point," said I. "There you are off to Persia with a millionaire, and rich yourself. How come you here in the South Seas, running a trader?"

He said, with a smile, that I had not yet heard of Jim's last bankruptcy. "I was about cleaned out once more," he said; "and then it was that Carthew had this schooner built, and put me in as supercargo. It's his yacht and it's my trader; and as nearly all the expenses go to the yacht, I do pretty well. As for Jim, he's right again: one of the best businesses, they say, in the West, fruit, cereals, and real estate; and he has a Tartar of a partner now — Nares, no less. Nares will keep him straight, Nares has a big head. They have their country-places next door at Saucelito, and I stayed with them time about, the last time I was on the coast. Jim has a paper of his own — I think he has a notion of being senator one of these days — and he wanted me to throw up the schooner and come and write his editorials. He holds strong views on the State Constitution, and so does Mamie."

"And what became of the other three Currency-Lasses after they left Carthew?" I inquired.

"Well, it seems they had a huge spree in the city of Mexico," said Dodd; "and then Hadden and the Irishman took a turn at the gold fields in Venezuela, and Wicks went on alone to Valparaiso. There's a Kirkup in the Chilean navy to this day,

I saw the name in the papers about the Balmaceda war. Hadden soon wearied of the mines, and I met him the other day in Sydney. The last news he had from Venezuela, Mac had been knocked over in an attack on the gold train. So there's only the three of them left, for Amalu scarcely counts. He lives on his own land in Maui, at the side of Hale-a-ka-la, where he keeps Goddedaal's canary; and they say he sticks to his dollars, which is a wonder in a Kanaka. He had a considerable pile to start with, for not only Hemstead's share but Carthew's was divided equally among the other four — Mac being counted."

"What did that make for him altogether?" I could not help asking, for I had been diverted by the number of calculations in his narrative.

"One hundred and twenty-eight pounds nineteen shillings and eleven pence halfpenny," he replied with composure. "That's leaving out what little he won at Van John. It's something for a Kanaka, you know."

And about that time we were at last obliged to yield to the solicitations of our native admirers, and go to the pastor's house to drink green cocoanuts. The ship I was in was sailing the same night, for Dodd had been beforehand and got all the shell in the island; and though he pressed me to desert and return with him to Auckland (whither he was now bound to pick up Carthew) I was firm in my refusal.

The truth is, since I have been mixed up with Havens and Dodd in the design to publish the latter's narrative, I seem to feel no want for Carthew's society. Of course I am wholly modern in sentiment, and think nothing more noble than to publish people's private affairs at so much a line. They like it, and if they don't, they ought to. But a still small voice keeps telling me they will not like it always, and perhaps not always stand it. Memory besides supplies me with the face of a pressman (in the sacred phrase) who proved altogether too modern for one of his neighbours, and

Qui nunc it per iter tenebricosum

as it were, marshalling us our way. I am in no haste to

— nos præcedens —

be that man's successor. Carthew has a record as "a clane shot," and for some years Samoa will be good enough for me.

We agreed to separate, accordingly; but he took me on board in his own boat with the hardwood fittings, and entertained me on the way with an account of his late visit to Butaritari, whither he had gone on an errand for Carthew, to see how Topelius was getting along, and, if necessary, to give him a helping hand. But Topelius was in great force, and had patronised and — well — outmanœuvred him.

"Carthew will be pleased," said Dodd; "for there's no doubt they oppressed the man abom-

inably when they were in the *Currency Lass*.   It's
diamond cut diamond now."

This, I think, was the most of the news I got
from my friend Loudon; and I hope I was well
inspired, and have put all the questions to which
you would be curious to hear an answer.

But there is one more that I dare say you are
burning to put to myself; and that is, what your
own name is doing in this place, cropping up (as
it were uncalled for) on the stern of our poor
ship? If you were not born in Arcadia, you linger
in fancy on its margin; your thoughts are busy
with the flutes of antiquity, with daffodils, and
the classic poplar, and the footsteps of the nymphs,
and the elegant and moving aridity of ancient art.
Why dedicate to you a tale of a caste so modern;
— full of details of our barbaric manners and un-
stable morals; — full of the need and the lust of
money, so that there is scarce a page in which the
dollars do not jingle; — full of the unrest and
movement of our century, so that the reader is
hurried from place to place and sea to sea, and
the book is less a romance than a panorama; —
in the end, as blood-bespattered as an epic?

Well, you are a man interested in all problems of
art, even the most vulgar; and it may amuse you
to hear the genesis and growth of *The Wrecker*.
On board the schooner *Equator*, almost within sight
of the Johnstone Islands (if anybody knows where
these are) and on a moonlit night when it was
a joy to be alive, the authors were amused with

several stories of the sale of wrecks. The subject tempted them; and they sat apart in the alleyway to discuss its possibilities. "What a tangle it would make," suggested one, "if the wrong crew were aboard. But how to get the wrong crew there?" — "I have it!" cried the other; "the so-and-so affair!" For not so many months before, and not so many hundred miles from where we were then sailing, a proposition almost tantamount to that of Captain Trent had been made by a British skipper to some British castaways.

Before we turned in, the scaffolding of the tale had been put together. But the question of treatment was as usual more obscure. We had long been at once attracted and repelled by that very modern form of the police novel or mystery story, which consists in beginning your yarn anywhere but at the beginning, and finishing it anywhere but at the end; attracted by its peculiar interest when done, and the peculiar difficulties that attend its execution; repelled by that appearance of insincerity and shallowness of tone, which seems its inevitable drawback. For the mind of the reader, always bent to pick up clews, receives no impression of reality or life, rather of an airless, elaborate mechanism; and the book remains enthralling, but insignificant, like a game of chess, not a work of human art. It seemed the cause might lie partly in the abrupt attack; and that if the tale were gradually approached, some of the characters introduced (as it were) beforehand, and the book started in the tone of a novel of manners and

35

experience briefly treated, this defect might be lessened and our mystery seem to inhere ·in life. The tone of the age, its movement, the mingling of races and classes in the dollar hunt, the fiery and not quite unromantic struggle for existence with its changing trades and scenery, and two types in particular, that of the American handyman of business and that of the Yankee merchant sailor — we agreed to dwell upon at some length, and make the woof to our not very precious warp. Hence Dodd's father, and Pinkerton, and Nares, and the Dromedary picnics, and the railway work in New South Wales — the last an unsolicited testimonial from the powers that be, for the tale was half written before I saw Carthew's squad toil in the rainy cutting at South Clifton, or heard from the engineer of his " young swell." After we had invented at some expense of time this method of approaching and fortifying our police novel, it occurred to us it had been invented previously by some one else, and was in fact — however painfully different the results may seem — the method of Charles Dickens in his later work.

I see you staring. Here, you will say, is a prodigious quantity of theory to our halfpenny worth of police novel; and withal not a shadow of an answer to your question.

Well, some of us like theory. After so long a piece of practice, these may be indulged for a few pages. And the answer is at hand. It was plainly desirable, from every point of view of convenience and contrast, that our hero and narrator should partly stand aside from those with whom he mingles, and be but a pressed-man in the dollar hunt. Thus it was that Loudon Dodd became a student of the plastic arts, and that our globe-trotting story came to visit Paris and look in at Barbizon. And thus it is, dear Low, that your name appears in the address of this epilogue.

For sure, if any person can here appreciate and read between the lines, it must be you — and one other, our friend. All the dominos will be transparent to your better knowledge; the statuary contract will be to you a piece of ancient history; and you will not have now heard for the first time of the dangers of Roussillon. Dead leaves from the Bas Breau, echoes from Lavenue's and the Rue Racine, memories of a common past, let these be your bookmarkers as you read. And if you care for naught else in the story, be a little pleased to breathe once more for a moment the airs of our youth.

LaVergne, TN USA
01 July 2010
188110LV00001B/115/P